Forbidden Seductions

ANNE MATHER
INDIA GREY
KIMBERLY LANG

Published in Great Britain 2015
by Mills & Boon, an imprint of Harlequin (UK) Limited,
Eton House, 18-24 Paradise Road, Richmond, Surrey, TW9 1SR

FORBIDDEN SEDUCTIONS © 2015 Harlequin Books S.A.

His Forbidden Passion, Craving the Forbidden and *Girls' Guide to Flirting with Danger* were first published in Great Britain by Harlequin (UK) Limited.

His Forbidden Passion © 2009 Anne Mather
Craving the Forbidden © 2011 India Grey
Girls' Guide to Flirting with Danger © 2011 Kimberly Kerr

ISBN: 978-0-263-25212-5
eBook ISBN: 978-1-474-00391-9

05-0515

Harlequin (UK) Limited's policy is to use papers that are natural, renewable and recyclable products and made from wood grown in sustainable forests. The logging and manufacturing processes conform to the legal environmental regulations of the country of origin.

Printed and bound in Spain
by CPI, Barcelona

HIS FORBIDDEN PASSION

BY
ANNE MATHER

Anne Mather says: 'I've always wanted to write—which is not to say I've always wanted to be a professional writer. On the contrary, for years I wrote only for my own pleasure, and it wasn't until my husband suggested that I ought to send one of my stories to a publisher that we put several publishers' names into a hat and pulled one out. The rest, as they say, is history. And now, more than a hundred and fifty books later, I'm literally—excuse the pun—staggered by what happened.

'I had written all through my infant and junior years, and on into my teens. The trouble was, I never used to finish any of the stories, and *Caroline*, my first published book, was the first book I'd actually completed. I was newly married then, and my daughter was just a baby. It was quite a job, juggling my household chores and scribbling away in exercise books every chance I got. Not very professional, as you can see, but that's the way it was.

'I now have two grown-up children, a son and daughter, and two adorable grandchildren, Abigail and Ben. My e-mail address is mystic-am@msn.com, and I'd be happy to hear from any of my readers.'

CHAPTER ONE

CLEO was almost sure she'd seen the woman before.

She didn't know when or where she might have seen her, or if the feeling was real or just imagined. But there was an odd sense of familiarity when she looked at her that refused to go away.

She shook her head rather impatiently. Sometimes she was far too sensitive for her own good. But there was no doubt that the woman had been staring at *her* ever since she'd joined the queue at the checkout, so perhaps that was why she looked familiar. Perhaps she resembled someone the woman used to know.

There was obviously a perfectly innocent explanation. Just because she didn't like being stared at didn't mean the woman meant her any harm. Paying for the milk that had sent her to the store in the first place, Cleo determinedly ignored the persistent scrutiny, and then nearly jumped out of her skin when the woman spoke to her.

'It's Ms Novak, isn't it?' she asked, blocking Cleo's way as she would have moved past her. 'I'm so pleased to meet you at last. Your friend said I might find you here.'

Cleo frowned. She could only mean Norah. Which meant the woman must have been to their apartment first. She sighed. What was Norah thinking of, offering her whereabouts to a complete stranger? With all the odd things that happened these days, Cleo would have expected her to have more sense.

'I'm sorry,' she said, albeit against her better judgement. 'Should I know you?'

The woman smiled and Cleo realised she was older than she'd appeared from a distance. Cleo had assumed she was in her forties, but now she saw she was at least fifty. The sleek bob of copper hair was deceiving, but the trim figure and slender legs were not.

She wasn't very tall. She had to tilt her head to meet Cleo's enquiring gaze. But her make-up was skilful, her clothes obviously expensive, and what she lacked in stature she more than made up for in presence.

'I apologise,' she said, her accent vaguely transatlantic, drawing Cleo out of the store by the simple method of continuing to talk to her. The cool air of an autumn evening swirled about them and the woman shivered as if it wasn't to her liking. 'Of course,' she went on, pausing on the forecourt. 'I should have introduced myself at once. We haven't met, my dear, but I'm Serena Montoya. Your father's sister.'

Of all the things she might have said, that had to be the least expected, thought Cleo incredulously. For a moment she could only stare at her in disbelief.

Then, recovering a little, she said with a mixture of shaky amusement and relief, 'My father didn't have a sister, Ms Montoya. I'm sorry.' She started to move away. 'I'm afraid you've made a mistake.'

'I don't think so.' Serena Montoya—if that really was her name—put out scarlet-tipped fingers and caught the sleeve of Cleo's woollen jacket. 'Please,' she pleaded. 'Listen to me for a moment.' She sighed and removed her fingers again when Cleo gave her a pointed look. 'Your father's name was Robert Montoya—'

'No.'

'—and he was born on the island of San Clemente in the Caribbean in 1956.'

'That's not true.' Cleo stared at her impatiently. Then, with a sound of resignation, 'Well, yes, my father was born on San Clemente, but I'm not absolutely sure of the date, and his name was Henry Novak.'

'I'm afraid not.' Grasping Cleo's wrist, this time with a firmness that wouldn't be denied, Serena Montoya regarded her with determined eyes. 'I am not lying to you, Ms Novak. I know you've always thought that Lucille and Henry Novak were your parents, but they weren't.'

Cleo couldn't believe this was happening. 'Why are you doing this?' she demanded. 'Why are you insisting that this man, Robert Montoya—*your brother*—is my father?'

'Was,' Serena corrected her regretfully. 'Robert was your father. He died some years ago.'

Cleo's voice broke on a sob. 'It's a ridiculous assertion and you know it.'

'It's true.' Serena was inflexible. Resisting Cleo's efforts to pull away, she continued flatly, 'Believe me, Ms Novak, when my father—your grandfather—told me what had happened, I didn't want to believe it either.'

'Now, that I can believe,' said Cleo a little grimly. 'Well, don't worry, Ms Montoya. Obviously your father is suffering from delusions. Unfortunately my real parents were killed in a rail accident six months ago or they would have told you that themselves.'

'Yes, we know about the accident.' Serena was full of surprises. 'That's when my father first learned where you were living.' She paused. 'And he is not delusional. Please, Cleo, come and have a drink with me and let me explain—'

Cleo fell back a step and this time the woman let her go. 'How do you know my name?'

'How do you think?' Serena sounded as if she was getting bored now. 'It's Cleopatra, isn't it?' And, seeing the unwilling confirmation on Cleo's face, she added, 'It was your maternal grandmother's name, too. She was called Cleopatra Dubois and her daughter, Celeste, was your mother. Celeste Dubois was one of the most beautiful women on the island.' She gave Cleo a considering look. 'I hesitate to say it, but you look a lot like her.'

Cleo's lips tightened. 'Was she black?'

Serena frowned. 'Does that matter?'

Cleo shook her head. 'Only a white person would ask such a question.' Her lips curled. 'Yes, it matters.'

'OK.' Serena considered. 'Well, yes, I suppose she was— black. Her skin was—um—coffee coloured. Not black, exactly, but not white either.'

That was enough. Cleo refused to listen to any more. If the description of her so-called 'mother' had been meant to disarm her, it had failed abysmally. She was used to vapid flattery. Usually from men, it was true. But she'd had to deal with it all her life.

'Look, I have to go,' she said, assuring herself that if there had been any truth in what the woman was saying, she'd have heard about it by now. Her parents had not been liars, whatever Serena Montoya said. And Cleo had loved them far too much to even countenance such a suggestion.

Besides which, she'd been the sole executor of her parents' estate. And she'd found nothing among their papers to arouse any kind of suspicion in her mind.

Except that photograph, she remembered now, half unwillingly. At the time, she'd thought little of it. It was a picture of her mother with another woman, a woman who she'd realised looked a lot like her. But there'd been nothing on the back of the picture, nothing to say who the woman might be. And Cleo had put it down to her own imagination. There were probably hundreds of people in the world that she bore a resemblance to.

Like Serena Montoya…

But no, she banished that thought, and to her surprise the other woman didn't try to detain her any longer.

'All right,' she said evenly. 'I realise this has been as much of a shock to you as it was to me.'

You got that right, thought Cleo savagely, but she didn't voice the thought. Nor was she foolish enough to believe that this was the end of the matter.

'You need time to assimilate what I've told you,' Serena went on, almost conversationally, drawing velvet-soft leather gloves over her ringed fingers as she spoke. 'But don't take too long, will you, my dear? Your grandfather is dying. Are you going to deny him a last chance to meet his only granddaughter?'

Cleo arrived back at the apartment she shared with Norah Jacobs some thirty minutes later.

Actually, it was normally only a five-minute walk from the supermarket to Minster Court, where the apartment was situated. But Cleo had taken a detour through the park to give herself time to think.

At any other time, nothing would have persuaded her to enter the park alone and after dark, but right now she wasn't thinking very coherently. She'd just been told that her mother and father—the two people in the world she'd always thought she could depend on—had lied about her identity. That far from being alone now, as she'd believed, she had an aunt and a grandfather—and who knew what else?—who were—well, white.

She didn't want to believe it. She wanted things to go back to the way they were before she'd decided she couldn't do without milk on her cornflakes in the morning.

If she hadn't gone to the supermarket...

But that was silly. Sooner or later, the Montoya woman would have caught up with her. And things weren't going to change any time soon. Not unless Serena Montoya was playing the biggest hoax Cleo had ever heard of.

And why would she do that? What did she have to gain by it? She hadn't struck Cleo as being the kind of woman who'd put herself out for a complete stranger. Not unless her own father *was* dying, of course. And he had another agenda she had yet to reveal.

Norah was waiting for her in the rather cramped living room of the apartment. The whole place was pushed for space, but rents in this part of London were prohibitive, and Cleo had jumped at the chance to share expenses with the other girl.

Norah was blonde and pretty and inclined to plumpness. The exact opposite of Cleo in so many ways. But the two girls had been friends since their schooldays and, despite the limitations of their surroundings, they generally got along very well.

Now, however, Norah looked positively anxious. 'Here you are!' she exclaimed in relief, as soon as Cleo opened the door. 'I've been worried sick. Where have you been?' Then, her brows drawing together as Cleo moved into the light of the living room, 'What's wrong? You look as if you've seen a ghost.'

Cleo shook her head without saying anything. Walking past her friend, she rounded the breakfast bar that separated the tiny kitchen from the rest of the living space and stowed the milk in the fridge.

Then, straightening, she said, 'Why on earth would you tell a complete stranger where I was?'

'Oh…' The colour in Norah's cheeks deepened. 'So she found you.'

'If you mean Serena Montoya, then yes, she did.'

'Serena Montoya? Is that her name?' Norah tried to lighten the conversation, but she could tell Cleo wasn't distracted by her efforts. 'Well, she said she was your aunt,' she offered lamely. 'What was I supposed to say? She didn't look like a con artist to me.'

'Like you would know,' said Cleo drily. Norah's many unsuccessful attempts to find herself a decent man were legendary. Coming back into the living room, Cleo flung herself onto the sofa, regarding her friend moodily. 'Honestly, Norah, I thought you had more sense.'

'So she's not your aunt?'

'No, she's not my aunt,' stated Cleo with more force than conviction. 'I mean, didn't anything about her give you a clue? Be honest, Norah. Do I look like Serena Montoya's niece?'

'You could be.' Norah wasn't prepared to back down. 'In fact, although you're taller than she is, you do have similar features.' She paused. 'Montoya. That's a Spanish name, isn't it?'

'I don't know. I believe she lives in the Caribbean, so it could be.' Cleo was impatient. 'But my parents were black, Norah. Not Spanish. You know that.'

She hunched her shoulders, reluctant now to remember the rare occasions when she'd questioned her identity herself. She hadn't looked a lot like her parents, and she had wondered if one or both of them might have Latin blood.

But those questions had aroused such animosity that she'd kept any further doubts to herself. And she refused to believe they'd been lying to her. She'd loved them too much for that.

'Oh, well…' Norah was philosophical. 'So what else did she say? There must be some sort of connection to bring her here.'

'There is no connection.' Cleo was exasperated. Then, seeing Norah's indignation, she went on, 'All right. She said that Mom and Dad weren't my real parents. That my biological father's name was actually Robert Montoya.' She paused. 'Her brother.'

'Oh, my God!'

'Yeah, right.' Cleo felt a sudden sense of apprehension at the sudden possibility that it might be true. 'That's why I looked a bit—spaced-out when I came in, I suppose. It's not every day someone tells you you're not who you'd always thought you were.'

Norah bit her lip. 'But you think she's lying?'

'Damn right!' Cleo stared at her emotively. 'Of course she's lying. How can you ask such a thing? You knew my parents. Did they strike you as the kind of people who'd keep a secret like that?'

'Well, no.' Norah sighed. 'All the same, I have sometimes

thought that you didn't look a lot like them, Cleo. I mean, OK, your skin is darker than mine, but you're not a blonde, are you? And you've got that gorgeous straight black hair.'

'Don't go there, Norah.'

Getting to her feet again, Cleo turned abruptly away, heading for the small bedroom that Norah had had decorated for her when she moved in.

She didn't want to consider that there might be even a grain of truth in what Serena Montoya had said. To do so would tear the whole fabric of her life up to this time apart.

She should have asked more questions, she acknowledged. She should have asked the woman outright what proof she had to substantiate her claim.

Instead, all she'd done was keep on denying something that she now saw in retrospect had to have some meaning. Maybe not the meaning Serena Montoya had put upon it, but a reason why she'd contacted her.

Dominic Montoya was standing staring out of the hotel's fourteenth-floor windows when Serena strode into the suite. The lights of the capital were spread out below him, a teeming, noisy metropolis, much different from his family's estate back home.

The door's automatic closing mechanism prevented Serena from slamming it, but the oath she uttered caused her nephew to turn and regard her with mocking green eyes.

'It must have gone well,' he remarked, as Serena charged across the room to where a tray of drinks resided on a bureau. He watched as she splashed vodka and ice into a glass and raised it to her lips before adding, 'I assume you found her.'

Serena swallowed half her drink before replying. Then, her lips tightening, she said, 'Yes, I found her.' Her blue eyes sparkled coldly. 'But you can go and see her yourself next time.'

Dominic pushed his thumbs into the back pockets of his jeans and rocked back on the heels of his leather boots. 'So there is to be a next time,' he remarked casually. 'Have you made that arrangement?'

'No.' Serena was stubborn. 'But one of us will have to bite the bullet, won't we?' She shook her head. 'Your grandfather's going to have a hissy fit.'

Dominic's dark brows drew together enquiringly, and Serena thought, not for the first time, what a damnably attractive man he was. A small core of resentment uncurled inside her. Whatever happened, her father would never blame him.

Ever since her brother, Robert, had found the infant, Dominic, wandering the streets of Miami when he was barely three years old, it had always been that way. Dominic was that most fortunate of beings: the favoured grandchild.

The *only* grandchild until now, Serena reflected irritably. Although her brother had married when he was in his early twenties, she never had. She'd had offers, of course, when she was younger. But their mother's premature death when Serena was in her teens had persuaded her that her father needed her as his hostess, and she'd never looked back.

Now, discovering her brother had had an adulterous affair with Celeste Dubois had really thrown her. She'd always thought they were close. She'd been shattered when he died. But recently, her father had revealed the circumstances of the affair, how he—and he alone—had helped Robert keep the child's existence a secret.

She shook her head and Dominic thought he could guess what she was thinking. He knew she'd never forgive Robert for deceiving her and Dominic's adoptive mother, Lily. It was the fact that Lily couldn't have children that had made his own adoption so much easier.

And he knew how lucky he'd been to find such loving, caring parents. His own biological mother had never wanted him, and she'd been only too happy for someone else to take responsibility for him.

He had once tried to find his mother, when he was a teenager and curious about his roots. But he'd discovered she'd died of an overdose, just weeks after he'd been adopted, and he'd realised again how fortunate he was that Robert had found him.

Perhaps that was why he viewed the present situation with much less anguish than Serena. OK, it had been a shock to all of them, particularly his mother, who, like Serena, had trusted her husband completely.

And it was going to be hard for her. The old man—his grand-father—had a lot to answer for, bringing the girl to their attention all these years after Robert's death. He must have had an attack of conscience, Dominic decided, brought on by the sudden discovery of prostate cancer earlier in the year.

'So why is my grandfather going to have a—what was it you said—a hissy fit?' Dominic questioned now, and Serena turned resentful eyes in his direction.

'Because she's the image of her mother,' she retorted shortly. 'Or the way she used to look before she died.' She shook her head. 'You know, I knew Celeste had had a baby, but I never dreamt it might be Robert's child.'

'Obviously, no one did. Except perhaps my grandfather.'

'Oh, yes, he knew.' Serena was bitter. 'But how could Robert do that to Lily? I thought he loved her.'

'I know he did.' Dominic's tone was mild. 'This woman—Celeste—was probably just a momentary madness.'

'A momentary sexual madness.' Serena wasn't prepared to compromise. 'Or maybe to prove he wasn't impotent, hmm?' She flopped down into one of the tapestry-covered armchairs that flanked the pseudo-marble fireplace. 'How could he, Dom? Would you do that to a woman you professed to love?'

'Uh—no.' Dominic was indignant. 'But we're not talking about me, Serena. And your brother's dead. Someone has to defend him. He wasn't a bad man, for God's sake. Can't you cut him a little slack?'

Serena sighed. 'It's not easy.'

'Anyway, I doubt if Robert would approve of what your father's doing, if he were alive.' Dominic was persuasive.

'And I dare say at the time he thought what he was doing was right.'

'Getting rid of the evidence, you mean?'

'Oh, 'Rena…' Dominic came to squat on his haunches beside her chair. 'I'm sure he had the child's best interests at heart. Her mother was dead and I doubt if my mother would have welcomed her into the family then.'

'I doubt if she would either,' agreed his aunt forcefully. 'So what makes you think Lily will feel any differently now?'

Dominic sighed and pushed himself to his feet again. 'I doubt she will,' he admitted honestly. 'But it's not her call, is it? It's your father's decision.'

'Well, I think the whole thing is disgusting. I don't know how I kept my temper when that —that ignorant girl refused to believe me.' She snorted. 'She has no idea what she's being offered.'

'Perhaps she doesn't care,' suggested Dominic quietly. 'So— did you manage to convince her?'

'I don't know.' Serena got up to pour herself another drink and then resumed her seat. 'She may think about what I've said, but I don't particularly care. She's not at all what I expected.'

Dominic's brows rose. 'Because she looks like the Dubois woman?' he probed shrewdly, and Serena turned an indignant face up to his.

'Of course, you would think that,' she said crossly. 'You're a man. Men always made fools of themselves over the Dubois women. Or so I've heard.' She sighed. 'But all right. Perhaps I am a bit jealous. One thing's for sure, she doesn't look a lot like Robert.'

'Not at all?'

Serena made a frustrated sound. 'Well, obviously she does a little,' she admitted. 'She has his nose and his mouth and his height.'

'But she's black?'

'No.' Serena shifted a little uncomfortably. 'Well, not obviously so. She's just—beautiful. Slim and dark and gorgeous. Just like her mother, as I say.'

Dominic couldn't suppress a grin. 'No wonder you didn't like her,' he teased and a rueful smile tugged at his aunt's mouth.

'Well, she was arrogant,' she said defensively. 'Like she was doing me a favour by speaking to me at all.'

'Oh, dear.' Dominic was amused. 'But let's face it, you are a complete stranger to her. She was probably suspicious of your motives.'

Serena considered. 'She really believes the Novaks were her parents, you know.'

'Well, I suppose they were.' Dominic shrugged. 'The only parents she's known, anyway. For the past twenty-odd years, she's believed she had no other relatives.'

'Twenty-two years,' said Serena pedantically. 'I guess you were about seven or eight when she was born.'

'There you are, then.'

'But didn't she ever have any doubts?' Serena frowned.

'Children tend to believe what their parents tell them,' said Dominic reasonably. 'Unless they find them out in a lie. And it can't have been easy for the Novaks either.'

'They weren't poor,' said Serena pointedly. 'According to Dad, Robert paid them a small fortune to take the baby to England and pass it off as their own.'

'There are other problems besides financial ones,' Dominic remarked drily, but Serena wasn't listening to him.

'They'd already made arrangements to emigrate,' she said. 'And the money must have been a real bonus.' She grimaced. 'I suppose the fact that Celeste had died in childbirth made it easier for Robert to escape the consequences of his actions.'

Dominic decided not to pursue the subject. Serena was never going to agree that neither her brother nor the Novaks had had it all their own way.

He doubted his father had found it easy to turn away his own child—his own flesh and blood—even for the sake of his marriage. He must have regretted it sometimes, however much he'd loved his wife.

'Well, it's in your hands now, darling,' declared Serena half maliciously. 'I've done my best and it obviously wasn't good enough. Let's hope you have more success.'

CHAPTER TWO

CLEO buttoned the neckline of her leather jacket and wrapped a blue and green striped scarf around her collar.

There was no point in pretending she wasn't going to be frozen sitting watching a rugby football match. Despite Eric's promise that they'd be protected by the roof of the stands, there wouldn't be any heating at all.

Why had she agreed to go with him? she wondered. It wasn't as if she wanted him to get the wrong impression about their relationship. He was a good friend; a good neighbour. But that was all.

The truth was that since Serena Montoya's visit, she'd spent every evening on edge, waiting for the doorbell to ring. Although it was three days now since that encounter at the supermarket, she couldn't believe the woman wouldn't try to see her again. An evening out, even at a rugby match with Eric Morgan, was better than staying in on her own.

Norah had a date. She wouldn't be home until much later, whereas Cleo's job as an infant-school teacher meant she was home most afternoons by five o'clock.

After stepping into short sheepskin-lined boots, she considered the beanie lying on the table beside her. What the woollen hat lacked in style, it more than made up for in warmth and comfort.

But, on the other hand, she didn't want Eric to think she was

a wimp. And wearing a woolly hat was strictly for the birds.
All the same…

With a muffled exclamation, she picked up the beanie and
jammed it onto her head. She could always say she'd worn it
to keep her hair tidy, she thought, viewing her reflection in the
mirror without satisfaction. It wasn't easy to keep the tumbled
mass of silky dark hair in check. It was long enough to wear in
a braid, but she'd caught it up in a ponytail this evening.

At least no one could say she looked beautiful at present.
Quite the contrary, she'd decided firmly. But then she grimaced.
She'd told herself she wouldn't think about what the Montoya
woman had said, so where had that come from?

When the doorbell rang at half-past six, she felt none of the
apprehension she'd experienced in recent days when anyone
came to the apartment. It just meant Eric was a few minutes
early, and, as he only lived in the apartment upstairs, he didn't
have far to come.

'Hang on,' she called, snatching up her purse and her mobile
phone and stuffing them into her pockets. Then, pulling the
door open, she carolled, 'See! I am rea—'

But it wasn't Eric.

In fact it wasn't anyone she knew and she felt a moment's
panic. Strange men just didn't come calling this late in the day.
Particularly not tall, dark men, with deep-set eyes and hollow
cheekbones, and the kind of dangerous good looks that seldom
went with a caring disposition.

He wasn't a particularly handsome man. His features were
too harsh, too masculine, to be described in such modest terms.
Nevertheless, he was disturbingly attractive. He disturbed her
in a way she recognised as being wholly sexual. And that was
not good.

'Um…' Her voice failed her for a moment and she saw his
eyes—green eyes, she observed—narrow perceptively. Then,
clearing her throat, she continued tightly, 'Can I help you?'

'I hope so.'

His voice was as smooth as molasses and twice as sensual.

Cleo's stomach plunged alarmingly. She wasn't used to having this kind of reaction to a man and she struggled to compose herself.

He had to be looking for Norah, she thought, though her friend had never mentioned meeting anyone like him. One thing was for sure: she'd never seen him before.

'You must be Cleopatra,' he went on, supporting himself with one hand raised against the jamb, and she stiffened.

His action had caused the sides of his dark cashmere overcoat to fall open to reveal an Italian-made suit that had probably cost more than Cleo made in a year at her job. A matching waistcoat was buttoned over a dark blue shirt that looked as if it was made of silk, dark trousers cut lovingly to reveal muscled thighs and long, powerful legs.

Even without the name he'd used causing her a shiver of apprehension, his appearance alone sent a frisson of awareness feathering down her spine.

No one she knew called her Cleopatra. No one except Serena Montoya, of course. Dear heaven, this man must be something to do with her.

'Who—who are you?' she got out uneasily, suddenly conscious of her less than glamorous appearance. Snatching off the beanie, she thrust it into her pocket. 'I—I was just going out.'

'I had sort of gathered that,' remarked the man, faint amusement tugging at the corners of his lean mouth. 'I guess I've come at a bad time.'

Cleo pressed her lips together for a moment and then said, 'If—if Ms Montoya sent you, there wouldn't be a good time.' And let him make what he liked of that.

The man's hand dropped from the frame of the door and he straightened. 'I have to assume you didn't like Serena,' he commented drily, and Cleo made a sound of impatience.

'I neither like nor dislike her,' she said, not altogether honestly. 'And my name's Cleo. Not Cleopatra.'

'Ah.' He glanced up and down the hall before looking at her

again. 'Well, Cleo—whether you like it or not, sooner or later we have to talk.'

'Why?'

'I think you know the answer to that as well as I do,' he replied levelly.

'Because some old man says I'm his son's daughter?' demanded Cleo tersely. 'I don't think so.'

'No.' The man shook his head. 'Not just because my grandfather says it's so—'

'Your grandfather?' Cleo felt as if the ground beneath her feet had shifted a little. 'You—you're Ms Montoya's son?'

He laughed then, his lips parting to reveal a row of even white teeth. What else? thought Cleo irritably. The man was far too sure of himself.

Then he sobered, his grin totally disarming her. 'No,' he said, and she didn't know why she wasn't relieved by his explanation. 'My name is Dominic Montoya. Serena's my aunt.'

Cleo swallowed. 'I see,' she said. But what did that mean?

'She's yours, too,' he added, unsteadying her still further. 'Robert was my father, as well.'

Cleo couldn't speak. This man was her *brother?* She didn't believe it. She didn't *want* to believe it.

'That's impossible,' she managed at last, and he pulled a wry face.

'Yeah, well, that's the way it is.' He shrugged dismissively. 'Get used to it.'

'It can't be true—'

'Cleo?'

She had never been more relieved to hear Eric Morgan's voice. The young man from the apartment on the floor above was coming down the stairs just along the hall from her door.

'Is everything OK?' he asked, coming to join them, and Cleo could tell from his tone that he'd heard at least some of what they'd been saying.

His eyes flickered suspiciously over the man standing by her door, but Cleo had to admit his words had more bluster than substance. In his navy duffel coat and club scarf, Eric was at least half a foot shorter than Dominic Montoya, and in any physical contest she doubted he'd stand a chance.

Nevertheless…

'It's fine, Eric,' she said now, grateful for his concern. She gestured towards her visitor. 'Mr Montoya was just leaving.'

Dominic knew a momentary sense of irritation. Serena had been right, he thought impatiently. Cleopatra—Cleo—whatever she called herself, was arrogant. And stubborn. It would serve her right if he and his aunt abandoned the whole business.

But she was labouring under a misapprehension if she thought his grandfather would give up. Jacob Montoya was not that kind of man.

'Are you ready, Cleo?'

The little man was annoying, inserting himself between them as if he had a right to be there, and Dominic had to bite his tongue to prevent himself from making a foolish mistake. If he wanted to speak to her again, he had to keep this civil. But the temptation to blow them both off was incredibly appealing.

'OK,' he said now, taking a step back from the door, his eyes holding hers with a narrowed insistence. 'Enjoy your evening—uh—Cleo. We'll talk again, when you have more time.'

He strode away, descending the stairs without a backward glance, and Cleo expelled a breath that was neither relieved nor convincing. She'd wanted him to go, she told herself. So why did she feel this sense of frustration? Why did she care that she'd been less than polite?

'You OK, Cleo?'

Eric was obviously aware that something wasn't quite right, but Cleo was in no mood to explain things to him now.

'Just a misunderstanding,' she said, pulling out her woolly hat again and putting it on. 'Shall we go?'

'But who was that man?' Eric asked, as she turned out the light and locked her door. 'Does he work for the education authority?'

As if, thought Cleo bitterly, and then wondered if it wouldn't be easier to pass Dominic Montoya off as someone she'd met at work.

But no, she was no good at lying. 'He's not important,' she said, starting down the stairs so that Eric was compelled to follow her. 'I hope it doesn't rain. I haven't brought an umbrella.'

Cleo noticed the car as soon as she came out of school the following afternoon.

It was already getting dark. A slight drizzle was falling and the huge black SUV idling at the kerb just outside the playground entrance did look slightly sinister.

The children had long gone, so she knew she didn't have to worry about infant predators. Just an adult one, perhaps, with his quarry already in his sights.

Putting up her umbrella, she angled it so that she couldn't see the SUV any more and, stepping onto the pavement, turned determinedly towards the bus stop. She'd timed her exit to coincide with the bus's timetable. A woman alone didn't linger long in this area, particularly after dark.

The SUV was facing in the opposite direction, so she reckoned that if her bus was on time she ought to be able to board it before the car turned round.

But she hadn't accounted for the fact that the vehicle might simply use its reverse gear. And the road was quiet enough, so it presented no danger.

Even so, the main thoroughfare frequented by the city's buses was just ahead and she quickened her pace. She didn't want to run, even though every nerve in her body was urging her to do so.

Then the car stopped just ahead of her, the driver's door was pushed open and a man got out. A tall man, wearing jeans and a sports jacket over a black T-shirt. He was at once familiar and unfamiliar, and Cleo found she was clutching her shoulder bag to her chest, as if for protection.

'Hi,' he said, apparently indifferent to the weather, rain sparkling on his dark hair in the light from the street lamp. He came round the bonnet of the car to block her path. 'I'm sorry. Did I scare you?'

Cleo expelled a nervous breath. 'No. Why would you think that?' she asked sarcastically. 'I'm often stalked by strange men after school.'

Dominic sighed. 'I wasn't stalking you.'

'What would you call it, then?'

'I was waiting for you,' he said mildly. 'Come on. I'll give you a lift home.'

'That's not necessary.'

'Dammit, I know it's not *necessary*!' exclaimed Dominic tersely. He blew out a breath, calming himself. 'OK. What would you rather do? Go to a pub and have a drink? Or come back to the hotel and speak to Serena? It's all the same to me.'

'And what if I don't want to do any of those things?' Cleo asked, aware that the words sounded childish even to her ears.

'Oh, please…' Dominic counted to five before continuing, 'This isn't going to go away, Cleo. Your grandfather has terminal cancer. Do you want him to go to his grave knowing his only granddaughter was too stubborn—or too proud—to admit that she might be wrong?'

Cleo met his gaze defiantly for a moment, and then she looked away. 'No,' she mumbled reluctantly.

'So what's it to be?'

'What do you mean?' She was wary.

'Your place, a bar, or the hotel? It's your call.' Dominic glanced about him. 'Make up your mind. I'm getting wet.'

Cleo hesitated.

If she took him back to the apartment, there was a risk that Norah might come home early. And so far she hadn't had a chance to tell her friend about his visit the night before.

But equally, she had no desire to go to his hotel room. What if Serena wasn't there? That troubled her, too, more than she wanted to admit.

'Um—perhaps we could have a drink,' she murmured at last, and Dominic breathed a sigh of relief.

'OK,' he said, 'where? Is there somewhere near here?'

'No, not here,' said Cleo quickly, and Dominic arched a quizzical brow.

'No?'

'You wouldn't like any of the pubs around here,' Cleo assured him firmly, looping the strap of her bag over her shoulder again, almost poking him in the eye with her umbrella as she did so.

But she didn't want to have to explain to any of her colleagues, who might be lurking in the saloon bar of the King's Head, what she was doing having a drink with a—well, sexy stranger, who was evidently far out of her usual sphere of escorts.

'Where, then?'

He sounded impatient and Cleo licked dry lips before saying awkwardly, 'There's a hotel at the next crossroads. Could we go there?'

'You tell me.' Dominic swung open the passenger-side door. 'D'you want to get in?'

'Oh—yes. Thanks.' Cleo closed her umbrella without causing any more damage and climbed into the front of the car.

It smelled deliciously of warmth and leather, and when Dominic got in beside her she detected his shaving lotion also. It wasn't obvious; just pleasantly subtle. But it created an intimacy around them that caused Cleo to shift a little nervously in her seat.

'Is something wrong?'

Dominic had noticed and was looking her way now. Cleo managed a convulsive shake of her head.

'Just getting comfortable,' she murmured, far too aware of the taut fabric moulding his thigh just inches from her own.

She endeavoured to concentrate on the vehicle. It was superbly sprung, superbly comfortable, and Cleo was half sorry she was only going to enjoy it for such a short time. But perhaps it was just as well. She was far too aware of the man beside her.

Her brother!

But no. There had to be some other explanation. A surreptitious glance in Dominic's direction assured her that they were nothing alike. They were both dark-haired, of course, but so were at least a third of the population. And he owed the colour of his skin to the heat of a Caribbean sun, whereas she—

'Is this the place you meant?'

She'd hardly been aware of them moving, let alone that he'd driven in the right direction and was now slowing for the turn into the grounds of the hotel she'd mentioned.

'Oh—yes,' she said, recovering herself with an effort. 'I—er—I can't stay long. I've got a lot of marking to do tonight.'

Dominic didn't make any comment. Instead, he pulled into a parking bay, shoved open his door again and thrust long legs out of the car. Cleo hurriedly followed suit and he slammed her door behind her, pressing the fob to lock the vehicle.

Cleo had only been in the hotel once before and that had been on the occasion of a friend's wedding. The reception had been held in the conference room and she remembered lots of seafood, vol-au-vents and cheap champagne.

On reflection, she thought perhaps it hadn't been the wisest place to bring a man like Dominic Montoya. He was bound to think it was seedy and not up to his usual standard.

In fact, the lobby was encouraging. Someone had placed a large tub of late chrysanthemums on a table in the middle of the floor, and the signs indicating the various public rooms of the hotel were well-lit.

'Shall we go into the cocktail bar?' she asked, with a confidence she was far from feeling. 'I imagine we can get tea or coffee in there.'

'Tea or coffee?' Dominic's lips twitched. 'Well, yeah, if that's what you want.'

'It is.' Cleo spoke firmly. 'I don't drink, Mr Montoya.'

She started across the floor and to her relief he accompanied her. But she couldn't help being aware of the speculative glances they were attracting from female staff and patrons alike. They were probably wondering what a hunk like him was doing with someone like her, she thought ruefully.

Even in casual clothes, Dominic Montoya exuded an air of power and authority that was hard to ignore. Whereas she, in a dark green sweater, khaki trousers and an orange parka jacket felt—and probably looked—as if she was out of her depth.

Thankfully, the cocktail bar was almost empty at this hour of the afternoon. They had their choice of tables and Cleo chose one that was both clearly visible from the bar and near the exit.

A waitress came at once to take their order, not turning a hair when Dominic requested coffee for two.

'Is that OK with you?' he asked, taking the armchair opposite. 'I can't say I'm a great fan of tea myself.'

'Coffee's fine,' agreed Cleo tensely. 'Thank you.'

'Hey, no problem,' he responded, picking up a coaster and flicking it absently between his fingers. Long brown fingers, Cleo noticed unwillingly. 'So…' He arched his brows enquiringly. 'Have you thought any more about what I told you?'

Cleo hunched her shoulders. 'Yes, I've thought about it,' she admitted. She'd literally thought about little else, unfortunately.

'And?'

'And I don't see how what you say can be true,' she offered carefully.

'Why not?'

'Um—' She moistened dry lips before continuing, 'If you and I are supposed to be—brother and sister, we don't look much alike, do we?'

Now, why had she chosen that particular item out of all the things he and his aunt had told her to question first? She was pathetic!

'Well, that's easily explained.' Dominic lay back in his chair, steepling his fingers and regarding her over them with lazy green eyes. 'I was adopted. Your father's wife couldn't have any children.'

'Will you stop calling him my father?' exclaimed Cleo fiercely, even while the relief she felt was zinging through her veins.

He *wasn't* her brother.

But then, what did it matter? She probably wasn't his adopted sister either.

Probably?

The waitress arrived with the coffee and the few minutes she took unloading her tray gave Cleo time to think. What was she supposed to make of his answer? That his wife's inability to give him a child was why Robert Montoya had had an affair with Celeste Dubois?

It annoyed her that the woman's name sprang so easily to mind. She'd only heard it mentioned a couple of times and yet it felt as if it was emblazoned on her soul.

The waitress poured the coffee, and offered cream and sugar. Cleo accepted, but her companion declined. Then the young woman departed again, but not without a calculated backward glance at Dominic. Which he didn't return, Cleo noted, annoyed at herself for doing so.

Dominic tasted his coffee and then pulled a face. 'When will the English learn to brew a decent cup?' he demanded, shaking his head. He intercepted the look she cast him and gave a rueful grin. 'I bet you could do better than this.'

'I doubt it.' Cleo wasn't prepared to be cajoled into an invitation. She put down her cup. 'Why don't you tell me why you think the Novaks aren't my real parents?'

CHAPTER THREE

'IN OTHER words, why don't I cut to the chase?' suggested Dominic drily, and Cleo nodded.

Serena had been right, he thought resignedly. Ms Novak was one tough lady. And she wasn't going to be distracted by a few compliments, even if her face had betrayed a very different reaction when she'd discovered they weren't related after all.

Dominic wasn't a conceited man, but he hadn't lived for thirty years without becoming aware that women liked him. And Cleo Novak liked him as a man—if not as her nemesis. He'd bet his life on it.

But that didn't even figure in the present situation. There were enough women in his life already, and he had no intention of doing to her what his father had done to her mother. Lily Montoya was going to find this very hard as it was without him showing a quite inappropriate interest in the girl.

Nevertheless, she was very attractive…

He expelled an impatient breath and said crisply, 'OK, why don't you tell me about yourself? Before we get into the heavy stuff, I'd like to hear about your life with the Novaks.'

'With my parents, you mean?'

Cleo was stubborn, but he already knew that.

'Right,' he agreed. 'With your parents.' He paused. 'What did Henry—what did your father do for a living?'

Cleo hesitated. 'He did a lot of jobs. He was a taxi driver for a time, and a postman. When he and my mother died, they were working for an old lady in Islington. She let them occupy the basement of her house in exchange for gardening and—well, household duties.'

'Really?'

Dominic frowned. So what had happened to the not inconsiderable sum of money his father had given them? Evidently Cleo had had a good education, so that was something. But it sounded as if her adoptive father hadn't stuck at any job for very long.

Still, that wasn't his concern. 'But you didn't live with them?' he prompted and, after a moment, Cleo fixed him with a defiant look.

'Is this important?' she demanded. 'Why do you want to know so much about me? I thought you had all the answers.'

'Hardly.' Dominic's tone was rueful. 'Well, OK, we'll leave it there for now—'

'For now?'

'Yeah, for now,' he said, his tone hardening. He paused. 'I suppose I should tell you how you came to be living with the Novaks, shouldn't I?'

Cleo gave a dismissive shrug. 'If you must.'

'Oh, I must,' he told her a little harshly. 'Because whatever spin you choose to put upon it, you are Robert Montoya's daughter, and I can prove it.'

'How?'

Cleo sounded suspicious now and Dominic decided that was better than indifference. She was regarding him with dark, enquiring eyes and, for the first time, he saw a trace of his father in her cold defiance.

Putting a hand into his inner pocket, he pulled out a folded sheet of worn parchment and handed it to her. Half guessing what it might be, Cleo opened it out with trembling fingers.

And found herself looking at a birth certificate, with Robert Montoya's name securely in the place where a father's name should be.

Without bothering to check the mother's name, or the identity of the infant concerned, she thrust the sheet back at him. 'This isn't mine,' she declared tremulously. 'My birth certificate is with the papers my parents left.'

'Your *second* birth certificate,' Dominic amended flatly. 'My father bribed the authorities in San Clemente to produce another certificate with the Novaks' name on it.' He patted the paper he was holding with the back of his hand. 'But this is the original, believe me.'

Cleo felt as if she couldn't breathe. 'You're lying!'

'I don't lie,' said Dominic bleakly. 'Unlike your father, I'm afraid.'

Cleo shook her head. 'How do I know that's not the so-called second certificate?' she protested. 'Perhaps your father lied to you, too.'

Dominic didn't argue with her. He just looked at her from beneath lowered lids, thick black lashes providing a stunning frame for his clear green eyes.

And for the first time, Cleo began to worry about the consequences of her actions. What if he and his aunt were telling the truth? If they were, it followed that the Novaks had lied to her all these years. And that scenario was very hard to stomach.

Then he said quietly, 'There is such a thing as DNA, you know.'

'I don't know what to say,' she muttered at last, and saw a trace of compassion in his face.

'Why don't you take a proper look at this?' Dominic suggested, handing her the birth certificate again. 'Celeste insisted on having you registered before she died.'

Cleo swallowed and reluctantly looked at the sheet of parchment he'd given her. There was Robert Montoya's name, and her own, Cleopatra. She had been born in San Clemente, but her birth had been registered in Nassau, New Providence, both islands in the Bahamas.

Smoothing the sheet with quivering fingers, she said, 'If this is real, why did your father send me away?'

'It's—complicated.' Dominic sighed. 'Initially, I don't suppose he intended to. Celeste would never have let him take you away. But…' He paused. 'Celeste died, and that changed everything. And there was no way Robert Montoya could have claimed you as his when his own wife was incapable of having children.'

'But she adopted you,' protested Cleo painfully, and Dominic felt a useless pang of anger towards the man who'd raised him.

'I was—different.'

'Not black, you mean?'

Cleo was very touchy and Dominic couldn't say he blamed her.

'No,' he said at last, although her mother's identity had played an important part in Robert's decision. He sighed. 'Celeste Dubois had worked for my father. She was an extremely efficient housekeeper and when she discovered she was pregnant—'

'Yes, I get the picture.' Cleo's lips were trembling now. She made a gesture of contempt. 'It wouldn't do for the household staff to get above themselves. What a delightful family you have, Mr Montoya.'

'They're your family, too,' he said wryly. 'And my name is Dominic. It's a little foolish to call me Mr Montoya in the circumstances, don't you think?'

'I don't know what to think,' said Cleo wearily. 'I just wish—' She shook her head. 'I just wish it would all go away.'

'Well, I'm afraid that's not going to happen.'

'Why? Because my grandfather is dying?' She sniffed back a sob. 'Why should I do anything for a man who didn't even acknowledge my existence for the first twenty-two years of my life?'

'You don't actually know how he felt.' Dominic had noticed the way she'd said 'my' grandfather and not 'your'. 'It wasn't the old man's decision to send you to London with the Novaks.'

'But he apparently went along with it.'

'Mmm.' Dominic conceded the point. 'But what's done is done. It's too late to worry about it now.'

Cleo sniffed again. 'Is that supposed to console me?'

'It's a fact.' Dominic spoke without emphasis. 'It may please you to know that he's going to get quite a shock when he sees you.'

'Why? He knows who my parents were.'

Dominic groaned. 'Will you stop beating yourself up over who your parents were? They don't matter. Well, only indirectly. I meant—' He broke off and then continued doggedly, 'You're a beautiful woman, Cleo. I'm sure many men have told you that. But I doubt if the old man has considered the effect you're going to have on island society.'

Cleo gave him a disbelieving look. 'You don't mean that.'

'Don't I?'

She hesitated. 'So—are you saying I have that effect on you, too?' she asked tightly, a faint trace of mockery in her voice.

Dominic sighed. 'I guess I'm as susceptible to beauty as the next man,' he conceded wryly. 'But I don't think your grandfather would approve of any relationship between us.' He grimaced. 'He doesn't approve of the way I live my life as it is.'

Cleo bent her head, suddenly despairing. She had never felt more gauche or so completely out of her depth in her life.

She should have known he wouldn't find her attractive. Despite what he'd said, she was convinced he was only being polite. Besides, a man like him was almost bound to have a girlfriend—girlfriends! He was far too charismatic for it not to be so.

But she couldn't help wondering what kind of woman he liked.

One thing was certain, she thought a little bitterly. He wouldn't choose someone like her, someone who hadn't even known who their real parents were until today.

'So—do you believe me?'

Cleo didn't lift her head. 'About what?'

He blew out a breath. 'Don't mess with me, Cleo. You know what I'm talking about.' He paused. 'I want to know how you feel.'

'Like you care,' she muttered, and Dominic had to stifle an oath.

'I care,' he said roughly. 'I know this has been tough on you. But believe me, there was no other way to deal with it.'

She moved her head in a gesture of denial. Then, unable to hide the break in her voice, she mumbled, 'I still can't believe it. Someone should have told me before now.'

'I agree.'

She cast a fleeting glance up at him. 'But you didn't think it was your place to do it?'

'Hey, I didn't know myself until a couple of weeks ago!' exclaimed Dominic defensively. 'Nor did Serena. She is seriously—peeved, believe me.'

Cleo sensed the word he'd intended to use was not as polite as 'peeved' but he controlled his anger.

'Are you seriously—peeved?' she asked, again without looking at him, and Dominic wondered what she expected him to say.

'Only with the situation,' he assured her, aware of a feeling of frustration that had nothing to do with her. 'I guess the Novaks had been told to keep your identity a secret. Maybe they would have told you—eventually. But they didn't get a chance.'

Cleo heaved a sigh, and when she turned her face up to his he saw the sparkle of tears overspilling her beautiful eyes.

'I've been such a fool,' she said tremulously. 'I'm sorry. It's just—too much to take in all at once.'

'I can see that.'

In spite of himself, Dominic felt his senses stir. She was so confused; so vulnerable. His grandfather should never have gifted him with this task.

'Hey,' he said gruffly, as the tears continued to flow. Leaning towards her, he used his thumb to brush the drops away. 'Don't cry.'

He was hardly aware of how sensual his action had been until he felt the heat of her tears against the pad of his thumb.

Fortunately, at this hour of an October afternoon, the subdued lights in the lounge created an oasis of intimacy around their table, and no one had seen what he'd done.

Or, perhaps, not so fortunately, thought Dominic, hastily dragging his hand away. But not before her eyes had met his in a look of total understanding.

And he knew that she knew that for a brief moment of madness he had wanted her. Wholly and completely. He'd wanted to penetrate the burning core of her and assuage the incredible hard-on he'd developed in the melting heart of her oh-so-tempting body.

Christ and all His saints!

Unable to sit still with such thoughts for company, Dominic got abruptly to his feet. He buttoned his jacket over the revealing bulge in his trousers, hoping against hope that she hadn't seen it. For pity's sake, what in hell was wrong with him?

The waitress, ever-vigilant, came to see if there was anything else she could get him. Yeah, thought Dominic grimly, a stiff whisky. But he was driving, so he shook his head.

'Just the bill,' he said, pulling out his wallet and handing over a couple of twenties. 'Keep the change,' he added, as she started to protest it was too much.

Then, turning back to Cleo, he said, 'If you're ready, I'll take you home.'

Cleo swallowed, her tears evaporating as she became aware, in some shameful corner of her mind, that she was to blame for his sudden agitation. She wasn't proud of her reaction, but she was only human, after all. And she couldn't deny the warm feeling that was swelling inside her.

Whether he liked it or not, Dominic wasn't indifferent to her. But she couldn't—shouldn't—allow it to go on.

'I'll get the bus,' she said, making a thing of pouring herself more coffee. 'I'm not finished. Thank you all the same.'

She could hear Dominic breathing as he stood beside her. And the very fact that she could hear his infuriated response should have warned her she was treading on thin ice.

But she certainly wasn't prepared for him to bend down and pour the contents of her cup into the coffee pot. Then, slamming the cup back onto the saucer, he said, 'You're finished. Let's go.'

The waitress was still hovering and Cleo knew she couldn't cause a scene. Apart from anything else, she might want to visit the hotel again, whereas Dominic, she was sure, was never likely to darken its doors again.

Gathering her bag, she forced a smile for the waitress's benefit, and then, pressing her lips together, preceded Dominic from the room.

They crossed the reception hall in silence, but when they emerged into the damp evening air Cleo stopped dead in her tracks.

'I meant what I said,' she declared stiffly. 'I would prefer to get the bus.'

'And I've said I'll take you home,' said Dominic, brooking no argument. His hand in the small of her back was anything but romantic. 'Move, Cleo. You know where I parked.'

She decided there was no point in fighting with him. Besides, the buses were usually full at this hour of the evening, and why look a gift horse in the mouth? If he insisted on driving her home, why not let him? It was obvious from his expression that he had nothing else on his mind.

Dominic, meanwhile, was struggling to come to terms with what had happened in the bar. For goodness' sake, what was there about Cleo Novak that caused every sexual pheromone in his body to go on high alert?

It was pathetic, he thought irritably. He wasn't a kid to get a hard-on every time a beautiful woman flirted with him.

But, as they neared the SUV and he used the remote to

unlock the doors, he had to admit she intrigued him. Dammit, when had the touch of a woman's skin ever had that effect on him?

Never.

Cleo didn't wait for him to open the door for her. Sliding inside, she settled her bag on her lap, and pressed her knees tightly together. But a pulse was palpitating insistently inside her head and it was mirrored by the sensual heat she could feel between her legs.

Drawing a breath, she tried to concentrate on the car park outside the windows of the vehicle. Several people were leaving as they were, but others were just arriving.

Staff, maybe, she reflected, aware that she didn't really care. She just wanted to be home, safe inside the locked door of the apartment. She didn't want to think about Dominic, or her grandfather, or how she felt about the couple she'd always believed were her parents. She just wanted to get into bed and bury her head under the covers.

'I assume this road will take us to Notting Hill,' Dominic said after a moment, and she was forced to pay attention to her surroundings.

'Yes,' she muttered. 'But you can drop me in Cheyney Walk, if you like.'

'I think I can find Minster Court,' he said coolly and she remembered that he'd been there before. 'You'd better give me your cellphone number. If you do intend to obey your grandfather's wishes and come to San Clemente, there are arrangements to be made, right?'

Cleo's throat dried. Of course. They expected her to go to San Clemente. But how could she do that? She didn't even know where it was.

She'd been silent for too long, and with a harsh exclamation Dominic said, 'About what happened at the pub…'

'Your ruining my coffee, you mean?' she countered, grateful for the reprieve, but he wasn't amused by her attempt at distraction.

'No,' he said flatly. 'Forget about the damn coffee. You know what I'm talking about.'

'Do I?'

'Yes.' His strong fingers tightened on the wheel and she couldn't help wondering how it would feel to have those long fingers gripping her just as tightly. 'It was a mistake, right? I never should have touched you. And I want you to know, it'll never happen again.'

'All right.'

Cleo made her voice sound indifferent and he cast a frustrated glance in her direction.

'I mean it,' he persisted. 'I want you to know, I'm not that kind of man.'

'But you think I'm that kind of woman, hmm?' she suggested contemptuously, and he groaned.

'Of course not—'

'Well, forget it—Dominic. You're my brother, remember?'

Dominic wished to hell he were her brother. Her *real* brother, that was. Then he wouldn't be having this crisis of conscience.

'I haven't forgotten.' His tone was carefully controlled. 'Now, do you have that number? By my estimation, we should leave within the week. Do you have a passport?'

Cleo caught her breath. 'I can't leave within a week,' she protested. 'I have a job.'

'Ask for leave of absence,' said Dominic impatiently. 'Tell them it's a family emergency.'

Cleo gasped. 'Like they're going to believe that.'

'Why not?'

'Why do you think? They know I just…buried…my parents six months ago.'

Dominic felt a reluctant sense of compassion. 'Well, I guess you're going to have to tell them the truth,' he murmured drily, and she gave him an indignant look.

'I can't do that.' She turned her head to stare out of the window again. 'My God, how am I supposed to convince Mr Rodgers of something that I hardly believe myself?'

Dominic frowned. 'How about telling them that you've just discovered you've got a grandfather living in San Clemente? I assume they know that the Novaks came from the Caribbean?'

Cleo's lips quivered. 'You think it's so easy, don't you? But this is my life, my career; the way I earn my living. I can't just screw it up on a whim.'

Dominic bit back the urge to tell her that, unless he was very much mistaken, earning a living was going to be so much less of a challenge in the future. Jacob Montoya was a very wealthy man and he'd already hinted to Dominic that he wanted to try and make amends for his son's failings.

But when Cleo continued to look doubtful, he had to say something.

'You could always offer a few weeks' salary in lieu of leave of absence,' he murmured quietly, and Cleo's eyes widened in alarm.

'I couldn't do that. I couldn't *afford* to do that.' In the light from the street lamps outside, Dominic was almost sure her colour deepened. 'Besides, what would people think?'

'Does that matter?'

'Of course it matters.' Cleo was indignant. 'I need this job, Mr Montoya. I don't want anyone to assume I have independent means because I don't.'

Dominic sighed. 'I don't think money's going to be a problem for you in the future,' he said drily. 'Jacob—Jacob Montoya, that is, your grandfather—is a wealthy man—'

'And you think I'd take money from him.' Cleo was appalled. 'I don't want his money. I don't really want to have anything to do with him. It's only because he's—'

'Dying?' suggested Dominic helpfully, and she gave him a brooding look.

Then, when he said nothing more, she murmured unhappily, 'I suppose if I told Mr Rodgers—he's the head teacher—that I needed the time off on compassionate grounds, he might agree.' She bit her lip. 'I don't know.'

'Well, it's worth a try,' observed Dominic, deciding to reserve any stronger reaction until later. One way or another, she was going to be on that flight to San Clemente. He hadn't come this far to back off now.

'Mmm.'

She still sounded uncertain and Dominic was almost sorry when he saw the turn into Minster Court ahead of them.

There was so much more he should have said, he thought impatiently. Not least that her welcome might not be all that she expected. His own adoptive mother still lived at Magnolia Hill, the Montoyas' estate on the east side of the island, and she was totally opposed to his grandfather's decision to bring his son's daughter back to the island.

The fact that the girl was Lily's late husband's daughter had come as a terrible shock to her. She'd had no idea that the reason Celeste's baby had been spirited so hastily to England had been to prevent her from finding out the truth. Celeste's death had sealed her lips once and for all.

But it was all out in the open now, and Dominic didn't envy any of them having to deal with the fallout.

'You can stop here,' Cleo said suddenly, and Dominic realised they were outside the old Victorian block in which her apartment was situated.

And, when he did so, she pulled a pen and a scrap of paper from her bag and scribbled her mobile-phone number on it.

'There you are,' she said. And then, although she didn't really want to pursue it, she added, 'Shouldn't I have some way of getting in touch with you? Just in case I can't get the time off.'

Dominic's jaw hardened. But he had to answer her. 'We're staying at the Piccadilly Freemont,' he said flatly. 'But I'll be in touch myself in a day or so.'

'Don't worry.' Cleo's lips twisted. 'If I speak to your aunt, I won't say anything to embarrass you.'

'I doubt you could,' retorted Dominic shortly, thrusting open the car door.

However, before he could alight, Cleo's hand on his sleeve

arrested him. 'Stay here,' she said, the determined pressure of her fingers penetrating his jacket and feeling ridiculously like a hot brand on his forearm. 'I don't need an escort into my own house.'

'OK.' He slammed the door shut again and forced a mocking smile that didn't quite reach his eyes. 'I'll give you a call tomorrow evening.'

'If you like.'

Cleo pushed open the door and slid out of the car, looping the strap of her bag over her shoulder before slamming the door behind her.

Then, reluctantly aware of how vulnerable she suddenly seemed, Dominic jerked the car into gear and pulled away.

But he knew the frustration he was feeling was unlikely to be expunged by relating his conversation with Cleo to Serena. When he reached the hotel, he eschewed that responsibility and headed rather aggressively into the bar.

CHAPTER FOUR

'NOT long now.'

Cleo had been gazing out of the aircraft window, mesmer-ised by the incredible blue of the sea below them. But now she was forced to drag her eyes away and look at Serena Montoya, who'd come to seat herself in the armchair opposite.

'Really?' she said, knowing that 'How exciting!' or 'I can't wait' would have been more appropriate. But, in all honesty, she didn't know how she felt.

Serena had changed her clothes, she noticed. The woollen trouser suit she'd worn to board the British Airways jet in London had disappeared, and now she looked cool and relaxed in cotton trousers and a patterned silk shirt.

Cleo wouldn't have been surprised if she'd had a shower as well. The small bathroom behind the panelled door was very luxurious. Much different from the service facilities supplied on commercial transport.

But then, this wasn't a commercial aircraft.

After clearing Customs in Nassau, they'd boarded this small executive jet for the short flight to San Clemente. The jet was apparently owned by the Montoya Corporation, which had been another eye-opener for Cleo, who was still recovering from the shock of travelling first class for the first time in her life.

'Are you looking forward to meeting your grandfather?'

asked Serena casually, and Cleo was instantly aware that her words had attracted Dominic's attention.

He was seated across the aisle, papers and a laptop computer spread out on the table in front of him. He'd been working almost non-stop since they'd left London, leaving Cleo and Serena to fend for themselves.

Now he cast his aunt a warning look. 'Leave it, Rena,' he said sharply and Cleo saw the older woman's face take on a sulky look.

'I was only asking a perfectly reasonable question,' she protested, moving her shoulders agitatedly.

'I know exactly what you were doing,' Dominic retorted flatly. 'Leave her alone. She'll have to deal with it soon enough.'

Serena made an impatient sound. 'You make it sound like a punishment,' she said, flicking a non-existent thread of cotton from her trousers. 'He is her grandfather, for heaven's sake.'

'Rena!'

Serena snorted. 'Since when have you appointed yourself her champion?' she demanded. 'You've hardly said a word to either of us since we left London.'

'I've been working.' Dominic returned his attention to his papers. He shuffled several of them together and stowed them in the briefcase at his side. Then he looked at his aunt again. 'Why don't you call Lily and tell her we'll be landing in about twenty minutes?'

Twenty minutes!

Cleo's stomach took a dive.

It was all happening far too quickly for her. Despite the nine-hour journey from London, and this subsequent flight to San Clemente, it felt much too soon to be facing their arrival.

'Why don't you ring her?' she heard Serena say, as Cleo struggled to come to terms with this new development. 'She's your mother.'

'And your sister-in-law,' murmured Dominic mildly, apparently not at all put-out by his aunt's obvious frustration. 'But, OK. If you want me to ring her, I will.'

'No, I'll do it.'

With a gesture of irritation, Serena sprang up from her seat and disappeared through another door which Cleo knew led into one of the bedrooms. There were phones in this cabin but evidently it was to be a private conversation.

Or a warning?

The pilot had given Cleo a brief tour of the aircraft when she'd first climbed on board. And, as well as this comfortable cabin where they were sitting, there were both double and single bedrooms on the plane. Together with a couple of bathrooms, one of which Cleo had been glad to take advantage of.

'Don't mind Serena,' remarked Dominic now, continuing to gather his papers together. 'Believe it or not, she's a little nervous, too.'

Cleo reserved judgement on that, but evidently it wasn't a problem he suffered from.

She didn't make any comment, returning her attention to the view. She had to pinch herself at the thought that this was where she'd been born; this was where she actually came from. Was that the reason Henry and Lucille Novak had never shown any desire to come back?

She shivered, but now the distant shapes of several islands were appearing below them. And, as the plane banked to make its approach to the small airport on San Clemente, she saw the wakes of several boats moving purposefully across the sparkling water.

Her stomach hollowed again as the sea seemed to rush up to meet them, and she tried to concentrate on the sails of a large yacht that seemed to be making a run towards the island, too.

'That looks like Michael Cordy's yacht,' observed Dominic suddenly, and she realised he'd come to stand beside her chair and was leaning rather unnervingly towards the window.

It seemed such a reckless thing to do in such a small plane

that was already tilting far too much for Cleo's liking. Her hands sought the leather arms of the chair, gripping so tightly her knuckles whitened, and, as if becoming aware of her anxiety, Dominic dropped down into the seat Serena had vacated.

'It's OK,' he said reassuringly. 'Rick's a good pilot.'

'I'm sure.' Cleo licked her lips, her words tight and unconvincing. Then, forcing herself to relax, she glanced out of the window again. 'Is—is that the island? Just there?'

She pointed and Dominic leaned forward again, forearms resting along his spread thighs, his posture unconsciously sensual. Cleo's eyes were irresistibly drawn to the innocent bulge between his legs, and she had to force herself to look away.

Fortunately, he hadn't appeared to notice.

'Yeah, that's San Clemente,' he said, with evident pride. 'It always looks smaller from the air.'

'Do you think so?' Cleo had been thinking it looked bigger than she'd expected. 'Do you get many visitors?'

Dominic lounged back again, propping an ankle across his knee. 'Tourists, you mean?' And at her nod, 'We get a few. We don't have any high-rise hotels or casinos, stuff like that. But our visitors tend to like the beach life, and we do have some fantastic scuba-diving waters around the island.'

He was watching her again, and Cleo shifted a little nervously. 'Do you go scuba-diving?' she asked, and Dominic pulled a wry face.

'When I have the time,' he said. 'But since the old man's been ill, that isn't very often.'

'The old man?' Cleo frowned.

'Jacob Montoya. Our grandfather,' he said flatly. 'Remember?'

'Oh, yes.' Cleo bit her lip.

Dominic's brows drew together then. 'I should tell you,' he said, 'the Montoya Corporation is involved in a lot of different businesses. Leisure; casinos; oil. And recently we acquired a telecommunications network, that should keep the company solvent in the years to come.'

Cleo's jaw had dropped. 'I had no idea,' she whispered, and Dominic expelled a weary sigh.

'I know that,' he said. 'But don't let it worry you. No one expects you to take it all in at once.'

And wasn't that the truth? she thought unsteadily. She was having a hard time dealing with any of it. Even though the Montoyas had delayed their departure for a week to give her time to make her arrangements, it still hadn't been enough.

Not that people hadn't been understanding. Her head teacher, Mr Rodgers, had found her explanation quite fascinating, and he barely knew the half of it. Still, with his help, she had been able to persuade the local education authority that this was an emergency, and they'd given her a couple of weeks' unpaid leave.

Norah had been helpful, too, offering to go shopping with her, encouraging her to see this journey as the opportunity it really was.

'You don't know how I envy you,' she'd said, refusing Cleo's offer to pay her share of their expenses while she was away. 'You make the most of it, girl. You may never get a chance like this again.'

But, in spite of numerous good wishes, Cleo's actual involvement felt no easier. She was out of her comfort zone, she thought. Not to mention—literally and figuratively—out of her depth.

Suddenly aware that the silence in the cabin had become deafening, Cleo rushed impulsively into speech.

'Do—do you work for your grandfather?'

'*Our* grandfather,' Dominic amended drily. Then, with a lift of his shoulders, 'I guess I do.'

'What he means is, he runs the corporation,' broke in another voice sardonically. 'Don't let him fool you, Cleo. Without Dominic, there'd be no Montoya Corporation at all.'

Dominic got abruptly to his feet. Returning to where he'd

left his laptop, he began stuffing the rest of his belongings into his bag.

'Did you speak to Mom?' he asked, the coolness of his tone an indication that he wasn't pleased with her, and Serena pulled a face at Cleo before answering him.

'Uh—yes,' she said, as if there was any doubt about the matter. 'She says the old man can't wait for Cleo to arrive.'

Dominic shook his head. Serena was bound and determined to make this as difficult for the girl as it was possible to be.

'Lily also said she thinks she should make some other arrangement if this is going to be a long-term commitment.' She gave Dominic a sly look. 'She's even talking of moving in with you.' She paused. 'Now, wouldn't that be a happy development?'

Dominic scowled, and, although Cleo didn't even know the woman yet, it seemed painfully obvious that Dominic's mother had already taken a dislike to her.

'Um—perhaps I could stay at a hotel,' she ventured, just as the pilot's voice came over the intercom, advising them to buckle up as they'd be landing shortly.

Dominic gave her an impatient look as he seated himself in his own chair and fastened his seat belt. 'No,' he said flatly. 'You'll be staying at Magnolia Hill.' His lips twisted. 'Believe me, your grandfather won't have it any other way.'

Lily Montoya was standing on the veranda when Dominic, Serena and Cleo arrived at the house.

Cleo guessed she'd been waiting for them, evidently as curious to see her late husband's illegitimate daughter as she was to greet her son.

Cleo was conscious of the older woman's eyes assessing her as she stepped out of the back of the open-topped Rolls-Royce that had been sent to meet them. But then Lily flung herself into Dominic's arms, hugging him and chiding him and accusing him of being away for far too long.

Dominic treated his mother's exuberance with as much

patience as affection, his eyes meeting Cleo's over the woman's shoulder filled with a rueful resignation.

Nevertheless, it was obvious his mother had missed him terribly. And, despite his efforts to introduce her to Cleo, she persisted in distracting him with news about some woman he had apparently been seeing.

What did she think? Cleo wondered. That her son might be as unreliable towards his responsibilities as her husband had been? Or that Cleo was some kind of femme fatale, sent to take revenge on her mother's behalf?

Shaking her head, she looked about her, unwillingly aware that Magnolia Hill was even more beautiful than she had imagined. A huge antebellum-style mansion, its whitewashed facade was faced by a row of Doric columns that blended with the ornate pediment at the roofline.

Tall windows, some with iron-railed balconies on the upper floor, framed a porticoed doorway. Shallow steps stretched along the front of the building, leading up to a marble-paved veranda.

And, within the shadows of the veranda, a handful of cushioned iron chairs and a pair of bistro tables offered a relaxing place to escape the late-afternoon sun.

It was all quite overwhelming. The breathtaking views she'd seen on the short journey from the small airport had hardly prepared her for so much beauty and elegance. Magnolia Hill was quite simply the most beautiful house she'd ever seen.

The house's name was appropriate, too, she decided. It stood on a rise overlooking the land that surrounded it. A cluster of outbuildings, including cabins and barns and an enormous garage were set back among trees, while across palm-strewn dunes she could see the pink-white sands of an exquisite coral beach.

But the shadows were drifting over the island as the sun sank lower in the west and Cleo hoped it wasn't an omen. Despite her admiration for her surroundings, she hadn't forgotten how she came to be here.

She steeled herself with the thought that, in a matter of days, it would all be over and she'd be going home…

'Put the boy down, Lily.'

The gruff command enabled Dominic to free himself from his mother's clinging embrace and stride up the shallow steps to greet the elderly man who had appeared in the porticoed doorway of the house.

'Hey, Grandpa,' he said, shaking the man's hand and allowing him to place a frail, but possessive, arm about his shoulders. 'How are you?'

'Better now that you're here,' Jacob Montoya assured him roughly, affection thick in his voice. He looked beyond his grandson to where the three women stood together. His eyes flicked swiftly over his daughter and daughter-in-law before settling finally on Cleo. 'You brought her, then?'

'Did you think I wouldn't?' Dominic's tone was wry. 'I know an order when I hear one.'

'It wasn't an order,' his grandfather protested fiercely. But then he let go of the younger man to move along the veranda. 'Cleopatra?' he said, his voice quavering a little. 'You're the image of your mother, do you know that?'

'It's Cleo,' she murmured uncomfortably, aware that he'd said nothing to his daughter yet. 'How—how do you do?'

Jacob shook his head. He still had a shock of grey hair and despite the fact that there was no blood connection, he looked not unlike his grandson. They possessed the same air of power and determination.

They were both big men, too. In his youth, Jacob must have been as tall as Dominic. But now age, and his illness, had rounded his shoulders and attenuated the muscled strength that his grandson had in spades.

Still, his eyes glittered with a sharp intelligence that no physical weakness could impair. And, although his stature was a little uncertain, the hand he held out to Cleo was as steady as a rock.

'Come here…Cleo,' he said, ignoring Serena when she hurried up the steps to take his arm.

'Where's your stick?' she hissed, but Jacob only gave her an impatient look.

'I'm not an invalid, Rena,' he muttered. 'Leave me be.'

Cleo went up the steps rather timidly, which annoyed her a little, but she couldn't deny it. She couldn't help being intimidated by this man who was, incredibly, her grandfather.

She was also aware that both Serena and Lily Montoya were watching her. Probably hoping she'd fall flat on her face, she thought bitterly. It was becoming more and more obvious that neither of them really wanted her here.

Jacob was still holding out his hand and, with a feeling of trepidation, Cleo put her hand into it and felt the dry brown fingers close about her moist skin.

'My granddaughter,' Jacob said, and she was almost sure there was a lump in his throat as he spoke the words. 'My God, girl, you're beautiful!'

Cleo didn't know what to say. Out of the corner of her eye, she could see Dominic propped against one of the pillars. He'd taken off his jacket and folded his arms, watching their exchange with narrowed green eyes.

What was he thinking? she wondered. And why, at this most significant moment in her life, did she feel as if he was the only friend she had?

Which was ridiculous really. She hardly knew him, for heaven's sake. Oh, sure, there'd been that moment in the cocktail lounge of the hotel back in England when she'd sensed he was attracted to her. But that had just been a brief aberration, brought on, no doubt, by the fact that he hadn't seen his girlfriend for a week at least.

Nevertheless, almost unconsciously, she'd begun to depend on him, and it was only now that she realised she didn't even know where he lived. She knew he didn't live at Magnolia Hill.

Serena had said as much. But was he going to leave her here at the mercy of his aunt and his mother?

'This must all be very strange for you.' Jacob was speaking again and Cleo had to concentrate hard to understand what he was saying. 'I want you to know, I've anticipated this day with great excitement and emotion.'

Cleo didn't know how to answer him. How did you speak to a man you'd never met before, but who was as closely related to you as any man alive?

'I—I didn't believe it,' she offered at last, flashing Dominic a glance of pure desperation.

This had been such an incredibly long and nerve-racking day, and exhaustion was causing a tension headache to tighten all the skin at her temples.

'But Dominic must have told you what happened?' Jacob persisted, drawing her hand through his arm and turning towards the door into the house. 'I'm sure he explained—'

'Give her a break, old man.'

Dominic himself had stepped into their path, his jacket slung carelessly over one shoulder, and Cleo felt an immense sense of relief that he'd understood her panic.

'What do you mean?'

Jacob's tone was confrontational, but Dominic only exchanged a challenging look with Serena before saying smoothly, 'Can't you see she's tired? This has been a long day for her and I dare say what she'd really appreciate is a little time to herself. Why don't you let Serena show her to her room? Then she can have a shower and rest. She'll feel far more like answering your questions when she's not dropping on her feet.'

Jacob scowled, but he turned to Cleo with reluctant concern. 'Is this true, my dear?' he asked, and Cleo wet her lips before replying.

'I would like a chance to freshen up,' she agreed weakly. 'If you don't mind?'

'If I don't mind?' Jacob snorted. 'You must do whatever you feel like doing, my dear. I'm hoping you'll consider Magnolia

Hill your home; that you'll regard Dominic, Serena and myself as your family.' His lips tightened as he glanced back along the veranda. 'And Lily, of course.'

Dominic's mother looked as if the last thing she wanted to do was welcome her husband's illegitimate daughter into the family. But it was obvious from the tight smile that touched her lips, and from the fact that she didn't contradict him, that even she didn't fly in the face of her father-in-law's commands.

'Good.' Dominic sounded pleased. 'Now that's settled, perhaps Sam can fetch Cleo's bags from the car?'

CHAPTER FIVE

CLEO slept for almost twelve hours.

After that meeting with her grandfather, Serena had shown her to the rooms she was to occupy and suggested she might like her supper served there.

'I know my father won't approve. He can't wait to talk to you,' she said. 'But I think both Dominic and I are of the opinion that you need time to get your bearings before facing any more questions.'

At the time, Cleo had demurred. The sooner she got the initial interview with her grandfather over, the sooner she could think about going home. Because whatever Jacob Montoya had said, Magnolia Hill was not her home and never would be.

But it was not to be.

After the manservant had delivered her luggage and Cleo had denied needing any help with her unpacking, she'd spent a little time exploring her apartments.

A spacious living room, simply furnished with comfortable chairs and sofas, some of which sat beneath the long windows, flowed into an even more spacious bedroom. Here, French doors opened onto a balcony that overlooked a floodlit swimming pool at the back of the house, the huge colonial bed allowing its occupant to take full advantage of the view.

It had been getting dark, so she'd been unable to see much beyond the gardens. Besides, the marble-tiled bathroom had distracted her attention.

A large marble tub was sunk into the floor, while alongside it was a jacuzzi bath, with lots of jets for massaging the body. There were twin hand basins, also in marble, and an enormous shower cubicle, its circling walls made incredibly of glass tiles.

There were mirrors everywhere, throwing back her reflection from every angle, flattering or otherwise. When she first shed her clothes, Cleo spent a little time fretting over her appearance. In her opinion, her breasts were too small and her hips were too big, and she shivered at the thought of Dominic seeing her in a swimsuit.

But, despite these inappropriate feelings towards her adopted brother, by the time Cleo had had a shower and washed her hair, she could hardly keep her eyes open.

Wrapping her hair in one of the fluffy towels she found on a rack in the bathroom, she dragged her suitcase across the floor and extracted a bra and panties. Then, stretching out on the satin luxury of the bedspread, she closed her eyes.

She awakened to fingers of sunlight finding their way between the slats of the window blind. It was evidently morning, but for a moment she couldn't remember where she was. Only that the bed, and most particularly the room, were unfamiliar.

Then her memory reasserted itself, and, unable to suppress a little gasp of dismay, she pushed herself up on her elbows and looked about her.

Her first realisation was that someone had been into her room while she was sleeping. The bedspread she'd been lying on had been drawn back and she was now covered with a fine Egyptian cotton sheet. Also, the blinds hadn't been drawn when she'd lain down on the bed. So who had checked up on her?

One of the servants, perhaps? Or Serena? She wouldn't put it past the older woman to want to satisfy herself that Cleo wasn't going to appear again that night. But what had she told Jacob Montoya? Had she let him think that Cleo had chosen to go to bed rather than spend the evening with him?

She sighed. It was too late now to worry about such a possibility. And her grandfather—she was amazed at how easily the word came to her mind—had said to treat the place as her home. Not that she would. As she'd thought the night before, she could only ever be a visitor here. Too many things had happened to consider anything else.

Sliding her legs out of bed, Cleo got to her feet and was relieved to find she felt totally rested. If a little sticky, she conceded, aware that, despite the air conditioning, moving brought a film of moisture to her skin. Beyond the windows, the sun was evidently gaining in strength. What time was it? she wondered. And where had she left her watch?

She eventually found it in the bathroom. She'd adjusted the time on the plane and she saw now that it was barely seven o'clock. Nudging the bedroom blind aside, she peered through the French windows. It was a glorious morning and, despite herself, she felt her spirits rise.

There didn't appear to be anyone about and, unlatching the window, she pushed it open. Warmth flooded into the room and with it came the tantalising scent of tropical blossoms and the unmistakable tang of the sea.

She saw now that beyond the gardens was the beach she'd glimpsed so briefly on her arrival. Feathery palm trees framed the blue waters of the Atlantic, a frill of foam creaming along the shore.

Slipping between the vertical blinds, she stepped out onto the balcony. Below her, the swimming pool sparkled in the sunlight, tubs of shrubs and hibiscus and oleander marking the curve of a patio that was half-hidden from her view.

A maid appeared with a watering can, evidently intent on her task, and although Cleo was inclined to step back inside she resisted the impulse. After all, her bra and panties were no more revealing than a bikini. It was amazing, she could stand here in the sunlight, when it had been wet and cloudy yesterday morning in London.

She wondered what time her grandfather got up. Whether he'd expect her to join him for breakfast. Her nerves jangled a little at the prospect, though from what she'd seen the night before, he didn't seem a very intimidating figure.

Unlike Dominic…

Her pulse quickening, she wondered if Dominic had stayed the night at Magnolia Hill. Had he ever lived here at all? He'd told her his parents had had their own house when he'd explained about Celeste—her mother. Goose pimples feathered her skin at the memory.

But still, she couldn't stop thinking about where he might be at this moment. Perhaps he lived with his girlfriend, though that thought was less easy to engage. Whatever, it was really no concern of hers, so she should just get over it. Before she saw him again and let him guess how she felt…

A shadow moved at the far side of the pool.

For the first time, she noticed that there were cabanas there; small cabins where a person using the pool could change their clothes.

A man had emerged from one of the cabanas. A tall man, bare-chested, with a towel draped around his neck. He was wearing swimming shorts that barely skimmed his hip bones. Wet shorts that clung to every corded sinew.

As she watched, he used the towel to dry his hair, and she saw the growth of dark hair beneath his arms and arrowing down his chest. His skin was brown and sleek with muscle, his stomach flat above long, powerful legs.

Cleo's palms were suddenly damp. She didn't have to wonder any longer about Dominic. He'd obviously been swimming. But how long had he been there? And was he able to see her?

Her throat drying, Cleo eased herself back into her bedroom. Then, allowing the blinds to fall back into place, she took a moment to calm her racing heart. Wherever he lived he'd evidently spent the night at Magnolia Hill, she thought breathlessly. Would he be joining his grandfather for breakfast, too?

She was spending far too much time speculating about

Dominic Montoya. Impatient with herself, Cleo smoothed her palms down her thighs and knelt beside her suitcase.

What to wear? That was the problem. Well, not a bikini, she assured herself, with another glance in the mirror. The tank suit Norah had persuaded her to buy was probably going to remain unworn in her case.

Half an hour later, she emerged from the bathroom in narrow-legged lemon shorts and a white cotton T-shirt. Smart, but casual, she thought, remembering something else Norah had told her. It wasn't cool to look overdressed.

Besides, the last thing she wanted was for anyone to get the impression that she was looking for admiration. Or sex, she added grimly, abruptly recalling the last months of her mother's life.

She decided she could hardly blame Lily Montoya for being hostile. After all, her husband had had an affair with Celeste. But as for her being attracted to her adopted brother... Cleo sucked in a breath. There was no way history was going to repeat itself.

Her hair was still a little wet, so she found an elasticated band in her bag and looped it up in a ponytail. Then, stepping into thonged sandals, she checked her appearance once more before opening her door.

The place seemed very quiet. Without the knowledge that there were at least half a dozen servants working in the house, she might have thought she and Dominic were its only occupants.

She blew out a breath, inwardly chiding herself. She had to stop punctuating every thought with Dominic. He meant nothing to her. How could he? She hardly knew him. And it went without saying that she meant nothing to him.

A long hallway with a window at the end led to the staircase. However, before reaching the downward curve of a scrolled iron banister, the landing opened out into a pleasant sitting area. From here, it was possible to overlook the lower foyer, circular leaded windows allowing sunlight to stream into the stairwell.

As Cleo started down, she saw the huge potted fern that filled the turn of the staircase. Tendrils of greenery clung to the iron and brushed her fingers as she passed. There was something almost sensual about its twining fronds, she mused ruefully. Or perhaps she was just extra-sensitive this morning.

Certainly, she had climbed this staircase the night before. But then, exhaustion, and a certain amount of tension, had clouded her view. Not that she was any less tense this morning, she thought, pausing to admire the view from an arching window. Even the sight of the alluring shoreline couldn't quite rid her of the feeling that she shouldn't be here.

A West Indian maid appeared below her. She looked up at her with expectant eyes, and Cleo wondered what she was thinking. 'Can I help you, Ms Novak?' she asked, and Cleo was relieved to find she hadn't been introduced to the staff as Cleo Montoya.

'Um—you could tell me if Mr Montoya is up yet,' she said, deciding she might as well be proactive. If her grandfather wanted to see her, there was no point in her dragging her heels.

The maid gestured across the delicately patterned tiles of the foyer. 'Mr Dominic is having breakfast on the terrace,' she said politely. 'You like I should show you the way?'

'Oh—no.' Cleo had no desire to spend any more time with Dominic than she had to. 'I meant—Mr Montoya Senior. What time does he usually get up?'

'Your grandfather has breakfast in his room at about seven a.m.,' remarked a disturbingly familiar voice from behind her. Cleo turned to find Dominic standing in the arched entry to the adjoining room. 'He'll be down later.'

Thankfully, he was dressed now. Albeit in khaki cargo shorts and a tight-fitting black T-shirt that exposed taut muscles and a wedge of brown flesh at his waist.

Which seemed far too casual to her way of thinking. It was easier to keep him at arm's length in a formal suit and tie.

He had evidently heard their voices and come to investigate. The acoustics in the foyer must have allowed the sound to circulate around the ground-floor rooms. Cleo realised belatedly that she should have thought of that.

However, the maid turned towards him with evident enthusiasm. 'Ms Novak was just lookin' for Mr Jacob, sir,' she said, sashaying towards him, hips swinging, arms akimbo. 'You want more coffee, Mr Dominic? You do, just say the word and Susie'll get it for you.'

Dominic's lips tightened as he saw Cleo's reaction to the implied intimacy of the girl's words, and there was an edge to his voice when he said, 'You can get Ms Novak some breakfast instead. Fruit, cereal, rolls, coffee.' He arched his brows at Cleo. 'Does that about cover it?'

'I...' Cleo had hardly heard what he'd said and now she struggled to answer him. 'I—I guess so,' she muttered. 'Thank you.'

'No problem.' Dominic turned once more to the maid. 'On the terrace, Susie. As quick as you can, right?'

Susie pursed sulky lips, but she knew better than to argue that it wasn't her job to serve meals when she'd already offered to get him fresh coffee.

'Yes, sir,' she said tersely, her hands dropping to her sides as she marched away, and Cleo hoped she hadn't made another enemy.

Meanwhile, Dominic was trying to master his own frustration. Dammit, Cleo probably thought he exercised some medieval droit de seigneur over the female members of the household staff and it irritated the hell out of him.

Not that it mattered what Cleo thought, he reminded himself. Only it did.

'Did you sleep well?'

Dominic gestured for her to come and join him and, although she would have preferred to make her own way, Cleo had little choice but to obey him.

'Very well,' she responded, making sure she didn't brush

against him as she preceded him into the room behind him. 'I'm sorry if your grandfather expected me to join him yesterday evening, but I'm afraid I just flaked out.'

'I know.'

Dominic was far too sure of himself, and Cleo gave him a wary look.

'You know?'

'Yeah.' He nodded. 'Serena had one of the maids check up on you.' He grimaced. 'You could have fallen asleep in the bath. We wouldn't want you to drown yourself before you had a chance to get to know us.'

Cleo pressed her lips together. 'I wasn't likely to do that,' she said, but Dominic only gave her a wry smile.

'All the same…' he murmured lightly. 'The old man would never have forgiven himself if anything had happened to you.'

'Just the old man?' Cleo found herself saying provocatively, and saw the way Dominic's expression darkened.

'Don't play games with me, Cleo,' he said warningly. 'You're not equipped to deal with the fallout.'

Cleo's lips parted, but she didn't say anything more. Her face flaming, she turned away, grateful to transfer her attention to less disquieting subjects.

But he was right, she thought. She wasn't used to provoking anyone, least of all a man who always seemed to bring out the worst—or was it the bitch?—in her.

It was quite a relief to study her surroundings.

Darkly upholstered sofas and chairs stood out in elegant contrast to the backdrop of pale walls and even paler wooden floors.

Long windows, some of them open to admit the delicious breeze off the ocean, boasted filmy drapes that moved seductively in the morning air.

'We'll go outside,' said Dominic after a moment, and Cleo realised he had crossed the room and was now standing by French doors that opened onto a stone terrace.

She followed, as slowly as she dared, taking in the exquisite appointments of the room. Low tables; cut-glass vases filled with flowers; thick candles in chunky silver holders.

There was even a grand piano, its lid lifted, hidden away in one corner of the enormous apartment. And dramatic oil paintings in vivid colours that added their own particular beauty to the walls.

'You have a beautiful home,' she said a little stiffly, wanting to restore some semblance of normality, but Dominic's lips only twisted rather mockingly at her words.

'It's not my home,' he reminded her carelessly, stepping aside to let her pass him. 'But I'm sure your grandfather is hoping you'll make it yours.'

Cleo's jaw dropped. 'You're not serious!'

'What about?' Dominic ignored her startled expression. 'I assure you, I do have my own house a couple of miles from here on Pelican Bay.'

'No—' Cleo was almost sure he was deliberately misunderstanding her '—that's not what I meant.'

They'd emerged onto the terrace now and Cleo could see where a tumble of pink and white bougainvillea hid the low wall that separated the paved patio from the pool.

She was briefly silenced by the view. By the pool, shimmering invitingly; by the rampant vegetation and flowering trees that surrounded it; by the ever-constant movement of the ocean beyond the rolling dunes.

Aware of Dominic's silence, she turned to him and said, 'About my grandfather—he doesn't really expect me to stay here, does he?'

Dominic shrugged, his compassion reluctantly stirred by her obvious confusion. 'It's what he wants,' he said simply. 'I think he's hoping to make up for all those years when he didn't know you.'

Cleo chewed on her lower lip. 'But why now?'

Dominic sauntered towards a circular table set in the shade of a brown and cream striped canopy. Then, picking up his coffee, he glanced at her over his shoulder. 'Why do you think?'

Cleo groped for a convincing answer. 'Because he's ill?'

'Because he's dying,' Dominic amended flatly. 'Because he's been forced to face the fact of his own mortality.' He paused. 'According to his lawyer, he's been looking for you for some time.'

Cleo frowned. 'And did—did my mother and father know this?'

'The Novaks?' Dominic shrugged. 'I shouldn't think so.'

He raised his cup to his lips and swallowed the remainder of his coffee, his dark head tilted back, the brown column of his throat moving rhythmically.

Cleo was unwillingly fascinated, but she managed to drag her eyes away and say, 'So—he waited until they were dead?'

Dominic lowered his cup to its saucer and regarded her resignedly. 'What are you saying? You think the old man had something to do with their deaths?'

'Heavens, no.' Cleo was horrified. 'They died in a train crash, you know that.' She hesitated, and then went on a little emotionally, 'They'd been to visit some friends who'd relocated to North Wales and were on their way back. Apparently the train became derailed at a crossing. It was an accident. A terrible accident.' Her voice broke then. 'I miss them so much.'

'I'm sure you do.'

The sympathy in Dominic's voice was almost her undoing, but she managed to hold herself together.

Dominic, meanwhile, was having a hard time controlling the urge he had to comfort her. But he hadn't forgotten what happened when he touched her. How uncontrollable his own reaction could be.

'Anyway,' she went on, unaware of his agitation, 'your aunt said that was when—when he decided to contact me.'

'Yeah.' Dominic sucked in a breath. 'He'd known the Novaks wouldn't take kindly to any intervention from him. But after—well, after the funeral, he had a firm of investigators find out all about you.'

'But how did he know about the train crash?'

'Again, according to his lawyer, he'd already traced the Novaks to Islington. It wasn't until after the funeral he discovered that you weren't living with them.'

Cleo frowned. 'I moved out a couple of years ago, when Mom and Dad went to live with Mrs Chapman. I was just finishing college and I'd got the job at St Augustine's, so I didn't want to move away.'

'So you decided to share an apartment with a friend?'

'More or less.'

Dominic realised she was unaware of it, but this was the first time she'd been totally relaxed with him.

And he was enjoying her company far too much.

Nevertheless, it was impossible to ignore the fact that he was possibly her only ally here. His grandfather had his own agenda, no doubt, but both Serena and his mother resented her. That went without saying.

And her vulnerability stirred him in a way he'd never felt before. In her simple T-shirt and shorts, her dark hair caught up in a ponytail, she looked so young and—dammit, innocent.

He scowled. He had to stop feeling responsible for her, he told himself. The old man wouldn't like it; wouldn't like the idea that she depended on Dominic and not himself.

But it was that sense of responsibility that had made Dominic accept his grandfather's invitation to stay the night at Magnolia Hill. Despite the fact that Sarah Cordy, his current girlfriend, had made him promise to go and see her as soon as he got back...

'Norah—that's the girl I live with,' Cleo was saying now, completely unaware of his frustration, 'she was finding the rent of the apartment too much for just one person, so she offered me the chance to share.' She smiled disarmingly. 'I jumped at it.'

'And Eric? Where does he fit in?'

Dominic heard the words leave his lips with a feeling of incredulity. Dammit, whoever Eric was, it was nothing to do with him. But it was too late to take them back now.

'Eric?' Cleo's lips rounded. 'Oh, yes, you met Eric, didn't you?' A teasing smile tilted her mouth. 'Did he scare you?'

'Are you kidding me?'

Dominic had answered without thinking, but now he realised she'd just been baiting him.

'Oh, yeah, very clever,' he grunted. 'The guy really had me quaking at the knees.'

'And they're such nice knees, aren't they?' Cleo giggled, stepping back to get a better look. 'Mmm, you definitely wouldn't win any knobbly-knees contest.'

'Any what?' he was demanding, advancing on her half threateningly, when they both became aware that they were no longer alone.

His mother was standing at the far side of the terrace, amazingly holding the tray that contained Cleo's breakfast in her hands.

Her blue eyes were glacial as they rested on Cleo's flushed face. Then warmed slightly when they moved to her son.

'Am I interrupting?' she asked, indicating the tray. 'I intercepted Susie in the foyer and she said you'd asked for this, Dominic.' Her smile was thin. 'I thought you'd already had breakfast.'

'I have.'

Dominic was fairly sure the tray wasn't all his mother had got from Susie, but he kept his thoughts to himself.

'It's Cleo's breakfast,' he said pleasantly. 'Here.' He went towards her. 'Let me take it from you.'

'I can manage,' she said.

But somehow—Dominic didn't want to think it was deliberate—the tray slipped from her hands.

Cleo jumped back as cups and saucers shattered on the stone paving, Fruit juice and hot coffee splashed in all directions, the latter burning as it touched her bare feet.

She bent automatically to pick up a rolling peach, its skin as soft as her own, thought Dominic savagely. But bruised now, as she was, by his mother's careless hands.

Then her eyes moved anxiously to his and he turned to give his mother an enigmatic look.

'Oh, dear me!' Lily Montoya pressed her clasped hands to her breast. 'I'm so clumsy.'

And if Cleo hadn't seen the look the woman had cast her earlier, she might have believed she meant it.

CHAPTER SIX

'IT DOESN'T matter.' Dominic was dismissive, almost as if destroying an expensive porcelain coffee service was of no matter. 'I'll get Susie to bring another tray.'

'Oh, please, don't!'

Cleo's cry arrested him. She didn't think she could bear to be alone with Lily Montoya at this moment.

She hadn't asked to come here, she told herself as the other woman's expression hardened. And, although she had sympathy for Lily's feelings, Dominic's mother shouldn't blame her because her husband hadn't been able to keep his trousers zipped.

'Cleo—' Dominic began, when the clatter of a stick against stone made them all turn.

'Dom! Dom!' Jacob Montoya stumped heavily across the terrace, sharp eyes taking in the scene and finding it wanting. 'What's going on here, boy? Has your mother been throwing china around again?'

'I dropped the tray, Jacob.' Lily was defensive. 'I'm not in the habit of breaking things.'

'If you say so.' Jacob spoke indifferently. 'I just hope you're not trying to intimidate our guest.'

Lily's lips tightened. '*Your* guest, Jacob. Not mine. Or Dominic's.'

'Ma!' Dominic intervened now, aware that Cleo's face was rapidly losing all colour. 'Can't you see, Cleo had no part in

Dad's defection? You can't blame her for something she knew nothing about.'

'And that's the truth,' broke in his grandfather staunchly, but Lily wasn't listening to him.

Taking a handkerchief out of her handbag, she held it to her nose, her eyes seeking Dominic's in mute appeal. 'I'm not to blame either,' she whispered tearfully. 'I thought you would understand how I felt.'

'I do.' Dominic could feel himself weakening, but he knew deep inside that his mother was far more capable of manipulating the situation to her own ends than Cleo. 'Just cool it, hmm, Ma? We all need to learn to get along together, right?'

Lily sniffed. 'I think you're asking too much, Dominic. This is my home—'

'But it's my house,' Jacob Montoya interrupted, his voice surprisingly forceful. 'And so long as I own Magnolia Hill, I'll say who can or can't stay here.'

Cleo stifled a groan. She pressed cold hands to her face, wishing the paving stones of the terrace would just open up and swallow her.

This was so much worse than she'd anticipated. She'd been anxious about Dominic's mother, of course, but she'd never expected the woman to take such an instantaneous dislike to her.

And the fact that Lily lived here, at Magnolia Hill, just emphasised the problem. Someone should have warned her about this before she agreed to come here.

'Look, we're upsetting Cleo,' said Dominic impatiently, and his mother let out a wounded cry.

'You're upsetting *me,* Dominic,' she protested, her eyes wide and indignant. 'But that doesn't matter, apparently.'

'Oh, please…' Cleo couldn't take any more of this. She looked from her grandfather to Dominic and then back again. 'I—I never wanted to stay here. And I certainly don't want to upset anyone. I'd be much happier if I could just find a room at a bed-and-breakfast—'

'Forget it!'

Before Dominic could voice his own protest, his grandfather had intervened.

'You're staying here, girl,' Jacob said flatly. 'That's a given. And if my daughter-in-law isn't happy with that, then I suggest she finds somewhere else to stay, not you.'

'Oh, but—' began Cleo, only to have Dominic intercede this time.

'Would you rather Cleo stay at Turtle Cove with me, Ma?' he suggested, and, as he'd expected, his mother couldn't hide her dismay at this proposal.

'That—that would be totally inappropriate!' she exclaimed, aghast, and Jacob actually laughed.

'Good move, Dom,' he said, before shuffling across the terrace to where Cleo was standing and throwing a reassuring arm about her shoulders. 'It'll all work out, you'll see,' he added, giving her a protective squeeze. 'So we'll hear no more about bed-and-breakfasts, OK?'

Cleo wanted to move out of his embrace. Whatever he said, she'd never feel at home here. But she had the feeling she was supporting Jacob as much as he was supporting her, so she merely shook her head.

'Now,' he went on cheerfully, 'I'm guessing that was your breakfast that ended up on the ground, am I right?' Her expression gave him her answer, and he nodded. 'Good. Then we'll have breakfast together.'

'You've had breakfast, Father.'

Lily wasn't going to give in without a fight, it seemed, but Jacob only gave her a warning look. 'I can have two breakfasts, can't I?' he demanded. Then he looked at Cleo again. 'But I think we'll have it in the morning room. This place needs cleaning up and the atmosphere doesn't suit me at the moment.'

Dominic watched Cleo and Jacob make their way across the terrace and into the house. Then he turned to look at his mother.

'You OK?'

'Like you care.' Lily was near to tears.

'Of course I care,' said Dominic heavily. 'But antagonising the old man isn't going to do you any good.' He paused. 'She's his granddaughter. She has every right to be here, and you know that.'

Lily pursed her lips. 'You like her, don't you?'

'Uh—yeah.' Dominic was wary. 'She's my adoptive sister. What's not to like?'

'Correction, she's your father's by-blow,' retorted Lily angrily. 'She's not related to us by any means whatsoever.'

'OK.' Dominic closed his eyes for a moment. 'But she's still a Montoya, in everything but name. Whatever names you choose to call her, she's still the legitimate heir to Magnolia Hill.'

Lily's lips parted. 'Did your grandfather tell you that?' she asked, appalled.

'No.' Dominic didn't know what the old man might decide about the house. 'But she does have a place here, Ma. Goodness knows, it was hard enough to persuade her to come.'

Lily frowned. 'You're joking!'

'No, I'm not.' Dominic was weary of this. 'Look, I've got to go. I promised Josh I'd call into the office as soon as I got back.'

'Oh, yes, it's all right for you, isn't it?' muttered Lily resentfully. 'My father left you God knows how many millions, and Jacob's already given you virtual control of the Montoya Corporation. Whereas I—I—'

'Can do exactly what you like,' Dominic interrupted her flatly. 'You chose to come and live here when Dad died. But there's nothing stopping you from buying another house.'

Lily gasped. 'This is my home!' She straightened her shoulders. 'I never thought I'd hear you say otherwise.'

'I'm not saying otherwise,' protested Dominic, wishing he'd never started this. 'I just want you to be happy.'

'Then you should never have brought that girl here,' declared his mother forcefully. 'I don't know what Sarah's going to think.'

'Sarah's not my keeper, Ma!'

'No, but she is your girlfriend, Dominic. She deserves some loyalty, don't you think? Or are you blinded by this other young woman's doubtful charms?'

Dominic stifled an oath. 'You're exaggerating the situation,' he said harshly. 'Sarah's a friend, that's all. I'll go and see her in my own good time.'

'I think she thinks she's rather more than that,' said his mother tightly. 'But in any event, I'd make my peace with her before she hears about your apparent attachment for your grandfather's—um—folly—from someone else.'

Dominic scowled. 'What the hell is that supposed to mean?'

'You can't deny you and the Novak girl were acting very cosy when I walked onto the terrace,' Lily asserted, pushing the tissue she'd been using back into her bag.

Dominic raked long fingers through his hair. 'Don't call her the Novak girl!' he exclaimed frustratedly. 'Anyway, what do you mean, we were acting cosy? What did you *think* we were doing?'

'I don't know, do I?'

'Oh, for pity's sake!' Dominic was rapidly losing his temper and it was an effort to rein it in. 'I was trying to get her to relax, that's all. If you'd get your head out of your—' He broke off, before he said something unforgivable, and continued, 'Get to know her, Ma. You might like her, too.'

'I don't think so.'

Lily was inflexible and Dominic gave up. 'I'm going to change,' he said. 'I need to get into town.'

Hunched shoulders was his only answer and, blowing out an impatient breath, Dominic started for the door.

There was no point in saying any more, he realised. He'd probably said more than he should already. But, dammit, Cleo needed someone other than his grandfather to fight her corner.

Breakfast with her grandfather was surprisingly enjoyable.

And, although Cleo knew it was due in no small part to

Jacob's determination to put her at her ease, she found him amazingly easy to talk to.

Much like Dominic, she admitted unwillingly. Except that when she was talking to her grandfather, there was no sexual tension between them.

As there was with Dominic.

A shiver of remembrance prickled her spine. She didn't know what might have happened if his mother hadn't interrupted them as she had. Or was that simmering awareness between them only in her mind, not his? There was no doubt it played an integral part in the way she reacted to him.

But it was pleasant, sitting in the sunlit luxury of the morning room, overlooking the gardens of the house and the blue-green waters of the Atlantic beyond.

Crisp lemon-yellow linen, gleaming silver flatware, cut glass and bone china, all set on a circular table in the shaded curve of the windows.

Jacob began by saying how sorry he was that she'd lost her parents—even if he was thinking that she'd had no blood tie to them at all. Nevertheless, he was kind enough to express his condolences; to help her to relax and feel there was someone else, besides herself, who cared.

Her apology for not appearing again the night before was quickly dealt with.

'Dominic was right,' he assured her, gnarled fingers surprisingly dark against her creamy skin. 'I should have realised you were tired. Instead of expecting you to be as excited to see me as I was to see you.'

Cleo had no answer to that. Easy-going as he was, she hadn't to forget how she came to be here. But it wasn't as easy to hold a grudge in such beautiful surroundings. And hadn't he been as much a victim of circumstance as she was?

No!

Fortunately, her grandfather was happy to lead the conversation. He seemed quite content to describe the island and its history, entertaining her with stories of the illegal rum-running that had gone on during Prohibition in the United States.

Surprisingly, he'd also mentioned the slavery that had taken place during the late-eighteenth and early-nineteenth centuries, too. He'd shocked her by admitting that there were few families on San Clemente who could claim there was no mixed blood in their ancestry.

Indeed, she'd been so engrossed in what he was saying that it wasn't until the meal was over that Cleo realised how much about her own life he'd gleaned. Just the odd question here and there, but she'd found herself telling him about her job and about Norah, forgetting for a few moments exactly who he was.

He was a clever man, she mused, accepting his invitation to sit on the terrace for a while after breakfast. He'd probably already known half of what she'd told him. But by getting her to confide in him, he'd created a bond between them that would be that much harder to break.

'Perhaps you'd like a swim,' he remarked, apparently aware that Cleo had been eyeing the cool waters below the terrace with some envy. 'Later this afternoon, you might enjoy a walk along the shoreline. I'd like to take you myself, but for now I can recommend the pool.'

'Oh, no.' Cleo shook her head. Then, in an outright lie, 'I don't have a swimsuit, Mr Montoya.'

'If you can't call me Grandpa, call me Jacob,' he said a little tersely then, continuing his earlier suggestion. 'A swimsuit is no problem.' He gestured with his stick towards the cabanas. 'You'll find everything you need in one of the cabins. Serena always keeps a selection of swimwear for unexpected guests.'

'But I'm not really an unexpected guest, am I?' Cleo regarded him with cautious eyes. 'I think I'd rather hear why you've brought me here now. When—well, for over twenty years you've ignored my existence.'

Jacob sighed. 'It must seem that way, mustn't it?'

'It is that way,' said Cleo flatly. 'And although I appreciate that you're ill—'

'My being ill is the least of it!' exclaimed her grandfather fiercely. 'Is that what they told you? That because I'm dying I've had a change of heart?'

Cleo felt a little nervous now. She didn't want to upset him, goodness knew.

'And—and isn't that true?' she ventured, aware that she was treading into deep water. But she had a right to know, she told herself. She'd spent too many years in the dark.

The old man's fingers massaged the head of his cane for a few pregnant moments, and then he said, 'How much has Dominic told you?'

'Oh…' Cleo could feel her body getting hot now and she shifted a little uncomfortably beneath his knowing eyes. 'Well, he told me that—that Celeste—'

'Your mother.'

'All right, my mother—used to work for the Montoyas.'

'Yes, she did. She worked for Robert and Lily. I believe Dominic was very fond of her. But he was only a young boy at the time.'

'Dominic knew her?'

'Of course. She lived with the family. And until—well, until my son took a fancy to her, Lily and Celeste were good friends.'

'Friends!'

Cleo was scornful, but Jacob only shook his head. 'Yes, friends,' he insisted. 'We have no class system here on the island, Cleo. Your mother worked for my son and his wife, this is true, but she was never regarded as one of the servants.'

'So what happened?'

'You know what happened.' Jacob grimaced. 'Robert fell in love with her. Oh, yes.' He held up a hand as Cleo would have interrupted him. 'Robert did love Celeste. I am assured of that. But he loved his wife as well and he knew that their relationship would destroy Lily if she found out.'

Cleo bent her head. 'How convenient that Celeste died.'

Jacob made a sound of resignation. 'I suppose it does seem that way to you. And I accept the fact that your growing up on the island would have been a constant threat.'

'To your son!'

'And to Lily,' Jacob agreed heavily. 'She couldn't have children, you know. If she could, things might have been different.'

'I don't think so.'

Cleo couldn't help the faintly bitter edge that had entered her voice now, and Jacob stretched out a hand and gripped her arm.

'No one knows what might have happened if circumstances had been different,' he said, holding her troubled gaze with his. 'I'm not totally convinced Robert would have let you go to England. But after Celeste's death, he was a changed man.'

Cleo made a helpless gesture. 'And where did my—the Novaks fit into the equation?'

'Well…'

Jacob released her arm and lay back in his chair. He was looking very pale and Cleo realised this must be a terrible strain on him. She half wished someone—even Lily—would interrupt them. But the breeze was all that stirred the feathery palms.

'Henry was a decent man,' her grandfather said at last. 'But he was ambitious. He thought that moving to England would help him achieve the success he was striving for. He and Lucille had no children, and Lucille and Celeste had been friends. It wasn't too difficult to persuade them to adopt her daughter.'

Cleo caught her breath. Her mother—her adoptive mother—and her real mother had been friends! That at least accounted for the faded photograph she'd found among her parents' papers, after they were dead.

She frowned now. 'But it must have been a drain on their resources. I mean, my father—Henry, that is—didn't have a job to go to, did he?'

'No.' Jacob moistened his lips. 'We—Robert and I—oiled the wheels of the removal for him. It was…the least we could do.'

Cleo stared at him. 'You mean, you paid him to adopt me?' She was dismayed. 'Oh God. No one told me that!'

'Don't take it so hard, my dear.' Jacob blew out a breath. 'You have to understand, the Novaks were not wealthy people.'

'Even so…'

'They looked after you, didn't they? They loved you, I'm sure. And, judging by the way you've turned out, they did a damn good job of it as well.'

Cleo shook her head, aware that her eyes burned with unshed tears. It was all too much for her to handle. First the news that she wasn't who she'd always thought she was. And now—horror of horrors—the fact that her parents had had to be paid to adopt her.

Well, they weren't her parents, of course, she reminded herself. She mustn't forget that. And it was true, they had loved her and she'd loved them. But how much of their love had been fabricated? she wondered. She would never know now.

'This has been very hard for you,' murmured her grandfather regretfully. 'And believe me, if I could have done it any other way, I would. But we, Robert and I, respected the Novaks' wishes not to contact you. They wanted you to have nothing more to do with this family, and I suppose I can't blame them for that. But when I discovered they'd been killed in that accident—'

'All bets were off,' said Cleo bitterly, and her grandfather bowed his head in mute acknowledgement.

There was silence for a while. The breeze continued to bring a blessed freshness to the air, and the water in the pool rippled invitingly.

Glancing at her grandfather, Cleo saw he'd closed his eyes and she wondered a little anxiously if he was all right. But his chest was rising and falling rhythmically, so she felt a little better. Probably, he'd just fallen asleep.

She wished she'd agreed to take a swim now. The idea of

submerging herself in the cool water was just as attractive as it had been before.

But she was glad they had had this conversation. At least she knew now why the Novaks had adopted her. Even if she felt as if the world as she'd known it had been destroyed.

Pushing herself to her feet, she walked to the edge of the terrace and stood looking down at the marble dolphin that continuously spouted water into the pool. She wished she could be as unfeeling as the fountain. But she was far too emotional for that.

'Why don't you?' her grandfather's voice interrupted her reverie. 'Have that swim?' he suggested, and she turned to gaze at him with incredulous eyes.

'How did you know—?'

'What you were thinking?' His lined face creased into a grin. 'We're family, remember?'

Cleo shook her head. 'I think you're just very intuitive,' she said.

'Well, whatever I am, why don't you take me at my word?' He nodded towards the cabanas. 'Humour me, Cleo. I'd love to watch my beautiful granddaughter enjoying herself at last.'

Cleo had her doubts, but the temptation was greater. Besides, she suspected Jacob would relax if she proved she hadn't taken offence over what he'd told her.

And, after all, she'd wanted to know the truth, hadn't she? She'd asked him to tell her how she'd come to be living with—with the Novaks. Not the other way about.

The cabana smelled of pine and salt water. Although it was a freshwater pool, she guessed the cabins were used by anyone who wanted to change. As Jacob had said, there was a fitted rail with a row of colourful swimsuits. Tank suits and bikinis, but not a one-piece outfit in sight.

Blowing out a breath, she examined the suits rather disappointedly. But short of abandoning the idea, she would have to choose one of them to wear.

And, after all, there was no one about—well, except Lily.

But she couldn't see Dominic's mother caring to watch her take a swim.

She emerged from the cabana wearing the plainest tank suit in the collection. It was a deep blue, with white piping highlighting every seam and hem.

It left a narrow wedge of skin exposed at her midriff, but that didn't worry her. She was used to that after wearing cropped T-shirts at home.

However, the high-sided briefs made her wonder with unwilling humour if she should have taken Norah's advice and had a Brazilian wax before taking off her clothes.

Still, it was too late now. She left the cabana, pulling the elastic band off her hair and folding her hair in half before securing it again.

With her arms upraised, her breasts were lifted and the skimpy briefs threatened to reveal more than they concealed. And it was at that precise moment she saw Dominic, across the pool, standing beside her grandfather's chair.

CHAPTER SEVEN

THE breath whooshed out of her lungs with a rush. Her body suffused with heat, yet goose pimples pebbled all over her skin.

She wanted to pull her arms down, to draw the cuffs of her briefs over her buttocks. To somehow compose herself so that he wouldn't see how his appearance had affected her.

But for some reason, her limbs were frozen like a statue. And she thought how ironic it was that only minutes before she'd been imagining how unfeeling the marble dolphin was.

She wasn't unfeeling; she was hot and unsteady. Her only consolation was that surely he couldn't see the pointed hardness of her breasts outlined against the blue silk of her top.

Dominic, meanwhile, looked cool and indifferent. He was wearing another suit, although there was no formal vest or waistcoat in sight. Just Italian silk and pale grey cotton, his tie a splash of charcoal against his shirt.

She could always slip into the pool, Cleo thought, managing to bring her hands down at last, feeling the slick of moisture in her palms.

But that would be a rude and cowardly gesture. And she had no intention of proving Lily's opinion was right.

Dominic meanwhile was wishing he'd never stepped onto the terrace. He'd seen his grandfather sitting there, alone, and he'd assumed Cleo had gone back to her room. All he'd intended was to clear the air with the old man before leaving.

But now his eyes were riveted on the young woman who'd just emerged from the cabana.

God, she was beautiful, he thought. But there was something more than beauty alone that drew him to her. Sarah was beautiful, but he had never felt this way in her presence. Never felt his stomach clenching with awareness, or the wild rush of blood to his groin.

She had a sexual appeal that was beyond anything he had experienced before. And he couldn't help comparing his feelings to the feelings his adoptive father had had for her mother.

He could almost scent her, he mused grimly, even while he rejected the notion. She made him feel like some kind of jungle predator, his senses spinning with the thought of her naked in his arms.

Dammit!

'Is something wrong?'

The old man was far too perceptive, and Dominic had to physically force a hollow smile to his lips.

'I didn't realise Cleo was here,' he said, aware that his answer begged even more questions. He pushed his fists into his jacket pockets. 'Well, as you're in such good hands, I'll be on my way.'

'It's a pity you can't stay,' remarked his grandfather sagely. 'I know how much you like a swim in the pool.'

'I had one earlier,' said Dominic shortly, not best-pleased at being reminded. The brief glimpse of Cleo he'd seen on her balcony was still far too dominant in his mind.

With her hair tumbled about her shoulders, she'd drawn his eyes instinctively. In her skimpy bra and panties, she'd looked even more seductive than she did now.

'Oh, well…'

Dominic was fairly sure the old man wasn't deceived, but he wasn't about to stay around to find out.

'I'll see you tomorrow,' he said. 'You know I'm having

dinner with Sarah this evening. She was pretty peeved when I didn't get over to see her last night.'

'She'll get over it.' Jacob spoke absently, lifting a hand to Cleo as he spoke. 'Just so long as you remember we're having a special dinner here tomorrow evening. I want to introduce Cleo to our friends and neighbours. I want them to know how proud of her I am.'

Dominic stifled a sigh. 'OK.'

'Oh, and by the way…' Jacob looked up at him now '…I never thanked you for bringing my granddaughter to me, Dom. You've no idea how much it means to me to have her here.'

Dominic pulled a wry face. 'I have a pretty good idea,' he said, squeezing his grandfather's shoulder with genuine affection. 'Look after yourself, old man. And don't be overdoing things to try and impress her, yeah?'

'Then you're going to have to spend a little time with her yourself, Dom,' said Jacob staunchly. 'Introduce her to your friends. I'd like for you all to get along.'

Yeah, right.

Dominic didn't voice the words, but he wasn't deceived by the old man's suggestion. Jacob knew Sarah for one would be as keen to make a friend of Cleo as his mother.

Dominic prepared for the celebratory dinner at Magnolia Hill with little enthusiasm.

He was in no hurry to spend an evening refereeing a slanging match between his grandfather and his mother. And, judging from what Lily had said when he'd spoken to her on the phone earlier, her opinion of their unexpected guest hadn't improved with time.

He was less sure of Serena.

According to his mother, his aunt was playing a waiting game, neither applauding Cleo's arrival, nor making any attempt to alienate the girl.

Which was Serena all over, thought Dominic wryly, sliding his arms into the sleeves of a dark blue silk shirt. She must know that her position as her father's hostess could be in jeopardy and she'd be holding her cards very close to her chest.

As for Cleo herself...

Dominic buttoned his shirt with impatient fingers, studying his reflection in his dressing-room mirror without liking. He really didn't want to see her again. Not with the image of her as he'd last seen her, beside the pool, still tormenting his mind.

Of course, he'd had a valid excuse for not calling to see his grandfather the night before. The old man had known he was having dinner with Sarah, so Dominic had contented himself with a phone call instead.

Not that his dinner with Sarah had been a particularly enjoyable occasion. She'd still been brooding about his absence the previous evening, and Dominic was beginning to think their affair had run its course. Her mood had soured their meeting, and he'd been glad to get back to his own house.

He'd known Sarah had expected him to stay over. But even after she'd thrown off her petulance, he'd had enough. He doubted he could have sustained a convincing conversation. And as for going to bed with her...

Dominic closed his eyes for a moment. Then, zipping up his trousers, he emerged into the bedroom.

Sarah was standing in the middle of the floor. She had evidently been debating the merits of surprising him in either his bathroom or his dressing room, and her face fell when she saw he was fully dressed.

Dominic had half forgotten he'd invited her to the dinner party. When he'd first arrived at her house the night before, it had seemed the natural thing to do. Now, though, he was definitely regretting it...

'You're ready,' she said disappointedly, and Dominic was inordinately relieved he hadn't spent any more time than was necessary in the shower.

'What did you expect?' he asked, coming to bestow a light kiss on her expectant mouth. 'We have to be there in twenty minutes.'

'There's no rush.' Sarah's lips pouted.

'There is,' said Dominic flatly, stepping past her to pick up his cellphone from the low table beside the king-size bed. 'I promised Grandpa I wouldn't be late.'

'Oh, Grandpa!'

Sarah spoke contemptuously, and Dominic couldn't help noticing how her lips thinned when she was agitated.

Even in her apricot sequinned mini-dress, that exposed her slim legs to advantage, and with her cap of blonde hair curling confidingly under her chin, her face had a sulky arrogance that detracted somewhat from its pale beauty.

'Yes, Grandpa,' agreed Dominic, not prepared to argue. He glanced towards her. 'I assume Nelson is waiting outside. Why don't you go ahead? I've got a couple of calls to make before I leave.'

'But you're coming with me, aren't you?'

Sarah was indignant, and Dominic ran a weary hand round the back of his neck.

'I thought I'd drive my own car,' he said, aware that he was behaving badly. But, dammit, if he allowed the Cordys' chauffeur to drive them, Sarah would expect to spend the night at Turtle Cove when they got back.

So what was wrong with that?

Everything!

Sarah got the message, as he'd known she would.

'You're still sulking,' she said accusingly. 'Just because I was a bit short with you last night—not without good reason, mind you—you've decided to punish me in return.'

'Don't be ridiculous!'

Dominic wanted to laugh out loud at the ludicrousness of that statement.

'I just think it would be easier if I didn't have to rely on Nelson,' he said. 'Grandpa may decide he wants a post-mortem after the party is over. It will save you hanging around when I don't know when I'll be ready to leave.'

Sarah pursed her lips. 'Why can't Jacob wait until tomorrow

if he needs to discuss anything with you? For heaven's sake, Dom, you're in charge of the Montoya interests, not him.'

'Don't let Grandpa hear you saying that,' remarked Dominic, trying to lighten the mood. 'Anyway, it's a good idea, isn't it? And I am still pretty jet-lagged, you know.'

Sarah considered for a moment, and then came to rest her head against his shoulder. 'I'm a bitch, aren't I?'

'No.' Dominic's conscience couldn't allow her to think that. 'Look—we can spend time together when I'm not so committed,' he said, not altogether truthfully. He put an arm about her shoulders and gave her a hug. 'Right now, things are a bit…hectic. I'm sorry.'

'You mean because that girl is here,' said Sarah peevishly. 'I don't know what your grandfather's thinking of, bringing your father's bastard daughter to Magnolia Hill.'

Dominic's jaw hardened. 'I wish you wouldn't talk about her like that, Sarah,' he said coldly. 'You sound just like my mother. You can't hold Cleo responsible for what her father and mother did before she was born.'

Sarah's lips curled. 'But can you understand why—with a sweet wife like Lily—your father could risk impregnating a woman like Celeste Dubois? I mean—it's disgusting!'

'Yeah, well…'

Unfortunately, Dominic could understand his father's situation exactly.

But that was something he had no intention of acting on, so they weren't that alike, after all.

Cleo was standing beside her grandfather's chair when she saw Dominic come out of the house with a slim blonde young woman clinging to his arm.

It was evening, and beyond the candle-lit beauty of the terrace it was already pitch-dark. Only the muted roar of the sea reminded her of the walk she'd taken earlier, the perfumed scents of the flowers overlaid by the expensive fragrances worn by their female guests.

Cleo was already tired of keeping a smile plastered to her lips. Her grandfather—and Serena—had introduced her to so many people that she'd had no hope of remembering all their names.

She did know they were here for two reasons, however. One, to please her grandfather; and two, to get a look at Robert Montoya's bastard.

Ever since her grandfather's guests started arriving, she'd been aware of their interest and speculation. Aware, too, that many of the whispered conversations, taking place behind discreetly raised glasses, concerned her and her likeness not just to her mother, but to her father, as well.

Not that anyone had mentioned it to her. They'd all been very cordial, very polite. Though she couldn't exactly call them friendly.

Which was probably due to the fact that Dominic's mother had stood glaring at her all evening, making her attitude towards her father-in-law's behaviour all too obvious.

'At last,' she heard her grandfather mutter now, and guessed Dominic's late arrival was what he meant. 'Where the devil has he been?' he demanded of no one in particular. 'I told him I wanted him to be here to welcome our guests.'

Cleo thought she had an idea why his grandson's arrival had been delayed. The way the young woman with him was hanging on his arm was a fair indication, and she was sure they'd shared more than a car ride here.

Whatever, it was nothing to do with her, she assured herself fiercely. She'd be going back to England before too long and then she'd never see any of them again.

Not surprisingly, Dominic made a beeline for his grandfather, only stopping briefly along the way when one or other of Jacob's guests spoke to him.

With an easy confidence Cleo could only envy, he parried all their greetings with a rueful aside or a laughing retort, leaving an admiring group of men as well as women in his wake.

Sarah, who'd been forced to let go of his arm, followed him across the terrace. In a strapless, sequin-studded mini-dress, that suited her petite figure, she was every bit as glamorous as Cleo had anticipated Dominic's girlfriend would be.

Certainly, her outfit was far more expensive than the simple jade slip dress Cleo was wearing; her skin with that delicate look of porcelain, that made Cleo's skin look almost dusky.

'Hey, Grandpa!' Dominic exclaimed when he reached them, squatting down beside the old man's chair, his expression rueful. 'I guess I'm in the doghouse, yeah?'

Jacob gave an impatient shake of his head. 'That depends what you've got to say for yourself,' he declared drily. 'Where the hell have you been?'

'Sarah's car broke down,' Dominic replied without hesitation, and Cleo felt her own jaw drop at the total incredulity of his excuse.

'Say what?' Jacob stared at him. 'Can't you do better than that, boy?'

'It's true,' said Dominic, glancing up into Cleo's doubtful face.

Obviously she didn't believe him either, he thought, wishing it didn't matter to him. Then, straightening, he turned to Sarah, 'Do you want to tell them or shall I?'

'Oh…' Sarah pouted prettily, and Cleo wondered it if was possible to hate someone when you'd never even been introduced to them. 'Well, Nelson—that's my father's chauffeur, Mr Montoya—'

'Yes, I know who Nelson Buffett is,' Jacob interrupted her shortly, and with a little sigh she went on.

'Well, Nelson thought Daddy had put gas in the car and Daddy thought Nelson had.' She spread her hands innocently. 'It turns out, neither of them had.'

'So you ran out of gas?'

'Yes.'

Sarah nodded, her eyes drifting irresistibly to Cleo, and

Dominic realised he was being damnably ignorant in not introducing them.

But he was loath to do it. Cleo looked so beautiful this evening, and he was unwilling to give Sarah a chance to hurt her feelings as his mother had done.

Instead, he turned back to his grandfather. 'Hey, it was lucky we weren't travelling together,' he said, and saw the way Cleo's eyes widened again. 'I came along about ten minutes later in the SUV and I offered to go and get some gas for them.'

Jacob sniffed. 'And couldn't young Buffett have phoned the garage and had them bail him out?' he asked, and once again Sarah joined in.

'He did ring the garage in San Clemente, Mr Montoya, but there's nobody there at this time of the evening. And we couldn't leave poor Nelson to walk home, could we?'

Jacob grimaced. 'I suppose not,' he said grudgingly. He looked up at Cleo. 'I guess we're going to have to forgive him, eh, my dear? Oh, and by the way, you haven't met Dominic's girlfriend, have you?' He paused. 'This is Sarah, Cleo. Why don't you ask her what she'd like to drink?'

Sarah's polite words belied the flush of irritation that stained her cheeks. 'I've been here often enough to get my own drink, thank you. Or Dom can get it, can't you, darling?' She linked her arm with his again. 'How do you do—er—Cleo? Are you enjoying your stay at Magnolia Hill?'

'Very much,' Cleo was beginning, when her grandfather caught her hand in both of his.

'We're hoping she might consider making her home on San Clemente,' he said, in a voice that carried right across the terrace. 'Isn't that right, Dom? You're all for it, aren't you?'

The old devil!

Dominic's teeth ground together for a moment. The old man knew he'd never discussed any such thing, despite his suspicions of what Jacob had in mind.

But before he could make any response, Cleo said awkwardly, 'I don't think we've ever talked about that—er—Jacob.'

She refused to call him 'Grandfather' in front of all these people, even if that was the way she was beginning to think of him. 'I certainly don't think this is the time or the place—'

'Nonsense!' But Jacob seemed to realise he'd embarrassed her and he patted her hand reassuringly. 'We'll leave it for now.' He glanced round. 'Now where's Luella with the canapés? I told her I wanted them serving as soon as all the guests had arrived.'

There was a significant relaxing of the atmosphere as Jacob got determinedly to his feet. Refusing the help of either his grandson or his granddaughter, he stomped off towards the buffet tables that were set up beneath a sheltering canopy.

Catching Cleo's eye, Dominic realised that she was more upset by what had happened than either himself or Sarah. He was used to his grandfather's blunt way of speaking, but Cleo wasn't, and, detaching himself from Sarah's clinging hands, he said, 'Come on. I'll get us all a drink.' He nodded towards Cleo's glass. 'Is that a pina colada?'

'This?' Cleo was taken aback. 'Um—no. It's just pineapple juice,' she said, aware of Sarah's displeasure at this turn of events. 'And I don't need another drink, thank you.'

'Well, I do,' said Dominic flatly. And before he'd given any thought to his actions, he'd gripped Cleo's elbow with a decisive hand and turned her towards the bar set up beside the swimming pool.

He regretted it instantly. He hadn't forgotten how soft her skin was, or erased the memory of her scent, that tonight was a mixture of musk and spice and some tropical fragrance. But he had blanked it from his mind.

Now, however, it was back, more potent than before.

The side of her breast was so warm and sexy against his suddenly moist fingers. And if she was wearing a bra, it was doing little to hide the way her nipples had peaked and were pressing unrestrainedly against the thin fabric of her dress.

Oh, God!

His arousal was as painful as it was inappropriate. With

Sarah—the girl he'd brought to the party, dammit—following closely behind, he had no right to be feeling as if the ground was shifting beneath his feet.

Yet it was. And, heaven knew, he wanted to touch Cleo. Not as he was touching her now, but privately, intimately. To bury his hands in her silky hair and bury another part of his body— that was hot and hard and pulsing with life—in some place equally soft, but tight and wet as well.

He wondered if she'd heard his hoarse intake of breath, the surely audible pounding of his heart. She must have felt his fingers tightening almost involuntarily, because she turned to look at him, her eyes almost as wide and elemental as his own.

He abruptly let her go, surging ahead to where a handful of waiters tended the comprehensive array of drinks his grandfather had provided.

'Scotch,' he said without hesitation. 'No. No ice. Just as it is.' Then he raised the single malt to his lips and swallowed half of it before turning to address the two girls.

Cleo was wishing she'd accompanied her grandfather, after all. She was far too aware of Dominic, far too conscious of the fact that in other circumstances she wouldn't have wanted him to let her go.

Everything about him disturbed her: from the lean, muscular strength of his body to the intensely masculine perfume of his skin.

When he'd taken her arm, his heat had surrounded her. The hardness of his fingers gripping her arm had felt almost possessive. She'd wanted to rub herself against him, like a cat that was wholly sensitive to his touch.

She still felt that way, she thought unsteadily, and then had to compose herself when Sarah caught her gaze. Was the other woman aware that Dominic was a fallen angel? That beneath his enigmatic exterior beat the heart of a rogue male?

'How long do you expect to stay on the island?'

Sarah got straight to the point and Cleo told herself she was grateful.

'I— Just a few more days,' she said, aware that she'd lowered her voice in the hope that Dominic wouldn't hear her.

'Oh…' Sarah looked slightly taken aback. But pleased, Cleo thought. Perhaps she'd expected a more aggressive kind of response.

Though why should she? She and Dominic had looked very much a couple when they'd arrived tonight.

'So you're not planning on making your home here?'

Sarah was persistent, and Cleo wished she could just leave her and Dominic to sort out their own problems.

'Not at the moment,' she replied at last, not wanting to say anything to offend her grandfather. But she was grateful when someone else attracted Sarah's attention.

She didn't really dislike the girl, she assured herself. It was just that they had nothing in common.

Except Dominic…

'Here!'

She was forced to look at him again when Dominic took her drink from her and thrust another glass into her hand.

'What is this?' she protested, managing to instil a convincing edge of indignation in her voice. 'I said I didn't want another drink.' She sniffed suspiciously. 'Ugh—this is alcoholic!'

'Damn right,' agreed Dominic, finishing his own drink and turning to ask the waiter for a refill. 'This is supposed to be a celebration. You can't celebrate with a pineapple juice and soda.'

'Who says?' Cleo leant past him to replace the glass on the table that was serving as a bar, intensely aware of him beside her. She cast a nervous glance behind her. 'I wonder where your grandfather is. I think I ought to go and find him.'

Dominic sucked in a breath. Her bare arm had brushed along his midriff as she deposited the glass and he felt as if someone had scorched him with a burning knife.

'Don't,' he said barely audibly, his voice rough with emotion. 'The old man knows what he's doing.' He blew out a tortured breath that seared along her hairline. 'God knows, I wish I did.'

Startled eyes lifted to his, liquid dark eyes that Dominic felt he could have happily drowned in.

'I—I don't know what you mean,' she said, a catch in her breathing, and his hard-on threatened to drag him to his knees.

You do, his eyes accused her. But then Sarah was beside them, and Cleo hurriedly made good her escape.

CHAPTER EIGHT

CLEO walked along the shoreline in the coolness of early morning.

It was barely light and, apart from a few seabirds, she was alone on the beach.

All the guests had left in the early hours. They'd stayed much longer than she'd expected, particularly as her grandfather had retired soon after midnight.

In his absence, Serena had done her best to provide entertainment for their guests. Earlier in the evening, a group of West Indian musicians had arrived, and although Cleo had anticipated a lot of noisy percussion, she couldn't have been more wrong.

These musicians used their steel drums to produce melodic liquid sounds that played on the senses as well as the mind. Rippling chords of magic that filled any awkward silences with rhythm and enchantment.

The area around the pool had been cleared and there'd been some dancing. But, even though Cleo had danced with a couple of Jacob's friends, she'd avoided the younger men like the plague.

The last thing she needed was for these people—who probably neither liked her nor trusted her—to get the idea that she was like her mother. She didn't know much about Celeste, of course. Only what her grandfather had told her. But nothing could alter the fact that she'd had an affair with a married man.

Her employer, no less.

She supposed, from the Montoyas' point of view, the evening had been a success. She'd been introduced to San Clemente society, and Jacob's intentions towards her had been made plain for all to see.

But they were wrong.

There'd been a subtle change in the atmosphere after her grandfather had retired. No one had been rude, but their questions about her life in England had seemed more pointed somehow. She'd got the feeling they regarded her with a mixture of curiosity and blame.

But it wasn't her fault that her father had seduced her mother, she told herself fiercely. And if they had fallen in love…

She had made sure she'd kept out of Dominic's way. And with Sarah constantly at his side, it hadn't been too difficult. Besides, with talk of a possible wedding on everyone's lips, she'd had little to contribute.

She'd wondered a couple of times if Sarah was speaking more loudly for her benefit. She was obviously suspicious of Cleo, and she and Dominic's mother seemed to have a lot in common.

Whatever, Cleo had been glad to leave the party herself at about 2 a.m. She hadn't been tired, exactly, but she'd definitely had enough of being treated like the skeleton at the feast.

Now it was a little before six, and she'd left the house with a feeling of deliverance. She'd wanted to get away; not just from Magnolia Hill, but from her thoughts.

The tide was coming in. The cool water brushed against her toes, and Cleo kicked off her sandals and allowed the waves to swirl about her feet.

She'd been mad to come down to the beach in high-heeled wedges anyway. But then, she was still wearing the dress she'd worn the evening before. Having spent the last three hours lying sleepless on her bed, it had seemed like too much trouble to change.

She'd stopped to examine the pearly spiral of a conch shell when she felt the distinct vibration of footsteps on the sand.

Lifting her head, she saw a man approaching, his profile still indistinct in the morning half-light. He was some distance away, but he was running in her direction. Long legs pumping rhythmically, arms swinging to match his muscular pace.

It looked like Dominic, but it couldn't be him. He had brought Sarah to the party. It was a cinch he'd taken her home. To his home, if she was any judge of the other girl's intentions, thought Cleo ruefully. There was no way he'd have stayed at Magnolia Hill.

But it was Dominic!

As he drew nearer, Cleo recognised his height and his muscular build. Broad shoulders, narrow hips and a tight butt, she conceded reluctantly. Outlined to perfection in black Lycra shorts.

He obviously enjoyed running, judging by the damp patches on his black cotton vest, and the streams of perspiration running down his chest. Despite the fact that she'd had no sleep, her adrenalin kicked up another notch.

'Hi.' Dominic slowed as he reached her, his eyes taking in the fact that she hadn't changed from what she'd been wearing the night before. 'Going somewhere special?'

Cleo's chin jutted. She wouldn't allow him to make fun of her. 'I haven't been to bed,' she said, as if that wasn't already obvious. 'I'm sorry. Is that a problem for you?'

Privately Dominic thought it was one hell of a problem, judging from the way he reacted to her. But after last evening's fiasco, he was determined to keep things simple.

'Not for me,' he said, bending forward and bracing himself with his hands on his knees to avoid looking at her. He was uncomfortably aware that his quickened heartbeat was as much mentally as physically induced.

But eventually, he had to straighten. 'So,' he said evenly, 'did you enjoy the party? I seem to remember the guest of honour disappeared.'

Cleo forced herself to look at the horizon. The faintest trace of pink was brushing the ocean and she pretended an interest in the view. 'I wasn't the guest of honour,' she said tensely. 'Or if I was, your guests didn't know it.'

Dominic scowled. 'What's that supposed to mean? What did they say to you?'

'Oh—nothing.'

Cleo wished she hadn't started this. Not when he was standing so close that the heat of his body enveloped her in its spell. She could smell his sweat; smell *him*; and her mouth was suddenly as dry as parchment. Even her legs felt unsteady as she met his accusing gaze.

'Forget it,' she said, trying to behave naturally. 'Why aren't you at—what was it you called your house—Pelican Bay?' She paused, and then added brightly, 'Did Sarah stay over as well?'

Dominic ignored her question. 'I want to know what's upset you,' he said. 'Did my mother say something? Did Sarah?'

'Heavens, no.' Cleo spread her hands, not allowing herself to look at him again. 'But, let's face it, your guests didn't just come to be polite. They were—curious. About me.'

Dominic stifled a groan. 'They were curious, sure—'

'I rest my case.' Cleo permitted herself another brief glance in his direction. 'Curious—and suspicious. They think I want Jacob's money!' She made a sound of disgust. 'If they only knew!'

'Only knew what?'

Dominic's hand reached for her bare arm and instantly her skin felt as if he'd burned her. The pain that flared in the pit of her stomach was purely sexual, its fiery tendrils spreading down both her legs.

She knew an urgent need to press herself against him, to allow the fever smouldering inside her to take control. But no matter how sorry he was, how sympathetic, he could do nothing physically to ease her pain.

'It doesn't matter,' she said, stepping back from him,

breaking his hold, and Dominic raked frustrated fingers though his hair.

But it was just as well one of them had some sense, he conceded, even if he could have done without her conscience asserting itself right now.

He felt the ache between his legs, glanced down and saw the unmistakable swell of his erection. What did this woman do to him? he wondered. One touch and his body took control.

'I think you're exaggerating people's reactions,' he said harshly, in an effort to ground himself. But even to his own ears, his voice was edged with strain.

'Well, I don't want your grandfather's money,' she said. 'So tell that to whoever's prepared to listen. I'll be leaving here in a few days anyway. Then it won't matter either way.'

Dominic stared at her with anguished eyes. Dammit, he didn't want to see her go. But to tell her that would be madness. He wasn't interested in making that kind of commitment, to her or anyone else.

He had to put any thought of a relationship between them out of his mind...

With a muffled oath, he abandoned any attempt to reason with her. Turning, he plunged into the water, hoping against hope that the ocean would ease his mangled emotions.

Cleo's lips parted in astonishment when she saw what he was doing. Dominic had gone into the water still wearing his vest and shorts. Was he mad or simply reckless? Why did it matter so much what he did?

She stared after him, watching as he struck out strongly into the current. The weight of his clothes didn't appear to hamper his progress, but she was anxious just the same.

Allowing herself to tread a little deeper into the shallows, she wished she had the nerve to do something reckless. And as the salty water swirled about her ankles, she could feel the erratic beating of her heart.

Dominic had almost disappeared. His head appeared only

fleetingly above the waves. She prayed he knew what he was doing. That he had the sense to know when to turn back.

A thin line of gold was fringing the horizon now, and in the growing light she saw—much to her relief—that he was swimming back to shore. She envied him his skill, the strength with which his arms attacked the waves and defeated them. He looked like a dark, powerful predator moving through the water, and she knew if she had any sense she'd be long gone before he reached the beach.

But still she waited.

Dominic reached the shallows and, pushing himself to his feet, he walked towards her. He was dripping water everywhere, from his hair, from his arms, from his legs. Even from his lashes as he blinked to clear his gaze.

Pushing his hair back with both hands, he caught Cleo's gaze and held it. He knew she'd been watching him, had felt her staring at him, even with so many yards of ocean between them. And, as her eyes dropped down his body, he realised his swim had done nothing to kill his lust.

With a feeling of inevitability, he closed the gap between them. Then, before she could do anything to stop him, he reached out and jerked her into his arms.

His mouth found hers and it was just as sweet and lush and hot as he had imagined. His tongue licked, probed, seeking and finding entry. And she opened to him eagerly, it seemed, welcoming his invasion.

Cleo's world spun. To try and steady herself, she clutched his hips above the cropped waistband of his shorts. And found smooth muscled flesh, narrow bones that moved beneath her fingers. Raw, uncontrolled passion in the way his body ground against hers.

'Cleo!'

She heard his strangled groan as if from a distance. But whatever protest it might have signalled made little difference to his urgent assault on her emotions.

His tongue mated with hers, velvet-soft and undeniably

sexual. Cleo felt as if she was drowning in sensation, the will to keep a hold on her senses as fleeting as the clouds that briefly veiled the sun.

Dominic deepened the kiss, his hands slipping the narrow straps of her dress off her shoulders. He seemed to delight in the silky smoothness of her olive-toned skin.

As the thin fabric dropped away, Cleo made a futile attempt to stop it. Drawing back from his kiss, she gazed at him wildly, her breathing as uneven as her pounding heartbeat.

'Let me,' Dominic insisted, removing her fingers. And, as the dress fell to her waist, he cupped her breasts in his eager hands.

His thumbs rubbed abrasively over the tender dusky nipples. They were already tight, he saw, and swollen with need. Then, dropping onto his knees in front of her, he let the dress fall about her ankles. He apparently didn't care that it was now as wet as he was. Instead, he buried his face against her quivering mound.

Cleo's legs shook. Try as she might, she couldn't seem to think coherently, let alone push him away. She was naked, but for the lacy thong that Norah had assured her was all she needed under the flimsy chiffon. And when Dominic licked her navel, she let out a trembling cry.

Dominic's body felt as if it was on fire. As he pressed his face against her softness, his lungs quickly filled with her exotic scent. She was satin and silk, the rarest of spices, and oh, so responsive. His hands gripped the backs of her thighs. He wanted to rip the scrap of lace away.

It barely did the job anyway, he acknowledged. Dark curls spilled out at either side, and he wondered if those hidden lips were moist. He guessed they were, slick with the arousal rising to his nostrils. His hands moved to cup her rounded bottom. Just touching her like this was both a heaven and a hell.

He wanted to touch her everywhere, he wanted to touch her and taste her, and spread those gorgeous legs so he could—

Sanity struck him like a peen hammer. They were here—on a private beach, it was true—but one of his grandfather's groundsmen raked the sand every morning. How would Cleo feel if someone saw them? While he might not have any inhibitions, Dominic was fairly sure Cleo would.

Abandoning the erotic image of laying her down on the warm sand and relieving the hard-on he'd had since he'd first seen her on the beach, Dominic got reluctantly to his feet.

Dammit, he thought, he'd been semi-aroused since their confrontation the night before. If you could call what had happened between them a confrontation. Whatever, he'd wanted her then and he wanted her now.

God help him!

Even so, he couldn't deny himself the pleasure of lifting one of her pouting breasts to his mouth and suckling briefly on its puckered tip. She tasted so good; so irresistible. How could he let her go?

Desire sparked anew, and he opened his lips wide and allowed her nipple to brush the roof of his mouth. It was all unbearably sensual, this carnal need he had to make her want him as much as he wanted her. His hands followed the sensitive hollow of her spine, arching her against him, letting her feel what she was doing to him.

The unmistakable roar of the tractor arrested him before he could drag his sodden vest over his head and gather her against him. He'd wanted to feel those button-hard nipples against his bare chest, but it was too late.

'For pity's sake, let me go!'

Dominic didn't know whether Cleo's frantic words sourced a belated resistance on her part or a sudden awareness of the tractor's approach. But they were a shocking reminder of what he was doing; or what he'd *done*.

With a feeling of remorse, he stumbled back from her. But when he would have bent to pick up her dress, she beat him to it, wrenching it away from his grasp.

Giving it only the most perfunctory of shakes, she stepped into it, hauling the straps up over her shoulders and recoiling from the damp clamminess of the skirt.

Cleo had heard the engine, but she was wondering who could be driving along the sand at this hour of the morning. Whoever it was, she should be grateful, she thought, avoiding Dominic's eyes with an urgency that bordered on paranoia.

Dear heaven, what had she been thinking of? How had she allowed such a thing to happen? After everything she'd said. How could she have been so stupid?

The dress was gritty as well as wet, its abrasive folds like sandpaper against her sensitive skin. How on earth was she going to get into the house unnoticed? She could imagine how she would feel if anyone—her mind switched instinctively to Lily—saw her.

'Cleo, dammit—'

Dominic put out a hand as she snatched up her sandals and started away from him. But she easily evaded his touch.

'Go home, Dominic,' she said, her voice as unsteady as her legs. But she couldn't blame him entirely. 'This—this never happened.'

'We both know it did,' said Dominic harshly as the tractor rolled into view. He swore then. 'Look, why don't you let me take you back to my house? We can dry your dress—'

'Yeah, right.' Cleo regarded him incredulously. 'Do you honestly think I'd go anywhere with you?'

Then, her eyes widening at the sight of the heavy vehicle, she backed away from him. Stumbling a little, she turned and hurried away towards the house.

Dominic swore again. Raking frustrated hands through his hair, he watched her disappear through the trellis gate that led into his grandfather's garden.

He hoped to God that she didn't encounter his mother. Lily Montoya was already suspicious of the girl and she wouldn't mince her words. If she discovered Cleo in that state and then learned that Dominic had been on the beach with her, she'd certainly demand an explanation.

One that he didn't have to give, admitted Dominic grimly. He had the feeling that his whole day was only going to go from bad to freaking worse.

CHAPTER NINE

'WHAT the hell did you think you were doing with my grand-daughter?'

It was later that morning.

Dominic didn't know if Cleo had made it into the house without encountering either Serena or his mother. But, evidently, nothing escaped the eagle eye of his grandfather.

Dominic himself was hardly in the mood for an argument. He'd returned to his own house to shower and change before heading for the Montoya Corporation's headquarters in San Clemente.

Then, striding into his own suite of offices, he'd informed his staff that he wasn't to be disturbed.

Not that that counted for anything when Jacob Montoya demanded to see him. He'd heard the old man giving his assistant hell even through the door of the outer office. By the time Jacob appeared, Dominic was on his feet and ready to defend himself. He thought it was typical that the old man should have chosen today to make one of his infrequent forays into town.

Dominic's PA, Hannah Gerard, a pleasant-faced woman of middle years, hovered anxiously behind the visitor.

'May I get you some coffee, Mr Montoya?' she asked, including both men in her enquiry.

However, it was Jacob who waved his stick somewhat irritably and said, 'Not now, woman. I want to talk to my grandson. We'll let you know if we want anything. Now, scoot!'

Hannah's face flushed with embarrassment and Dominic moved swiftly round the desk to take the woman's arm. 'That's OK, Hannah,' he said gently, urging her towards the door. 'As Mr Montoya says, we're good. I'll let you know if we need anything, right?'

'Yes, sir.'

Hannah was obviously relieved to return to her own office, and Dominic closed the door and leant back against it for a moment, viewing his visitor with curious eyes.

Jacob wasn't usually so brusque with his employees. Dominic's nerves tightened at the scowling expression on his grandfather's face.

'Is something wrong?'

'You tell me.'

Jacob shifted to lower himself into the armchair opposite Dominic's desk. He hooked his walking stick over the arm and then delivered his bombshell.

'What the hell did you think you were doing with my grand-daughter?'

Dominic sucked in a breath and then blew it out again on a long sigh.

There was no point in denying that he'd been with Cleo. Somehow—God knew how!—Jacob knew. Or thought he did.

He exchanged a look with the old man, wondering if someone had seen them and reported to him. What had they seen? Everything? His lower body heated at the memory. Or was Jacob just fishing because he'd found out Cleo had been soaked to the skin?

Now he pushed himself away from the door and circled his desk. Then, spreading his hands on its granite surface, he said evenly. 'What did you think I was doing?'

'Don't get clever with me, Dom. I know what you were doing. I saw you.' Jacob's lips curled triumphantly. 'You forget, I get up early in the mornings and my balcony overlooks the beach.'

Dominic stifled an inward groan.

He remembered all too clearly what they—what *he*—had been doing. Even from a distance it would have been impossible not to see that he had kissed her. And almost stripped her naked, kneeling on the sand, pressing his face into her—

'You damn near had sex with her!' exclaimed his grandfather angrily. 'Didn't you care that people might see you? Your mother, perhaps?'

Dominic shrugged and, pushing back from the desk, sank down into his own chair. 'I didn't think,' he said honestly. 'It was a mistake.' He paused. 'It won't happen again.'

'Damn right!' Jacob scowled at him with piercing blue eyes. 'I thought you had more sense. Can't you see the girl's fragile; vulnerable?'

Dominic's eyes darkened. 'You've made your point, old man. You don't have to labour it. I made a mistake and I'm sorry, OK? I'm not about to ruin her life.'

'The way your father ruined her mother's?' suggested Jacob maliciously. 'No, I won't let you do that.'

Dominic groaned. 'Look, is there any point to this? I've said I'm sorry and I am.'

His jaw tightened. Sorry his grandfather had had to be involved, anyway.

Jacob hesitated, his manner softening. 'But you like the girl, don't you? Silly question, of course you do. All that dark silky hair and smooth almond flesh. Kind of gets under your skin, doesn't she?'

Dominic's jaw dropped. 'Are you saying—?'

'That she gets under my skin?' Jacob swore impatiently. 'Get over yourself, boy. I'm not talking personally.' His scowl returned. 'I'm only saying I can see how a young buck like yourself might be smitten. She's certainly got more about her than the girls you usually bring to Magnolia Hill.'

Dominic stared at him in disbelief. 'A few minutes ago you were reminding me of my responsibilities.'

'I know, I know.' Jacob moved his stick agitatedly. 'But maybe I was too rash. Maybe you and Cleo should get together.

My grandson and my granddaughter. Yes, that is a very appealing image.'

'No!'

Dominic spoke heatedly, and his grandfather regarded him with calculating eyes.

'You haven't heard what I have to say yet,' he said harshly. 'Don't go second-guessing me before I tell you what I have in mind.'

'I don't care what you have in mind,' retorted Dominic grimly. 'I was out of line this morning. I admit it. But if you think you can manipulate me as you manipulated Serena, you've got another think coming. And if you don't like it, well—tough.'

His grandfather didn't react as he'd expected however. Instead of arguing with him, a mocking smile tipped up the old man's mouth.

'OK, OK,' he said. 'If that's the way you feel, I'll say no more about it.' He reached across the desk and pressed the button for the intercom. 'Let's have that coffee, shall we? You look as if you need something to kick you into shape.'

Dominic dragged weary hands down his face, feeling the scrape of stubble he'd been too preoccupied to shave. He didn't feel as if he'd won the argument. He felt agitated and frustrated in equal measures.

When Hannah knocked timidly at the door, Jacob summoned her in. And then ordered coffee for two with the kind of charming diffidence that left the woman wondering if she'd only imagined his anger earlier.

'So,' he said, when she'd departed again, 'what are you planning on doing for the rest of the day? I had thought of bringing Cleo into town, showing her around, giving her a taste of what she's been missing all these years. What do you think?'

Dominic gnawed at his lower lip. 'What do you mean? Showing her around? You don't intend to bring her here, do you?'

'Why not?' The old man was irritatingly bland. 'You have no objections, do you?'

'No.' But Dominic's nerves tightened at the thought of seeing Cleo again. 'I—just don't think she'll want to do that, that's all.'

'Why?' Jacob was suspicious. 'What has she said to you?'

'Nothing.' Dominic blew out a resigned breath. 'Hell, old man, she doesn't talk to me.'

'No, I noticed that,' remarked his grandfather sharply, and Dominic ran damp palms over the arms of his chair. 'But I want you to know, I'm hoping to persuade Cleo to make her home on San Clemente. And I don't want you doing anything to queer my pitch.'

Dominic shook his head. 'You'll probably do that yourself,' he muttered, and the old man gave him an angry look.

'What are you talking about?'

'Oh—' Dominic wished he'd never started this '—I just don't think she's happy here.'

'She didn't enjoy the party?' Jacob could be disconcertingly astute. 'I noticed she was still wearing the dress she wore last night when I saw you two this morning. Did someone upset her? Did *you* upset her?'

Then he snorted. 'No, don't answer that. Of course you upset her. Trying to seduce her. My God, don't you have any respect for her at all?'

'Of course I do.' Dominic spoke fiercely, refusing to admit that his behaviour might have had any bearing on the way Cleo was feeling. He groaned. 'Look, you can't expect everyone you know to like her, just because you say so, old man.'

'So someone did say something to upset her last night. After I'd gone to bed, I'll wager.' He scowled. 'Go on. You might as well tell me what it was.'

Dominic sighed. 'Maybe,' he said reluctantly, 'maybe—people asked questions. They were curious about her. You can't blame them for that.'

'Can't I?'

The return of Hannah with the tray of refreshments provided a welcome break in the conversation.

Dominic thanked her and assured her he could handle it, and after she'd gone he poured them both a cup of the strong beverage.

Then, sinking down into his chair again, he allowed himself a moment's respite. But he knew his grandfather too well to imagine that the old man would leave it there.

'They blame her, don't they?' Jacob said, making no attempt to drink his coffee. 'Those idiots blame her for what her parents did.' He thumped his cane on the floor. 'Dammit, Dom, it's unreasonable. It wasn't her fault.'

'I know.' Dominic replaced his cup in its saucer. 'And, in time, people will begin to see her for the—the attractive young woman she is.'

'As you do?' Jacob was sardonic. 'Or are you like them, Dom? Was the way you treated Cleo this morning an example of how you really feel about her?'

Cleo was standing beside the pool looking down into the blue water, when her grandfather came to join her.

It was the morning after that disastrous encounter with Dominic on the beach, and she was relieved she hadn't seen him since.

The previous day, she'd had only Serena and Lily for company. Dominic had evidently left before breakfast, and when she'd ventured downstairs again it was to find she had the morning room to herself.

Not that she'd been hungry. Some orange juice, a cup of coffee and a fresh nectarine satisfied her, and she was grateful not to have to explain herself to anyone else.

Lunch had been a different affair.

Both Serena and Lily had joined her at the table, Serena taking the time to inform her that her grandfather had gone into town.

'He's gone to the office to see Dominic,' she'd said tersely, in answer to her sister-in-law's query. 'But he should be resting, Lily, not risking his health over something he can do nothing about.'

Or some*one*, Cleo had reflected uneasily, when Lily cast a speculative glance her way. But she didn't see how she could be held responsible for her grandfather's behaviour. She hadn't even spoken to him since last night.

'Jacob always was a stubborn man,' Lily had declared carelessly. 'But Dominic won't let him do anything silly. Whatever ideas may have been put into his head.'

Cleo had caught her breath at this.

'I hope you're not implying that I had anything to do with Jacob's going into town!' she'd exclaimed defensively. And even Serena had been taken aback by the fierceness of her tone.

'Why, no.'

For once, Lily had seemed at a loss for words, and Cleo pressed on.

'But you were implying that I might have had some ulterior motive for coming here, weren't you? Do you think I want Jacob's money, Mrs Montoya? Do you honestly believe that any amount of money could compensate me for everything I've lost?'

Lily had swallowed a little nervously. 'That's easy to say, Ms Novak—'

'No, it's not easy to say, Mrs Montoya.'

Cleo had had enough of being the silent victim, and although she'd been fighting back tears, she'd had to speak out.

'I was happy in England, believe it or not. Six months ago, I hadn't a care in the world.'

Well, that hadn't been precisely true. But everyone had problems, even a wealthy woman like Lily, who must have been as devastated by her husband's betrayal as Cleo herself.

'I—I had a good home,' she'd continued, a little huskily. 'A loving family; a job I like.' She paused. 'When my parents— the only parents I'd ever known—were killed, I was shattered. I didn't think anything worse could happen to me. And then—

and then Serena turned up and told me that my whole life up until that point had been a lie.'

'I'm sure Lily didn't mean to offend you, Cleo,' Serena had broken in anxiously, evidently aware of the bigger picture here. She'd known Jacob wouldn't be at all pleased if he thought the other women in his household had been upsetting his grand-daughter.

'Is that true?'

Cleo had held Dominic's mother's gaze, her own eyes dark and sparkling with unshed tears. And, with a little shrug, Lily had given a little ground.

'Perhaps I have been a little hasty in judging you, Ms Novak,' she'd conceded, tracing the rim of her plate with a purple-tipped nail. Her shoulders lifted again. 'We shall see.'

Her reluctance to admit anything had been apparent, but to avoid any further unpleasantness, Cleo had let it go. Besides, how could she sustain her animosity towards a woman who had been as innocent a victim as herself?

In any case, Serena had smoothed the waters with a comment about the lobster pâté she'd been spreading on wafer-thin biscuits. Dominic's mother had seemed equally eager to change the subject and that was that.

Not that Lily had spoken directly to Cleo throughout the rest of the meal, though she had considered her from time to time from behind the shelter of her wine glass. What had she really been thinking? Cleo had wondered. Did Lily still believe she'd wanted to come here?

The rest of the day had been something of an anticlimax. Serena had offered to take her shopping in San Clemente, but Cleo had politely refused her invitation. She was fairly sure the offer had only been made as a kind of sweetener, and she had no desire to impose her company on anyone else.

Instead, she'd spent some time by the pool before returning to her room and flaking out for a couple of hours. Her sleepless night had caught up with her, and it was nearing dinner time when she'd gone downstairs again.

Only to find there was just to be Serena and herself for the evening meal.

'My father sends his apologies,' Serena had said. 'But that trip into town has worn him out. He tries to do too much and his body betrays him.' She'd forced a smile. 'He'll be all right tomorrow.'

'You're sure?'

Cleo had found she was really concerned, and Serena had given her a reassuring look.

'Oh, yes,' she'd said. 'He wants you to join him for breakfast. Believe me, nothing will stop him from spending as much time with you as he can.'

And now, as proof of that statement, Jacob took Cleo's arm.

'Come along,' he said. 'We can talk over breakfast. I thought you might like to try Luella's maple pancakes. They're Dominic's favourites.' He gave her a calculating sideways glance. 'It's a pity he's not here.'

Cleo permitted herself a slight smile of acquiescence, but she didn't say anything. If her grandfather had known what had been going on, he might not have been so generous towards the younger man.

She contemplated for a moment what Jacob might say if she told him. But she'd never been a sneak and she wouldn't start now.

They ate in the morning room, as they had two days ago, and Cleo did her best to do justice to the pancakes Luella had supplied. They were delicious, but once again she wasn't hungry. She thought ruefully that if she stayed here long, she'd soon be as thin as Serena.

'I thought I'd take you into San Clemente today,' Jacob said, pouring himself more coffee. 'We'll have lunch with Dom. On the yacht, I think. It's time you learned a little more about the Montoya Corporation.'

'Oh…' Cleo's throat dried. The last thing she wanted to do was spend time in Dominic's company. 'Um—will your grandson's girlfriend be joining us, too?'

Jacob pulled a wry face. 'Do you mean Sarah?' he asked. 'No, I shouldn't think so. Why?' His brows ascended. 'Did you and she get along?'

Cleo bent her head over her plate. 'I only spoke to her very briefly,' she murmured, and her grandfather gave a mocking snort.

'I didn't think you two had much in common,' he said, and, glancing up, Cleo found him grinning. ''Cept maybe Dom himself, hmm? How about that?'

'What do you mean?'

The words were out before she could prevent them, and Jacob arched a sardonic brow.

'Well, you like your brother, don't you, Cleo? It seemed to me when you arrived that you'd come to depend on him, quite a lot.'

Cleo pressed her lips together. 'He's not my brother.'

'As good as.' Jacob was dismissive. 'Why's it matter, anyway? You're both my grandchildren. And when I'm gone and Serena's married, you'll be the only Montoyas left.'

Cleo's jaw dropped. 'I didn't know Serena was getting married.'

'Nor does she—yet.' The old man grimaced. 'But she and Michael Cordy—that's Lily's cousin—have been friends since they were children. And since his first wife died, he's been looking for a replacement.'

Cleo stared at him incredulously. 'But does she love him?'

'Well…' Jacob considered. 'She's turned him down a time or two in the past. Under some mistaken impression that I needed her here. But that was before he married someone else.' He chuckled. 'It's amazing how much more attractive something becomes if it's forbidden fruit.' He paused. 'I guess you know that.'

'Me?' Cleo heard the squeak in her voice and struggled to control it. 'How should I know?'

'Why—your father and your mother. What did you think I

meant?' asked Jacob innocently. 'If their relationship wasn't forbidden fruit, then I don't know what it was.'

'Oh…' Cleo swallowed a little convulsively, not totally convinced that he was being completely honest.

But he couldn't know about her and Dominic. How could he? Not unless Dominic had spilled the beans, and something told her that that was the last thing he would do.

'Anyway—how about it?' Jacob asked. 'This trip I've got planned for us? You'd like to see the town of San Clemente, wouldn't you? This island's your home, Cleo. I want you to love it just as much as I do.'

The idea of loving anything—or anybody—was not something Cleo wanted to think about at that moment. Whatever Jacob said, how could she even think of staying here? Apart from all the obvious problems, there was still Dominic. She was not going to become his mistress as her mother had become Robert's.

Now, however, she chose her words with care.

'I—I would like to see San Clemente, of course,' she said. 'But perhaps we could just drive through the town instead of stopping for lunch.' She paused. 'Serena told me you tired yourself out yesterday. I don't think it's wise to risk your health by doing too much today.'

'Rubbish!' Jacob was impatient. 'When you don't know how much time you've got left, you don't put off until tomorrow what you can do today. Believe me, my dear, I have no intention of killing myself. As I say, we'll have lunch on the yacht. You'll like that. Then I'll have a rest in one of the cabins, while Dominic gives you a tour of the town.'

Cleo stifled a moan. 'Dominic may not want—may not have time,' she amended quickly, 'to take me sightseeing.'

'He'll make time,' declared her grandfather confidently. 'He's his own boss. No one tells him what to do.'

Except you, thought Cleo unhappily, but Jacob only winked at her.

'Now, are you finished?' he asked. 'Good. Then go and get

your handbag or whatever else you need. I'll have Sam bring the car round, so don't be long.'

Cleo wanted to protest.

She wanted to say that Dominic wouldn't want to have lunch with someone for whom he evidently had so little respect.

She wanted to suggest Jacob start making arrangements for her to return to England at the end of this week instead of next.

But over all her objections, she felt an unmistakable surge of excitement.

And how ridiculous was that?

CHAPTER TEN

DOMINIC lounged in his chrome and white leather chair, one arm hooked over its back, and wished the glass he was holding contained whisky.

Wine was all very well, and his grandfather was something of a connoisseur. But Dominic needed something stronger. Something to stop his eyes from straying in Cleo's direction every chance they had.

He'd tried to concentrate on his surroundings. They were having lunch on the sundeck of the company's yacht, shaded from too much brilliance by a huge canopy, and it was certainly a spectacular setting.

The little town of San Clemente climbed the hill behind the marina, colour-washed walls and red-tiled roofs providing a stunning backdrop to the blue, blue water.

A breeze blew up off the water, rattling the ties of the other yachts moored in the adjoining slips. It lifted the fringe of the canopy; caused a silky coil of Cleo's hair to curl about her shoulder.

Dammit!

The trouble was, she looked so bloody attractive. She was wearing an off-the-shoulder top of some bronze-coloured fabric that hugged her breasts and outlined her hips. Knee-length shorts exposed bare calves and narrow ankles. She wore a gold chain round her ankle, drawn to his attention by provocative four-inch heels.

There were huge gold rings in her ears, too, that brushed her bare shoulders every time she moved her head. Her hair was drawn loosely back from her face and tied at her nape with a chiffon scarf. But that didn't stop errant strands escaping and causing him no end of grief.

He swallowed the remainder of the wine in his glass and reached for the bottle of Merlot as his grandfather spoke.

'Isn't this nice?' the old man said, including both of them in his sharp appraisal. 'My two grandchildren and myself, having lunch together. What could be nicer, eh, Dom?'

'Indeed,' Dominic said drily, refilling his wine glass with a surprisingly steady hand. Considering the rest of his body was taut with frustration, he thought he managed it very well. 'What could be nicer?'

Cleo cast a wary look in his direction. She had few doubts that Dominic wasn't enjoying the meal. From the moment they'd arrived at the Montoya Corporation's offices, she'd sensed his resistance to the outing. If there'd been any way he could have got out of joining them without offending his grandfather, she was sure he would have done so.

But, apart from the respect Dominic evidently had for the old man, Jacob was seriously ill, and his time was limited. It would have taken a more ruthless man than Dominic to deny such a simple request.

'I hope you're not drinking too much, boy.' Jacob was nothing if not direct. He nodded to Dominic's plate, where the better part of his risotto was congealing in the heat. 'You've hardly touched your food.'

Dominic gave a thin smile. 'I wasn't hungry, old man,' he said evenly. 'It's too hot for eating.' He paused before raising his glass to his lips again. 'Particularly when you're wearing a suit.'

'Then get changed!' exclaimed Jacob at once. 'You know I'm expecting you to give Cleo a tour of San Clemente later this afternoon.'

'Oh, that's not necessary—' began Cleo hurriedly, but her grandfather ignored her.

'Me, I'm going to have a rest.' Jacob blew out a breath. 'But you're right. It is hot.'

Cleo turned her head to look at him, aware of an anxiety that was as unexpected as it was misplaced. She hardly knew him, she thought, yet she already felt concerned about him.

Dominic was concerned, too. Putting down his wine glass, he said, 'Perhaps you ought to get Sam to take you back to Magnolia Hill.'

'I can rest here just as well as at Magnolia Hill,' Jacob retorted shortly. 'Just help me down to the cabin, will you, Dom? It'll be cooler below deck.'

Cleo chewed anxiously at her lower lip as Dominic got up and helped his grandfather from his chair. One of the crew appeared, possibly expecting to clear the table, but Jacob only waved the man away.

'Cleo and Dom haven't finished,' he said, albeit a little breathlessly as his grandson supported him towards the stairs to the lower deck. 'Bring my granddaughter some coffee, will you? I think she'd prefer that to the wine.'

By the time Dominic came back, Cleo was sipping her second cup of coffee.

Her eyes darted instantly to his dark face, the enquiry evident in her troubled gaze. 'Is he all right?' she asked, putting her cup down as he crossed the deck towards her. 'The cabins are air-conditioned, aren't they? He'll be able to breathe more easily if the air is cooler.'

'Yeah, he'll be OK.' Dominic flung himself back into his chair and regarded her with an intensity of purpose she couldn't possibly sustain. 'How about you?'

'Me?' Cleo considered picking up her cup again, if only for protection, but she was afraid she might spill its contents. 'I'm OK.' She glanced determinedly about her. 'This certainly is a beautiful place.'

'Yes, it is.' Dominic pulled in a long breath and then went for the jugular. 'I wondered if you'd come.'

Cleo's eyes widened. 'Your grandfather invited me,' she said, and he noted she was back to saying 'your' grandfather and not 'my'. 'Besides, I wanted to see something of the island before I leave.'

Dominic's stomach hollowed. 'You're leaving!'

'In a few days, yes,' said Cleo, concentrating on her finger nudging at her saucer. 'I'd have thought you'd be pleased. If I'm not here, I'm not a threat, am I?'

'A threat!' Dominic's tone hardened. 'A threat to whom?'

Cleo pressed her lips together. 'You know.'

'What the hell's that supposed to mean?' Dominic stared at her, his eyes as cold as green ice. 'If you're implying that I might be upset if the old man decides to leave all his money to you—'

'No!' Cleo had to look at him now, anguish in her dark gaze. 'I'd never think anything like that.' She licked her lips with an agitated tongue. 'You can't think I want Jacob's money! Any of it! I shouldn't be here. I don't belong here. I—I just want to get on with my life.'

'This is your life now,' stated Dominic harshly. He hated the look of horror he'd brought to her face. But she had to understand that Jacob wasn't about to let her go, not without a whole raft of conditions. 'And you do belong here, Cleo. As much as any of us, actually.'

'No—'

'Yes.' With some reluctance Dominic got up from his seat and came to take the one his grandfather had vacated beside her. 'You're Robert's daughter. You can't get away from that. Jacob won't let you.'

Cleo blew out an unsteady breath and Dominic realised she was trembling. Tiny goosebumps had blossomed all over those pale almond shoulders, enveloping the smooth skin of her throat and puckering the rounded curve of her breasts.

And he had to touch her.

To comfort her, he defended himself. But the minute his hand contacted the fine bones of her shoulder, he wanted to do so much more.

In consequence, his voice was harsher than it should have been when he said, 'Is the prospect of staying here so terrible?'

Cleo glanced sideways at him. 'Not terrible, no,' she said tensely. 'But, please, let me go. This isn't helping anyone.'

It's helping me, thought Dominic unevenly, aware of his pulsing arousal.

But she was right. He was behaving like an idiot.

Yet, 'Don't you like me touching you?' he asked thickly, all too aware of the warmth of her bare thigh brushing his trousered leg. 'That's not the impression I got before.'

'Bastard!'

The word was barely audible, but the way she thrust back her chair and got to her feet showed how angry she was. Casting a contemptuous glance over her shoulder, she strode across the deck to the rail, and for a moment Dominic had the uneasy feeling that she intended to jump over the side.

But all she did was grip the rail with both hands and stare out across the water. He guessed her knuckles must be white, judging by the taut muscles tensing in her arms. The stiff line of her spine was eloquent of the resentment she was feeling, the sweet curve of her buttocks above those spectacular thighs made him itch to cup them in his hands.

Dear God!

He dragged his hands through his hair, aware that this wasn't the way he'd intended to play it. Dammit, she had a low enough opinion of him as it was without him making it ten times worse. Yet something about her got under his skin. When he was with her, he couldn't think about anything—or anyone—else.

Common sense was telling him to go and get changed into something cooler and take her into town. He'd promised his grandfather he'd look after her, and that didn't include touching her every chance he got.

Getting to his feet, he stood for a moment regarding that

rigid back, and then, almost of their own volition, his feet moved in her direction.

He stopped directly behind her, but she didn't turn. She must have heard his approach, he thought impatiently, waving the ever-attentive waiter away. The soles of his Oxfords made a distinct sound against the floor of the deck.

'Talk to me,' he said, his breath fluttering the wisps of sable silk that had escaped her scarf. 'Dammit, Cleo, I'm not the only one involved here. You wanted me yesterday morning. You can't deny it. If I hadn't called a halt…'

Cleo clamped her jaws together. She had nothing to say to him. But he was right. However passionately she might try to convince herself that he'd been totally to blame for what had happened, nothing could alter the fact that she'd been completely blown away by his kisses, had been drowning in the sensuous beauty of his mouth.

Her silence angered Dominic. Drawing the wrong conclusions, he did something he would never have done if she'd only admitted there were faults on both sides.

Moving closer, he placed a hand on the rail at either side of her. Now she was imprisoned against the chrome-plated barrier, his lean body taut against her back.

She moved then, tried to turn, but he wouldn't let her. With the scent of her warm body rising to his nostrils and the agitated movements she was making only adding to his unwilling response, there was no way he was going to let her go.

Pressing closer, he let her feel the unmistakable thrust of his arousal. Wedged one leg between hers to feel her sensual heat.

The little moan that issued from her lips when he bent his head and bit the soft skin at the side of her neck was almost his undoing.

It was so fragile, so anguished, and a knot twisted in his belly at the sound. But the desire to turn her round and feel her breasts pucker against his chest was consuming any lingering sense he had left.

'Dominic…'

Her whispered protest only added to the urgent need he had to touch her. The sinuous pressure of her thighs against his pelvis almost drove him crazy with need.

'I want you,' he said, his voice barely recognisable to his own ears, it was so thick and hoarse with emotion. 'I don't care about anything else. I just want to feel you naked in my arms.'

'And then what?' Cleo challenged him unsteadily, even as her treacherous body arched back against him.

She so much wanted to give in. But she had to remember who he was, *what* he was: a man who apparently cared for nothing but his own needs.

She took a deep breath. 'Perhaps you're thinking, like mother, like daughter. That I'm no better than Celeste. That just because a white man looked at her—a married man, moreover—she was happy to let him screw her brains out.'

'No!'

Dominic swore then, his voice harsh with self-loathing. Hauling her round to face him, he grasped her tilted chin in one less-than-gentle hand.

'D'you think that's what all this is about?' he demanded, trying to ignore her quivering lips, her eyes, that were the mirror of her soul. 'Some sick desire to follow in my father's footsteps?' His jaw clenched. 'For God's sake, Cleo, I thought you knew me better than that.'

Cleo trembled. 'But I don't know you at all!' she exclaimed, her hands gripping his biceps, feeling the muscles grow taut beneath the fine cotton of his shirt. 'I don't know anything about you.'

She was trying to hold him back, but it was a losing battle. He was so much stronger than she was, so much more deter-mined to have his way.

'You do know me,' he said savagely. His thumb scraped painfully across her lower lip. 'Dammit, you know how I feel about you.'

'Do I?'

Her eyes widened and now he could see tears sparkling in

the corners. And the desire he'd had to hurt her as she was hurting him was strangled by his need to comfort her.

'Cleo—'

'You want I should clear now, Mr Dominic, sir?'

Dominic couldn't believe it. One of the yacht's younger—less experienced—stewards had appeared at the top of the steps that led down to the domestic area of the vessel carrying a tray.

Forced to let go of Cleo, Dominic swung round, ready to deliver a cutting denial. But Cleo's hand on his sleeve was a silent rebuke.

'All right,' he muttered. 'Why not?' He gave the youth an affirming nod. 'I guess we're finished here.'

Then, striding away towards the companionway, he cast a look back at Cleo. 'Wait for me,' he commanded harshly. 'I won't be long.'

CHAPTER ELEVEN

THE phone rang as Dominic was getting ready to go for his morning run.

He was tempted to ignore it. But it just might be his grandfather, and he and the old man were not on such good terms at the moment.

Calling to Ambrose, his houseman, that he'd get it, Dominic returned to the foyer and picked up the receiver.

'Yeah,' he said flatly, and then stifled an oath when Sarah came on the line.

He'd managed to avoid talking to Sarah for the last couple of days. He'd had Hannah tell her he was out when she'd rung him at the office, and Ambrose had orders not to tell anyone but Jacob that he was in the house.

He'd known Cleo wouldn't ring. Since that afternoon on the yacht, he'd neither seen nor spoken to her. Mostly because Jacob had ordered him to stay away from Magnolia Hill.

She'd been gone when he'd returned to the sundeck that day. The young steward had stammered out the news that the young lady had walked off into town.

Dominic had known right away that he hadn't a hope in hell of finding her in the busy little town. The straw market adjoined the harbour and it was the easiest thing in the world to get lost among the many booths and stalls.

Besides, he'd suspected she'd find some way to get back to Magnolia Hill, and she had. She evidently hadn't wanted to disturb her grandfather, but equally she'd have rather done anything than wait for him.

Which, of course, was why he and Jacob were barely speaking to one another. Jacob had had no hesitation in blaming Dominic for Cleo's sudden departure from the yacht.

'You'd better keep your hands off her in future,' he'd warned his grandson, not at all convinced by Dominic's explanation that Cleo had left the yacht of her own volition. 'If anything happens to that girl, boy, I'll know exactly who to blame.'

Dominic had had to accept that that was fair comment. And he had to admit that neither of them had known a minute's peace until Serena had rung to say Cleo had returned to the house in a taxi.

She'd been curious, too, and he'd thought he could imagine the subsequent conversation between her and his mother. But he'd been so relieved that Cleo was home safely, nothing else had mattered.

'Dominic; darling.' Sarah's voice was amazingly amicable in the circumstances. He'd have expected accusations and tantrums, but instead she sounded much the same as she always did. 'What have you been doing? I've been trying to reach you for days.'

Dominic blew out a weary breath. 'I'm sorry about that,' he said evenly. 'Was there something urgent you wanted to speak to me about?'

'Nothing really, darling.' Sarah was a little less conciliatory now. 'Where have you been? I even asked your grandfather where you were, but he said he hadn't seen you either.'

Did he, now?

Dominic's jaw compressed. He wouldn't have put it past the old man to make some provocative comment and enjoy the fallout.

But it seemed Jacob was prepared to let his grandson lead his own life, so long as it didn't involve Cleo. And so long as he wasn't expected to pick up the pieces if anything went wrong.

'I've been pretty busy,' he said at last, despising himself for prevaricating. He was going to have to be honest with her, so why not now?

But how the hell did you tell someone that you were in lust with another woman? That since meeting Cleo, he hadn't been able to think of anyone else?

Besides, as he kept telling himself, this crazy infatuation would pass. It had to. Once Cleo returned to England, he'd get over this madness that was controlling his life.

If she returned to England.

He scowled. If his grandfather had his way, she'd only return there long enough to settle her affairs before returning to San Clemente and making her home here.

'So what does that mean?' Sarah's voice was considerably cooler now. 'I was under the impression that you had executive assistants and managers to handle the day-to-day operation of the company for you.' She paused. 'Or is what you're really saying that you're so busy with your grandfather's houseguest that you haven't got time for me?'

Dominic stifled a groan, raking a frustrated hand through the thickness of his hair. How was he supposed to answer that?

The truth was, she was right, but he couldn't tell her that on the telephone. That was the cowardly way out, and, although he might be a bastard, he had no intention of deliberately hurting her.

'OK,' he said at last. 'I suppose I have been neglecting you lately. But…' He closed his eyes for a moment, trying to decide how best to proceed. 'I knew you didn't like Cleo—'

'I didn't say that.'

Sarah didn't let him finish, and Dominic heaved a sigh. 'You didn't have to,' he said. 'That night at Magnolia Hill, you practically ignored her.'

'All right.' Sarah seemed to realise she couldn't go on denying it. 'I don't like her. I admit it. You mother doesn't like her either. All that fuss over one dinner party!'

'A dinner party that was supposed to have been arranged to

welcome Cleo to the island,' retorted Dominic, feeling his control slipping again. 'Not as a reason for you and my mother to sharpen your claws.'

'Dominic!'

Sarah caught her breath now, and Dominic realised he'd gone too far.

'Yeah, yeah,' he said wearily. 'That was a little harsh.'

'A little?'

'All right, a lot.' He blew out a breath. 'I'm sorry. I guess I'm not in the best of moods at the moment.'

Sarah hesitated. 'Is it her; Cleo?' she ventured after a moment. 'I mean, I suppose it is pretty difficult for you, her staying at Magnolia Hill and all. You and your grandfather have always been so close, and if he's thinking of making her his heir—'

'Where the hell did that come from?' Dominic demanded angrily.

But he knew. His mother. They were her words, not Sarah's.

'I just meant—'

'Yeah, I know what you meant.'

Dominic's tone was harsh, but somehow he managed to get a handle on his emotions. It wasn't her fault and he had to stop behaving as if it was.

'Look,' he said, immediately regretting it, 'are you free this evening?'

Sarah gasped. 'I—I think so.'

'Good.' Dominic tamped down his disappointment. 'Then how about we have dinner together? I've heard there's a new restaurant opened on Bay Street—'

'I'd prefer it if we could have dinner at Turtle Cove,' Sarah interrupted him appealingly. 'It seems ages since we've had dinner together. Just the two of us, you know. Alone.'

Dominic bit back an instinctive denial. 'Why not?' he conceded after a moment, realising it would be easier to talk without an audience. 'Shall we say—eight o'clock? Eight-thirty?'

'So late?' Sarah was plaintive. But then, with a little sigh of resignation, she agreed. 'Eight o'clock. I'll look forward to it.'

'Yeah.' Dominic almost put down the receiver without responding. 'Um—so will I.'

Cleo left the house by the back entrance.

She'd discovered there was a second staircase that descended to a rear lobby, and she'd become accustomed to using it whenever she didn't want to encounter anyone else.

Which usually only happened after her grandfather had retired for the night.

During the day she'd adapted to life at Magnolia Hill very well, she thought. Perhaps the fact that there was a limit to the length of time she would stay here was a contributing factor.

As things stood, she'd made it plain to Jacob that she didn't feel she belonged here. This was Serena's home, not hers. And so far he seemed to have accepted that.

Consequently, her relations with the other women in the household had improved considerably. Since their confrontation over the lunch table, even Lily seemed to have revised her opinion of her. So much so that on a couple of occasions recently she'd actually thawed enough to ask Cleo about her life in England.

If Cleo suspected that Lily's intention was to remind her of her roots, she didn't say anything. And at least both women had stopped regarding her as a threat to their own positions in Jacob's life. She didn't think they thought she was a gold-digger any longer. And Jacob was so delighted to have her here that no one wanted to deny him his last chance of happiness.

The only cloud on the horizon was Dominic.

It was several days since she'd seen him; several days since he'd visited Magnolia Hill. She didn't like to think that she was to blame for his apparent estrangement from his grandfather. But deep inside, she knew she was.

There was no one about and Cleo tramped through the dunes

and down onto the beach. Kicking off her flip-flops, she allowed her toes to curl into the moist sand.

Heaven, she thought. She would miss this when she went back to England. Would miss a lot, if she was honest. She'd begun to care about her grandfather, and it troubled her that when she returned to England she might never see him again.

She sniffed, aware that she was suddenly near to tears. She hadn't thought she was a particularly emotional person, but since she'd come to San Clemente she found her eyes filling with tears at the most inappropriate moments.

Like just after Dominic had kissed her for the first time, she mused, when she'd stumbled, wet and dishevelled, back to the house.

And after their confrontation on the yacht. When she'd been desperate to escape the probable outcome of his lovemaking.

No, not his lovemaking, she corrected herself fiercely as she started to walk along the shoreline. They hadn't made love, thank God, although goodness knew she'd wanted to.

She'd wanted him, she admitted now. Just as he'd said. But she'd denied it. Though not in words, she thought bitterly. Just by running away. And how convincing was that?

She'd been walking briskly for some time when all at once she realised she was running out of beach. A rocky groyne provided a natural barrier between this cove and the next. And, because she felt too edgy to go back yet, she slipped on her flip-flops again and climbed up onto the rocks.

It was higher than she'd thought, and she was glad she'd taken the time to change before heading out. Cotton shorts and a strappy vest were far more suitable for rock-climbing than the camisole dress she'd worn for dinner with her grandfather.

The deserted strip of beach beyond the barrier was appealing. Moonlight illuminated a stretch of sand similar to the one she'd just walked along, and the idea of going further was tempting.

No one would miss her, if she was late back, she knew. Lily had gone out for the evening and Serena had already retired to her rooms for the night. She, too, was supposed to be having an early night, but there was no reason to feel guilty, just because she'd left the house.

Clambering down the other side of the outcrop, she bit her lip when she almost lost her footing. She grimaced. It would be just like her to fall and sprain her ankle; to have to spend the night camped out on the rocks.

But nothing more daunting happened. She gained the beach at the other side of the rocks and once again kicked off her sandals. She dismissed the sudden thought that she might be trespassing on someone's private property. If she was discovered, she had a perfectly good excuse.

She'd walked perhaps a couple of hundred yards when she saw the house just ahead of her.

She'd been thinking of other things, not least how she was going to feel when she got back to England, and the sudden appearance of the building caused her to come to an abrupt stop.

It was standing on a slight rise. Single-storeyed; built of mellow brick. Perhaps not as big as Magnolia Hill, but still immensely impressive.

She caught her breath in alarm. So she was trespassing, she thought. Clearly, this beach belonged to the house.

And it was occupied, too. Lights streamed from a dozen windows, highlighting the terrace gardens, giving colour to the moon-bleached vegetation that hedged a cantilevered deck.

Sliding glass doors to the deck stood open. And even as she watched, her eyes wide and incredulous, a man and a woman emerged from the house to confront one another across its lamp-lit area.

A man Cleo knew only too well, she realised disbelievingly. And a woman she hardly knew at all.

Sarah.

Cleo knew she should retreat. If she slunk away into the shadows, no one need ever know she'd been there. This was evidently Dominic's house, Dominic's beach, Dominic's property.

The house he must have left that morning when she'd encountered him on the beach below Magnolia Hill.

But she didn't move.

Dominic and Sarah were arguing.

Or rather Sarah was arguing. Dominic's stillness was an indication of his mood. Sarah kept waving her arms about, shifting from one foot to the other. Making accusations, if her pointing finger was any guide. Though Cleo knew her judgement could be sadly flawed.

Then Sarah stepped forward and slapped Dominic's face.

The sound was clearly audible and Cleo pressed her hand to her mouth to silence her automatic gasp of dismay. For heaven's sake, what was going on?

She half expected Dominic to respond then. In her world, women didn't get away with striking their partners without expecting some kind of retaliation.

But Dominic didn't move. Didn't do anything. And Sarah burst into uncontrollable sobbing, making Cleo feel even worse for witnessing her distress.

She had to leave, she told herself. Now. This minute. She was no better than a voyeur, watching something she had no right to see.

But couples had arguments all the time, she assured herself as a form of justification. Though that didn't excuse her behaviour. Not at all. So why didn't she just go back to Magnolia Hill?

'Don't you have anything else to say?'

Sarah's words were suddenly audible and once again Cleo stifled a gasp. Instead of backing away, she'd moved forward, and now only the bushes that grew in the angle of the deck protected her from discovery.

To her horror, Dominic's gaze turned towards the garden then, and she felt a momentary sense of panic that somehow he'd seen her and was about to expose her.

But then Sarah spoke again, and his attention was distracted.

'I'm leaving,' she declared, scrubbing at her eyes with a

damp tissue. 'I don't think there's any point in my staying any longer, do you?'

'Probably not.'

Dominic's response was spoken in a neutral tone and Sarah let out an anguished cry.

'You're a bastard, Dominic Montoya,' she accused him bitterly. 'And I hate you!'

Once again, Dominic made no response and Sarah's face contorted.

'I can't talk to you when you're in this mood,' she said angrily. 'I'm going home.'

Pushing past him, she strode into the house. A few moments later, Cleo heard the sound of a car's engine, and then the unmistakable squeal of rubber as the vehicle took off.

Only then did she realise she'd been holding her breath. Expelling it weakly, she allowed her head to tip forward, feeling a distinct surge of relief.

She hadn't realised how tightly she'd been wound until the tension eased, and she moistened lips that had become dry and parched.

'You can come up now.'

Her relief was short-lived.

Her head jerked up to find Dominic looking down at her. Arms resting on the rail of the deck, he was regarding her with a mixture of curiosity and derision. And she realised that when she'd thought he'd seen her, he had.

CHAPTER TWELVE

CLEO tried to gather her scattered wits.

'Perhaps I don't want to come up,' she said, tugging the ponytail she'd made of her hair with nervous fingers. Then, because curiosity was a two-way street, 'How did you know I was here?'

'Oh, please.' Dominic's lazy voice scraped across her nerves, making her heart beat even faster than it was doing already. 'If you want to go sneaking about, don't wear a white top.'

Cleo glanced down at her vest. 'It's not white,' she said pedantically. 'It's cream.'

'Oh, well, excuse me.' Dominic was sarcastic now. 'Don't wear a *cream* top, then.'

Cleo squared her shoulders. 'In any case, I wasn't sneaking about,' she added defensively. 'I didn't know this was your house.'

'No?'

'Not until I saw you, no.' She was indignant. 'You usually come to Magnolia Hill by car.'

'Yeah.' Dominic conceded her point. 'Half a dozen miles by road. Less than a mile across the sand. Go figure.'

Cleo drew in a breath and took a step backward. 'I think I ought to be going—'

'So you don't want to see where I live?'

Of course she did. Cleo swallowed. But, 'Not particularly,' she said tightly. 'Serena will be wondering where I am.'

'You think?' Dominic's dark brows arched at the blatant lie. 'If I know my dear aunt, she's probably tucked up in bed at this moment, watching her soaps. Serena's a great soap fan. Did you know?'

Cleo shrugged, causing one of the bootlace straps to tip off her shoulder. Hurriedly replacing it, she said, 'She went to her room. That's all I know.'

'Well, take my word for it.' Dominic scowled, impatient with himself for getting involved with her again. 'So—do you want to have a drink with me? A non-alcoholic drink,' he amended swiftly. 'Then I'll drive you home.'

'I can take myself home, thank you,' said Cleo firmly, but her eyes drifted irresistibly towards the flight of wooden steps that led up to the deck.

She'd be a fool if she accepted any invitation from him, she told herself fiercely. She didn't trust him, and after the way he'd just treated Sarah...

'Better you than me, then,' Dominic remarked carelessly, and she had to concentrate hard to remember what she'd said. 'The tide's coming in,' he continued. 'The rocks are dangerously slippery when they're wet.'

Now, why had he said that? Dominic wondered half frustratedly. Why the hell was he persisting with this when it was obvious she was just as dangerous to his peace of mind?

Cleo had turned round now and was looking rather anxiously towards the ocean. Sure enough, the distance, between where she was standing and the water, had definitely narrowed in the last few minutes.

He felt her indecision. Felt it in the looks she cast up at him, the uneven breath she blew out before she spoke again.

'Why—why should I trust you to take me home?' she asked, but he could tell that she was weakening. 'You were cruel to Sarah. She was in tears when she left here.'

Dominic grunted. The nerve of the woman.

'I have no intention of discussing my relationship with Sarah with you,' he stated flatly. He turned away from the rail. 'Do what you like.'

Cleo sighed and looked along the beach. She could see that the waves were indeed starting to splash over the rocky promontory. And realised that to return to Magnolia Hill that way would be far more scary than she'd thought.

Dominic had entered his living room and was pouring himself another whisky when he heard her coming up the steps outside.

Swallowing a mouthful of the single malt, he stared grimly at his reflection in the mirror above the fieldstone hearth. And scowled at his image, wondering why the hell he hadn't just pretended not to see her.

Inviting her into his house had to be the craziest thing he'd ever done. He didn't want her here, he told himself. He didn't want to be reminded of her every time a shadow moved across his vision, didn't want to smell her distinctive fragrance in places he'd hitherto regarded as his own personal territory.

He didn't want her making a mockery of his life.

Despite the sexual chemistry between them—and he couldn't deny that—there was no way they could have an affair. She'd never forgive his father for the way he'd treated her mother and, if history was repeating itself, she wanted no part of it.

But he still wanted her. That was a given. Wanted her with an urgency that he'd never felt before.

He wondered how she'd feel if he told her that the reason Sarah had rushed out of here in tears was because, despite all her efforts, she'd failed to arouse even a trace of the excitement he was feeling now.

It had not been a pleasant evening. Dominic hated having to play the villain. Usually, his relationships ended by mutual consent.

Or did they? Perhaps he'd only been kidding himself. If Sarah was to be believed, his reputation was in shreds. But then, that begged the question of why she had gone out with him. And why she should be so bitter because they were breaking up.

Certainly, Dominic had begun to wish he'd insisted on meeting her at a restaurant. Surely with other diners around, Sarah wouldn't have resorted to threats. She'd actually accused him of cheating on her. She'd had some wild notion that he'd already slept in Cleo's bed.

Wild indeed!

Still, threatening to tell his grandfather about the affair he was purportedly having with Cleo had been one step too far. And, although she'd evidently regretted it afterwards, Dominic had had enough.

She should have resorted to tears sooner, he thought with a trace of self-mockery. Few men were immune to a woman's tears.

He heard footsteps crossing the deck and then silence. Cleo had paused between the sliding doors and was waiting for him to acknowledge her.

He didn't turn. Not immediately. Let her stew for a while, he thought savagely. He'd had a basinful of that, goodness knew.

But then she cleared her throat, a nervous little sound, and his stomach muscles clenched. He couldn't do this, he thought firmly. What the hell did she think was going on here?

A pulse in his jaw jerked as he swung round to face her. 'Come in, why don't you?' he said harshly. 'And shut the door before we get eaten alive.'

Cleo hesitated a moment. Then she stepped inside onto cool Italian marble tiles, and slid the window closed behind her.

She was in a huge room, a beautiful room, with a high, arching ceiling. Dark wood predominated, starkly elegant against pale upholstered walls.

There were several chairs and sofas positioned about the room, some in honey-soft leather, others in plush velvet or brocade. And a thick Chinese rug in shades of cream and topaz.

The large stone fireplace was presently filled with exotic

blossoms: anthurium and bird of paradise; delicate orchids and calla lilies. And her own reflection was thrown back at her in the mirror above the mantel.

Dominic was standing beside the fireplace, a half-filled tumbler of what she guessed was whisky in his hand. He wasn't wearing a tie and his shirt was half-open down his chest. The shirt was black, like his trousers, and exposed a triangle of brown flesh lightly covered with coarse dark hair.

Lord, but he looked good, Cleo thought, feeling her awareness of him deepen. There was a heaviness in her limbs, a disturbing sense of moisture between her legs. She wanted to sit down, rather badly. If for no other reason than to hide the treacherous tremor in her knees.

She must keep her head, she warned herself fiercely. But she was beginning to understand how Celeste must have felt when Robert Montoya had taken her to his bed. Celeste must have tried to resist, to keep her head in the face of enormous provocation. But ultimately she'd surrendered to something maybe stronger than herself.

Meanwhile Dominic was facing his own demons. He knew, better than anyone, how dangerous the present situation was. This had never happened to him before, but that didn't alter the fact that there was a certain inevitability to it.

He could feel his own need in the thickness of his erection, and marvelled that only minutes before, when Sarah had been trying to arouse him, he had felt no reaction at all.

Hot blood pounded through his veins, insistent, demanding, intense. He felt both angry and vulnerable. Was he no longer in control of his own life?

Cleo was waiting for him to say something, and he nodded somewhat offhandedly towards a chilled cabinet standing at the opposite side of the room.

'Can I get you a drink? A *soft* drink,' he corrected himself with a tight smile.

'Thank you.' Cleo was struggling to remember why she'd come here. It certainly hadn't been her most sensible action to date. 'Um—a cola would be good.' She paused. 'If you have one.'

A cola!

Dominic shook his head as he crossed the room to open the cabinet. Pulling out a can, he reflected that at least there was no danger of her getting drunk and doing something rash.

Like coming on to him...

All the same, having her in his house was a torment. She looked so incredibly sexy in the skimpy vest and shorts. Unfortunately, he could remember only too well how she'd looked without any clothes. That creamy almond skin; the raw temptation of her mouth.

Frustration gripped him, and pulling the tab on the can, he poured it into a glass. Adding a straw, he decided she could have this one drink, then he'd take her back to Magnolia Hill. They'd both be infinitely safer with other people around.

His fingers brushed hers as he handed her the glass and immediately his good intentions foundered. He felt the contact radiating heat right to his groin.

He knew he should move away, should put the width of the room between them, but he just stood there. Watching as she sucked the ice-cold cola through the straw, imagining where he'd like to feel those sucking lips.

His next words shocked him almost as much as they shocked her.

'Let's go to bed,' he said abruptly, knowing there was no point in denying what he really wanted.

Cleo's eyes widened in disbelief. Almost choking, she whispered, 'Wh-what did you say?'

As if there was any doubt about it.

'I think you heard what I said,' retorted Dominic huskily, setting down his own glass and taking hers out of her unresisting fingers. 'I said, let's go to bed. I want to make love with you.'

Cleo looked uncomprehending. This couldn't be happening, she told herself. Not after everything that had gone before. He knew how she felt about Robert Montoya's relationship with Celeste, with her *mother*. How could he ask her to go to bed with him knowing how that other affair had turned out?

It didn't matter that his words had sent the blood streaming through her veins like wildfire. Or that, only moments before, she'd been having similar thoughts about him.

She was ashamed of herself for even thinking such things, particularly after the way he'd treated his girlfriend. She should be feeling sorry for Sarah; despising Dominic for attempting to use her to assuage his obvious frustration.

Her breathing had quickened and now she said a little breathlessly, 'What's the matter? Did Sarah turn you down?'

Dominic's green eyes grew icy. 'You can't turn down something that doesn't exist,' he said harshly. 'If you want chapter and verse, it was Sarah who was frustrated, not me.'

'But—why?' Cleo was confused. 'I—I thought you wanted her.'

'I thought so, too,' said Dominic flatly. 'But unfortunately I don't.' His eyes softened. 'I want you.'

Cleo drew a trembling breath. 'You—you don't mean that.'

'Oh, come on.' Dominic was impatient now. 'You can't deny there's something going on between us. You felt it that morning on the beach and you knew it when we were on the yacht. That's why you ran away.'

Cleo swallowed. 'I didn't run away.'

'Well, your grandfather sure as hell didn't take you.'

'Jacob was sleeping. I didn't want to disturb him.'

'Yeah, right.' Dominic's response was sardonic. 'And I suppose you didn't hear me ask you to wait for me.'

'I heard.'

'So?'

Cleo was defensive. 'I—got bored.'

'With me?'

Cleo couldn't answer that. Shaking her head, she turned away.

Never with you, she thought achingly, aware that, slowly but surely, he was wearing her resistance down.

'I'll take that as a no, then, shall I?' he asked softly, and the draught of his breath across her skin made her realise he had come to stand close behind her.

'You—you can take it any way you like,' she mumbled, feeling his heat surrounding her, enveloping her. Then, with a distinct effort, 'This—this isn't going to happen, Dominic.'

'Isn't it?'

Her shoulder was just too tempting and, bending his head, Dominic allowed his tongue to stroke her bare skin.

'N—no,' she said unconvincingly. 'Please—don't do that.'

'Why?' Dominic slipped the strap of the vest off her shoulder, his body quickening when he discovered she wasn't wearing a bra. 'Don't you like me touching you?'

Too much, thought Cleo tremulously, resisting the urge to give in to the torment and rest back against him.

'Come on,' he persisted, his hand slipping from her shoulder to the swollen curve of her breast. 'You want me. Why don't you admit it? And you know I want you.'

'I—I can't—'

'Yes, you can.' Dominic's arm slipped possessively about her waist, drawing her back against him. 'Feel that?' he said thickly. 'Then tell me you don't feel the same.'

'I don't.'

'Well, not precisely the same, obviously,' he muttered impatiently. 'But I bet if I slipped my finger beneath the hem of your shorts—'

'Don't you dare!'

For a moment indignation brought her to her senses, but when she would have twisted away from him, he wouldn't let her.

'Cool it,' he said, and, to her dismay, he peeled the other strap off her shoulder.

She tried to clutch the folds of the vest against her, but his hands were insistent. Cupping her breasts, he said hoarsely, 'Don't play with me, Cleo. I need you.'

'You don't need me,' protested Cleo fiercely. 'You want to have sex with me. Let's tell it as it is, as that seems to be the way you like it.'

'OK.' Dominic stifled a groan as her rigid body pressed into him. 'OK, I want to have sex with you.' He made a bitter sound. 'Please don't tell me you've never had sex with a man before.'

Cleo trembled. 'I'm not denying it,' she said. Although the couple of occasions she had allowed a man into her bed had hardly been memorable.

'So?'

'So what?'

'So why don't we just do it and put us both out of our misery?' he demanded unsteadily. 'It's what I want. It's what you want—'

'It's not what I wan—' she began, but she didn't finish her sentence.

With a groan of desperation, Dominic twisted her round in his arms and stifled her protest with his mouth.

Cleo's resistance crumbled. With Dominic's mouth hard on hers she could hardly breathe, let alone think. His tongue plunged hot and hungry between her teeth and she sank weakly against him.

It was all Dominic could do to remain upright. The temptation to throw her down on the Chinese carpet beneath their feet was very appealing, to peel those tantalising shorts down her legs and—

But that was as far as he dared take it without losing what little control he had left. Instead, with his mouth still plundering hers, he swept her up into his arms and carried her out of the living room. The corridor to his bedroom had never seemed so long, but at last he was able to push open the door.

Ambrose had switched on the lamps in the room, but the sheers at the windows had been drawn back and darkness pressed at the panes. A huge bed, covered with a thick chocolate coverlet, occupied a prominent position, and, kicking the door closed behind him, Dominic carried Cleo to the bed and lowered her onto it.

The bedcover was cool against Cleo's back, and when Dominic straightened she was able to take in the beauty of the room.

Pale wood, wide windows, a velvet-soft carpet on the floor. This was his bedroom, she thought, smoothing her damp palms against the figured silk of the coverlet. This was his bed, this huge expanse of thick, springy mattress and soft, downy pillows, wooden rails at both the head and the foot.

This was where he slept.

Where he'd probably slept with Sarah.

So why didn't it appal her that she was here?

It should.

But Sarah need never know, she told herself.

And wasn't that exactly what her father must have told her mother?

CHAPTER THIRTEEN

DOMINIC peeled off his shirt and came down beside her, and her eyes were briefly dazzled by the beauty of the man. He was all brown, tanned flesh, strong and dark and masculine. And he wanted her, Cleo Novak, she thought incredulously.

How amazing was that?

He moved over her, straddling her thighs. His trousered crotch was rough against her soft skin, but she barely noticed. Then he bent and rubbed his hair-roughened chest against her, warm, taut muscle against her naked breasts.

'God you have no idea how much I've wanted to do this,' he said hoarsely, and Cleo closed her eyes.

She suspected she had a fair idea, she thought. Probably as much as she had wanted him to touch her. Her head was spinning with the nearness of him, with the spicy scent of shaving soap and man.

When he drew back to caress her breasts with his hands, she trembled. His thumbs abraded the swollen peaks and she felt the flood of her own arousal.

'This—this is crazy, you know that,' she breathed, opening her eyes when she felt his mouth take the place of his fingers. Then, catching her breath, 'In heaven's name, what are you doing?'

Dominic lifted his head to give her a smouldering look. 'Don't you like it?' he asked, blowing softly on the damp tip of the breast he'd been suckling, and she gave a weak nod of submission.

'No one—no man, that is, or woman either,' she appended hastily, 'has—has ever done that to me before.'

Dominic's expression showed his satisfaction now. 'So you are a virgin, in some ways,' he murmured softly, and she caught her breath.

In lots of ways, she thought, wishing she had more experience in these matters. Wishing, too, that Dominic would take the rest of his clothes off. She felt too vulnerable, too exposed.

But Dominic seemed intent on robbing her of any dignity. Unbuttoning the waistband of her shorts, he pushed them down over her hips. Pushed her bikini briefs with them, she realised, feeling the cool draught of air against her skin.

'Please...' she protested, but Dominic only bent his head and nuzzled the flat plane of her stomach.

'Let me,' he said, his voice thickening, and she felt his fingers part the dusky curls at the apex of her legs and press intimately inside.

He felt her wetness, felt the little jerk she gave when he caressed her. And withdrew his fingers and brought them to his lips.

'Oh, Dominic,' she choked and this time he seemed to understand her feelings.

'Don't stop me, sweetheart,' he whispered. 'You taste as delicious as you look.'

But then, as her eyes widened and hot colour stained her cheeks, he took pity on her. 'OK, OK,' he said, rolling onto his side beside her. Giving her a rueful grin, he quickly unbuckled his belt.

He pushed his trousers down his legs with no trace of embarrassment. He exposed long, powerful limbs, liberally spread with night-dark hair. And Cleo, watching him, was mesmerised by his maleness, by the thick shaft rising proudly from its nest of curling hair.

He was so big, she thought, her heartbeat accelerating. So

big and hard and most definitely aroused. His erection reared its head and she swallowed uneasily. Was she really going to be woman enough for him?

A tiny drop of moisture sparkled on the tip of his erection, and Dominic saw her looking at it, looking at him.

'Did I say I wanted you?' he asked, bending to trace her lips with his tongue.

Then, capturing one of her hands, he closed it around his throbbing shaft. He kissed her again, feeling the innocent slide of her fingers, knowing just how close he was to the edge.

He sucked in a breath. 'Well, let's take that up a stretch,' he said a little raggedly. Her hand was making its own exploration and he knew he couldn't take much more.

He pulled her hair free of its confining band and pushed his hands into its vibrant texture. 'I'm mad for you.' He covered her cheeks and forehead with damp, urgent kisses. 'I want to be inside you, a part of you. I don't want to know where my body ends and yours begins.'

His mouth returned to hers, hot and demanding. And hers opened to him, her tongue seeking his in an eager mating dance. Then he drew back to trail kisses over her breasts and down her quivering body, the rough stubble of his jaw a sexual abrasive against her sensitive skin.

He felt her response in the way her body arched towards him. She didn't hold back, but lifted one leg to wind it seductively about his thigh.

She moaned, an abandoned, sensual little sound that rocked his universe. He knew he'd never wanted any other woman as he wanted her.

When his tongue found her core, she shifted in protest. But without drawing back Dominic parted her womanly folds to reveal her bud, already swollen with need.

'You—you can't,' she gasped, when he nudged her legs apart and she realised his intentions.

'Oh, I can,' he said hoarsely, tasting her essence. 'You're so ready for me.' He felt her buck against him. 'It would be so easy to make you come right now.'

Cleo knew it. Could feel her scattered senses urging him on.

But, 'Not—not like this,' she whispered, clutching handfuls of his hair, trying to drag him up to her. 'Dominic, I want you. I want to feel you inside me. Not—not just your tongue.'

Dominic groaned. 'I know,' he said unsteadily, and with a reluctant sigh he moved over her again. 'But you taste so good, I want more of it. More of everything. More of you.'

Her legs were parted and he slid his hands beneath her bottom to bring her closer. For a moment, she felt a sense of panic, remembering how big he was, wondering if she could do this.

But then, with an ease of movement she could only envy, he allowed his shaft to probe her moist entry. And then thrust smoothly into her slick sheath.

Her body expanded automatically. His thick erection stretched her and filled her with a completeness she'd never felt before.

She caught her breath and immediately he drew back to look down at her. 'Did I hurt you?' he demanded, but the sensual look in her eyes was answer enough.

'No, you didn't hurt me,' she said huskily, framing his anxious face in her palms, brushing an erotic thumb across his lips. 'It's incredible. You're incredible.' Her tongue circled her lips. 'Don't—stop—now.'

'As if I could,' said Dominic a little unsteadily, feeling his body tight against her womb.

He drew back again and then rocked forward, pinning her to the mattress, the friction of their two bodies moving together a tantalising provocation.

But he couldn't prolong the experience. Much as he would have liked to make this first consummation last forever it couldn't be done. Cleo was too hot, too eager, too wickedly delicious to allow him to take his time.

She delighted him, she enchanted him, she taught him there

was as much satisfaction in giving as to receive. His body felt as if it was on fire. The feeling was so intense, he felt there was a danger that they might both go up in flames.

His movements quickened as the urgency of the moment gripped him. Every time he was with this woman, he learned things about himself he'd never known before.

He felt the throbbing pulse of her body, felt the telltale shudder when her climax reached its peak. Felt her muscles clench around him, heard her moan with pleasure, felt the sensual rush of her release.

His own orgasm followed hers almost immediately, the shattering surge of his release arousing an anguished groan from him. His body shook as his sccd drained from him, a heated flood that left him weak and trembling with relief.

Cleo's head was spinning dizzily. It had been that way since Dominic started moving, since she'd felt the intimate brush of his pubic hair against her core.

The sensations he'd aroused she hadn't known existed. The climax she'd experienced was like nothing she'd known before.

And she realised that where sex was concerned she was totally out of her depth.

Her body was shaking, still developing the pleasurable pangs of the aftermath of what had happened. Occasionally she felt a twitch deep inside her, felt the softening heat of Dominic's shaft still buried to the hilt.

And remembered with another pang that they'd used no protection. She certainly hadn't thought about it and she suspected it had been the last thing on Dominic's mind when he'd penetrated her, flesh to flesh, skin to skin.

She shivered. It was just as well it wasn't the time of the month when she might have conceived a child, she thought gratefully. It easily could have been, and she could have found herself in exactly the same position as her mother.

The thought was sobering, and with a little wriggle she attempted to get away from him.

But Dominic wasn't asleep. She felt the instant hardening of his erection as he became aware of what she was trying to do.

'Hey,' he said huskily, cupping her face in his hand and rubbing his lips against hers. 'Don't go. I was just enjoying the sensation of lying here, anticipating my next move.' His smile was lazily possessive. 'Now, what do you think it should be?'

'I don't—that is, I have to go,' said Cleo disjointedly. 'Please—move, will you? I want to get up.'

'And I don't want you to get up,' retorted Dominic, his green eyes darkening with obvious impatience. 'I want to make love with you again.' His thumb was rough against her lips. 'All night, if I can make it.'

'No—'

'What do you mean, no?'

Dominic sounded a little peeved now, and Cleo wished she didn't have to do this. But it had gone far further than she had ever intended, and now she had to put an end to it.

'I mean…' She licked her lips, searching for the right words to tell him how she felt. 'This has been really—really—'

'Good? Mediocre? What?' Dominic pushed himself up on his elbows and stared down at her. 'Come on: tell it like it is, why don't you?'

'Oh, please…' Cleo moaned. 'OK, it was—wonderful,' she admitted unwillingly, and then wished she hadn't been so honest when he bent his head and thrust his tongue deep into her mouth.

'Yeah, for me, too,' he muttered, drawing back to caress her face with hungry eyes, and she felt him hardening inside her.

'But…'

He blinked at the negative connotation. 'But what?'

Cleo hesitated. 'It was—good, better than good. But it can't go on.'

'Why not?'

His body was losing that instinctive response and she wished she didn't have to do this.

'You know why,' she told him steadily. 'Not least…' She paused. 'Please—don't make me have to say her name.'

'Sarah?' Dominic scowled. 'Of course, you mean Sarah.'

'Who else?' Cleo gave him a reproving look. 'You can't pretend she doesn't exist.'

'Lord!' Dominic was impatient. 'Do we have to talk about Sarah now?' He blew out a breath. 'You know what, I think you're only using Sarah as an excuse. If you're that desperate to get away from me, be my guest.'

Cleo stared at him for another significant moment. And then, taking him at his word, she gathered all her strength and scrambled out from under him.

Her sudden withdrawal was obviously unexpected, and Dominic rolled onto his back, his hand forming a protective shield for his maleness.

Meanwhile, Cleo hustled across the wide bed in a hasty effort to put some space between them.

Dominic scowled, turning his head to watch her. 'Don't worry,' he said harshly. 'I'm not planning on jumping you, Cleo. For pity's sake, we need to talk about this like adult human beings.'

'Get our stories straight, do you mean?' Cleo wasn't mollified by his appeal. 'Oh, yes, I'm sure that's what your father must have told my mother.'

Dominic's scowl was confused now. 'What's that supposed to mean?'

'She was having an illicit relationship with your father,' retorted Cleo painfully. 'And in many ways, our relationship is the same.'

'No, it's not!'

Dominic hauled himself upright as he spoke, apparently giving up on his attempt to consider her modesty. His eyes were dark with anger as he stared at her and she quivered.

'There's nothing illicit about our relationship. For God's sake, we're two consenting adults. We don't have to consider anyone but ourselves.'

'You think?' Cleo's voice was tremulous. 'I doubt if your mother would agree.'

'My mother has nothing to do with this!' he exclaimed savagely. 'Cleo, I'm a man. I make my own decisions.'

'I had noticed.'

Cleo sniffed again, shaking her head as she looked about her for her clothes. Finding her panties on the floor, she hurriedly put them on without looking at him. She'd never dressed in front of a man before and this was so much worse because of what had been said.

But she could hardly take refuge in his bathroom, even if she wanted to. Not when her clothes were strewn all over his bedroom floor.

'Cleo, please!'

'There's nothing more to say,' she said, rescuing her vest and pulling it over her head.

Her hair was all over the place, but at least she was covered. She spied her shorts lying on the floor at the foot of the bed and snatched them up with some relief.

'Like hell!'

Dominic's anger was obviously growing. He was sitting on the edge of the bed glaring at her, and she couldn't help thinking how sad this whole situation had become.

But why should she expect anything else? She'd broken the rules and now she had to pay for it. It was Sarah she should be feeling sorry for, not herself.

'Cleo,' Dominic began again, 'don't do this to me.' He drew a breath. 'Come on, stay with me tonight.'

'You know I can't.' Hopping from one foot to the other, Cleo struggled to put on her shorts without falling over. 'It was good while it lasted, but don't let's pretend it was anything more than sex. Pure and simple.'

'There was nothing pure about it,' retorted Dominic. 'It wasn't simple either. Not as far as I'm concerned. It was damn complicated. It *is* damn complicated. Do you think I intended this to happen?'

'Do you think I did?' Cleo gasped indignantly. Her fingers stumbled in their attempt to fasten the button at her waist and she muttered a frustrated exclamation. 'Dammit! Dammit! This wasn't my idea.'

'No, it was mine.'

Dominic's tone had gentled, but in her haste to get her shorts on, she barely noticed. However, she had moved nearer to the bed, and now Dominic leant towards her and hooked his fingers into her waistband.

'Don't fasten that,' he said a little thickly, pulling her resisting body between his legs. 'Let me take them off again so you can come back to bed.'

'No!'

Despite the languor that had gripped her as soon as she was close to his naked body again, Cleo managed to overcome it.

Twisting away, she paused when there was some distance between them, and said, 'I want to go back to Magnolia Hill.' She was amazed at the determination in her voice. 'You—you said you'd take me back.'

'Yeah, I did, didn't I?'

Dominic closed his eyes for a long minute. She was right, he thought wearily. He had promised to drive her home. But, dammit, that was before she'd completely blown his mind.

'Cleo, sweetheart—'

He made one final attempt to appeal to her, but she wasn't interested.

'Don't call me that.' She squared her shoulders. 'Are you going to get dressed or do I have to call a cab?'

'Well, good luck with that.' Dominic's tone was dry. 'I don't know any cab drivers on San Clemente who'll turn out after midnight.'

Cleo couldn't believe it. It couldn't be after midnight. But it was.

The little ormolu clock standing on the cabinet beside the bed showed the time as twenty minutes past the hour. She had been away from Magnolia Hill since a little before nine o'clock.

Turning back to Dominic, she placed bravely defiant hands on her hips. 'OK, it's late. So—are you going to take me or do I have to walk?'

Dominic shook his head. 'Like you'd risk walking the better part of six miles in the dark,' he scoffed. 'Even if you knew which way to go—which you don't.'

'I could always try going back the way I came,' she retorted staunchly. 'The tide has probably turned by now.'

'You think?'

Her shoulders abruptly sagged. 'Oh, come on,' she said despairingly. 'Please, Dominic. Don't make me have to beg.'

Dominic's features lost all expression.

With a grim shrug of his shoulders, he got up from the bed. And, although she made a squeaky little sound and leapt back out of his way, he didn't even look at her.

Opening a drawer, he pulled out a pair of cargo shorts and yanked them, commando-style, up his legs. He used his zip but left the button at his waist unfastened. Then, without bothering with a shirt, he nodded pointedly towards the door.

'After you.'

Swallowing the sob that rose in her throat at his sudden coldness, Cleo preceded him from the room. She was half-afraid he might still try to stop her.

Half-afraid he wouldn't.

He didn't.

Barefoot, he led the way across an atrium-roofed foyer to the front doors of the house.

Muted ceiling lights gave the huge reception area a warmly elegant appearance, but Cleo scarcely noticed. She was too wrapped up in her own emotions, her own misery.

This was so much worse than she'd even imagined. Her heart was beating so fast, yet her feet wanted to drag.

She didn't want to leave him, she acknowledged bitterly. She wanted to stay, to be with him. To spend the rest of the night making love with him.

She loved him.

The realisation struck her like a blow to the solar plexus. And it terrified her.

After all her efforts to deny it, to tell herself she'd never do what her mother had done, she'd fallen in love with him.

Oh, she was such a fool!

Dominic didn't love her.

He *wanted* her. She believed that. But wanting wasn't the same as needing someone, and what had just happened had proved it.

CHAPTER FOURTEEN

'Is IT possible for you to arrange for me to go home? Today, preferably.'

It was the next morning and, after making certain enquiries, Cleo had found her way to Serena's apartments.

The older woman had bid her enter her suite, evidently expecting it to be one of the servants. Her eyes had widened considerably when she'd seen Cleo.

'To go home?' she echoed. In a thin silk negligee, Serena had been having breakfast on her balcony. But she'd left the table to answer the door. 'I... Does my father know about this?'

'No one knows,' said Cleo flatly. 'And I wanted to make all the arrangements before I tell Jacob.' She paused. 'I suspect he won't want me to go, but—'

'You suspect!' The emphasis in Serena's voice was much different from her own. 'Cleo, you know he won't agree to this. He wants you to stay here.'

'Well, I can't.' Cleo was determined. 'I'm sorry. I'm going to miss him—miss all of you,' she added a little ruefully. 'But you do understand, don't you? I have my own life. In England.'

Serena's brows drew together. 'I don't know what to say.'

'You don't have to say anything.' Cleo licked her dry lips. 'I think you know, as well as anyone, that my staying here would never have worked.'

'Initially.' Serena hesitated. 'Initially, I'd have said that. Did say it, actually. But things have changed.'

'No, they haven't.'

The last thing Cleo wanted was for Serena to try and persuade her to stay. She'd told herself she was prepared for Jacob's disappointment. Anything else would be too much for her to handle.

And after last night, there was no way she could remain at Magnolia Hill. Not after what had happened. She wasn't her mother. She'd never be satisfied with second-best. And it had been evident from Dominic's attitude that all he wanted was an affair.

She hadn't slept for what was left of the night and, in consequence, she wasn't thinking all that clearly. But one thing seemed perfectly obvious: she had to leave here before she lost all her self-respect.

Last night it had taken quite a hammering. Particularly during that ominously silent drive back to Magnolia Hill. Dominic hadn't spoken, except to advise her to fasten her seat belt, and when he'd dropped her at the house only courtesy had prevented him from driving away before she was safely inside.

As luck would have it, the rear door was still unlocked, and she'd merely lifted a hand in farewell before scuttling through it. She'd heard the SUV's wheels squeal as he'd executed a three-point turn, and prayed no one else had been awake to hear it, too.

And she'd known then how vulnerable she was. She'd wanted to appease him, she admitted painfully. And she *would* give in if she stayed here. It was only a matter of time before he wore her down.

Which mustn't happen.

'Does this have anything to do with Lily?' asked Serena now, and Cleo wondered if she dared use Dominic's mother as an excuse.

But, no. In actual fact, Lily had become the least of her worries. She doubted the other woman would ever like her, but she thought she had gained a bit of respect in her eyes.

Which would soon vanish if she ever found out about her

and Dominic, Cleo conceded bitterly. Lily was prepared to accept that her coming here was not her doing, but her attitude would soon change if she thought Cleo wasn't going back.

'I just want to go home,' Cleo said simply, and Serena shook her head.

'You know my father considers that this is your home, don't you?' she protested. She paused. 'Nobody knows how much time he has left. Couldn't you put your own life on hold for a few more weeks?'

Cleo sighed. 'You know I only got leave of absence for two weeks.'

'But I'm sure, in the circumstances—'

'No.' Cleo hated having to refuse her, to refuse Jacob, but what could she do?

'I have to go back,' she insisted. 'You know people don't accept me here.'

'They're beginning to.' Serena was persuasive. 'You have to give people time to get to know you, Cleo. No one knew of your existence until a few weeks ago.'

'Do you think I've forgotten?'

There was a trace of pain in Cleo's voice now. She'd been sure it wouldn't matter to her, but it did.

And Serena did something Cleo never would have expected. She stepped towards her and enfolded her in her arms.

'You have to put the past behind you, my dear,' she said gently. 'Believe me, we all feel regret for things that we did, things we didn't do. I more than most.'

Cleo had submitted to the embrace, but now she drew back to look at this woman who was, amazingly, her aunt.

'What do you mean?'

'Oh…' Serena pulled a wry face. 'Hasn't my father told you about Michael Cordy?'

A trace of colour entered Cleo's cheeks at her words and Serena nodded her head resignedly.

'I see he has,' she said. 'Did he tell you Michael asked me to marry him? Not once, but several times?' She grimaced.

'And, like a fool, I turned him down. I had the mistaken idea that my father needed me here.'

'I'm sure he did, Serena.' Cleo had never imagined she'd be comforting her aunt. 'When your mother died, he must have been desolate.'

'I suppose he was.' Serena tipped her head from side to side in a gesture that spoke of her uncertainty. 'But I was never woman enough for him. He could always walk all over me. He still does, if I let him.'

'Oh, Serena!' Cleo felt such sympathy for her. 'He loves you. You know he does. Perhaps his illness…'

'Do you honestly think his being ill has made a scrap of difference to the way he thinks of me; the way he thinks of all of us?' Serena was scornful. 'You know, perhaps I shouldn't be trying to persuade you to stay here. Heaven knows, if you did, your life would never be your own.'

Cleo sighed, releasing herself with some reluctance from Serena's arms. Then she put a little space between them.

'I have to go,' she said, hoping the other woman wouldn't ask for any more reasons. 'Will you—do what you can to arrange it?'

'And risk my father's wrath?'

'I am going to tell him what I plan to do,' said Cleo firmly. 'I wouldn't just leave without saying goodbye.'

'Well, good luck with that.' Serena pulled a wry face. 'Though I guess this proves that you're really his granddaughter.' She shook her head. 'Apart from Dominic, we all give in to him, one way or the other.'

She paused. 'But I'll speak to Rick Moreno. He's the pilot who brought you here. He flies into Nassau most days on company business or to pick up supplies. I might be able to arrange with him to take you with him.'

Cleo bit her lip. 'When?'

'When?' Serena frowned. 'Oh—in a day or two.'

'Tomorrow?'

Serena blew out a breath. 'Cleo—'

'Please.'

Serena shook her head. 'I'll do what I can, but I'm not promising anything. Your grandfather may have something to say about that.'

'Thanks.' Impulsively, Cleo stepped towards her again and kissed Serena's cheek. 'I appreciate it.'

Serena shook her head. 'I wish you wouldn't do this.' She sniffed. 'Just as we're getting to know one another.'

Cleo managed a rueful smile. But when she got outside the room again, and the door was securely closed behind her, she felt the hot tears rolling down her cheeks.

Dominic was sitting at his desk, staring broodingly into space, when his cellphone rang.

Flicking it open, he blinked when he saw who was calling him. The old man always used the office number when he wanted to get in touch with his grandson there and the very fact that he hadn't put this call on an entirely different footing.

'Grandpa!' Forcing a neutral tone, Dominic hoped he sounded less edgy than he felt. 'This is a surprise.'

The old man didn't say anything and Dominic's nerves tightened even more. 'To what do I owe this pleasure?'

'Like you don't know.'

The anger in the older man's voice was almost palpable and Dominic wearily closed his eyes and dragged a hand down his face.

'OK,' he said. 'I assume this is about Cleo.'

'You're sharp, I'll give you that.' But Jacob was sarcastic. 'You couldn't keep your hands off her, could you? After the way you swore to me that you had no intention of ruining her life as your father ruined her mother's.'

'I haven't.'

But the old man wasn't listening to him. 'Just tell me: did you sleep with her?'

Dominic heaved a sigh. 'Cleo?'

'Don't mess with me, boy. You know who I mean.'

'OK.' Dominic spoke flatly. 'Yes, I slept with her.'

'Damn you!'

'It's not what you think, old man.'

'No?' Jacob snorted. 'You're going to tell me next that you asked her to marry you. Oh, no, you couldn't do that because marriage isn't on your agenda.'

'Grandpa—'

'You make me sick, do you know that?'

Dominic groaned. 'If you'd let me speak—'

'And say what?'

'That I love her, dammit!' exclaimed Dominic harshly. 'You don't take any prisoners, do you?'

The silence that followed this pronouncement was ominous.

Dominic had expected the old man to say something, even if it was only to call him a liar. But Jacob said nothing, and that was more disturbing than his anger had been.

Unable to sit still while he waited for his grandfather to speak, Dominic pushed himself up from his chair and walked a little jerkily over to the window.

The three-storey block of offices that housed the Montoya Corporation overlooked the bay. A couple of hundred feet above the marina, up a narrow, winding street, it had an unparalleled view of the town and the harbour beyond.

But Dominic was blind to the beauty of his surroundings. Finally, he said, 'Well? Don't you have anything to say?'

'It's too late.'

Jacob's words struck his grandson like a sword to his ribs. 'What do you mean—it's too late?' he snarled. 'I've told you, I love her. I do. I'm going to see her today, to tell her—'

'Well, you should have thought of that sooner.' Jacob was contemptuous. 'But I guess this is all new for you. You don't usually offer marriage to the women you sleep with.'

Dominic bit his tongue on a savage retort. 'This is different,' he muttered. 'I needed time to think.'

'I bet you did.' Jacob snorted. 'Anyway, forget it. It's too late now. She's gone!'

'Cleo?' Dominic felt a sudden chill in the pit of his stomach. 'What the hell are you talking about?'

'I should have thought it was fairly obvious,' said his grandfather coldly. 'She left on this morning's flight.'

'You're kidding!'

'Would I kid about something like that? She's gone, I tell you. She wouldn't listen to anything I had to say. I tried to persuade her to stay on until the end of the two weeks' absence she'd been granted. But it was no use.'

'Jesus!'

'Yes, you might consider calling on Him for forgiveness, boy, because I sure as hell am going to find it hard to forgive you myself.'

Dominic's fist connected with the frame of the window. 'I'll go after her.'

'You won't.' Jacob was very definite about that. 'Don't you think you've done enough damage? She told me she never wants to see you again, and I believe her. If you want to do something useful, I suggest you clear up your own mess. Or is splitting up with Sarah Cordy not so urgent now that the girl you seduced has left the island?'

Dominic sucked in a breath. 'That's a foul accusation to make. Even from you.'

'Yes.' The old man sounded very weary suddenly. 'Yes, it was. And maybe not totally justified. You're a young man. Why shouldn't you sow a few wild oats? I know I did. But you knew how I felt about Cleo. Couldn't you have slaked your lust with someone else?'

'It wasn't lust,' said Dominic doggedly.

'Whatever.' His grandfather's lips turned down. 'It doesn't matter now.'

'It does matter.' Dominic raked frustrated hands through his hair. 'I'll go after her. I'll bring her back. If I tell her how you feel—'

'Do you think, I didn't tell her that?' Jacob was impatient now. 'For goodness' sake, Dominic, I did everything I could to persuade her to stay. But she was determined to leave, and I realise now we have to let her do this. At least for a little while. She's promised me she'll come back if I need her. And I don't want you—especially you—or any of us doing anything to muddy the waters. Do you hear?'

Cleo was standing in the queue at the British Airways check-in desk when someone said her name.

'Cleo?' the woman said, her voice horribly familiar. 'Cleo, are you leaving?'

Cleo hesitated only a moment before turning to face Sarah Cordy.

'Oh, hello,' she said reluctantly. She really didn't want to talk to Dominic's girlfriend at the moment. But politeness necessitated an answer, and with a slight smile she added. 'Yes, I have to get back to London.'

'Really?' Sarah's blue eyes widened. 'This is rather sudden, isn't it? I understood from Dom that you were staying for two weeks.'

'Change of plan,' said Cleo shortly, grateful when the desk clerk chose that moment to ask for her passport. Handing it over, she said, 'Are you going to London, too?'

Hopefully not with Dominic, she appended silently. That would really be too much for her to bear.

'Oh…'

Sarah looked taken aback for a moment. And then, as if a thought had occurred to her, a look of calculation crossed her face.

'Well, no,' she said a little smugly. 'I'm here to meet an associate of Dominic's actually. He asked me to stand in for him. I think he's grooming me for—well, you know.'

Cleo did know. Sarah meant when they were married. She wondered if a heart could split in two.

'Anyway, I think that's the flight that's just landed,' Sarah continued. 'I'd better get going. Enjoy your trip.'

Cleo nodded, but Sarah's departure was hardly a relief.

But then, as she was handed her boarding card, another thought entered her head. If Sarah was here to meet an associate of Dominic's, surely she was in the wrong area of the airport altogether.

She shrugged, and dismissed the thought. What did she know about airports, after all? She'd just be grateful when she was on the flight to London. It was two days since she'd left San Clemente and this was the first available booking she'd been able to make.

CHAPTER FIFTEEN

NORAH met Cleo on the landing outside their small apartment.

It was obvious the other girl had been waiting for her, and Cleo was instantly reminded of that other occasion when Serena Montoya had accosted her at the supermarket.

It was three months since she'd returned to London. Three months and spring had lifted its head at last. There were daffodils in the park and ducks on the pond, and a definite feeling of warmth invading the air.

Not the kind of warmth she'd known when she was in San Clemente, Cleo acknowledged. But England had other attractions for her. A sense of normality for one; a return to the places she was familiar with. The sights and sounds and people she loved.

Of course, she loved her grandfather, too. That realisation had come to her in the darkness of her bedroom and given her some sleepless nights. She worried about him constantly; wished there was some way she could make up to him for the way she'd left the island.

But going to live on San Clemente wasn't an option. She would go and see her grandfather if he needed her, but there was no way she could stay there and constantly come into contact with the man she loved.

Oh, yes. The sudden awareness that she'd felt that night at his house hadn't changed. She loved Dominic. But she would not allow history to repeat itself.

At least she wasn't pregnant.

She'd had a few scary moments, but her period had arrived only two days late that first month home. When she was feeling really low, she conceded it was a mixed blessing. Despite the fact that she told herself she never wanted to see Dominic again, the idea of having his child had been something else.

Was that how her mother had felt? she wondered. Was that why she'd gone ahead and had her child in spite of the obvious difficulties it involved? Had she loved her baby? Cleo felt fairly sure she must have. Which was another reason why she must never forget the past.

Now, as Norah bustled towards the stairhead, she looked at her friend with slightly apprehensive eyes.

'What's wrong?' Cleo asked, her stomach plunging alarmingly. 'Oh, God, it's not my grandfather, is it?'

Norah gave a helpless shrug. 'I don't know why she's here,' she said. 'She wouldn't tell me.'

'She? She?' Cleo's mouth was dry. 'You mean—Serena? Ms Montoya? Is she here?'

Norah shook her head. 'It's not the woman who came before. But I think she did say her name was Montoya.' She spread her hands. 'Anyway, I just wanted to warn you. After the last time…'

Cleo closed her eyes for a moment as they crossed the landing. The urge to turn round and go out again was tempting, but she couldn't leave Norah alone. The trouble was, there were only two other Montoyas it could be: either Dominic had married Sarah, as she'd evidently wanted, or it was Lily. And Cleo was fairly sure it wouldn't be his mother.

But it was.

Amazingly, Lily was seated on their shabby sofa. Despite the warmth of the apartment, she still had her cashmere overcoat clutched about her throat. Perhaps she felt the cold, thought Cleo, trying to distract herself. She couldn't think of a single reason why the woman should be here.

Norah made a beeline for her bedroom. 'I've made some

tea,' she said in passing, indicating the pot standing on the divider. 'If you need anything else, Cleo...'

'Thanks.' Cleo exchanged a look with her friend and then became aware that Lily had risen to her feet as soon as Norah left the room. 'Um—hello, Mrs Montoya. This is a—surprise.'

'A shock, I think.' For once Lily seemed almost approachable. Her smile—a smile Cleo had so rarely seen—came and went in quick succession.

Then, as if she were the hostess, she said, 'Won't you sit down, Cleo? I need to talk to you.' She took a deep breath. 'I've been so worried.'

Although Lily sank onto the sofa once more, Cleo didn't move.

'Grandfather,' she said, scarcely aware that she'd used the familiar form of address. 'I mean—has something happened? Is he worse?' Her voice broke. 'He hasn't—he hasn't—'

'Jacob's fine,' Lily assured her quickly. 'Well, as fine as can be expected, anyway. Isn't that what they always say?' She made an impatient gesture and then, evidently getting tired of looking up at her, she patted the seat beside her. 'Please, sit down, Cleo. You're making me nervous,'

You're making me nervous, thought Cleo, but she obediently loosened her jacket and subsided onto the sofa beside her.

'OK,' she said. 'I'll buy it. What are you worried about?'

Lily regarded her with wary eyes. 'You sound so harsh, my dear. I suppose I'm to blame for that.'

'No one's to blame.' Cleo wasn't about to discuss Dominic with his mother. 'But I am rather tired. It's been a long day.'

'And the last thing you expected was to find me at the end of it?'

Cleo pulled a wry face. 'Frankly, yes.'

'That's understandable.' Lily nodded. Then, glancing towards the kitchen, she said, 'You know, I think I will have a cup of tea, after all.'

Cleo tamped down her resentment and got to her feet.

Whatever was going on here, she wasn't going to find out until Lily was good and ready.

But what could it be? Had Lily found out about her and Dominic? Was she worried that Cleo might be pregnant? That her son might find himself in the same predicament as his father?

She didn't make herself a cup of tea. She simply poured a cup, added milk, and carried it across to Lily. 'Sugar?' she asked, hoping they had some.

But Lily merely shook her head. 'This is good,' she said, taking a sip. 'The English always make the best tea.'

Cleo was tempted to point out that she wasn't English. But it was too much trouble to attempt to justify herself to her.

Resuming her seat, she said, 'Are you going to tell me what all this is about? If you're afraid I might be planning on coming back to live on the island, you can relax. I shall be staying here.'

'Will you?'

Lily's lips twisted, and, although she'd professed herself satisfied with the tea, Cleo noticed she only swallowed a mouthful before setting the cup on the low table at her side.

'I'm hoping I can change your mind,' she went on, causing Cleo to stare at her disbelievingly. 'Oh, yes, my dear. I mean it. For my son's sanity, I think you have to come.'

'Dominic!' His name spilled from Cleo's lips almost automatically. And, despite all the promises she'd made to herself, she felt her heart skip a beat. She took a breath. 'Dominic sent you?'

'Heavens, no! He'd be furious if he knew I was here. Only—only his grandfather knows where I am. Like me, Jacob would do anything for his grandson.'

She pressed her hands together in her lap, breathing rather shallowly. 'I—I'm so afraid he's going to do something terrible to himself, Cleo. He's changed so much since you left. I—I don't think I know him any more.'

Cleo blinked. That was an exaggeration surely.

'I don't understand—'

'His grandfather's worried, too, of course. He blames himself for a lot of what happened.' She paused and then continued with some reluctance, Cleo felt. 'Dom wanted to come after you, you see, but Jacob made him swear he wouldn't do anything without his consent. He insisted you wouldn't want to see him. I think even Jacob thought you'd come round in your own time.'

'Come round?' Cleo gazed at her and Lily nodded.

'You should know,' she said. 'Your grandfather equates everything with money. He was sure the knowledge that you were his legitimate heir would persuade you to come back.'

Cleo gasped. 'I don't care about his money!'

'No. I think he realises that now.' Lily sighed. 'But I'm not here because of Jacob. I want you to know that my son needs you. I never thought I'd say such a thing, but in the circumstances, I don't have a lot of choice.'

Cleo shook her head. 'But what about Sarah?' Her hands were trembling and she trapped them between her shaking knees.

'Oh, well…' Lily was distracted. 'I suppose I hoped something might come of their relationship.' She sighed. 'She's such a lovely girl. And so suitable—'

She broke off abruptly, as if just realising who she was talking to. Then went on, rather heavily, 'But Dominic doesn't love Sarah. According to your grandfather, he loves you…'

She reached for her teacup and managed to raise it to her lips without spilling any, even though her hand was shaking, too.

'Not that he discussed it with anyone,' she went on, her voice wobbling. 'He doesn't discuss his personal feelings at all.' She set her cup down again with a noisy clatter. 'He spends every hour God sends either in that damn plane, flying all over the country, or at the office. We hardly see him. I'm very much afraid he's working himself to death.'

Cleo stared at her. Another exaggeration, she thought, even

as her stomach clenched at the images Lily was creating. 'Dominic has more sense than that.'

'How would you know?' Lily stared at her with resentful eyes. 'You're not his mother. I am.'

Thank goodness for that, thought Cleo, trying desperately to hang on to her own sanity. And that was a thought she'd never have believed she'd have.

'I still don't believe Dominic would do anything foolish,' she said doggedly. 'Surely Sarah—'

'Oh, Sarah's gone away,' said Lily at once. 'The Cordys have family in Miami and I've heard she's staying with them at present.' She hesitated. 'As a matter of fact, she had left the island, but then she came back the next day, apparently all ready to forgive him. I think someone had told her you'd gone back to England, and she must have thought she might still have a chance with him.'

Cleo's jaw dropped.

She was remembering that afternoon when she'd been checking in for her flight to London. She'd wondered why Sarah was in the departure hall when she was supposed to be meeting someone.

My God, Cleo thought now, Sarah had found out she was leaving and taken the next flight back to the island. She'd certainly never mentioned anything about Dominic himself.

Though would she? Cleo asked herself honestly. In Sarah's position, wouldn't she have kept her mouth shut, too? After all, Sarah had evidently wanted Dominic. Cleo guessed she must have been secretly clapping her hands.

'I'm sorry,' she said, but predictably Lily showed little sympathy for the other girl.

'Oh, the Cordys have always coveted Magnolia Hill,' she said carelessly. 'And when Michael had no success with Serena, they set their sights on her nephew instead. I doubt if there was any love involved, my dear, on either side. Even if Sarah's mother and I did encourage people to think there was.

I knew, as soon as I saw you and Dominic together, that you were the one.'

Cleo was stunned. 'I don't believe it.'

'Why not?' Lily's eyes narrowed. 'You are attracted to my son, are you not? It's not a one-sided affair?'

'No.' Cleo bent her head. 'But you don't like me, do you?'

The silence that followed this statement was formidable. Cleo knew she'd gone too far, but for far too long Lily had had it all her own way.

Then, with a little sigh, Lily said, 'I—resented you, Cleo. I admit it. You remind me so much of Celeste. I loved your mother, you know, and she betrayed me. I didn't know about that until Jacob told us what Robert—my husband—had done.'

Cleo drew a tremulous breath. 'I'm sorry.'

'Yes.' Lily lifted her shoulders. 'I was devastated when Celeste died, you know, and her mother took the baby away. Robert told me afterwards that it had died, too, and I had no reason to disbelieve him. I knew nothing about the plans he'd made with the Novaks. That he'd arranged for you to be taken to England with them. The first I heard about it was when Jacob dropped his bombshell. And by the time you arrived, I'd already convinced myself that you were as much to blame as Robert himself.'

Cleo hesitated. 'I've been told that my...father...arranged for me to be adopted by the Novaks because he didn't want to upset you.'

'To upset me!' Lily sounded a little bitter now. 'I fear Robert sent you away to protect himself. Celeste had died, the only witness to his betrayal. He saw a way out of his dilemma that saved him any disgrace and ensured you would always have a comfortable home.'

'But why?' Cleo was confused. 'If no one knew who my father was?'

'You look a lot like him,' said Lily at once. 'He must have seen that immediately. His eyes; his nose; his mouth. Now you even exhibit certain mannerisms he had. He knew I'd have guessed that he was your father and he couldn't allow that.'

'But I thought—because you couldn't have children of your own—'

'We'd adopted Dominic, hadn't we? There was no reason why we shouldn't have adopted you.' Lily sighed. 'My dear girl, that was why he told me you'd died. You see, on top of everything else, you were my half-sister's child.'

Cleo stared. 'I'm afraid I—'

Lily grimaced. 'Robert wasn't the first member of my family to betray his wife, Cleo. Cleopatra Dubois—your grandmother, the person your mother named you after—was my father's mistress many years ago. It was supposed to be a secret. As children, we weren't supposed to know about it. But everybody did. On an island like San Clemente, it's very hard to keep a secret to yourself.'

Cleo could only gaze at her in wonder. 'My father knew this, of course.'

'Of course.' Lily sounded resigned. 'He knew who she was long before she came to live with us. But, after we adopted Dominic, I needed help around the house, someone to look after Dominic when I wasn't there. Celeste offered to be a kind of au pair and I jumped at the chance. We were friends as well as sisters, however unlikely that sounds.'

Cleo was beginning to understand. So many things were slipping into place.

But Lily wasn't quite finished.

'Robert hid his affair with Celeste, as much because *she* didn't want to hurt me as for any sense of guilt he might have felt. Your father was an arrogant man in many ways, Cleo, but I loved him. I prefer not to think about what might have happened if both you and Celeste had survived.'

CHAPTER SIXTEEN

IT WAS strange to be back on San Clemente soil again.

Climbing down from the small aircraft that her grandfather had sent to meet her in Nassau, Cleo looked about her with an odd sense of homecoming.

Which was ridiculous, really. San Clemente had never been her home. Her father had seen to that. And whether her grandfather was right—that Robert had loved both Celeste and his wife and hadn't wanted to hurt Lily—or Lily's story that he was a selfish man who'd been trying to hide his own guilt was the real truth, she would never know.

The fact was, she was beginning to see that she had been an innocent victim of her mother's desires and her father's lust.

The sight of a tall figure, standing in the shade of the airport buildings, drove all other thoughts from her head.

'My God,' she breathed, barely audibly. It was Dominic. Her grandfather had said he would come to meet her himself. What on earth was Dominic doing here?

'You OK, Ms Novak?'

Rick Moreno, the young pilot, had followed her down the steps and was now regarding her with some concern. And Cleo realised she had come to a complete halt, standing there in the brilliant glare of the afternoon sun.

'Oh—er—yes. Yes, I'm fine,' she stammered, managing to put one foot in front of the other, heading somewhat uncertainly

for the shelter of the overhang where Dominic was waiting.
'Thanks, Mr Moreno. I think the sun must be getting to me.'

'No problem.'

Rick was carrying the suitcase she'd brought with her, and
when he saw Dominic he hailed the other man with a cheerful
smile.

'Hey, Mr Montoya,' he said. 'It's good to see you.' He held
up the suitcase. 'You got a car I can load this into?'

'Um—Mr Montoya may not have come to meet me,' said
Cleo hurriedly, trying not to stare too obviously at Dominic. She
glanced around. 'Isn't—isn't Jacob here?'

'No.'

Dominic's response was hardly welcoming, but heavens,
Cleo could see why Lily had swallowed her pride and come to
find her. If she was to blame for his appearance, she had a lot
to answer for.

He looked so gaunt. He'd evidently lost weight, and, although his suit was undoubtedly Armani, the trousers hung
loosely from his narrow hips.

'The Roller's over there,' he said, and Rick nodded his
understanding. He started in that direction, leaving Cleo and
Dominic alone.

Dominic didn't speak and, feeling obliged to make some
kind of contact, Cleo said a little awkwardly, 'I thought your
grandfather was going to meet me.'

'So did I.'

Once again, Dominic's reply was daunting.

But, gathering her courage, Cleo persisted. 'Well, thanks for
coming, anyway,' she murmured. Then, gesturing in Rick's direction, 'Shouldn't we follow him?'

Dominic regarded her without expression. 'What are you
doing here, Cleo?' he asked at last. His voice was as cold as an
Arctic winter. 'I understood you told the old man that you
never wanted to see me again.'

Oh…!

Cleo pulled her lower lip between her teeth. How was she

supposed to answer that? She had said as much, but the circumstances had been so different then.

Lifting her shoulders, she said, 'People change.'

'Do they?' Dominic wasn't convinced. 'Or isn't it a fact that people have their minds changed for them? Particularly if someone lays a guilt trip on them.'

'A guilt trip! No…' Cleo put out her hand to touch his sleeve, but Dominic shifted out of her reach. 'You don't understand.'

'No, I freaking don't,' he agreed harshly. 'But I want you to know that anything my mother has told you is just so much hot air! I don't want you here, Cleo. I don't need you. And if I'm the reason you've swallowed that stubborn pride of yours, then forget it! As far as I'm concerned, you can turn right around and go back where you came from.'

Cleo winced. He'd meant his words to hurt her and they had. But something—the conviction that Lily hadn't been lying, or perhaps the haunted expression in his eyes that, try as he might, he couldn't quite disguise—made her say,

'This is where I came from, Dominic. Don't you remember? You told me that.'

Dominic's jaw clamped. 'Do you think I care what I said to get you here? My grandfather was dying—he *is* dying—and I'd have said anything to get you on that plane. But this…' He made an impatient gesture. 'This is different. If you're here now, it's not because of anything I've said.'

Cleo pressed her lips together for a moment. This was going to be so much harder than she'd ever imagined. If she didn't know better, she'd have said he hated her. Perhaps he did hate her. After all, hatred was akin to love.

With a supreme effort, she pasted a smile on her lips. 'Well, we'll just have to see, won't we?' she said, in much the same tone as she'd have used to a child. 'Shall we get going?'

'Don't patronise me, Cleo.'

'I wouldn't dream of it,' she said pleasantly. She turned to the young pilot who had deposited his load and was now approaching. 'Thanks again, Mr Moreno. You're a star.'

Rick grinned at her, but then, seeing his employer's glowering expression, he quickly sobered. 'No problem, Ms Novak,' he said. He nodded politely at Dominic. 'I'll be flying out later tonight, Mr Montoya. Will you be needing me tomorrow?'

'I'll let you know.'

Dominic was abrupt and he immediately despised himself for taking his ill humour out on the other man. During the past few weeks, he and Rick had flown together many times, and the young pilot was always good-tempered and polite.

'Yes, sir.'

Rick executed a salute and then disappeared through the door that led into the terminal building to register his arrival. And, because she guessed their behaviour was being monitored by the airport staff, Cleo headed determinedly towards where the ancient Rolls-Royce convertible that her grandfather was so proud of was waiting.

Rick had stowed her suitcase in the boot. And after tossing her hand luggage into the back seat, Cleo pulled open the passenger door and tucked herself inside.

Dominic walked round the vehicle to the driver's side, yanking open the door and coiling his length behind the wheel. The sleeve of his jacket brushed her bare arm as he did so, and she wondered how he could bear to wear a suit on a day like this.

A faint smell of soap invaded the car at his entrance, and she noticed that the ends of dark hair that brushed his collar at the back were wet. He'd evidently had a shower, either at the house or at his office. Though, judging by the growth of stubble on his chin, he hadn't stopped to shave.

Even so, she felt a warm feeling inside her at the thought that he'd made an effort on her behalf. It sort of contradicted his assertion that he wanted her to leave. At once.

Or was she just clutching at straws?

She still hadn't the first idea how she was going to handle this. Was she even capable of doing so? Lily might have confidence in her abilities, but she had no confidence at all.

Taking a deep breath, she glanced his way. She had to get a conversation going, she thought as he drove out of the terminal parking area. She had to try and get him talking before they reached Magnolia Hill and he could abandon her without another word.

Clearing her throat, she said, 'Aren't you too hot? I mean, I assume you've been to the office, but do you really need your jacket on?'

'Do you really think it's any of your business?' he countered, checking the traffic. Then, with a mocking twist to his mouth, 'I bet you got the shock of your life when my mother turned up at your door.'

'How do you—?'

Cleo broke off, realising what she was admitting to, and Dominic's expression hardened at the obvious slip.

'How do I know she came to see you?' he remarked at last, taking pity on her. 'She told me herself. I think she hoped I'd be impressed.'

'And, of course, you weren't,' said Cleo tersely, resenting his superiority. 'Anyway, she was worried about you,' she added. 'Apparently she never sees you these days.'

'Well, she must have been worried to have got in touch with you,' he said, and Cleo caught her breath at the callousness of his words.

'Gee, thanks,' she said, trying not to show how small that made her feel. 'Well, I guess I was the last resort.'

Dominic scowled. Despite the way he felt about her—and right now he wished her any place else but here—he didn't like hurting her.

Dammit!

Not that she didn't deserve his contempt, he reminded himself savagely. She'd practically robbed him of any desire for living. And that was a heavy burden to shift.

'Look,' he said wearily, 'let's not pretend you wanted to come back here. And don't for a minute imagine that I knew in advance what my mother intended to do. I didn't. And if I had known, I'd have stopped her. Why can't she just leave me alone to get on with my life?'

'With your death, your mean!' exclaimed Cleo passionately, and Dominic gave her an incredulous look. 'Well, it's true,' she went on. 'What are you doing to yourself?' Her voice broke on a sob. 'What have I done to you?'

The car braked abruptly, and the small pick-up that had been following them along the coast road skidded wildly, almost swerving over the cliff.

The driver raised an angry fist as he went by, but Dominic wasn't paying him any attention. His eyes were fixed on Cleo's tormented face, and when she looked up and met his furious gaze, he shook his head.

'Oh, boy, she really did a number on you, didn't she?' he exclaimed. 'What the hell has she been saying? It must have been something pretty drastic to bring you back to San Clemente.'

Cleo fumbled in her pocket for a tissue. But she'd stuffed her denim jacket into her hand luggage before leaving the plane. Her sleeveless T-shirt and tight jeans left little room for extras.

Finally, abandoning her search, she rubbed her nose with the back of her hand. Then she ventured unevenly, 'I wanted to come back. I've wanted to come back every day since I left here.'

'Yeah, right.' Dominic was sardonic. Then, leaning forward, he rummaged in the glove compartment and pulled out a small pack of tissues.

He handed them to her and she was shocked to find his fingers were icy. 'You're good, Cleo, I'll give you that,' he said, his smile as cold as his flesh. 'Who came up with that explanation? No, don't tell me. It was my mother.'

Cleo felt the prick of tears behind her eyes. 'It wasn't your mother,' she retorted tightly. 'It's not made up. If—if you'd only listen to what I have to say—'

'Oh, yeah. And I'm supposed to believe that you were only waiting for an invitation to come back?'

'Not an invitation, no.' Cleo sighed. He was so hard; so un-forgiving. 'Can't you at least try and look at things from my side for a change?'

'Why should I?' Dominic's expression darkened. 'You've got a bloody nerve, coming here, expecting me to feel sympathy for you. I didn't ask you to come back. And you've only got my mother's word that I'd even want to lay eyes on you again.'

'Oh, Dominic!'

Cleo gazed at him with tear-wet eyes. She wouldn't have believed he could be so cruel. And the disturbing notion that Lily might have been wrong in her interpretation of events hit her with a mind-numbing blow.

'You—you have to understand how I felt when I left here,' she ventured huskily. 'All right. We'd slept together, and that was—that was amazing—'

Dominic's disbelieving gaze turned in her direction for a second, but then he forced himself to resume his contempla-tion of the ocean.

She didn't mean that, he assured himself. This was just another ploy on his mother's part to try and control his life.

'—but I—I couldn't be your mistress.'

Dominic's eyes raked her anxious face again. 'Had I asked you to be my mistress?' he demanded savagely. 'You'd better refresh my memory. I don't remember that at all.'

'No.' Cleo groaned. 'No, you hadn't actually said that—'

'Thank heaven for small mercies!' He was sarcastic.

'—but—but I was sure that was what you wanted.'

'Really?' He stared at her now, his eyes dark and dangerous. 'And you presumed to know my mind about this, just as you presumed to know better than me that night at Turtle Cove, right?'

Cleo blew out a nervous breath. 'I've explained about that.'

'Have you?'

'Yes.' Her tongue circled her lips. 'Can't you see I'm strug-gling here? I thought—I thought I had to get away from you before…before I did something I'd regret.'

'Like going to bed with me again?' Dominic's mouth curled. 'Yeah, I can see how that might have been a problem for you.'

'Oh, don't be so stupid!' Cleo glared at him through her tears. 'I was in love with you, all right? And I was afraid of getting hurt.' She pressed her palms to her hot cheeks. 'You can blame my mother, if you like, but that was the problem.'

Dominic's eyes darkened. 'Why would you think I'd hurt you?'

'Because of Sarah,' she answered simply. 'I thought you might be planning on marrying Sarah, and I couldn't have borne to live with that.'

Dominic was steeling himself against the urge to comfort her. Her tears tore him apart, but he still couldn't ignore what Sarah had said...

'So how do you explain what you said to Sarah at Nassau Airport?' he asked harshly.

'Sarah?' Cleo blinked, scrubbing the heels of her hands across her cheeks. 'What am I supposed to have said?'

'You didn't happen to tell her that you hoped you'd never see me again?'

'Or course not.' Cleo was horrified.

'But you don't deny you had a conversation with her?'

'It was hardly a conversation,' protested Cleo. 'And your name wasn't even mentioned. Oh—except when she told me you'd sent her to meet some business colleague of yours, but that was—'

'Say what?'

Dominic's expression was incredulous now and suddenly Cleo realised that her suspicions about the other girl were all true.

'There was no business colleague, was there?' she breathed. 'Your mother told me Sarah had left the island, but I didn't put it all together.'

'Put what together?'

'The fact that she wanted me to think you two were still a couple.'

'But how could you think that?' Dominic was struggling not to allow the feeling of euphoria that was building inside him to take control. 'You saw what happened between me and Sarah. Dammit, you must have heard something when you were hiding out in the bushes beneath my deck.'

'I wasn't hiding out in the bushes,' murmured Cleo unhappily. She shook her head. 'Oh—I'm no good at this at all.'

'You're better than me,' muttered Dominic, half turning in his seat towards her. 'I should have known Jacob's sudden frailty was too convenient. I guess he knows how weak and vulnerable I am.'

Dominic, weak and vulnerable?

Cleo didn't believe it. His brooding profile was very dear, but also very remote.

She wanted to reach out to him; to plunge her fingers into the silky dampness of his hair; to cradle his solemn face between her palms and make him see that her life wouldn't be worth living if he wasn't in it.

But she wasn't that courageous.

There was silence for a long time and then Dominic said softly, 'So you came back because my mother put the fear of God into you.'

'No.' Cleo held up her head. 'I came back because she convinced me you needed me.'

'And do you still think I do?'

'I don't know what to think,' she confessed huskily. 'But—but now I've seen you—'

'Yes?'

'—I think she might have had a point.'

Dominic grimaced. 'I look that bad, hmm?'

And suddenly, she couldn't take any more.

Uncaring what he thought, she reached out and grabbed the hair at the back of his neck, jerking him towards her. Then she recklessly pressed her mouth to his.

It was the first time she'd ever done such a thing, but she knew she had to do something to break through his iron control.

And, although his lips were only warm to begin with, they quickly heated beneath the sensuous pressure of hers.

She heard Dominic utter a savage protest, but the chemistry between them was undeniable. Despite any lingering resentment he might feel because of her prolonged absence, the instantaneous hunger of his own response made any kind of resistance futile.

'Dammit, Cleo,' he said hoarsely, and then his hands came almost convulsively to grip her shoulders, and he took control of the kiss.

Crushing her back against the leather squabs, he angled his mouth so that he could plunder the sweet cavity of hers with his tongue.

Her tongue came to meet his, a writhing, sensuous mating that gave as much as it took. And Dominic felt the anger he'd been nurturing all these weeks dissolving beneath the delicious vulnerability of her warm body.

Cleo's own relief was overwhelming. She'd been so afraid he wouldn't forgive her. Winding her arms about his neck, she pressed herself as close as the central console would allow.

But it wasn't close enough.

Finding the collar of his jacket, she pushed it off his shoulders, relieved to find that his skin was now much warmer to her touch. But she wanted to be even nearer and her fingers fumbled frantically with the buttons on his shirt.

Dominic sucked in a tortured breath when he felt her hands on his body, and his mouth dived urgently for the sensitive curve of her neck.

He felt hungry, feverish, and when she gave a little moan of pleasure he felt his own needs threatening to explode inside him.

'We have got to get out of here,' he muttered, covering her face with hot, addictive kisses. His hands slid down her arms to find the provocative thrust of her breasts, and he longed to tear the T-shirt over her head.

He wanted to touch her, much more intimately than their

present situation would allow. And, although right now he was crazy enough not to care, she meant so much more to him than a tumble in the back seat of his grandfather's car.

Pushing her back into the seat, he shrugged out of his jacket and tossed it into the back seat. Suddenly he was sweating, and it was such a good feeling.

'Where are we going?' asked Cleo, half-afraid he was going to take her to Magnolia Hill, and Dominic gave her a wry look as he started the car.

'Well, not to see your grandfather,' he said a little ruefully. 'The old devil can stew for a bit longer.'

'What do you mean?'

Cleo looked at him, her dark brows raised, and Dominic's foot pressed harder on the accelerator.

'He knew what he was doing when he asked me to come and meet you,' he said drily. 'He swore he was too tired to make the trip himself. And Serena was conveniently absent.'

'And did you mind?'

'Yes, I minded,' said Dominic honestly. 'He knew how I felt about you, and I couldn't conceive of any way you might want to see me again.'

'Dominic!'

'It's true.' He grimaced. 'I thought you'd come back because of something my mother had said. And I didn't want your— pity.'

'My pity!' Cleo caught her breath. 'Oh, darling…'

Dominic let out a tortured breath. 'Anyway, naturally he didn't want to ask Lily again, so—I was his only option. Or so he said.'

'Thank God!'

Cleo's response was fervent and, spreading her fingers over his thigh, she squeezed provocatively.

Dominic almost choked then. 'Please,' he said hoarsely, 'don't do that.'

'Why?' Cleo's smile was mischievous. 'Don't you like it?'

'I'll answer that when we get to Turtle Cove,' said Dominic, his look promising a delicious retribution, and Cleo shivered in delight.

The journey seemed to take forever. But at last Dominic turned between the stone gates that marked the extent of his property and drove swiftly up to the house.

They left the car on the forecourt, where a fountain sparkled brilliantly in the late-afternoon sun. But even before they reached the entry, Cleo was in Dominic's arms.

Ambrose, Dominic's houseman, appeared briefly in the open doorway, but he quickly made himself scarce. He could see his employer had everything he wanted for the moment, and his smile was a sign of his satisfaction, too.

They paused in the foyer only long enough for Dominic to haul Cleo's T-shirt over her head and to shed his own shirt. Then with his mouth still on hers they stumbled along the corridor to his bedroom.

Cleo thought it was odd seeing the place in daylight, but it was just as beautiful as she remembered. Dominic was just as beautiful, too, and her head swam as, between more of those soul-draining kisses, they peeled one another's clothes off.

Then he tumbled her onto the bed, and she felt his hot, aroused body between her legs.

'I want you—so much,' he muttered in a husky, impassioned voice.

And with her body throbbing with the uncontrolled hunger only he could assuage, Cleo gave herself up to the physical needs of passion...

EPILOGUE

CLEO's hair was still damp.

A silky strand was lying on the pillow beside Dominic's head and he coiled it round his finger.

It was so dark; even darker than his own, with a bluish tinge that gave it a lustrous vitality. It was so essentially her, and he loved it.

He loved everything about her, he thought, bringing the strand of hair to his lips. He inhaled, smelling his shampoo, and he liked the intimacy of that, too.

After their first frantic coupling, they'd taken a shower together. And he'd delighted in soaping her hair and her body, in covering every inch of her skin with his scent.

But, despite the smell of expensive lotions, he could still smell himself on her, and that pleased him.

It was hardly surprising, after all. Rubbing his hands all over her had aroused them both once again, and they'd made love beneath the cooling spray of water. He had pinned Cleo against the wall of the cubicle, and she'd wound her legs around his hips.

Amazingly, they'd made love again when they'd got back into bed. Dominic hadn't known he had it in him, but just thinking of making love with Cleo made him harden with desire.

She was the woman he loved, his soulmate; and he was

never going to let her go. They belonged together; they always had. And he could even feel grateful to his grandfather: without the old man's intervention, he might never have known her.

Cleo was sleeping now.

She was probably exhausted, he reflected. He was pretty tired, too. But he didn't want to miss a minute of the bliss in knowing they were together at last. He'd have plenty of time for sleep when they were married.

Married!

Cleo Montoya. He experimented with the name. Mrs Dominic Montoya. Yeah, that sounded really good.

It was getting dark outside, but he hadn't bothered to close the curtains. If anyone—his mother, Serena or his grandfather—chose to come and peer in at his windows, he really didn't care. He had nothing to hide, nothing to be ashamed of. He and Cleo were a couple.

And how amazing was that!

He stirred and Cleo's eyes flickered. Long, silky lashes lifted, and then she turned her head and encountered his gaze.

'What time is it?' she asked sleepily, and Dominic pulled her closer.

'About six,' he said softly. 'Are you hungry? I can have Ambrose fix us something to eat.'

Cleo's lips parted, and a dreamy expression entered her eyes. 'Is this really happening?' she whispered. 'Are we really together? This isn't just a dream, is it?'

'If it is, I'm having the same dream,' said Dominic, nuzzling her shoulder. 'No, sweetheart, it's not a dream. You're here, at Turtle Cove. In my bed.'

'Hmm, I like that,' she murmured, loving the feel of his stubble against her skin. 'But I suppose I'll have to go and see...*our*... grandfather. He must be wondering what's going on.'

'Oh, I think he has a fair idea,' said Dominic drily. 'I must have convinced all of them that I was in love with you. Why else would my mother have swallowed her pride and gone to see you?'

'Do you think he was worried?' asked Cleo anxiously. 'I wouldn't like to think I was to blame for any relapse in his condition.'

Dominic grinned. 'If Grandpa was worried, it was only over his part in the situation,' he said firmly. 'He was so sure you'd realise what you were giving up—financially, I mean—and come back.'

'But I never wanted his money!'

'Well, he knows that now,' agreed Dominic. 'And I dare say it did him good to sweat for a while.'

Cleo hesitated. 'But he is all right, isn't he?'

'He's OK.' Dominic was reflective. 'No one really knows how his condition will develop.'

Cleo drew a trembling breath. 'Well, I'm glad I'm going to see him again. I realised—I'm very fond of him.'

'That's good to know.' Dominic's eyes darkened. 'And how about me?'

Cleo gazed at him with her heart in her eyes. 'You know I love you,' she breathed. 'So much. That was why I had to go away. I couldn't bear the thought of seeing you and Sarah together.'

Dominic deposited a kiss on her nose. 'There was no way I could have married Sarah feeling as I do about you,' he said solemnly.

'No, but there were so many similarities between our relationship and that of my mother and father. I was afraid of what might happen next.'

'That you might get pregnant? You're not, are you?' he asked, raising his brows, and she giggled.

'Not yet,' she conceded, happily, and he pulled a wry face.

'Well, that's OK, I guess,' he said after a moment. 'I would like to have you to myself for a little while first.'

Cleo touched his cheek. 'I don't deserve you.'

'No.' Dominic grinned. 'But I'll forgive you.'

There was silence in the room for a few delicious moments and then Cleo stirred again.

'You know,' she said softly, 'Lily told me that Celeste was really her half-sister. Did you know that?'

'Hell, no!' Dominic was amused. 'Well, what do you know? My maternal grandfather wasn't as uptight as he liked people to think.'

Cleo nodded. 'Your mother said that my father wasn't the first male to be infatuated with the Dubois women.'

'And he's not the last,' Dominic reminded her staunchly. He bent and nipped the corner of her mouth with his teeth. 'Don't forget, you're a Dubois, too.'

'I haven't forgotten.'

'But there is a difference,' said Dominic, frowning, and Cleo felt a twinge of apprehension.

'What kind of a difference?'

'Well, I'm going to have the distinction of marrying a Dubois woman, if she'll have me.'

He touched her lips with his thumb. 'Will you have me, Cleo? Will you complete the circle and become my wife?'

And, of course, Cleo said yes.

CRAVING THE FORBIDDEN

BY
INDIA GREY

A self-confessed romance junkie, **India Grey** was just thirteen years old when she first sent off for the Mills & Boon Writers' Guidelines. She can still recall the thrill of getting the large brown envelope with its distinctive logo through the letterbox, and subsequently whiled away many a dull school day staring out of the window and dreaming of the perfect hero. She kept those guidelines with her for the next ten years, tucking them carefully inside the cover of each new diary in January, and beginning every list of New Year's Resolutions with the words Start Novel. In the meantime she gained a degree in English Literature and Language from Manchester University, and in a stroke of genius on the part of the gods of Romance met her gorgeous future husband on the very last night of their three years there. Ever since, she has been spent blissfully buried in domesticity and heaps of pink washing generated by three small daughters, but she has never really stopped daydreaming about romance. She's just profoundly grateful to have finally got an excuse to do it legitimately!

For my blog regulars
With thanks for listening, sharing and
making me smile.

CHAPTER ONE

'LADIES and gentlemen, welcome aboard the 16.22 East Coast Mainline service from King's Cross to Edinburgh. This train will be calling at Peterborough, Stevenage...'

Heart hammering against her ribs from the mad, last-minute dash down the platform carrying a bag that was about to burst at the seams, Sophie Greenham leaned against the wall of the train and let out a long exhalation of relief.

She had made it.

Of course, the relief was maybe a little misplaced given that she'd come straight from the casting session for a vampire film and was still wearing a black satin corset dress that barely covered her bottom and high-heeled black boots that were rather more vamp than vampire. But the main thing was she had caught the train and wouldn't let Jasper down. She'd just have to keep her coat on to avoid getting arrested for indecent exposure.

Not that she'd want to take it off anyway, she thought grimly, wrapping it more tightly around her as the train gave a little lurch and began to move. For weeks now the snow had kept falling from a pewter-grey sky and the news headlines had been dominated by The Big Freeze. Paris had been just as bad, although there the snow *looked* cleaner, but when Sophie had left her little rented apartment two days ago there had been a thick layer of ice on the inside of the windows.

She seemed to have been cold for an awfully long time.

It was getting dark already. The plate-glass windows of the office blocks backing onto the railway line spilled light out onto the grimy snow. The train swayed beneath her, changing tracks and catching her off guard so that she tottered on the stupid high-heeled boots and almost fell into an alarmed-looking student on his way back from the buffet car. She really should go and find a loo to change into something more respectable, but now she'd finally stopped rushing she was overwhelmed with tiredness. Picking up her bag, she hoisted it awkwardly into the nearest carriage.

Her heart sank. It was instantly obvious that every seat was taken, and the aisle was cluttered with shopping bags and briefcases and heavy winter coats stuffed under seats. Muttering apologies as she staggered along, trying not to knock cardboard cartons of coffee out of the hands of commuters with her bag, she made her way into the next carriage.

It was just as bad as the last one. The feeling of triumph she'd had when she'd made it onto the train in time ebbed slowly away as she moved from one carriage to the next, apologising as she went, until finally she came to one that was far less crowded.

Sophie's aching shoulders dropped in relief. And tensed again as she took in the strip of plush carpet, the tiny lights on the tables, the superior upholstery with the little covers over the headrests saying 'First Class'.

Pants.

It was occupied almost entirely by businessmen who didn't bother to look up from their laptops and newspapers as she passed. Until her mobile rang. Her ringtone—'Je Ne Regrette Rien'—had seemed wittily ironic in Paris, but in the hushed carriage it lost some of its charm. Holding the handles of her bag together in one hand while she scrabbled in the pocket of her coat with the other and tried to stop it falling open to reveal the wardrobe horror beneath, she was aware of heads turning, eyes looking up at her over the tops of glasses and from behind broadsheets. In desperation she hitched her bag onto the nearest table and pulled the phone from her pocket just in time to see Jean-Claude's name on the screen.

Pants again.

A couple of months ago she would have had a very different reaction, she thought, hastily pressing the button to reject the call. But then a couple of months ago her image of Jean-Claude as a free-spirited Parisian artist had been intact. He'd seemed so aloof when she'd first seen him, delivering paintings to the set of the film she was working on. Aloof and glamorous. Not someone you could ever imagine being suffocating or possessive or...

Nope. She wasn't going to think about the disaster that had been her latest romantic adventure.

She sat down in the nearest seat, suddenly too tired to go any further. You couldn't keep moving for ever, she told herself with a stab of bleak humour. In the seat opposite there was yet another businessman, hidden behind a large newspaper that he'd thoughtfully folded so that the horoscopes were facing her.

Actually, he wasn't *entirely* hidden; she could see his hands, holding the newspaper—tanned, long-fingered, strong-looking. Not the hands of a businessman, she thought abstractly, tearing her gaze away and looking for Libra. 'Be prepared to work hard to make a good impression,' she read. 'The full moon on the 20th is a perfect opportunity to let others see you for who you really are.'

Hell. It was the twentieth today. And while she was prepared to put on an Oscar-worthy performance to impress Jasper's family, the last thing she wanted was for them to see her for who she really was.

At that moment Edith Piaf burst into song again. She

groaned—why couldn't Jean-Claude take a hint? Quickly she went to shut Edith up and turn her phone off but at that moment the train swayed again and her finger accidentally hit the 'answer' button instead. A second later Jean-Claude's Merlot-marinated voice was clearly audible, to her and about fifteen businessmen.

'Sophie? Sophie, where are you—?'

She thought quickly, cutting him off before he had a chance to get any further. 'Hello, you haf reached the voicemail service for Madame Sofia, astrologist and reader of cards,' she purred, shaking her hair back and narrowing her eyes at her own reflection in the darkening glass of the window. 'Eef you leaf your name, number and zodiac sign, I get back to you with information on what the fates haf in store for you—'

She stopped abruptly, losing her thread, a kick of electricity jolting through her as she realised she was staring straight into the reflected eyes of the man sitting opposite.

Or rather that, from behind the newspaper, *he* was staring straight into *her* eyes. His head was lowered, his face ghostly in the glass, but his dark eyes seemed to look straight into her.

For a second she was helpless to do anything but look back. Against the stark white of his shirt his skin was tanned, which seemed somehow at odds with his stern, ascetic face. It was the face of a medieval knight in a Pre-Raphaelite painting—beautiful, bloodless, remote.

In other words, absolutely not her type.

'Sophie—is zat you? I can 'ardly 'ear you. Are you on Eurostar? Tell me what time you get in and I meet you at Gare du Nord.'

Oops, she'd forgotten all about Jean-Claude. Gathering herself, she managed to drag her gaze away from the reflection in the window and her attention back to the problem quite literally in hand. She'd better just come clean, or he'd keep ringing for the whole weekend she was staying with Jasper's family and rather ruin her portrayal of the sweet, starry-eyed girlfriend.

'I'm not on the Eurostar, no,' she said carefully. 'I'm not coming back tonight.'

'*Alors*, when?' he demanded. 'The painting—I need you here. I need to see your skin—to feel it, to capture contrast with lily petals.'

'Nude with Lilies' was the vision Jean-Claude claimed had come to him the moment he'd first noticed her in a bar in the Marais, near where they'd been filming. Jasper had been over that weekend and thought it was hilarious. Sophie, hugely flattered to be singled out and by Jean-Claude's extravagant compliments about her 'skin like lily petals' and 'hair like flames', had thought being painted would be a highly erotic experience.

The reality had turned out to be both extremely cold and mind-numbingly boring. Although, if Jean-Claude's gaze had aroused a similar reaction to that provoked by the eyes of the man in the glass, it would have been a very different story...

'Oh, dear. Maybe you could just paint in a few more lilies to cover up the skin?' She bit back a breathless giggle and went on kindly, 'Look, I don't know when I'll be back, but what we had wasn't meant to be for ever, was it? Really, it was just sex—'

Rather fittingly, at that point the train whooshed into a tunnel and the signal was lost. Against the blackness beyond the window the reflected interior of the carriage was bright, and for the briefest moment Sophie caught the eye of the man opposite and knew he'd been looking at her again. The grey remains of the daylight made the reflection fade before she had time to read the expression on his face, but she was left in no doubt that it had been disapproving.

And in that second she was eight years old again, holding her mother's hand and aware that people were staring at them, judging them. The old humiliation flared inside her as she heard her mother's voice inside her head, strident with indignation. *Just ignore them, Summer. We have as much right to be here as anyone else...*

'Sophie?'

'Yes,' she said, suddenly subdued. 'Sorry, Jean-Claude. I can't talk about this now. I'm on the train and the signal isn't very good.'

'*D'accord.* I call you later.'

'No! You can't call me *at all* this weekend. I-I'm...working, and you know I can't take my phone on set. Look, I'll call you when I get back to London on Monday. We can talk properly then.'

That was a stupid thing to say, she thought wearily as she turned her phone off. There was nothing to talk *about*. What she and Jean-Claude had shared had been fun, that was all. Fun. A romantic adventure in wintry Paris. Now it had reached its natural conclusion and it was time to move on.

Again.

Shoving her phone back into her pocket, she turned towards the window. Outside it was snowing again and, passing through some anonymous town, Sophie could see the flakes swirling fatly in the streetlamps and obliterating the footprints on the pavements, and rows of neat houses, their curtains shut against the winter evening. She imagined the people behind them; families slumped together in front of the TV, arguing cosily over the remote control, couples cuddled up on the sofa sharing a Friday evening bottle of wine, united against the cold world outside.

A blanket of depression settled on her at these mental images of comfortable domesticity. It was a bit of a sore point at the moment. Returning from Paris she'd discovered that, in her absence, her flatmate's boyfriend had moved in and the flat had been turned into the headquarters of the Blissful Couples Society. The atmosphere of companionable sluttishness in which she and Jess had existed, cluttering up the place with make-up and laundry and trashy magazines, had vanished. The flat was immaculate, and there were new cushions on the sofa and candles on the kitchen table.

Jasper's SOS phone call, summoning her up to his family home in Northumberland to play the part of his girlfriend for the weekend, had come as a huge relief. But this was the way it was going to be, she thought sadly as the town was left behind and the train plunged onwards into darkness again. Everyone pairing up, until she was the only single person left, the only one who actively didn't want a relationship or commitment. Even Jasper was showing worrying signs of swapping late nights and dancing for cosy evenings in as things got serious with Sergio.

But why have serious when you could have *fun*?

Getting abruptly to her feet, she picked up her bag and hoisted it onto the luggage rack above her head. It wasn't easy, and she was aware as she pushed and shoved that not only was the hateful dress riding up, but her coat had also fallen open, no doubt giving the man in the seat opposite an eyeful of straining black corset and an indecent amount of thigh. Prickling all over with embarrassment, she glanced at his reflection in the window.

He wasn't looking at her at all. His head was tipped back against the seat, his face completely blank and remote as he focused on the newspaper. Somehow his indifference felt even more hurtful than his disapproving scrutiny earlier. Pulling her coat closed, she sat down again, but as she did so her knee grazed his thigh beneath the table.

She froze, and a shower of glowing sparks shimmered through her.

'Sorry,' she muttered, yanking her legs away from his and tucking them underneath her on the seat.

Slowly the newspaper was lowered, and she found herself looking at him directly for the first time. The impact of meeting his eyes in glassy reflection had been powerful enough, but looking directly into them was like touching a live wire. They weren't brown, as she'd thought, but the grey of cold Northern seas, heavy-lidded, fringed with thick, dark lashes, compelling enough to distract her for a moment from the rest of his face.

Until he smiled.

A faint ghost of a smile that utterly failed to melt the ice in his eyes, but did draw her attention down to his mouth...

'No problem. As this is First Class you'd think there'd be enough legroom, wouldn't you?'

His voice was low and husky, and so sexy that her spirits should have leapt at the prospect of spending the next four hours in close confinement with him. However, the slightly scornful emphasis he placed on the words 'first' and 'class' and the way he was looking at her as if she were a caterpillar on the chef's salad in some swanky restaurant cancelled out his physical attractiveness.

She had issues with people who looked at her like that.

'Absolutely,' she agreed, with that upper-class self-assurance that gave the people who genuinely possessed it automatic admittance to anywhere. 'Shocking, really.' And then with what she hoped was utter insouciance she turned up the big collar of her shabby military-style coat, settled herself more comfortably in her seat and closed her eyes.

Kit Fitzroy put down the newspaper.

Usually when he was on leave he avoided reading reports about the situation he'd left behind; somehow the heat and the sand and the desperation never quite came across in columns of sterile black and white. He'd bought the newspaper to catch up on normal things like rugby scores and racing news, but had ended up reading all of it in an attempt to obliterate the image of the girl sitting opposite him, which seemed to have branded itself onto his retinas.

It hadn't worked. Even the laughably inaccurate report of counter-terrorist operations in the Middle East hadn't stopped him being aware of her.

It was hardly surprising, he thought acidly. He'd spent the last four months marooned in the desert with a company made up entirely of men, and he was still human enough to respond to a girl wearing stiletto boots and the briefest bondage dress beneath a fake army coat. Especially one with a husky night-club singer's voice who actually seemed to be complaining to the lovesick fool on the other end of the phone that all she'd wanted was casual sex.

After the terrible sombreness of the ceremony he'd just attended her appearance was like a swift shot of something extremely potent.

He suppressed a rueful smile.

Potent, if not particularly sophisticated.

He let his gaze move back to her. She had fallen asleep as quickly and neatly as a cat, her legs tucked up beneath her, a slight smile on her raspberry-pink lips, as if she was dreaming of something amusing. She had a sweep of black eyeliner on her upper lids, flicking up at the outside edges, which must be what gave her eyes their catlike impression.

He frowned. No—it wasn't just that. It was their striking green too. He could picture their exact shade—the clear, cool green of new leaves—even now, when she was fast asleep.

If she really was asleep. When it came to deception Kit Fitzroy's radar was pretty accurate, and this girl had set it off from the moment she'd appeared. But there was something about her now that convinced him that she wasn't faking this.

It wasn't just how still she was, but that the energy that had crackled around her before had vanished. It was like a light going out. Like the sun going in, leaving shadows and a sudden chill.

Sleep—the reward of the innocent. Given the shamelessness with which she'd just lied to her boyfriend it didn't seem fair, especially when it eluded him so cruelly. But it had wrapped her in a cloak of complete serenity, so that just looking at her, just watching the lock of bright coppery hair that had fallen across her face stir with each soft, steady breath made him aware of the ache of exhaustion in his own shoulders.

'Tickets, please.'

The torpor that lay over the warm carriage was disturbed by the arrival of the guard. There was a ripple of activity as people roused themselves to open briefcases and fumble in suit pockets. On the opposite side of the table the girl's sooty lashes didn't even flutter.

She was older than he'd first thought, Kit saw now, older than the ridiculous teenage get-up would suggest—in her mid-twenties perhaps? Even so, there was something curiously childlike about her. If you ignored the creamy swell of her cleavage against the laced bodice of her dress, anyway.

And he was doing his best to ignore it.

The guard reached them, his bland expression changing to one of deep discomfort when he looked down and saw her. His tongue flicked nervously across his lips and he raised his hand, shifting from foot to foot as he reached uneasily down to wake her.

'Don't.'

The guard looked round, surprised. He wasn't the only one, Kit thought. Where had that come from? He smiled blandly.

'It's OK. She's with me.'

'Sorry, sir. I didn't realise. Do you have your tickets?'

'No.' Kit flipped open his wallet. 'I—*we*—had been planning to travel north by plane.'

'Ah, I see, sir. The weather has caused quite a disruption to flights, I understand. That's why the train is so busy this evening. Is it a single or a return you want?'

'Return.' Hopefully the airports would be open again by Sunday, but he wasn't taking any chances. The thought of being stuck indefinitely at Alnburgh with his family in residence was unbearable.

'Two returns—to Edinburgh?'

Kit nodded absently and as the guard busied himself with printing out the tickets he looked back at the sleeping girl again. He was damned certain she didn't have a first-class ticket and that, in spite of the almost-convincing posh-girl accent, she wouldn't be buying one if she was challenged. So why had he not just let the guard wake her up and move her on? It would have made the rest of the journey better for him. More legroom. More peace of mind.

Kit Fitzroy had an inherent belief in his duty to look out for people who didn't have the same privileges that he had. It was what had got him through officer training and what kept him going when he was dropping with exhaustion on patrol, or when he was walking along a deserted road to an unexploded bomb. It didn't usually compel him to buy first-class tickets for strangers on the train. And anyway, this girl looked as if she was more than capable of looking after herself.

But with her outrageous clothes and her fiery hair and her slight air of mischief she had brightened up his journey. She'd jolted him out of the pall of gloom that hung over him after the service he'd just attended, as well as providing a distraction from thinking about the grim weekend ahead.

That had to be worth the price of a first-class ticket from London to Edinburgh. Even without the glimpse of cleavage and the brush of her leg against his, which had reminded him that, while several of the men he'd served with weren't so lucky, he at least was still alive...

That was just a bonus.

CHAPTER TWO

SOPHIE came to with a start, and a horrible sense that something was wrong.

She sat up, blinking beneath the bright lights as she tried to get her bearings. The seat opposite was empty. The man with the silver eyes must have got off while she was sleeping, and she was just asking herself why on earth she should feel disappointed about that when she saw him.

He was standing up, his back towards her as he lifted an expensive-looking leather bag down from the luggage rack, giving her an excellent view of his extremely broad shoulders and narrow hips encased in beautifully tailored black trousers.

Mmm... *That* was why, she thought drowsily. Because physical perfection like that wasn't something you came across every day. And although it might come in a package with industrial-strength arrogance, it certainly was nice to look at.

'I'm sorry—could you tell me where we are, please?'

Damn—she'd forgotten about the posh accent, and after being asleep for so long she sounded more like a barmaid with a sixty-a-day habit than a wholesome society girl. Not that it really mattered now, since she'd never see him again.

He shrugged on the kind of expensive reefer jacket men

wore in moody black and white adverts in glossy magazines. 'Alnburgh.'

The word delivered a jolt of shock to Sophie's sleepy brain. With an abrupt curse she leapt to her feet, groping frantically for her things, but at that moment the train juddered to an abrupt halt. She lost her balance, falling straight into his arms.

At least that was how it would have happened in any one of the romantic films she'd ever worked on. In reality she didn't so much fall into his waiting, welcoming arms as against the unyielding, rock-hard wall of his chest. He caught hold of her in the second before she ricocheted off him, one arm circling her waist like a band of steel. Rushing to steady herself, Sophie automatically put the flat of her hand against his chest.

Sexual recognition leapt into life inside her, like an alarm going off in her pelvis. He might look lean, but there was no mistaking the hard, sculpted muscle beneath the Savile Row shirt.

Wide-eyed with shock, she looked up at him, opening her mouth in an attempt to form some sort of apology. But somehow there were blank spaces in her head where the words should be and the only coherent thought in her head was how astonishing his eyes were, close up; the silvery luminescence of the irises ringed with a darker grey...

'I have to get off—now,' she croaked.

It wasn't exactly a line from the romantic epics. He let her go abruptly, turning his head away.

'It's OK. We're not in the station yet.'

As he spoke the train began to move forwards with another jolt that threatened to unbalance her again. As if she weren't unbalanced enough already, she thought shakily, trying to pull down her bulging bag from where it was wedged in the luggage rack. Glancing anxiously out of the window, she saw the lights of cars waiting at a level crossing slide past the window, a little square signal box, cosily lit inside, with a sign saying 'Alnburgh' half covered in snow. She gave another futile tug and heard an impatient sound from behind her.

'Here, let me.'

In one lithe movement he leaned over her and grasped the handle of her bag.

'No, wait—the zip—' Sophie yelped, but it was too late. There was a ripping sound as the cheap zip, already under too much pressure from the sheer volume of stuff bundled up inside, gave way and Sophie watched in frozen horror as a tangle of dresses and tights and shoes tumbled out.

And underwear, of course.

It was terrible. Awful. Like the moment in a nightmare just before you wake up. But it was also pretty funny. Clamping a hand over her open mouth, Sophie couldn't stop a bubble of hysterical laughter escaping her.

'You might want to take that back to the shop,' the man remarked sardonically, reaching up to unhook an emerald-green satin balcony bra that had got stuck on the edge of the luggage rack. 'I believe Gucci luggage carries a lifetime guarantee?'

Sophie dropped to her knees to retrieve the rest of her things. Possibly it did, but cheap designer fakes certainly didn't, as he no doubt knew very well. Getting up again, she couldn't help but be aware of the length of his legs, and had to stop herself from reaching out and grabbing hold of them to steady herself as the train finally came to a shuddering halt in the station.

'Thanks for your help,' she said with as much haughtiness as she could muster when her arms were full of knickers and tights. 'Please, don't let me hold you up any more.'

'I wouldn't, except you're blocking the way to the door.'

Sophie felt her face turn fiery. Pressing herself as hard as she could against the table, she tried to make enough space for him to pass. But he didn't. Instead he took hold of the broken bag and lifted it easily, raising one sardonic eyebrow.

'After you—if you've got everything?'

Alnburgh station consisted of a single Victorian building that had once been rather beautiful but which now had its boarded up windows covered with posters advertising family days out at the seaside. It was snowing again as she stepped off the train, and the air felt as if it had swept straight in from Siberia. Oh, dear, she really should have got changed. Not only was her current ensemble hideously unsuitable for meeting Jasper's family, it was also likely to lead to hypothermia.

'There.'

Sophie had no choice but to turn and face him. Pulling her collar up around her neck, she aimed for a sort of Julie-Christie-in-Doctor-Zhivago look—determination mixed with dignity.

'You'll be OK from here?'

'Y-yes. Thank you.' Standing there with the snow settling on his shoulders and in his dark hair he looked more brooding and sexy than Omar Shariff had ever done in the film. 'And thank you for…'

Jeepers, what was the matter with her? Julie Christie would never have let her lines dry up like that.

'For what?'

'Oh, you know, carrying my bag, picking up my…things.'

'My pleasure.'

His eyes met hers and for a second their gazes held. In spite of the cold stinging her cheeks, Sophie felt a tide of heat rise up inside her.

And then the moment was over and he was turning away, his feet crunching on the gritted paving stones, sliding his hands into the pockets of his coat just as the guard blew the whistle for the train to move out of the station again.

That was what reminded her, like a bolt of lightning in her brain. Clamping her hand to her mouth, she felt horror tingle down her spine at the realisation that she hadn't bought a ticket. Letting out a yelp of horror, followed by the kind of word Julie Christie would never use, Sophie dashed forwards towards the guard, whose head was sticking out of the window of his van.

'No—wait. Please! I didn't—'

But it was too late. The train was gathering pace and her voice was lost beneath the rumble of the engine and the squealing of the metal wheels on the track. As she watched the lights of the train melt back into the winter darkness Sophie's heart was beating hard, anguish knotting inside her at what she'd inadvertently done.

Stolen something. That was what it amounted to, didn't it? Travelling on the train without buying a ticket was, in effect, committing a criminal act, as well as a dishonest one.

An act of theft.

And that was one thing she would never, *ever* do.

The clatter of the train died in the distance and Sophie was aware of the silence folding all around her. Slowly she turned to walk back to pick up her forlorn-looking bag.

'Is there a problem?'

Her stomach flipped, and then sank like a stone. Great. Captain Disapproval must have heard her shout and come back, thinking she was talking to him. The station light cast dark shadows beneath his cheekbones and made him look more remote than ever. Which was quite something.

'No, no, not at all,' she said stiffly. 'Although before you go perhaps you could tell me where I could find a taxi.'

Kit couldn't quite stop himself from letting out a bark of laughter. It wasn't kind, but the idea of a taxi waiting at Alnburgh station was amusingly preposterous.

'You're not in London now.' He glanced down the platform

to where the Bentley waited, Jensen sitting impassively behind the wheel. For some reason he felt responsible—touched
almost—by this girl in her outrageous clothing with the snow-
flakes catching in her bright hair. 'Look, you'd better come
with me.'

Her chin shot up half an inch. Her eyes flashed in the station light—the dark green of the stained glass in the Fitzroy
family chapel, with the light shining through it.

'No, thanks,' she said with brittle courtesy. 'I think I'd
rather walk.'

That really *was* funny. 'In those boots?'

'Yes,' she said haughtily, setting off quickly, if a little unsteadily, along the icy platform. She looked around, pulling
her long army overcoat more tightly across her body.

Catching up with her, Kit arched an eyebrow. 'Don't tell
me,' he drawled. 'You're going to join your regiment.'

'No,' she snapped. 'I'm going to stay with my boyfriend,
who lives at Alnburgh Castle. So if you could just point me
in the right direction...'

Kit stopped. The laughter of a moment ago evaporated in
the arctic air, like the plumes of their breaths. In the distance
a sheep bleated mournfully.

'And what is the name of your...*boyfriend*?'

Something in the tone of his voice made her stop too, the
metallic echo of her stiletto heels fading into silence. When
she turned to face him her eyes were wide and black-centred.

'Jasper.' Her voice was shaky but defiant. 'Jasper Fitzroy,
although I don't know what it has to do with you.'

Kit smiled again, but this time it had nothing to do with
amusement.

'Well, since Jasper Fitzroy is my brother, I'd say quite a
lot,' he said with sinister softness. 'You'd better get in the car.'

CHAPTER THREE

INSIDE the chauffeur-driven Bentley Sophie blew her cheeks out in a long, silent whistle.

What was it that horoscope said?

The car was very warm and very comfortable, but no amount of climate control and expensive upholstery could quite thaw the glacial atmosphere. Apart from a respectfully murmured 'Good evening, Miss,' the chauffeur kept his attention very firmly focused on the road. Sophie didn't blame him. You could cut the tension in the back of the car with a knife.

Sophie sat very upright, leaving as much seat as possible between her fishnetted thigh and his long, hard flannel-covered one. She didn't dare look at Jasper's brother, but was aware of him staring, tense-jawed, out of the window. The village of Alnburgh looked like a scene from a Christmas card as they drove up the main street, past a row of stone houses with low, gabled roofs covered in a crisp meringue-topping of snow, but he didn't look very pleased to be home.

Her mind raced as crazily as the white flakes swirling past the car window, the snatches of information Jasper had imparted about his brother over the years whirling through it. Kit Fitzroy was in the army, she knew that much, and he served abroad a lot, which would account for the unseasonal tan. Oh, and Jasper had once described him as having a 'com-

plete emotion-bypass'. She recalled the closed expression
Jasper's face wore on the rare occasions he mentioned him,
the bitter edge his habitual mocking sarcasm took on when
he said the words 'my brother'.

She was beginning to understand why. She had only known
him for a little over three hours—and most of that time she'd
been asleep—but it was enough to find it impossible to believe that this man could be related to Jasper. Sweet, warm,
funny Jasper, who was her best friend in the world and the
closest thing she had to family.

But the man beside her was his *real* flesh and blood, so
surely that meant he couldn't be all bad? It also meant that
she should make some kind of effort to get on with him, for
Jasper's sake. And her own, since she had to get through an
entire weekend in his company.

'So, you must be Kit, then?' she offered. 'I'm Sophie.
Sophie Greenham.' She laughed—a habit she had when she
was nervous. 'Bizarre, isn't it? Whoever would have guessed
we were going to the same place?'

Kit Fitzroy didn't bother to look at her. 'Not you, obviously. Have you known my brother long?'

OK. So she was wrong. He was every bit as bad as she'd
first thought. Thinking of the horoscope, she bit back the urge
to snap, *Yes, as a matter of fact. I've known your brother for
the last seven years, as you would have been very well aware
if you took the slightest interest in him*, and kept her voice
saccharine sweet as she recited the story she and Jasper had
hastily come up with last night on the phone when he'd asked
her to do this.

'Just since last summer. We met on a film.'

The last bit at least was true. Jasper was an assistant direc-
tor and they had met on a dismal film about the Black Death
that mercifully had never seen the light of day. Sophie had
spent hours in make-up having sores applied to her face and

had had one line to say, but had caught Jasper's eye just as she'd been about to deliver it and noticed that he was shaking with laughter. It had set her off too, and made the next four hours and twenty-two takes extremely challenging, but it had also sealed their friendship, and set its tone. It had been the two of them, united and giggling against the world, ever since.

He turned his head slightly. 'You're an actress?'

'Yes.'

Damn, why did that come out sounding so defensive? Possibly because he said the word 'actress' in the same faintly disdainful tone as other people might say 'lap dancer' or 'shoplifter'. What would he make of the fact that even 'actress' was stretching it for the bit parts she did in films and TV series? Clamping her teeth together, she looked away—and gasped.

Up ahead, lit up in the darkness, cloaked in swirling white like a fairy castle in a child's snow globe, was Alnburgh Castle.

She'd seen pictures, obviously. But nothing had prepared her for the scale of the place, or the impact it made on the surrounding landscape. It stood on top of the cliffs, its grey stone walls seeming to rise directly out of them. This was a side of Jasper's life she knew next to nothing about, and Sophie felt her mouth fall open as she stared in amazement.

'Bloody hell,' she breathed.

It was the first genuine reaction he'd seen her display, Kit thought sardonically, watching her. And it spoke volumes.

Sympathy wasn't an emotion he was used to experiencing in relation to Jasper, but at that moment he certainly felt something like it now. His brother must be pretty keen on this girl to invite her up here for Ralph Fitzroy's seventieth birthday party, but from what Kit had seen on the train it was obvious the feeling wasn't remotely mutual.

No prizes for guessing what the attraction was for Sophie Greenham.

'Impressive, isn't it?' he remarked acidly.

In the dimly lit interior of the car her eyes gleamed darkly like moonlit pools as she turned to face him. Her voice was breathless, so that she sounded almost intimidated.

'It's incredible. I had no idea...'

'What, that your boyfriend just happened to be the son of the Earl of Hawksworth?' Kit murmured sardonically. 'Of course. You were probably too busy discussing your mutual love of art-house cinema to get round to such mundane subjects as family background.'

'Don't be ridiculous,' she snapped. 'Of course I knew about Jasper's background—*and* his family.'

She said that last bit with a kind of defiant venom that was clearly meant to let him know that Jasper hadn't given him a good press. He wondered if she thought for a moment that he'd care. It was hardly a well-kept secret that there was no love lost between him and his brother—the spoiled, pampered golden boy. Ralph's second and favourite son.

The noise of the Bentley's engine echoed off the walls of the clock tower as they passed through the arch beneath it. The headlights illuminated the stone walls, dripping with damp, the iron-studded door that led down to the former dungeon that now housed Ralph's wine cellar. Kit felt the invisible iron-hard bands of tension around his chest and his forehead tighten a couple of notches.

It was funny, he spent much of his time in the most dangerous conflict zones on the globe, but in none of them did he ever feel a fraction as isolated or exposed as he did here. When he was working he had his team behind him. Men he could trust.

Trust wasn't something he'd ever associated with home

life at Alnburgh, where people told lies and kept secrets and made promises they didn't keep.

He glanced across at the woman sitting beside him, and felt his lip curl. Jasper's new girlfriend was going to fit in very well.

Sophie didn't wait until the chauffeur came round to open the door for her. The moment the car came to a standstill she reached for the handle and threw the door open, desperate to be out of the confined space with Kit Fitzroy.

A gust of salt-scented, ice-edged wind cleared her head but nearly knocked her sideways, whipping her hair across her face. Impatiently she brushed it away again. Alnburgh Castle loomed ahead of her. And above her and around her too, she thought weakly, turning to look at the fortress-thick walls that stretched into the darkness all around her, rising into huge, imposing buildings and jagged towers.

There was nothing remotely welcoming or inviting about it. Everything about the place was designed to scare people off and keep them out.

Sophie could see that Jasper's brother would be right at home here.

'Thanks, Jensen. I can manage the bags from here.'

'If you're sure, sir...'

Sophie turned in time to see Kit take her bag from the open boot of the Bentley and turn to walk in the direction of the castle's vast, imposing doorway. One strap of the green satin bra he had picked up on the train was hanging out of the top of it.

Hastily she hurried after him, her high heels ringing off the frozen flagstones and echoing around the walls of the castle courtyard.

'Please,' Sophie persisted, not wanting him to put himself

out on her account any more than he had—so unwillingly—done already. 'I'd rather take it myself.'

He stopped halfway up the steps. For a split second he paused, as if he was gathering his patience, then turned back to her. His jaw was set but his face was carefully blank.

'If you insist.'

He held it out to her. He was standing two steps higher than she was, and Sophie had to tilt her head back to look up at him. Thrown for a second by the expression in his hooded eyes, she reached out to take the bag from him but, instead of the strap, found herself grasping his hand. She snatched hers away quickly, at exactly the same time he did, and the bag fell, tumbling down the steps, scattering all her clothes into the snow.

'Oh, knickers,' she muttered, dropping to her knees as yet another giggle of horrified, slightly hysterical amusement rose up inside her. Her heart was thumping madly from the accidental contact with him. His hand had felt warm, she thought irrationally. She'd expected it to be as cold as his personality.

'Hardly,' he remarked acidly, stooping to pick up a pink thong and tossing it back into the bag. 'But clearly what passes for them in your wardrobe. You seem to have a lot of underwear and not many clothes.'

The way he said it suggested he didn't think this was a good thing.

'Yes, well,' she said loftily, 'what's the point of spending money on clothes that I'm going to get bored of after I've worn them once? Underwear is a good investment. Because it's practical,' she added defensively, seeing the faint look of scorn on his face. 'God,' she muttered crossly, grabbing a handful of clothes back from him. 'This journey's turning into one of those awful drawing-room farces.'

Straightening up, he raised an eyebrow. 'The entire week-end is a bit of a farce, wouldn't you say?'

He went up the remainder of the steps to the door. Shoving the escaped clothes back into her bag with unnecessary force, Sophie followed him and was about to apologise for having the wrong underwear and the wrong clothes and the wrong accent and occupation and attitude when she found herself inside the castle and her defiance crumbled into dust.

The stone walls rose to a vaulted ceiling what seemed like miles above her head, and every inch was covered with muskets, swords, pikes and other items of barbaric medieval weaponry that Sophie recognised from men-in-tights-with-swords films she'd worked on, but couldn't begin to name. They were arranged into intricate patterns around helmets and pieces of armour, and the light from a huge wrought-iron lantern that hung on a chain in the centre of the room glinted dully on their silvery surfaces.

'What a cosy and welcoming entrance,' she said faintly, walking over to a silver breastplate hanging in front of a pair of crossed swords. 'I bet you're not troubled by persistent double-glazing salesmen.'

He didn't smile. His eyes, she noticed, held the same dull metallic gleam as the armour. 'They're seventeenth century. Intended for invading enemies rather than double-glazing salesmen.'

'Gosh.' Sophie looked away, trailing a finger down the hammered silver of the breastplate, noticing the shining path it left through the dust. 'You Fitzroys must have a lot of enemies.'

She was aware of his eyes upon her. Who would have thought that such a cool stare could make her skin feel as if it were burning? Somewhere a clock was ticking loudly, marking out the seconds before he replied, 'Let's just say we protect our interests.'

His voice was dangerously soft. Sophie's heart gave a kick, as if the armour had given her an electric shock. Withdrawing her hand sharply, she jerked her head up to look at him. A faint, sardonic smile touched the corner of his mouth. 'And it's not just invading armies that threaten those.'

His meaning was clear, and so was the thinly veiled warning behind the words. Sophie opened her mouth to protest, but no words came—none that would be any use in defending herself against the accusation he was making anyway, and certainly none that would be acceptable to use to a man with whose family she was going to be a guest for the weekend.

'I-I'd better find Jasper,' she stammered. 'He'll be wondering where I am.'

He turned on his heel and she followed him through another huge hallway panelled in oak, her footsteps making a deafening racket on the stone-flagged floor. There were vast fireplaces at each end of the room, but both were empty, and Sophie noticed her breath made faint plumes in the icy air. This time, instead of weapons, the walls were hung with the glassy-eyed heads of various large and hapless animals. They seemed to stare balefully at Sophie as she passed, as if in warning.

This is what happens if you cross the Fitzroys.

Sophie straightened her shoulders and quickened her pace. She mustn't let Kit Fitzroy get to her. He had got entirely the wrong end of the stick. She was Jasper's friend and she'd come as a favour to him precisely *because* his family were too bigoted to accept him as he really was.

She would have loved to confront Kit Superior Fitzroy with that, but of course it was impossible. For Jasper's sake, and also because there was something about Kit that made her lose the ability to think logically and speak articulately, damn him.

A set of double doors opened at the far end of the hallway and Jasper appeared.

'*Soph!* You're *here*!'

At least she thought it was Jasper. Gone were the layers of eccentric vintage clothing, the tattered silk-faced dinner jackets he habitually wore over T-shirts and torn drainpipe jeans. The man who came towards her, his arms outstretched, was wearing well-ironed chinos and a V-necked jumper over a button-down shirt and—Sophie's incredulous gaze moved downwards—what looked suspiciously like brogues.

Reaching her, this new Jasper took her face between his hands and kissed her far more tenderly than normal. Caught off guard by the bewildering change in him, Sophie was just about to push him away and ask what he was playing at when she remembered what she was there for. Dropping her poor, battered bag again, she wrapped her arms around his neck.

Over Jasper's shoulder, through the curtain of her hair, she was aware of Kit Fitzroy standing like some dark sentinel, watching her. The knowledge stole down inside her, making her feel hot, tingling, restless, and before she knew it she was arching her body into Jasper's, sliding her fingers into his hair.

Sophie had done enough screen and stage kisses to have mastered the art of making something completely chaste look a whole lot more X-rated than it really was. When Jasper pulled back a little a few seconds later she caught the gleam of laughter in his eyes as he leaned his forehead briefly against hers, then, stepping away, he spoke in a tone of rather forced warmth.

'You've met my big brother, Kit. I hope he's been looking after you.'

That was rather an unfortunate way of putting it, Sophie thought, an image of Kit Fitzroy, his strong hands full of her silliest knickers and bras flashing up inside her head. Oh, hell, why did she always smirk when she was embarrassed? Biting her lip, she stared down at the stone floor.

'Oh, absolutely,' she said, nodding furiously. 'And I'm afraid I needed quite a lot of looking after. If it wasn't for Kit I'd be halfway to Edinburgh now. Or at least, my underwear would.'

It might be only a few degrees warmer than the arctic, but beneath her coat Sophie could feel the heat creeping up her cleavage and into her cheeks. The nervous smile she'd been struggling to suppress broke through as she said the word 'underwear', but one glance at Kit's glacial expression killed it instantly.

'It was a lucky coincidence that we were sitting in the same carriage. It gave us a chance to…get to know each other a little before we got here.'

Ouch.

Only Sophie could have understood the meaning behind the polite words or picked up the faint note of menace beneath the blandness of his tone.

He's really got it in for me, she realised with a shiver. Suddenly she felt very tired, very alone, and even Jasper's hand around hers couldn't dispel the chilly unease that had settled in the pit of her stomach.

'Great.' Oblivious to the tension that crackled like static in the air, Jasper pulled her impatiently forwards. 'Come and meet Ma and Pa. I haven't stopped talking about you since I got here yesterday, so they're dying to see what all the fuss is about.'

And suddenly panic swelled inside her—churning, black and horribly familiar. The fear of being looked at. Scrutinised. Judged. That people would see through the layers of her disguise, the veils of evasion, to the real girl beneath. As Jasper led her towards the doors at the far end of the hall she was shaking, assailed by the same doubts and insecurities that had paralysed her the only time she'd done live theatre, in the seconds before she went onstage. What if she couldn't do it? What if the lines wouldn't come and she was left just being herself? Acting had been a way of life long before it became a way of making a living, and playing a part was second nature to her. But now...*here*...

'Jasper,' she croaked, pulling back. 'Please—wait.'

'Sophie? What's the matter?'

His kind face was a picture of concern. The animal heads glared down at her, as well as a puffy-eyed Fitzroy ancestor with a froth of white lace around his neck.

And that was the problem. Jasper was her closest friend and she would do anything for him, but when she'd offered to help him out she hadn't reckoned on all this. Alnburgh Castle, with its history and its million symbols of wealth and status and *belonging*, was exactly the kind of place that unnerved her most.

'I can't go in there. Not dressed like this, I mean. I—I came straight from the casting for the vampire thing and I meant to get changed on the train, but I...'

She opened her coat and Jasper gave a low whistle.

'Don't worry,' he soothed. 'Here, let me take your coat and you can put this on, otherwise you'll freeze.' Quickly he peeled off the black cashmere jumper and handed it to her, then tossed her coat over the horns of a nearby stuffed stag. 'They're going to love you whatever you're wearing. Particularly Pa—you're the perfect birthday present. Come on, they're waiting in the drawing room. At least it's warm in there.'

With Kit's eyes boring into her back Sophie had no choice but to let Jasper lead her towards the huge double doors at the far end of the hall.

Vampire thing, Kit thought scornfully. Since when had the legend of the undead mentioned dressing like an escort in some private men's club? He wondered if it was going to be the kind of film the boys in his unit sometimes brought back from leave to enjoy with a lot of beer in rest periods in camp.

The thought was oddly unsettling.

Tiredness pulled at him like lead weights. He couldn't face seeing his father and stepmother just yet. Going through the hallway in the direction of the stairs, he passed the place where the portrait of his mother used to hang, before Ralph had replaced it, appropriately, with a seven-foot-high oil of Tatiana in plunging blue satin and the Cartier diamonds he had given her on their wedding day.

Jasper was right, Kit mused. If there was anyone who would appreciate Sophie Greenham's get-up it was Ralph Fitzroy. Like vampires, his father's enthusiasm for obvious women was legendary.

Jasper's, however, was not. And that was what worried him. Even if he hadn't overheard her conversation on the phone, even if he hadn't felt himself the white-hot sexuality she exuded, you only had to look at the two of them together to know that, vampire or not, the girl was going to break the poor bastard's heart and eat it for breakfast.

The room Jasper led her into was as big as the last, but stuffed with furniture and blazing with light from silk-shaded lamps on every table, a chandelier the size of a spaceship hovering above a pair of gargantuan sofas and a fire roaring in the fireplace.

It was Ralph Fitzroy who stepped forwards first. Sophie was surprised by how old he was, which she realised was ridiculous considering the reason she had come up this weekend was to attend his seventieth birthday party. His grey hair was brushed back from a florid, fleshy face and as he took Sophie's hand his eyes almost disappeared in a fan of laughter lines as they travelled down her body. And up again, but only as far as her chest.

'Sophie. Marvellous to meet you,' he said, in the kind of upper-class accent that Sophie had thought had become extinct after the war.

'And you, sir.'

Oh, for God's sake—*sir*? Where had that come from? She'd be bobbing curtsies next. She was supposed to be playing the part of Jasper's girlfriend, not the parlourmaid in some nineteen-thirties below-stairs drama. Not that Ralph seemed to mind. He was still clasping her hand, looking at her with a kind of speculative interest, as if she were a piece of art he was thinking of buying.

Suddenly she remembered Jean-Claude's 'Nude with Lilies' and felt pins and needles of embarrassment prickle her whole body. Luckily distraction came in the form of a woman unfolding herself from one of the overstuffed sofas and coming forwards. She was dressed immaculately in a clinging off-white angora dress that was cleverly designed to showcase her blonde hair and peachy skin, as well as her enviable figure and the triple string of pearls around her neck. Taking hold of Sophie's shoulders, she leaned forwards in a waft of expensive perfume and, in a silent and elaborate pantomime, kissed the air beside first one cheek and then the other.

'Sophie, how good of you to come all this way to join us. Did you have a dreadful journey?'

Her voice still bore the unmistakable traces of a Russian accent, but her English was so precise that Sophie felt more than ever that they were onstage and reciting lines from a script. Tatiana Fitzroy was playing the part of the gracious hostess, thrilled to be meeting her adored son's girlfriend for the first time. The problem was she wasn't that great at acting.

'No, not at all.'

'But you came by train?' Tatiana shuddered slightly. 'Trains are always so overcrowded these days. They make one feel slightly grubby, don't you think?'

No, Sophie wanted to say. Trains didn't make her feel remotely grubby. However, the blatant disapproval in Kit Fitzroy's cool glare—now that had definitely left her feeling in need of a scrub down in a hot shower.

'Come on, darling,' Ralph joked. 'When was the last time you went on a train?'

'First Class isn't *too* bad,' Sophie said, attempting to sound as if she would never consider venturing into standard.

'Not really enough legroom,' said a grave voice behind her. Sophie whipped her head round. Kit was standing in the doorway, holding a bundle of envelopes, which he was scanning through as he spoke.

The fire crackled merrily away, but Sophie was aware that the temperature seemed to have fallen a couple of degrees. For a split second no one moved, but then Tatiana was moving forwards, as if the offstage prompt had just reminded her of her cue.

'Kit. Welcome back to Alnburgh.'

So, she wasn't the only one who found him impossible, Sophie thought, noticing the distinct coolness in Tatiana's tone. As she reached up to kiss his cheek Kit didn't incline his head even a fraction to make it easier for her to reach, and his inscrutable expression didn't alter at all.

'Tatiana. You're looking well,' Kit drawled, barely glancing at her as he continued to look through the sheaf of letters in his hand. He seemed to have been built on a different scale from Jasper and Ralph, Sophie thought, taking in his height and the breadth of his chest. The sleeves of his white shirt were rolled back to reveal tanned forearms, corded with muscle.

She looked resolutely away.

Ralph went over to a tray crowded with cut-glass decanters on a nearby table and sloshed some more whisky into a glass that wasn't quite empty. Sophie heard the rattle of glass against glass, but when he turned round to face his eldest son his bland smile was perfectly in place.

'Kit.'

'Father.'

Kit's voice was perfectly neutral, but Ralph seemed to flinch slightly. He covered it by taking a large slug of whisky. 'Good of you to come, what with flights being cancelled and so on. The invitation was…' he hesitated '…a courtesy. I know how busy you are. Hope you didn't feel obliged to accept.'

'Not at all.' Kit's eyes glittered, as cold as moonlight on frost. 'I've been away too long. And there are things we need to discuss.'

Ralph laughed, but Sophie could see the colour rising in his florid cheeks. It was fascinating—like being at a particularly tense tennis match.

'For God's sake, Kit, you're not still persisting with that—'

As he spoke the double doors opened and a thin, elderly man appeared between them and nodded, almost imperceptibly, at Tatiana. Swiftly she crossed the Turkish silk rug in a waft of Chanel No 5 and slipped a hand through her husband's arm, cutting him off mid-sentence.

'Thank you, Thomas. Dinner is ready. Now that everyone's here, shall we go through?'

CHAPTER FOUR

DINNER was about as enjoyable and relaxing as being stripped naked and whipped with birch twigs.

When she was little, Sophie had dreamed wistfully about being part of the kind of family who gathered around a big table to eat together every evening. If she'd known this was what it was like she would have stuck to the fantasies about having a pony or being picked to star in a new film version of *The Little House on the Prairie*.

The dining room was huge and gloomy, its high, green damask-covered walls hung with yet more Fitzroy ancestors. They were an unattractive bunch, Sophie thought with a shiver. The handsomeness so generously bestowed on Jasper and Kit must be a relatively recent addition to the gene pool. Only one—a woman in blush-pink silk with roses woven into her extravagantly piled up hair and a secretive smile on her lips—held any indication of the good looks that were the Fitzroy hallmark now.

Thomas, the butler who had announced dinner, dished up watery consommé, followed by tiny rectangles of grey fish on something that looked like spinach and smelled like boiled socks. No wonder Tatiana was so thin.

'This looks delicious,' Sophie lied brightly.

'Thank you,' Tatiana cooed, in a way that suggested she'd cooked it herself. 'It has taken years to get Mrs Daniels to cook things other than steak and kidney pudding and roast beef, but finally she seems to understand the meaning of low-fat.'

'Unfortunately,' Kit murmured.

Ignoring him, Ralph reached for the dusty bottle of Chateau Marbuzet and splashed a liberal amount into his glass before turning to fill up Sophie's.

'So, Jasper said you've been in Paris? Acting in some film or other?'

Sophie, who had just taken a mouthful of fish, could only nod.

'Fascinating,' said Tatiana doubtfully. 'What was it about?'

Sophie covered her mouth with her hand to hide the grimace as she swallowed the fish. 'It's about British Special Agents and the French Resistance in the Second World War,' she said, wondering if she could hide the rest of the fish under the spinach as she used to do at boarding school. 'It's set in Montmartre, against a community of painters and poets.'

'And what part did you play?'

Sophie groaned inwardly. It would have to be Kit who asked that. Ever since she sat down she'd been aware of his eyes on her. More than aware of it—it felt as if there were a laser trained on her skin.

She cleared her throat. 'Just a tiny role, really,' she said with an air of finality.

'As?'

He didn't give up, did he? Why didn't he just go the whole hog and whip out a megawatt torch to shine in her face while he interrogated her? Not that those silvery eyes weren't hard enough to look into already.

'A prostitute called Claudine who inadvertently betrays her Resistance lover to the SS.'

Kit's smile was as faint as it was fleeting. He had a way of making her feel like a third year who'd been caught showing her knickers behind the bike sheds and hauled into the headmaster's office. She took a swig of wine.

'You must meet such fascinating people,' Tatiana said.

'Oh, yes. Well, I mean, sometimes. Actors can be a pretty self-obsessed bunch. They're not always a laugh a minute to be around.'

'Not as bad as artists,' Jasper chipped in absently as he concentrated on extracting a bone from his fish. 'They hired a few painters to produce the pictures that featured in the film, and they turned out to be such prima donnas they made the actors look very down-to-earth, didn't they, Soph?'

Somewhere in the back of Sophie's mind an alarm bell had started drilling. She looked up, desperately trying to telegraph warning signals across the table to Jasper, but he was still absorbed in exhuming the skeleton of the poor fish. Sophie's lips parted in wordless panic as she desperately tried to think of something to say to steer the subject onto safer ground...

Too late.

'One of them became completely obsessed with painting Sophie,' Jasper continued. 'He came over to her in the bar one evening when I was there and spent about two hours gazing at her with his eyes narrowed as he muttered about lilies.'

Sophie felt as if she'd been struck by lightning, a terrible rictus smile still fixed to her face. She didn't dare look at Kit. She didn't need to—she could feel the disapproval and hostility radiating from him like a force field. Through her despair she was aware of the woman with the roses in her hair staring down at her from the portrait. Now the smile didn't look secretive so much as if she was trying not to laugh.

'If I thought the result would have been as lovely as that I would have accepted like a shot,' she said in a strangled voice, gesturing up at the portrait. 'Who is she?'

Ralph followed her gaze. 'Ah—that's Lady Caroline, wife of the fourth Earl and one of the more flamboyant Fitzroys.

She was a girl of somewhat uncertain provenance who had been a music hall singer—definitely not countess material. Christopher Fitzroy was twenty years younger than her, but from the moment he met her he was quite besotted and, much to the horror of polite society, married her.'

'That was pretty brave of him,' Sophie said, relief at having successfully moved the conversation on clearly audible in her voice.

The sound Kit made was unmistakably derisive. 'Brave, or stupid?'

Their eyes met. Suddenly the room seemed very quiet. The arctic air was charged with electricity, so that the candle flames flickered for a second.

'Brave,' she retorted, raising her chin a little. 'It can't have been easy, going against his family and society, but if he loved her it would have been worth the sacrifice.'

'Not if *she* wasn't worth the sacrifice.'

The candle flames danced in a halo of red mist before Sophie's eyes, and before she could stop herself she heard herself give a taut, brittle laugh and say, 'Why? Because she was too *common*?'

'Not at all.' Kit looked at her steadily, his haughty face impassive. 'She wasn't worth it because she didn't love him back.'

'How do you know she didn't?'

Oh, jeez, what was she doing? She was supposed to be here to impress Jasper's family, not pick fights with them. No matter how insufferable they were.

'Well…' Kit said thoughtfully. 'The fact that she slept with countless other men during their marriage is a bit of a clue, wouldn't you say? Her lovers included several footmen and stable lads and even the French artist who painted that portrait.'

He was still looking at her. His voice held that now-familiar note of scorn, but was so soft that for a moment Sophie was hypnotised. The candlelight cast shadows under his angular cheekbones and brought warmth to his skin, but nothing could melt the ice chips in his eyes.

Sophie jumped slightly as Ralph cut in.

'French? Thought the chap was Italian?'

Kit looked away. 'Ah, yes,' he said blandly. 'I must be getting my facts mixed up.'

Bastard, thought Sophie. He knew that all along, and he was just trying to wind her up. Raising her chin and summoning a smile to show she wouldn't be wound, she said, 'So—what happened to her?'

'She came to a sticky end, I'm afraid. Not nice,' Ralph answered, topping up his glass again and emptying the remains of the bottle into Sophie's. Despite the cold his cheeks were flushed a deep, mottled purple.

'How?' Her mind flashed back to the swords and muskets in the entrance hall, the animal heads on the wall. You messed with a Fitzroy—or his brother—and a sticky end was pretty inevitable.

'She got pregnant,' Kit said matter-of-factly, picking up the knife on his side-plate and examining the tarnished silver blade for a second before polishing it with his damask napkin. 'The Earl, poor bastard, was delighted. At last, a long-awaited heir for Alnburgh.'

Sophie took another mouthful of velvety wine, watching his mouth as he spoke. And then found that she couldn't stop watching it. And wondering what it would look like if he smiled—really smiled. Or laughed. What it would feel like if he kissed her—

No. *Stop.* She shouldn't have let Ralph give her the rest of that wine. Hastily she put her glass down and tucked her hands under her thighs.

'But of course, she knew that it was extremely unlikely

the kid was his,' Kit was saying in his low, slightly scornful voice. 'And though he was too besotted to see what was going on, the rest of his family certainly weren't. She must have realised that she'd reached a dead end, and also that the child was likely to be born with the rampant syphilis that was already devouring her.'

Sophie swallowed. 'What did she do?'

Kit laid the knife down and looked straight at her. 'In the last few weeks of her pregnancy, she threw herself off the battlements in the East Tower.'

She wouldn't let him see that he'd shocked her. Wouldn't let the sickening feeling she had in the pit of her stomach show on her face. Luckily at that moment Jasper spoke, his cheerful voice breaking the tension that seemed to shiver in the icy air.

'Poor old Caroline, eh? What a price to pay for all that fun.' He leaned forwards, dropping his voice theatrically. 'It's said that on cold winter nights her ghost walks the walls, half mad with guilt. Or maybe it's the syphilis—that's supposed to make you go mad, isn't it?'

'Really, Jasper. I think we've heard enough about Fitzroys.' Tatiana laid down her napkin with a little pout as Thomas reappeared to collect up the plates. 'So, Sophie—tell us about *your* family. Where do your people come from?'

People? Her *people*? She made it sound as if everyone had estates and villages and hordes of peasants at their command. From behind Tatiana's head Caroline the feckless countess looked at Sophie with amused pity. *Get yourself out of this one*, she seemed to say.

'Oh. Um, down in the south of England,' Sophie muttered vaguely, glancing at Jasper for help. 'We travelled around a lot, actually.'

'And your parents—what do they do?'

'My mother is an astronomer.'

It was hardly a lie, more a slip of the tongue. Astronomy/astrology...people got them mixed up all the time anyway.

'And your—'

Jasper came swiftly to the rescue.

'Talking of stars, how did your big charity auction go last week, Ma? I keep meaning to ask you who won the premiere tickets I donated.'

It wasn't the most subtle of conversational diversions, but it did the trick so Sophie was too relieved to care. As the discussion moved on and Thomas reappeared to clear the table she slumped back in her chair and breathed out slowly, waiting for her heartbeat to steady and her fight-or-flight response to subside. With any luck that was the subject of her family dealt with and now she could relax for the rest of the weekend.

If it were possible to relax with Kit Fitzroy around.

Before she was aware it was happening or could stop it her gaze had slid back to where he sat, leaning back in his chair, his broad shoulders and long body making the antique rosewood look as fussy and flimsy as doll's-house furniture. His face was shuttered, his hooded eyes downcast, so that for the first time since the train she was able to look at him properly.

A shiver of sexual awareness shimmered down her spine and spread heat into her pelvis.

Sophie had an unfortunate attraction to men who were bad news. Men who didn't roll over and beg to be patted. But even she had to draw a line somewhere, and 'emotion-bypass' was probably a good place. And after the carnage of her so-called casual fling with Jean-Claude, this was probably a good time.

'...really fabulous turnout. People were so generous,' Tatiana was saying in her guttural purr, the diamonds in her rings glittering in the candlelight as she folded her hands together and rested her chin on them. 'And so good to catch up with all the people I don't see, stuck out here. As a matter of fact, Kit—your name came up over dinner. A girlfriend of mine said you have broken the heart of a friend of her daughter's.'

Kit looked up.

'Without the name of the friend, her daughter or her daughter's friend I can't really confirm or deny that.'

'Oh, come on,' Tatiana said with a brittle, tinkling laugh. 'How many hearts have you broken recently? I'm talking about Alexia. According to Sally Rothwell-Hyde, the poor girl is terribly upset.'

'I'm sure Sally Rothwell-Hyde is exaggerating,' Kit said in a bored voice. 'Alexia was well aware from the start it was nothing serious. It seems that Jasper will be providing Alnburgh heirs a lot sooner than I will.'

He looked across at Sophie, wondering what smart response she would think up to that, but she said nothing. She was sitting very straight, very still. Against the vivid red of her hair, her face was the same colour as the wax that had dripped onto the table in front of her.

'Something wrong?' he challenged quietly.

She looked at him, and for a second the expression in her eyes was one of blank horror. But then she blinked, and seemed to rouse herself.

'I'm sorry. What was that?' With an unsteady hand she stroked her hair back from her face. It was still as pale as milk, apart from a blossoming of red on each cheekbone.

'Soph?' Jasper got to his feet. 'Are you OK?'

'Yes. Yes, of course. I'm absolutely fine.' She made an attempt at a laugh, but Kit could hear the raw edge in it. 'Just tired, that's all. It's been a long day.'

'Then you must get to bed,' Tatiana spoke with an air of finality, as if she was dismissing her. 'Jasper, show Sophie to her room. I'm sure she'll feel much better after a good night's sleep.'

Kit watched Jasper put his arm round her and lead her to the door, remembering the two hours of catatonic sleep she'd had on the train. Picking up his wine glass, he drained it thoughtfully.

It certainly wasn't tiredness that had drained her face of colour like that, which meant it must have been the idea of producing heirs.

It looked as if she was beginning to get an idea of what she'd got herself into. And she was even flakier than he'd first thought.

CHAPTER FIVE

ROTHWELL-HYDE.

Wordlessly Sophie let Jasper lead her up the widest staircase she'd ever seen. It was probably a really common surname, she thought numbly. The phone book must contain millions of Rothwell-Hydes. Or several anyway, in smart places all over the country. Because surely no one who lived up here would send their daughter to school down in Kent?

It was a second before she realised Jasper had stopped at the foot of another small flight of stairs leading to a gloomy wood-panelled corridor with a single door at the end.

'Your room's at the end there, but let's go to mine. The fire's lit, and I've got a bottle of Smirnoff that Sergio gave me somewhere.' He took hold of her shoulders, bending his knees slightly to peer into her face. 'You look like you could do with something to revive you, angel. Are you OK?'

With some effort she gathered herself and made a stab at sounding casual and reassuring. 'I'm fine now, really. I'm so sorry, Jasper—I'm supposed to be taking the pressure off you by posing as your girlfriend, but instead your parents must be wondering why you ended up going out with such a nutter.'

'Don't be daft. You're totally charming them—or you were until you nearly fainted face down on your plate. I know the fish was revolting, but really...'

She laughed. 'It wasn't that bad.'

'What then?'

Jasper was her best friend. Over the years she'd told him lots of funny stories about her childhood, and when you'd grown up living in a converted bus painted with flowers and peace slogans, with a mother who had inch-long purple hair, had changed her name to Rainbow and given up wearing a bra, there were lots of those.

There were also lots of bits that weren't funny at all, but she kept those to herself. The years when she'd been taken in by Aunt Janet and had been sent to an exclusive girls' boarding school in the hope of 'civilising' her. Years when she'd been at the mercy of Olympia Rothwell-Hyde and her friends...

She shook her head and smiled. 'Just tired. Honest.'

'Come on, then.' He set off again along the corridor, rubbing his arms vigorously. 'God, if you stand still for a second in this place you run the risk of turning into a pillar of ice. I hope you brought your thermal underwear.'

'Please, can you not mention underwear,' Sophie said with a bleak laugh. 'The contents of my knicker drawer have played far too much of a starring role in this weekend already and I've only been here a couple of hours.' Her heart lurched as she remembered again the phone conversation Kit had overheard on the train. 'I'm afraid I got off on completely the wrong foot with your brother.'

'Half-brother,' Jasper corrected, bitterly. 'And don't worry about Kit. He doesn't approve of anyone. He just sits in judgment on the rest of us.'

'That's why I'm here, isn't it?' said Sophie. 'It's Kit's opinion you're worried about, not your parents'.'

'Are you kidding?' Jasper said ironically. 'You've met my father. He's from the generation and background that call gay men "nancy boys" and assume they all wear pink scarves and carry handbags.'

'And what's Kit's excuse?'

Pausing in front of a closed door, Jasper bowed his head. Without the hair gel and eyeliner he always wore in London his fine-boned face looked younger and oddly vulnerable.

'Kit's never liked me. I've always known that, growing up. He never said anything unkind or did anything horrible to me, but he didn't have to. I always felt this…*coldness* from him, which was almost worse.'

Sophie could identify with that.

'I don't know,' he went on, 'now I'm older I can understand that it must have been difficult for him, growing up without his mother when I still had mine.' He cast her a rueful look. 'As you'll have noticed, my mother isn't exactly cosy—I don't think she particularly went out of her way to make sure he was OK, but because I was her only child I did get rather spoiled, I guess…'

Sophie widened her eyes. 'You? Surely not!'

Jasper grinned. 'This is the part of the castle that's supposed to be haunted by the mad countess's ghost, you know, so you'd better watch it, or I'll run away and leave you here…'

'Don't you dare!'

Laughing, he opened the door. 'This is my room. Damn, the fire's gone out. Come in and shut the door to keep any lingering traces of warmth in.'

Sophie did as she was told. The room was huge, and filled with the kind of dark, heavy furniture that looked as if it had come from a giant's house. A sleigh bed roughly the size of the bus that had formed Sophie's childhood home stood in the centre of the room, piled high with several duvets. Jasper's personal stamp was evident in the tatty posters on the walls, a polystyrene reproduction of Michelangelo's *David*, which was rakishly draped in an old school tie, a silk dressing gown and a battered trilby. As he poked at the ashes in the grate

Sophie picked her way through the clothes on the floor and went over to the window.

'So what happened to Kit's mother?'

Jasper piled coal into the grate. 'She left. When he was about six, I think. It's a bit of a taboo subject around here, but I gather there was no warning, no explanation, no good-bye. Of course there was a divorce eventually, and apparently Juliet's adultery was cited, but as far as I know Kit never had any contact with her again.'

Outside it had stopped snowing and the clouds had parted to show the flat disc of the full moon. From what Sophie could see, Jasper's room looked down over some kind of inner courtyard. The castle walls rose up on all sides—battlements like jagged teeth, stone walls gleaming like pewter in the cold, bluish light. She shivered, her throat constricting with reluctant compassion for the little boy whose mother had left him here in this bleak fortress of a home.

'So she abandoned him to go off with another man?'

Sophie's own upbringing had been unconventional enough for her not to be easily shocked. But a mother leaving her child...

'Pretty much. So I guess you can understand why he ended up being like he is. Ah, look—that's better.'

He stood back, hands on hips, his face bathed in orange as the flames took hold. 'Right—let's find that bottle and get under the duvet. You can tell me all about Paris and how you managed to escape the clutches of that lunatic painter, and in turn I'm going to bore you senseless talking about Sergio. Do you know,' he sighed happily, 'he's having a tally of the days we're apart tattooed on his chest?'

The ancient stones on top of the parapet were worn smooth by salt wind and wild weather, and the moonlight turned them to beaten silver. Kit exhaled a cloud of frozen air, propping his elbows on the stone and looking out across the battlements to the empty beach beyond.

There was no point in even trying to get to sleep tonight, he knew that. His insomnia was always at its worst when he'd just come back from a period of active duty and his body hadn't learned to switch off from its state of high alert. The fact that he was also back at Alnburgh made sleep doubly unlikely.

He straightened up, shoving his frozen fingers into his pockets. The tide was out and pools of water on the sand gleamed like mercury. In the distance the moon was reflected without a ripple in the dark surface of the sea.

It was bitterly cold.

Long months in the desert halfway across the world had made him forget the aching cold here. Sometimes, working in temperatures of fifty degrees wearing eighty pounds of explosive-proof kit, he would try to recapture the sensation, but out there cold became an abstract concept. Something you knew about in theory, but couldn't imagine actually *feeling*.

But it was real enough now, as was the complicated mix of emotions he always experienced when he returned. He did one of the most dangerous jobs on the planet without feeling anything, and yet when he came back to the place he'd grown up in it was as if he'd had a layer of skin removed. Here it was impossible to forget the mother who had left him, or forgive the studied indifference of the father who had been left to bring him up. Here everything was magnified: bitterness, anger, frustration...

Desire.

The thought crept up on him and he shoved it away. Sophie Greenham was hardly his type, although he had to admit that doing battle with her at dinner had livened up what would otherwise have been a dismal evening. And at least her presence had meant that he didn't feel like the only outsider.

It had also provided a distraction from the tension between him and his father. But only temporarily. Ralph was right—Kit hadn't come up here because the party invitation was too thrilling to refuse, but Ralph's seventieth birthday seemed like a good time to remind his father that if he didn't transfer the ownership of Alnburgh into Kit's name soon, it would be too late. The estate couldn't possibly survive the inheritance tax that would be liable on it after Ralph's death, and would no doubt have to be sold.

Kit felt fresh anger bloom inside him. He wasn't sure why he cared—his house in Chelsea was conveniently placed for some excellent restaurants, was within easy taxi-hailing range for women he didn't want to wake up with, and came without ghosts. And yet he did care. Because of the waste and the irresponsibility and the sheer bloody shortsightedness, perhaps? Or because he could still hear his mother's voice, whispering to him down the years?

Alnburgh is yours, Kit. Don't ever forget that. Don't ever let anyone tell you it's not.

It must have been just before she left that she'd said that. When she knew she was going and wanted to assuage her guilt; to feel that she wasn't leaving him with nothing.

As if a building could make up for a mother. Particularly a building like Alnburgh. It was an anachronism. As a home it was uncomfortable, impractical and unsustainable. It was also the place where he had been unhappiest. And yet he knew, deep down, that it mattered to him. He felt responsible for it, and he would do all he could to look after it.

And much as it surprised him to discover, that went for his brother too. Only Jasper wasn't at risk from dry rot or damp, but the attentions of a particularly brazen redhead.

Kit wondered if she'd be as difficult to get rid of.

* * *

Sophie opened her eyes.

It was cold and for a moment her sleep-slow brain groped to work out where she was. It was a familiar feeling—one she'd experienced often as a child when her mother had been in one of her restless phases, but for some reason now it was accompanied by a sinking sensation.

Putting a hand to her head, she struggled upright. In the corner of the room the television was playing quietly to itself, and Jasper's body was warm beside her, a T-shirt of Sergio's clasped in one hand, the half-empty bottle of vodka in the other. He had fallen asleep sprawled diagonally across the bed with his head thrown back, and something about the way the lamplight fell on his face—or maybe the shuttered blankness sleep had lent it—reminded her of Kit.

Fragments of the evening reassembled themselves in her aching head. She got up, rubbing a hand across her eyes, and carefully removed the bottle from Jasper's hand. Much as she loved him, right now all she wanted was a bed to herself and a few hours of peaceful oblivion.

Tiptoeing to the door, she opened it quietly. Out in the corridor the temperature was arctic and the only light came from the moon, lying in bleached slabs on the smooth oak floorboards. Shivering, Sophie hesitated, wondering whether to go back into Jasper's room after all, but the throbbing in her head was more intense now and she thought longingly of the paracetamol in her washbag.

There was nothing for it but to brave the cold and the dark.

Her heart began to pound as she slipped quickly between the squares of silver moonlight, along the corridor and down a spiralling flight of stone stairs. Shadows engulfed her. It was very quiet. Too quiet. To Sophie, used to thin-walled apartments, bed and breakfasts, buses and camper vans on makeshift sites where someone was always strumming a guitar or playing indie-acid-trance, the silence was unnatural.

Oppressive. It buzzed in her ears, filling her head with whistling, like interference on a badly tuned radio.

She stopped, her chest rising and falling rapidly as she looked around.

Passageways stretched away from her in three directions, but each looked as unfamiliar as the other. Oh, hell. She'd been so traumatised earlier that she hadn't paid attention to Jasper when he pointed out her room...

But that could be it, she thought with relief, walking quickly to a door at the end of the short landing to her left. Gingerly she turned the handle and, heart bursting, pushed open the door.

Moonlight flooded in from behind her, illuminating the ghostly outlines of shrouded furniture. The air was stale with age. The room clearly hadn't been opened in years.

This is the part of the castle that's supposed to be haunted by the mad countess's ghost, you know...

Retreating quickly, she slammed the door and forced herself to exhale slowly. It was fine. No need to panic. Just a question of retracing her steps, thinking about it logically. A veil of cloud slipped over the moon's pale face and the darkness deepened. Icy drafts eddied around Sophie's ankles, and the edge of a curtain at one of the stone windows lifted slightly, as if brushed by invisible fingers. The whistling sound was louder now and more distinctive—a sort of keening that was almost human. She couldn't be sure it was just in her head any more and she broke into a run, glancing back over her shoulder as if she expected to see a swish of pink silk skirt disappearing around the corner.

'I'm being stupid,' she whispered desperately, fumbling at the buttons of her mobile phone to make the screen light up and act as a torch. 'There's no such thing as ghosts.' But even as the words formed themselves on her stiff lips horror prickled at the back of her neck.

Footsteps.

She clamped a hand to her mouth to stifle her moan of terror and stood perfectly still. Probably she'd imagined it—or possibly it was just the mad drumming of her heart echoing off the stone walls…

Nope. Definitely footsteps.

Definitely getting nearer.

It was impossible to tell from which direction they were coming. Or maybe if they were ghostly footsteps they weren't coming from any particular direction, except beyond the grave? It hardly mattered—the main thing was to get away from here and back to Jasper. Back to light and warmth and TV and company. Shaking with fear, she darted back along the corridor, heading for the stairs that she had come down a few moments ago.

And then she gave a whimper of horror, icy adrenaline sluicing through her veins. A dark figure loomed in front of her, only a foot or so away, too close even for her to be aware of anything beyond its height and the frightening breadth of its shoulders. She shrank backwards, bringing her hands up to her face, her mouth opening to let out the scream that was rising in her throat.

'Oh, no, you don't…'

Instantly she was pulled against the rock-hard chest and a huge hand was put across her mouth. Fury replaced fear as she realised that this was not the phantom figure of some seventeenth-century suitor looking for the countess, but the all-too-human flesh of Kit Fitzroy.

All of a sudden the idea of being assaulted by a ghost seemed relatively appealing.

'Get *off* me!' she snapped. Or tried to. The sound she actually made was a muffled, undignified squawk, but he must have understood her meaning because he let her go immediately, thrusting her away from his body as if she were contam-

inated. Shaking back her hair, Sophie glared at him, trying
to gather some shreds of dignity. Not easy when she'd just
been caught behaving like a histrionic schoolgirl because she
thought he was a ghost.

'What do you think you're *doing*?' she demanded.

His arched brows rose a fraction, but other than that his
stony expression didn't change. 'I'd have thought it was obvious. Stopping you from screaming and waking up the entire castle,' he drawled. 'Is Jasper aware that you're roaming
around the corridors in the middle of the night?'

'Jasper's asleep.'

'Ah. Of course.' His hooded gaze didn't leave hers, but
she jumped as she felt his fingers close around her wrist,
like bands of iron, and he lifted the hand in which her mobile phone was clasped. His touch was as cold and hard as
his tone. 'Don't tell me, you got lost on the way to the bathroom and you were using the GPS to find it?'

'No.' Sophie spoke through clenched teeth. 'I got lost on
the way to my bedroom. Now, if you'd just point me in the
right—'

'*Your* bedroom?' He dropped her wrist and stepped away.
'Well, it definitely won't be here. The rooms in this part of
the castle haven't been used for years. But why the hell aren't
you sharing with Jasper? Or perhaps you prefer to have your
own...*privacy*?'

He was so tall that she had to tilt her head back to look at
his face. The place where they were standing was dark and
it was half in shadow, but, even so, she didn't miss the faint
sneer that accompanied the word.

'I just thought it wouldn't be appropriate to sleep with
Jasper in his parents' house, that's all,' she retorted haughtily. 'It didn't feel right.'

'You do a passable impression of indignant respectabil-
ity,' he said in a bored voice, turning round and beginning to

walk away from her down the corridor. 'But unfortunately it's rather wasted on me. I know exactly why you want your own bedroom, and it has nothing to do with propriety and everything to do with the fact that you're far from in love with my brother.'

It was those words that did it. *My brother.* Until then she had been determined to remain calm in the face of Kit Fitzroy's towering arrogance; his misguided certainty and his infuriating, undeniable sexual magnetism. Now something snapped inside her.

'No. You're *wrong*,' she spat.

'Really?' he drawled, turning to go back along the passageway down which she'd just come.

'*Yes!*'

Who the hell was he to judge? If it wasn't for him Jasper wouldn't have had to ask her here in the first place, to make himself look 'acceptable' in the contemptuous eyes of his brother.

Well, she couldn't explain anything without giving Jasper away, but she didn't have to take it either. Following him she could feel the pulse jumping in her wrist, in the place where his fingers had touched her, as fresh adrenaline scorched through her veins.

'I know you think the worst of me and I can understand why, but I just want to say that it wasn't—*isn't*—what you think. I would *never* hurt Jasper, or mess him around. He's the person I care most about in the world.'

He went up a short flight of steps into the corridor Sophie now remembered, and stopped in front of the door at the end.

'You have a funny way of showing it,' he said, very softly. 'By sleeping with another man.'

He opened the door and stood back for her to pass. She didn't move. 'It's not like that,' she said in a low voice. 'You don't know the whole story.'

Kit shook his head. 'I don't need to.'

Because what was there to know? He'd seen it all count-less times before—men returning back to base from leave, white-lipped and silent as they pulled down pictures of smiling wives or girlfriends from their lockers. Wives they thought they could trust while they were away. Girlfriends they thought would wait for them. Behind every betrayal there was a story, but in the end it was still a betrayal.

Folding her arms tightly across her body, she walked past him into the small room and stood by the bed with her back to him. Her hair was tangled, reminding him that she'd just left his brother's bed. In the thin, cold moonlight it gleamed like hot embers beneath the ashes of a dying fire.

'Is it common practice in the army to condemn without trial and without knowing the facts?' she asked, turning round to face him. 'You barely even *know* Jasper. You did your best to deny his existence when he was growing up, and you're not exactly going out of your way to make up for it now, so please don't lecture me about not loving him.'

'That's *enough*.'

The words were raw, razor-sharp, spoken in the split sec-ond before his automatic defences kicked in and the shutters came down on his emotions. Deliberately Kit unfurled his fists and kept his breathing steady.

'If you think finding your way around the castle is con-fusing I wouldn't even try to unravel the relationships within this family if I were you,' he said quietly. 'Don't get involved in things you don't need to understand.'

'Why? Because I won't be around long enough?' she de-manded, coming closer to him again.

Kit stiffened as he caught the scent of her again—warm, spicy, delicious. He turned away, reaching for the door handle. 'Goodnight. I hope you have everything you need.'

He shut the door and stood back from it, waiting for the

adrenaline rush to subside a little. Funny how he could work a field strewn with hidden mines, approach a car loaded with explosives and not feel anything, and yet five feet five of lying redhead had almost made him lose control.

He hated deception—too much of his childhood had been spent not knowing what to believe or who to trust—and as an actress, he supposed, Sophie Greenham was quite literally a professional in the art.

But unluckily for her he was a professional too, and there was more than one way of making safe an incendiary device. Sometimes you had to approach the problem laterally. If she wouldn't admit that her feelings for Jasper were a sham, he'd just have to prove it another way.

CHAPTER SIX

SOPHIE felt as if she'd only just fallen asleep when a knock at the door jolted her awake again. Jasper appeared, grinning sheepishly and carrying a plate of toast in one hand and two mugs of coffee in the other, some of which slopped onto the carpet as he elbowed the door shut again.

'What time is it?' she moaned, dropping back onto the pillows.

Jasper put the mugs down on the bedside table and perched on the bed beside her. 'Nearly ten. Kit said he'd bumped into you in the middle of the night trying to find your room, so I thought I'd better not wake you. You've slept for Britain.'

Sophie didn't have the heart to tell him she'd been awake most of the night, partly because she'd been frozen, partly because she'd been so hyped up with indignation and fury and the after-effects of what felt like an explosion in the sexual-chemistry lab that sleep had been a very long time coming.

He picked up a mug and looked at her through the wreaths of steam that were curling through the frigid air. 'Sorry for leaving you to wander like that. Just as well you bumped into Kit.'

Sophie grunted crossly. 'Do you think so? I thought he was the ghost of the nymphomaniac countess. No such luck.'

Jasper winced. 'He didn't give you a hard time, did he?'

'He thought it was extremely odd that we weren't sharing

a room.' Sophie reached for a coffee, more to warm her hands on than anything. 'I'm not exactly convincing him in my role as your girlfriend, you know. The thing is, he overheard me talking to Jean-Claude on the train and now he thinks I'm a two-timing trollop.'

'Oops.' Jasper took another sip of coffee while he digested this information. 'OK, well, that is a bit unfortunate, but don't worry—we still have time to turn it around at the party to-night. You'll be every man's idea of the perfect girlfriend.'

Sophie raised an eyebrow. 'In public? In front of your parents? From my experience of what men consider the perfect girlfriend, that wouldn't be wise.'

'Wicked girl,' Jasper scolded. 'I meant demure, devoted, hanging on my every word—that sort of thing. What did you bring to wear?'

'My Chinese silk dress.'

With a firm shake of his head Jasper put down his mug. 'Absolutely *not*. Far too sexy. No, what we need is something a little more…understated. A little more *modest*.'

Sophie narrowed her eyes. 'You mean frumpy, don't you? Do you have something in mind?'

Getting up, Jasper went over to the window and drew back the curtains with a theatrical flourish. 'Not something, some*where*. Get up, Cinderella, and let's hit the shops of Hawksworth.'

Jasper drove Ralph's four-by-four along roads that had been turned into ice rinks. It was a deceptively beautiful day. The sun shone in a sky of bright, hard blue and made the fields and hedgerows glitter as if each twig and blade of grass was encrusted with Swarovski crystals. He had pinched a navy-blue quilted jacket of Tatiana's to lend to Sophie, instead of the military-style overcoat of which Kit had been so scathing. Squinting at her barefaced reflection in the drop-down mirror on the sun visor, she remarked that all that was missing was a silk headscarf and her new posh-girl image would be complete. Jasper leaned over and pulled one out of the glove compartment. She tied it under her chin and they roared with laughter.

They parked in the market square in the centre of a town that looked as if it hadn't altered much in the last seventy years. Crunching over gritted cobblestones, Jasper led her past greengrocers, butchers and shops selling gate hinges and sheep dip, to an ornately fronted department store. Mannequins wearing bad blonde wigs modelled twinsets and patterned shirtwaister dresses in the windows.

'Braithwaite's—the fashion centre of the North since 1908' read the painted sign above the door. Sophie wondered if it was meant to be ironic.

'After you, madam,' said Jasper with a completely straight face, holding the door open for her. 'Evening wear. First floor.'

Sophie stifled a giggle. 'I love vintage clothing, as you know, but—'

'No buts,' said Jasper airily, striding past racks of raincoats towards a sweeping staircase in the centre of the store. 'Just think of it as dressing for a part. Tonight, Ms Greenham, you are *not* going to be your gorgeous, individual but—let's face it—slightly eccentric self. You are going to be perfect Fitzroy-fiancée material. And that means Dull.'

At the top of the creaking staircase Sophie caught sight of herself in a full-length mirror. In jeans and Tatiana's jacket, the silk scarf still knotted around her neck a lurid splash of colour against her un-made-up face, dull was exactly the word. Still, if dull was what was required to slip beneath Kit Fitzroy's radar that had to be a good thing.

Didn't it?

She hesitated for a second, staring into her own wide eyes, thinking of last night and the shower of shooting stars that had exploded inside her when he'd touched her wrist; the static that had seemed to make the air between them vibrate as they'd stood in the dark corridor. The blankness of his expression, but the way it managed to convey more vividly than a thousand well-chosen words his utter contempt...

'What do you think?'

Yes. Dull was good. The duller the better.

'Hello-*o*?'

Pasting on a smile, she turned to Jasper, who had picked out the most hideous concoction of ruffles and ruches in the kind of royal blue frequently used for school uniforms. Sophie waved her hand dismissively.

'Strictly Come Drag Queen. I thought we were going for dull—that's attention-grabbing for all the wrong reasons. No—we have to find something *really* boring...' She began rifling through rails of pastel polyester. 'We have to find the closest thing The Fashion Capital of the North has to a shroud... Here. How about this?'

Triumphantly she pulled out something in stiff black fabric—long, straight and completely unadorned. The neck was cut straight across in a way that she could imagine would make her breasts look like a sort of solid, matronly shelf, and the price tag was testament to the garment's extreme lack of appeal. It had been marked down three times already and was now almost being given away.

'Looks good to me.' Jasper flipped the hanger around, scrutinising the dress with narrowed eyes. 'Would madam like to try it on?'

'Nope. It's my size, it's horrible and it's far too cold to get undressed. Let's just buy it and go to the pub. As your fiancée I think I deserve an enormous and extremely calorific lunch.'

Jasper grinned and kissed her swiftly on the cheek. 'You're on.'

* * *

The Bull in Hawksworth was the quintessential English pub: the walls were yellow with pre-smoking-ban nicotine, a scarred dartboard hung on the wall beside an age-spotted etching of Alnburgh Castle and horse brasses were nailed to the blackened beams. Sophie slid behind a table in the corner by the fire while Jasper went to the bar. He came back with a pint of lager and a glass of red wine, and a newspaper folded under his arm.

'Food won't be a minute,' he said, taking a sip of lager, which left a froth of white on his upper lip. 'Would you mind if I gave Sergio a quick call? I brought you this to read.' He threw down the newspaper and gave her an apologetic look as he took out his phone. 'It's just it's almost impossible to get a bloody signal at Alnburgh, and I'm always terrified of being overheard anyway.'

Sophie shrugged. 'No problem. Go ahead.'

'Is there a "but" there?'

Taking a sip of her wine, she shook her head. 'No, of course not.' She put her glass down, turning the stem between her fingers. In the warmth of the fire and Jasper's familiar company she felt herself relaxing more than she had done in the last twenty-four hours. 'Except,' she went on thoughtfully, 'perhaps that I wonder if it wouldn't be easier if you came clean about all this.'

'Came out, you mean?' Jasper said with sudden weariness. 'Well, it wouldn't. It's easier just to live my own life, far away from here, without having to deal with the fallout of knowing I've let my whole family down. My father might be seventy, but he still prides himself on the reputation as a ladies' man he's spent his entire adult life building. He sees flirting with anything in a skirt as a mark of sophisticated social interaction—as you may have noticed last night. Homosexuality is utterly alien to him, so he thinks it's unnatural full stop.' With an agitated movement of his hand he knocked his pint glass so that beer splashed onto the table. 'Honestly, it would finish him off. And as for Kit—'

'Yes, well, I don't know what gives Kit the right to go around passing judgment on everyone else, like he's something special,' Sophie snapped, unfolding the paper as she moved it away from the puddle of lager on the table. 'It's not as if he's better than you because he's straight, or me because he's posh—'

'Holy cow,' spluttered Jasper, grasping her arm.

Breaking off, she followed his astonished gaze and felt the rest of the rant dissolve on her tongue. For there, on the front of the newspaper—in grainy black and white, but no less arresting for it—was Kit. Beneath the headline *Heroes Honoured* a photograph showed him in half profile, his expression characteristically blank above his dress uniform with its impressive line of medals.

Quickly, incredulously, Jasper began to read out the accompanying article.

'Major Kit Fitzroy, known as "the heart-throb hero", was awarded the George Medal for his "dedication to duty and calm, unflinching bravery in the face of extreme personal risk". Major Fitzroy has been responsible for making safe over 100 improvised explosive devices, potentially saving the lives of numerous troops and civilians, a feat which he describes as "nothing remarkable".'

For long moments neither of them spoke. Sophie felt as if she'd swallowed a firework, which was now fizzing inside her. The barmaid brought over plates of lasagne and chips and retreated again. Sophie's appetite seemed to have mysteriously deserted her.

'I suppose that does give him the right to act like he's a

bit special, and *slightly* better than you and me,' she admitted shakily. 'Did you know anything about this?'

'Not a thing.'

'But wouldn't your father want to know? Wouldn't he be pleased?'

Jasper shrugged. 'He's always been rather sneery about Kit's army career, maybe because he's of the opinion people of our class don't work, apart from in pointless, arty jobs like mine.' Picking up his pint, he frowned. 'It might also have something to do with the fact his older brother was killed in the Falklands, but I don't know. That's one of those Things We definitely Do Not Mention.'

There seemed to be quite a lot of those in the Fitzroy family, Sophie thought. She couldn't stop looking at the photograph of Kit, even though she wanted to. Or help thinking how attractive he was, even though she didn't want to.

It had been easy to write him off as an obnoxious, arrogant control-freak but what Jasper had said about his mother last night, and now this, made her see him, reluctantly, in a different light.

What was worse, it made her see herself in a different light too. Having been on the receiving end of ignorant prejudice, Sophie liked to think she would never rush to make ill-informed snap judgments about people, but she had to admit that maybe, just maybe, in this instance she had.

But so had he, she reminded herself defiantly. He had dismissed her as a shallow, tarty gold-digger when that most definitely wasn't true. The gold-digger part, anyway. Hopefully tonight, with the aid of the nunlike dress and a few pithy comments on current affairs and international politics, she'd make him see he'd been wrong about the rest too.

For Jasper's sake, obviously.

As they left she picked up the newspaper. 'Do you think they'd mind if I took this?'

'What for?' Jasper asked in surprise. 'D'you want to sleep with the heart-throb hero under your pillow?'

'No!' Annoyingly Sophie felt herself blush. 'I want to swot up on the headlines so I can make intelligent conversation tonight.'

Jasper laughed all the way back to the car.

Ralph adjusted his bow tie in the mirror above the drawing room fireplace and smoothed a hand over his brushed-back hair.

'I must say, Kit, I find your insistence on bringing up the subject of my death in rather poor taste,' he said in an aggrieved tone. 'Tonight of all nights. A milestone birthday like this is depressing enough without you reminding me constantly that the clock is ticking.'

'It's not personal,' Kit drawled, mentally noting that he'd do well to remember that himself. 'And it is boring, but the fact remains that Alnburgh won't survive the inheritance tax it'll owe on your death unless you've transferred the ownership of the estate to someone else. Seven years is the—'

Ralph cut him off with a bitter, blustering laugh. 'By someone else, I suppose you mean you? What about Jasper?'

Alnburgh is yours, Kit. Don't let anyone tell you it's not.

In the pockets of his dinner-suit trousers Kit's hands were bunched into fists. Experience had taught him that when Ralph was in this kind of punchy, belligerent mood the best way to respond was with total detachment. He wondered fleetingly if that was where he first picked up the habit.

'Jasper isn't the logical heir,' he said, very evenly.

'Oh, I don't know about that,' Ralph replied with unpleasant, mock joviality. 'Let's look at it this way—Jasper is probably going to live another sixty or seventy years, and, believe me, I have every intention of lasting a lot more than seven years. Given your job I'd say you're the one who's pushing your luck in that department, don't you think? Remember what happened to my dear brother Leo. Never came back from the Falklands. Very nasty business.'

Ralph's eyes met Kit's in the mirror and slid away. He was already well on the way to being drunk, Kit realised wearily, and that meant that any further attempt at persuasion on his part would only be counterproductive.

'Transfer it to Jasper if you want.' He shrugged, picking up the newspaper that lay folded on a coffee table. 'That would certainly be better than doing nothing, though I'm not sure he'd thank you for it since he hates being here as much as Tatiana does. It might also put him at further risk from ruthless gold-diggers like the one he's brought up this weekend.'

The medals ceremony he'd attended yesterday was front-page news. Idly he wondered whether Ralph had seen it and chosen not to say anything.

'Sophie?' Ralph turned round, putting his hands into his pockets and rocking back on the heels of his patent shoes. 'I thought she was quite charming. Gorgeous little thing, too. Good old Jasper, eh? He's got a cracker there.'

'Except for the fact that she couldn't give a toss about him,' Kit commented dryly, putting down the paper.

'Jealous, Kit?' Ralph said, and there was real malice in his tone. His eyes were narrowed, his face suddenly flushed. 'You think you're the one who should get all the good-looking girls, don't you? I'd say you want her for yourself, just like—'

At that moment the strange outburst was interrupted by Jasper coming in. Ralph broke off and turned abruptly away.

'Just like what?' Kit said softly.

'Nothing.' Ralph pulled a handkerchief from his pocket and mopped his brow. As he turned to Jasper his face lost all its hostility. 'We were just talking about you—and Sophie.'

Heading to the drinks tray, Jasper grinned. 'Gorgeous, isn't she? And really clever and talented too. Great actress.'

In his dinner suit and with his hair wet from the shower Jasper looked about fifteen, Kit thought, his heart darkening against Sophie Greenham.

'So I noticed,' he said blandly, going to the door. He turned to Ralph. 'Think about what I said about the estate transfer. Oh, and I promised Thomas I'd see to the port tonight. Any preference?'

Ralph seemed to have recovered his composure. 'There's an excellent '29. Though, on second thoughts, open some '71.' His smile held a hint of challenge. 'Let's keep the really good stuff for my hundredth, since I fully intend to be around to celebrate it.'

Crossing the portrait hall in rapid, furious strides, Kit swore with such viciousness a passing waiter shot behind a large display of flowers. So he'd failed to make Ralph see sense about the estate. He'd just have to make sure he was more successful when it came to Sophie Greenham.

It was just as well she hadn't eaten all that lasagne at lunch-time, Sophie reflected grimly, tugging at the zip on the side of the black dress. Obviously, with hindsight, trying it on in the shop would have been wise—all the croissants and baguettes in Paris must have taken more of a toll than she'd realised. Oh, well—if it didn't fit she'd just have to wear the Chinese silk that Jasper had decreed was too sexy...

Hope flared inside her. Instantly she stamped it out.

No. Tonight was not about being sexy, or having fun, she told herself sternly. Tonight was about supporting Jasper and showing Kit that she wasn't the wanton trollop he had her down as.

She thought again of the photo in the paper—unsmiling, remote, heroic—and her insides quivered a little. Because, she realised with a pang of surprise, she actually didn't want him to think that about her.

With renewed effort she gave the zip another furious tug. It shot up and she let out the lungful of air she'd been holding, looking down at the dress with a sinking heart. Her cell-like bedroom didn't boast anything as luxurious as a full-length mirror, but she didn't need to see her whole reflection to know how awful she looked. It really was the most severely unflattering garment imaginable, falling in a plain, narrow, sleeveless tube from her collarbones to her ankles. A slit up one side at least meant that she could walk without affecting tiny geishalike steps, but she felt as if she were wrapped in a roll of wartime blackout fabric.

'That's *good*,' she said out loud, giving herself a severe look in the little mirror above the sink. Her reflection stared back at her, face pale against the bright mass of her hair. She'd washed it and, gleaming under the overhead light, the colour now seemed more garish than ever. Grabbing a few pins, she stuck them in her mouth, then pulled her hair back and twisted it tightly at the back of her neck.

Standing back again, she pulled a face.

There. Disfiguring dress and headmistress hair. Jasper's dull girlfriend was ready for her public, although at least Sophie had the private satisfaction of knowing that she was also wearing very naughty underwear and what Jasper fondly called her 'shag-me' shoes. Twisting round, she tried to check the back view of the dress, and gave a snort of laughter as she noticed the price ticket hanging down between her shoulder blades.

Classy and expensive was always going to be a hard look for the girl who used to live on a bus to pull off, as Olympia Rothwell-Hyde and her cronies had never stopped reminding her. Attempting to do it with a label on her back announcing just how little she'd paid for the blackout dress would make it damned impossible.

She gave it a yank and winced as the plastic cut into her

fingers. Another try confirmed that it was definitely a job for scissors. Which she didn't have.

She bit her lip. Jasper had already gone down, telling her to join them in the drawing room as soon as she was ready, but there was no way she could face Tatiana, who would no doubt be decked out in designer finery and dripping with diamonds, with her knock-down price ticket on display. She'd just have to slip down to the kitchens and see if the terrifying Mrs Daniels—or Mrs Danvers as she'd privately named her when Jasper had introduced her this morning—had some.

The layout of the castle was more familiar now and Sophie headed for the main stairs as quickly as the narrow dress would allow. The castle felt very different this evening from the cavernous, shadowy place at which she'd arrived last night. Now the stone walls seemed to resonate with a hum of activity as teams of caterers and waiting-on staff made final preparations in the staterooms below.

It was still freezing, though. In the portrait hall the smell of woodsmoke drifted through the air, carried on icy gusts of wind that the huge fires banked in every grate couldn't seem to thaw. It mingled with the scent of hothouse flowers, which stood on every table and window ledge.

Sophie hitched up the narrow skirt of her dress and went more carefully down the narrow back stairs to the kitchens. It was noticeably warmer down here, the vaulted ceilings holding the heat from the ovens. A central stone-flagged passageway stretched beyond a row of Victorian windows in the kitchen wall, into the dimly lit distance. To the dungeons, Jasper had teased her earlier.

The dungeons, where Kit probably locked up two-timing girlfriends, she thought grimly, shivering in spite of the relative warmth. The noise of her heels echoed loudly off the stone walls. The glass between the corridor and the kitchen was clouded with steam, but through it Sophie could see that

Mrs Daniels' domain had been taken over by legions of uni-
formed chefs.

Of course. Jasper had mentioned that both she and Thomas
the butler had been given the night off. Well, there was no
way she was going in there. Turning on her high heel, she
hitched up her skirt and was hurrying back in the direction
she'd just come when a voice behind her stopped her in her
tracks.

'Are you looking for something?'

Her heart leapt into her throat and she spun round. Kit
had emerged from one of the many small rooms that led off
the passageway, his shoulders, in a perfectly cut black dinner suit, seeming almost to fill the narrow space. Their eyes
met, and in the harsh overhead bulk light Sophie saw him
recoil slightly as a flicker of some emotion—shock, or was
it distaste?—passed across his face.

'I was l-looking for M-Mrs Daniels,' she said in a strangled
voice, feeling inexplicably as if he'd caught her doing something wrong again. God, no wonder he had risen so far up
the ranks in the army. She'd bet he could reduce insubordi-
nate squaddies to snivelling babies with a single glacial glare.
She coughed, and continued more determinedly. 'I wanted to
borrow some scissors.'

'That's a relief.' His smile was almost imperceptible. 'I
assume it means I don't have to tell you that you have a price
ticket hanging down your back.'

Heat prickled through her, rising up her neck in a tide of
uncharacteristic shyness.

Quickly she cleared her throat again. 'No.'

'Perhaps I could help? Follow me.'

Sophie was glad of the ringing echo of her shoes on the
stone floor as it masked the frantic thud of her heart. He had
to duck his head to get through the low doorway and she followed him into a vaulted cellar, the brick walls of which were

lined with racks of bottles that gleamed dully in the low light. There was a table on which more bottles stood, alongside a knife and stained cloth like a consumptive's handkerchief. Kit picked up the knife.

'Wh-what are you doing?'

Hypnotised, she watched him wipe the blade of the knife on the cloth.

'Decanting port.'

'What for?' she rasped, desperately trying to make some attempt at sensible conversation. Snatches of the article in the newspaper kept coming back to her, making it impossible to think clearly. *Heart-throb hero. Unflinching bravery. Extreme personal risk.* It was as if someone had taken her jigsaw puzzle image of him and broken it to bits, so the pieces made quite a different picture now.

His lips twitched into the faint half-smile she'd come to recognise, but his hooded eyes held her gravely. The coolness was still there, but they'd lost their sharp contempt.

'To get rid of the sediment. The bottle I've just opened last saw daylight over eighty years ago.'

Sophie gave a little laugh, squirming slightly under his scrutiny. 'Isn't it a bit past its sell-by date?'

'Like lots of things, it improves with age,' he said dryly, taking hold of her shoulders with surprising gentleness and turning her round. 'Would you like to try some?'

'Isn't it very expensive?'

What was it about an absence of hostility that actually made it feel like kindness? Sophie felt the hair rise on the back of her neck as his fingers brushed her bare skin. She held herself very rigid for a second, determined not to give in to the helpless shudder of desire that threatened to shake her whole body as he bent over her. Her breasts tingled, and beneath the severe lines of the dress her nipples pressed against the tight fabric.

'Put it this way, you could get several dresses like that for the price of a bottle,' he murmured, and Sophie could feel the warm whisper of his breath on her neck as he spoke. She closed her eyes, wanting the moment to stretch for ever, but then she heard the snap of plastic as he cut through the tag and he was pulling back, leaving her feeling shaky and on edge.

'To be honest, that doesn't say much about your port,' she joked weakly.

'No.' He went back over to the table and picked up a bottle, holding it up to the light for a second before pouring a little of the dark red liquid into a slender, teardrop-shaped decanter. 'It's a great dress. It suits you.'

His voice was offhand. So why did it make goosebumps rise on her skin?

'It's a very *cheap* dress.' She laughed again, awkwardly, crossing her arms across her chest to hide the obvious outline of her nipples, which had to be glaringly obvious against the plainness of the dress. 'Or is that what you meant by it suiting me?'

'No.'

He turned to face her, holding the slim neck of the decanter. She couldn't take her eyes off his hands. Against the white cuffs of his evening shirt they looked very tanned and she felt her heart twist in her chest, catching her off guard as she thought of what he had done with those hands. And what he had seen with those eyes. And now he was looking at her with that cool, dispassionate stare and she almost couldn't breathe.

'I haven't got a glass, I'm afraid.' He swirled the port around in the decanter so it gleamed like liquid rubies, and then offered it up to her lips. 'Take it slowly. Breathe it in first.'

Oh, God.

At that moment she wasn't sure she was capable of breathing at all, but it was as if he had some kind of hypnotist's hold over her and somehow she did as he said, her gaze fixed unblinkingly on his as she inhaled.

It was the scent of age and incense and reverence, and instantly she was transported back to the chapel at school, kneeling on scratchy woollen hassocks to sip communion wine and trying to ignore the whispers of Olympia Rothwell-Hyde and her friends, saying that she'd go to hell because everyone knew she hadn't even been baptised, never mind confirmed. What vicar would christen a child with a name like Summer Greenham?

She pulled away sharply just as the port touched her lips, so that it missed her mouth and dripped down her chin. Kit's reactions were like lightning—in almost the same second his hand came up to cup her face, catching the drips of priceless liquor on the palm of his hand.

'I'm sorry,' she gasped. 'I didn't mean to waste it—'

'Then let's not.'

It was just a whisper, and then he was bending his head so that, slowly, softly, his mouth grazed hers. Sophie's breathing hitched, her world stopped as his lips moved downwards to suck the drips on her chin as her lips parted helplessly and a tidal wave of lust and longing was unleashed inside her. It washed away everything, so that her head was empty of questions, doubts, uncertainties: everything except the dark, swirling whirlpool of need. Her body did the thinking, the deciding for her as it arched towards him, her hands coming up of their own volition to grip his rock-hard shoulders and tangle in his hair.

This was what she knew. This meeting of mouths and bodies, this igniting of pheromones and stoking of fires—these were feelings she understood and could deal with expertly. Familiar territory.

Or, it had been.

Not now.

Not *this*…

His touch was gentle, languid, but it seared her like a blow-torch, reducing the memory of every man who'd gone before to ashes and dust. One hand rested on her hip, the other cupped her cheek as he kissed her with a skill and a kind of brooding focus that made her tremble and melt.

And want *more*.

The stiff fabric of the hateful dress felt like armour plating. She pressed herself against him, longing to be free of it, feeling the contours of the hard muscles of his chest through the layers of clothes that separated them. Her want flared, a fire doused with petrol, and as she kissed him back her fingers found the silk bow tie at his throat, tugging at the knot, working the shirt button beneath it free.

And suddenly there was nothing gentle in the way he pulled her against him, nothing languid about the pressure of his mouth or the erotic thrust and dart of his tongue. Sophie's hands were shaking as she slid them beneath his jacket. She could feel the warmth of his body, the rapid beating of his heart as he gripped her shoulders, pushing her backwards against the ancient oak barrels behind her.

Roughly she pushed his jacket off his shoulders. His hands were at her waist and she yanked at her skirt, pulling it upwards so that he could hitch her onto a barrel. She straddled its curved surface, her hips rising to press against his, her fingers twisting in his shirt front as she struggled to pull it free of his trousers.

She was disorientated with desire. Trembling, shaking, unhinged with an urgency that went beyond anything she'd known before. The need to have him against her and in her.

'Now…please…'

She gasped as he stepped backwards, tearing his mouth

from hers, turning away. A physical sensation of loss swept through her as her hands, still outstretched towards him, reached to pull him back into her. Her breath was coming in ragged, thirsty gasps; she was unable to think of anything beyond satisfying the itch and burn that pulsed through her veins like heroin.

Until he turned back to face her again and her blood froze.

His shirt was open to the third button, his silk tie hanging loose around his neck in the classic, clichéd image from every red-blooded woman's slickest fantasy. But that was where the dream ended, because his face was like chiselled marble and his hooded eyes were as cold as ice.

And in that second, in a rush of horror and pain, Sophie understood what had just happened. What she had just done. He didn't need to say anything because his expression—completely deadpan apart from the slight curl of his lip as he looked at her across the space that separated them—said it all.

She didn't hesitate. Didn't think. It was pure instinct that propelled her across that space and made her raise her hand to slap his face.

But her instinct was no match for his reflexes. With no apparent effort at all he caught hold of her wrist and held it absolutely still for a heartbeat before letting go.

'You unutterable bastard,' she breathed.

She didn't wait for a response. Somehow she made her trembling legs carry her out of the wine cellar and along the corridor, while her horrified mind struggled to take in the enormity of what had just happened. She had betrayed Jasper and given herself away. She had proved Kit Fitzroy right. She had played straight into his hands and revealed herself as the faithless, worthless gold-digger he'd taken her for all along.

CHAPTER SEVEN

So in the end it hadn't even been as hard as he'd thought it would be.

With one quick, angry movement Kit speared the cork in another dusty bottle and twisted it out with far less care and respect than the vintage deserved.

He hadn't exactly anticipated she would be a challenge to seduce, but somehow he'd imagined a little more in the way of token resistance; some evidence of a battle with her conscience at least.

But she had responded instantly.

With a passion that matched his own.

His hand shook, and the port he was pouring through the muslin cloth into the decanter dripped like blood over the backs of his fingers. Giving a muttered curse, he put the bottle down and put his hand to his mouth to suck off the drops.

What the hell was the matter with him? His hands were usually steady as a rock—he and his entire team would have been blown to bits long ago if they weren't. And if he hesitated, or questioned himself as he was doing now...

He had done what he set out to do, and her reaction was exactly what he'd predicted.

But his wasn't. His wasn't at all.

* * *

Wiping her damp palms down the skirt of the horrible dress, Sophie stood in the middle of the portrait hall, halfway between the staircase and the closed doors to the drawing room. She was still shaking with horror and adrenaline and vile, unwelcome arousal and the urge to run back up to her bedroom, throw her things into her bag and slip quietly out of the servants' entrance was almost overwhelming. Wasn't that the way she'd always dealt with things—the way her mother had shown her? When the going got tough you walked away. You told yourself it didn't matter and you weren't bothered, and just to show you meant it you packed up and moved on.

The catering staff were putting the finishing touches to the buffet in the dining room, footsteps ringing on the flagstones as they brought up more champagne in ice buckets with which to greet the guests who would start arriving any minute. Sophie hesitated, biting down on her throbbing lip as for a moment she let herself imagine getting on a train and speeding through the darkness back to London, where she'd never have to see Kit Fitzroy again...

She felt a stab of pain beneath her ribs, but at that moment one of the enormous doors to the drawing room opened and Jasper appeared.

'Ah, there you are, angel! I thought you might have got lost again so I was just coming to see if I could find you.'

He started to come towards her, and Sophie saw his eyes sweep over her, widening along with his smile as he came closer.

'Saints Alive, Sophie Greenham, that *dress*...'

'I know,' Sophie croaked. 'Don't say it. It's dire.'

'It's not.' Slowly Jasper circled around her, looking her up and down as an incredulous expression spread across his face. 'How *could* we have got it so wrong? It might have been cheap as chips and looked like a shroud on the hanger, but on you it's bloody dynamite.' He gave a low whistle. 'Have you seen yourself? No red-blooded, straight male will be able to keep his hands off you.'

She gave a slightly hysterical laugh. 'Darling, don't you believe it.'

'Soph?' Jasper looked at her in concern. 'You OK?'

Oh, hell, what was she doing? She'd come here to shield him from the prejudices of his family, and so far she'd only succeeded in making things more awkward for him. The fact that his brother was the kind of cold-blooded, ruthless bastard who would stop at nothing to preserve the purity of the Fitzroy name and reputation was all the more reason she should give this her all.

'I'm fine.' Digging her nails into the palms of her hands, she raised her chin and smiled brightly. 'And you look gorgeous. There's something about a man in black tie that I find impossible to resist.'

Wasn't that the truth?

'Good.' Jasper pressed a fleeting kiss to her cheek and, taking hold of her hand, pulled her forwards. 'In that case, let's get this party started. Personally, I intend to get stuck into the champagne right now, before guests arrive and we have to share it.'

Head down, Kit walked quickly in the direction of the King's Hall—not because he was in any hurry to get there, but because he knew from long experience that looking purposeful was the best way to avoid getting trapped into conversation.

The last thing he felt like doing was talking to anyone.

As he went up the stairs the music got louder. Obviously keen to recapture his youthful prowess on the dance floor Ralph had hired a swing band, who were energetically working their way through the back catalogue of The Beatles. The strident tones of trumpet and saxophone swelled beneath the vaulted ceiling and reverberated off the walls.

Kit paused at the top of the flight of shallow steps into the huge space. The dance floor was a mass of swirling silks and velvets but even so his gaze was instantly drawn to the girl in the plain, narrow black dress in the midst of the throng. She was dancing with Ralph, Kit noticed, feeling himself tense inexplicably as he saw his father's large, practised hand splayed across the small of Sophie's back.

They suited each other very well, he thought with an inward sneer, watching the way the slit in Sophie's dress opened up as she danced to reveal a seductive glimpse of smooth, pale thigh. Ralph was a lifelong womaniser and philanderer, and Sophie Greenham seemed to be pretty indiscriminate in her favours, so there was no reason why she shouldn't make it a Fitzroy hat-trick. He turned away in disgust.

'Kit darling! I thought it must be you—not many people fill a dinner jacket that perfectly, though I must say I'm rather disappointed you're not in dress uniform tonight.'

Kit's heart sank as Sally Rothwell-Hyde grasped his shoulders and enveloped him in a cloud of asphyxiating perfume as she stretched up to kiss him on both cheeks. 'I saw the picture on the front of the paper, you dark horse,' she went on, giving him a girlish look from beneath spidery eyelashes. 'You looked utterly mouth-watering, and the medal did rather add to the heroic effect. I was hoping to see it on you.'

'Medals are only worn on uniform,' Kit remarked, trying to muster the energy to keep the impatience from his voice. 'And being in military dress uniform amongst this crowd would have had a slight fancy-dress air about it, don't you think?'

'Very dashing fancy dress, though, darling.' Leaning in close to make herself heard above the noise of the band, Sally fluttered her eyelashes, which were far too thick and lustrous to be anything but fake. 'Couldn't you have indulged us ladies?'

Kit's jaw clenched as he suppressed the urge to swear. To Sally Rothwell-Hyde and her circle of ladies who lunched, his uniform was just a prop from some clichéd fantasy, his medals were nothing more than covetable accessories. He doubted that it had crossed her mind for a moment what he had gone through to get them. The lost lives they represented.

His gaze moved over her sunbed-tanned shoulder as he looked for an escape route, but she wasn't finished with him yet. 'Such a shame about you and Alexia,' she pouted. 'Olympia said she was absolutely heartbroken, poor thing. She's taken Lexia skiing this weekend, to cheer her up. Perhaps she'll meet some hunky instructor and be swept off her skis…'

Kit understood that this comment was intended to make him wild with jealousy, but since it didn't he could think of nothing to say. Sophie was still dancing with Ralph, but more slowly now, both of his hands gripping her narrow waist while the band, ironically, played 'Can't Buy Me Love'. She had her back to Kit, so as she inclined her head to catch something his father said Kit could see the creamy skin at the nape of her neck and suddenly remembered the silky, sexy underwear that had spilled out of her broken bag yesterday. He wondered what she was wearing under that sober black dress.

'Is that her replacement?'

Sally's slightly acerbic voice cut into his thoughts, which was probably just as well. Standing beside him, she had followed the direction of his stare, and now took a swig of champagne and looked at him pointedly over the rim of her glass.

'No,' Kit replied shortly. 'That's Jasper's girlfriend.'

'Oh! *Really*?' Her ruthlessly plucked eyebrows shot up and she turned to look at Sophie again, murmuring, 'I must say I never really thought there was anything in those rumours.' Before Kit could ask her what the hell she meant her eyes had narrowed shrewdly. 'Who is she? She looks vaguely familiar from somewhere.'

'She's an actress. Maybe you've seen her in something.' His voice was perfectly steady, though his throat suddenly felt as if he'd swallowed gravel.

'An actress,' Sally repeated thoughtfully. 'Typical Jasper. So, what's she like?'

Lord, all that champagne and he didn't have a drink himself. Where the hell were the bloody waiters? Kit looked around as his mind raced, thinking of a suitable answer. *She's an unscrupulous liar and as shallow as a puddle, but on the upside she's the most alive person I've ever met and she kisses like an angel...*

'I'll get Jasper to introduce you,' he said blandly, moving away. 'You can see for yourself.'

Just as Sophie was beginning to suspect that the band were playing the Extended-Groundhog-Club-Remix version of 'Can't Buy Me Love' and that she would be locked for ever in Ralph Fitzroy's damp and rather-too-intimate clutches, the song came to a merciful end.

She'd been relieved when he'd asked her to dance as it had offered a welcome diversion from the task of Avoiding Kit, which had been the sole focus of her evening until then.

'Gosh—these shoes are murder to dance in!' she exclaimed brightly, stepping backwards and forcing Ralph to loosen his death-grip on her waist.

Ralph took a silk handkerchief from the top pocket of his dinner jacket and mopped his brow. Sophie felt a jolt of unease at the veins standing out in his forehead, the dark red flush in his cheeks, and suddenly wondered if it was lechery that had made him cling to her so tightly, or necessity. 'Darling girl, thank you for the dance,' he wheezed. 'You've made an old man very happy on his birthday. Look—here's Jasper to reclaim you.'

Slipping through the people on the dance floor, Jasper raised his hand in greeting. 'Sorry to break you two up, but I have people demanding to meet you, Soph. Pa, you don't mind if I snatch her away, do you?'

'Be my guest. I need a—' he broke off, swaying slightly, looking around '—need to—'

Sophie watched him weave slightly unsteadily through the crowd as Jasper grabbed her hand and started to pull her forwards. 'Jasper—your father,' she hissed, casting a worried glance over her shoulder. 'Is he OK? Maybe you should go with him?'

'He's fine,' Jasper said airily. 'This is the standard Hawksworth routine. He knocks back the booze, goes and sleeps it off for half an hour, then comes back stronger than ever and out-parties everyone else. Don't worry. A friend of my mother's is dying to meet you.'

He ran lightly up the steps and stopped in front of a petite woman in a strapless dress of aquamarine chiffon that showed off both her tan and the impressive diamonds around her crêpey throat. Her eyes were the colour of Bombay Sapphire gin and they swept over Sophie in swift appraisal as Jasper introduced her.

'Sophie, this is Sally Rothwell-Hyde, bridge partner-in-crime of my mother and all round bad influence. Sally—the girl of my dreams, Sophie—'

An icy wash of panic sluiced through her.

Great. Just *perfect*. She'd thought that there was no way that an evening that had started so disastrously could get any worse, but it seemed that fate had singled her out to be the victim of not one but several humiliating practical jokes. Just as Olympia Rothwell-Hyde used to do at school.

'Pleased to meet you,' Sophie cut in quickly before Jasper said her surname.

'Sophie…'

Sally Rothwell-Hyde's face bore a look of slight puzzlement as her eyes—so horribly reminiscent of the cold, china-doll blue of her daughter's—bored into Sophie. 'I'm trying to place you. Perhaps I know your parents?'

'I don't think so.'

Damn, she'd said that far too quickly. Sweat was prickling between her shoulder blades and gathering in the small of her back, and she felt slightly sick. She moistened her lips. Think of it as being onstage, she told herself desperately as the puzzled look was replaced by one of surprise and Sally Rothwell-Hyde gave a tinkling laugh.

'Gosh—well, if it isn't that I can't think what it could be.' Her eyes narrowed. 'You must be about the same age as my daughter. You're not a friend of Olympia's, are you?'

Breathe, Sophie told herself. She just had to imagine she was in the audience, watching herself playing the part, delivering the lines. It was a fail-safe way of coping with stage fright. Distance. Calm. Step outside yourself. Inhabit the character. And above all resist the urge to shriek, *'A friend of that poisonous cow? Are you insane?'*

She arranged her face into a thoughtful expression. 'Olympia Rothwell-Hyde?' She said the loathed name hesitantly, as if hearing it for the first time, then shook her head, with just a hint of apology. 'It doesn't ring any bells. Sorry. Gosh, isn't it warm in here now? I'm absolutely dying of thirst after all that dancing, so if you'll excuse me I must just go and find a drink. Isn't it ironic to be surrounded by champagne when all you want is water?'

She began to move away before she finished speaking, glancing quickly at Jasper in a silent plea for him to rein back his inbred chivalry and keep quiet. He missed it entirely.

'I'll get—'

'No, darling, please. You stay and chat. I'll be back in a moment.'

She went down the steps again and wove her way quickly through the knots of people at the edge of the dance floor. Along the length of the hall there were sets of double doors out onto the castle walls and someone had opened one of them, letting in a sharp draft of night air. Sophie's footsteps stalled and she drank it in gratefully. It was silly—she'd spent the twenty-four hours since she'd arrived at Alnburgh freezing half to death and would have found it impossible to imagine being glad of the cold.

But then she'd have found it impossible to imagine a lot of the things that had happened in the last twenty-four hours.

A waiter carrying a tray laden with full glasses was making his way gingerly along the edge of the dance floor. He glanced apologetically at Sophie as she approached. 'Sorry, madam, I'm afraid this is sparkling water. If you'd like champagne I can—'

'Nope. Water's perfect. Thank you.' She took a glass, downed it in one and took another, hoping it might ease the throbbing in her head. At the top of the steps at the other end of the hall she could see Jasper still talking to Olympia Rothwell-Hyde's mother, so she turned and kept walking in the opposite direction.

She would explain to Jasper later. Right now the only thing on her mind was escape.

Stepping outside was like slipping into still, clear, icy water. The world was blue and white, lit by a paper-lantern moon hanging high over the beach. The quiet rushed in on her, as sudden and striking an assault on her senses as the breathtaking cold.

Going forwards to lean on the wall, she took in a gulp of air. It was so cold it flayed the inside of her lungs, and she let it go again in a cloud of white as she looked down. Far, far beneath her the rocks were sharp-edged and silvered by moonlight, and she found herself remembering Kit's voice as he told her about the desperate countess, throwing herself off the walls to her death. Down there? Sophie leaned further over, trying to imagine how things could have possibly been bleak enough for her to resort to such a brutal solution.

'It's a long way down.'

Sophie jumped so violently that the glass slipped from her hand and spiralled downwards in a shower of sparkling droplets. Her hand flew to her mouth, but not before she'd sworn, savagely and succinctly. In the small silence that followed she heard the sound of the glass shattering on the rocks below.

Kit Fitzroy came forwards slowly, so she could see the sardonic arch of his dark brows. 'Sorry. I didn't mean to startle you.'

Sophie gave a slightly wild laugh. 'Really? After what happened earlier, forgive me if I don't believe that for a second and just assume that's exactly what you meant to do, probably in the hope that it might result in another "accident" like the one that befell the last unsuitable woman to be brought home by a Fitzroy.'

She was talking too fast, and her heart was still banging against her ribs like a hammer on an anvil. She couldn't be sure it was still from the fright he'd just given her, though. Kit Fitzroy just seemed to have that effect on her.

'What a creative imagination you have.'

'Somehow it doesn't take too much creativity to imagine that you'd want to get rid of me.' She turned round, looking out across the beach again, to avoid having to look at him. 'You went to quite a lot of trouble to set me up and manipulate me earlier, after all.'

He came to stand beside her, resting his forearms on the top of the wall.

'It was no trouble. You were depressingly easy to manipulate.'

His voice was soft, almost intimate, and entirely at odds with the harshness of the words. But he was right, she acknowledged despairingly. She had been a pushover.

'You put me in an impossible position.'

'It wasn't impossible at all,' he said gravely. 'It would have been extremely workable, *if* I'd ever intended to let it get that far, which I didn't. Anyway, you're right. I do want to get rid of you, but since I'd have to draw the line at murder I'm hoping you'll leave quietly.'

'Leave?' Sophie echoed stupidly. A drumbeat of alarm had started up inside her head, in tandem with the dull throb from earlier. She hadn't seen this coming, and suddenly she didn't know what to say any more, how to play it. What had started off as being a bit of a game, a secret joke between her and Jasper, had spun out of control somewhere along the line.

'Yes. Leave Alnburgh.'

In contrast with the chaotic thoughts that were rushing through her brain, his voice was perfectly emotionless as he straightened up and turned to face her.

'I gather from Tatiana that Jasper's planning to stay on for a few days, but I think it would be best if you went back to London as soon as possible. The rail service on Sundays is minimal, but there's a train to Newcastle at about eleven in the morning and you can get a connection from there. I'll arrange for Jensen to give you a lift to the station.'

Sophie was glad she had the wall to lean on because she wasn't sure her legs would hold her up otherwise. She didn't turn to look at him, but was still aware of his height and the power contained in his lean body. It made her quail inside but it also sent a gush of hot, treacherous longing through her. She laughed awkwardly.

'Well, Major Fitzroy, you've got it all worked out, haven't you? And what about Jasper? Or have you forgotten him?'

'It's Jasper I'm thinking of.'

'Ah.' Sophie smacked herself comically on the forehead. 'Silly me, because I thought all this was for your benefit. I thought you wanted me gone because my face and my clothes and my accent don't fit and because I'm not scared of you like everyone else is. Oh, yes, and also because, no matter how much you'd like to pretend otherwise, you weren't entirely faking what happened earlier.'

For a second she wondered if she'd gone too far as some emotion she couldn't quite read flared in the icy fathoms of his eyes, but it was quickly extinguished.

'No.' His voice was ominously soft. 'I want you gone because you're dangerous.'

The anger that had fuelled her last outburst seemed suddenly to have run out. Now she felt tired and defeated, as the stags on the walls must have felt when the Fitzroy guns had appeared on the horizon.

'And what am I supposed to tell him?'

Kit shrugged. 'You'll think of something, I'm sure. Your remarkable talent for deception should make it easy for you to find a way to let him down gently. Then he can find someone who'll treat him with the respect he deserves.'

'Someone who also fits your narrow definition of suitable.' Sophie gave a painful smile, thinking of Sergio. The irony would have been funny if it hadn't all got so serious, and so horribly humiliating. 'Gosh,' she went on, 'who would have guessed that under that controlling, joyless exterior beat such a romantic heart?'

'I'm not romantic.' Kit turned towards her again, leaning one hip against the wall as he fixed her with his lazy, speculative gaze. 'I just have this peculiar aversion to unscrupulous social climbers. As things stand at the moment I'm prepared to accept that you're just a pretty girl with issues around commitment and the word "no", but if you stay I'll be forced to take a less charitable view.'

From inside came a sudden chorus of 'Happy Birthday to You.' Automatically Sophie looked through the window to where everyone had assembled to watch Ralph cut his birthday cake. The light from the huge chandeliers fell on the perma-tanned backs of the women in their evening dresses and made the diamonds at their throats glitter, while amongst them the dinner-suited men could have been the rich and the privileged from any era in the last hundred years.

I really, really do not belong here, Sophie thought.

Part of her wanted to stand up to Kit Fitzroy and challenge his casual, cruel assumptions about her, as her mother would have done, but she knew from bitter experience that there was no point. Inside, through the press of people, she could see Sally Rothwell-Hyde, all gleaming hair and expensive white teeth, as she sang, and suddenly Sophie was sixteen again, standing in the corridor at school with her packed trunk and her hockey stick beside her, watching through the glass doors of the hall as the other girls sang the school hymn and she waited for Aunt Janet to arrive.

She clenched her teeth together to stop them chattering, suddenly realising that she was frozen to the bone. Inside the rousing chorus of 'Happy Birthday' was coming to an end. If she went in now she could probably slip past unnoticed and reach the staircase while all eyes were focused on the cake.

Lifting her chin, she met Kit Fitzroy's eyes. They were as cold and silvery as the surface of the moonlit sea.

'OK. You win. I'll go.' She faked a smile. 'But do me a favour—spend some time with Jasper when I'm gone, would you? You'll like him when you get to know him.'

She didn't wait for his reply. Turning on her heel, holding herself very upright, she walked back to the door and pulled it open, stepping into the warmth just as the party-goers finished singing and burst into a noisy round of cheering and applause. Sophie paused as her eyes adjusted to the brightness in the hall. At the top of the steps at the far end an elaborate cake made to look like Alnburgh Castle stood on a damask-covered table, the light from the candles glowing in its battlements briefly illuminating Ralph's face as he leaned forwards to blow them out.

He seemed to hesitate for a moment, his mouth opening in an O of surprise. And then he was pitching sideways, grasping the tablecloth and pulling it, and the cake, with him as he fell to the floor.

CHAPTER EIGHT

'Somebody *do* something!'

Tatiana's voice, shrill with panic, echoed through the sudden silence. Before Sophie had time to process what had happened Kit was pushing past her, shrugging his jacket off as he ran across the hall towards the figure on the floor. The stunned onlookers parted to let him through, recognising by some mutual instinct that he was the person to deal with this shocking turn of events. As the crowd shifted and fell back Sophie caught a glimpse of Ralph's face. It was the colour of old parchment.

Kit dropped to his knees beside his father, undoing his silk bow tie with swift, deft fingers and working loose the button at his throat.

'Does anyone know how to do mouth-to-mouth or CPR?' he shouted.

The tense silence was broken only by the shuffling of feet as people looked around hopefully, but no one spoke. Before she could think through the wisdom of what she was doing Sophie found herself moving forwards.

'I do.'

Kit didn't speak or look up as she knelt down opposite him. Bunching up his dinner jacket, he put it beneath Ralph's feet.

'Is he breathing?' she asked in a low voice.

'No.'

Tatiana, supported now on each side by male guests, let out a wail of distress.

'Jasper,' Kit barked icily, 'take her to the drawing room. You can phone for an ambulance from there. Tell them the roads are bad and they'll need to send a helicopter. Do it *now*.'

Bastard, thought Sophie in anguish, glancing round to where Jasper was standing, his face ashen against his black dinner jacket, his eyes wide and glassy with shock. How dared Kit talk to him like that at a time like this? But his voice seemed to snap Jasper out of his trance of shock and he gathered himself, doing as he was told.

'Breathing or heart?'

He was talking to her, Sophie realised. 'Breathing,' she said quickly, and regretted it almost straight away. At the moment she could barely breathe for herself, never mind for Ralph too, but there was no time for second thoughts.

Kit had already pulled his father's shirt open and started chest compressions, his lips moving silently as he counted. Sophie's hand shook as she tilted Ralph's head back and held his jaw. His skin had a clammy chill to it that filled her with dread, but also banished any lingering uncertainty.

OK, so she'd only done this on fellow actors in a TV hospital drama, but she'd been taught the technique by the show's qualified medical advisor and right now that looked like Ralph's best hope. She had to do it. And fast.

Kit's hands stilled. 'Ready?'

For the briefest second their eyes met, and she felt an electrical current crackle through her, giving her strength. She took in a breath and bent her head, placing her mouth over Ralph's and exhaling slowly.

The seconds ticked by, measured only by the steady tide of her breath, the rhythmic movement of Kit's hands. They took it in turns, each acutely aware of the movements of the other. It was like a dance in which she let Kit lead her, watch-

ing him for cues, her eyes fixed unwaveringly on his as she
waited for his signal. Fifteen rapid compressions. Two long,
slow breaths.

And then wait.

Sophie lost track of time. She lost track of everything except Kit's eyes, his strong, tanned hands locked together on
Ralph's grey chest...the stillness of that chest. Sometimes
she thought there were signs of life—too tenuous for her to
feel relief, too strong for her to give up, so again and again
she bent her head and breathed for Ralph, willing the life and
heat and adrenaline of her own body into the inert figure on
the floor.

And then at last as she lifted her head she saw Ralph's
chest convulse in a sharp, gasping breath of his own. Her
gaze flew to Kit's face as he looked down at his father, pressing his fingers to Ralph's neck, waiting to see if a pulse had
returned. Except for the small frown of concentration between his brows it was expressionless, but a muscle twitched
in his jaw.

And then Ralph breathed again and Kit looked at her.

'Good girl.'

The sound of running feet echoed through the hall, breaking the spell. Sophie's head jerked round and she was surprised to see that the guests had all vanished and the huge
room was empty now—except for the helicopter paramedics
coming towards them, like orange-suited angels from some
sci-fi film.

Kit got to his feet in one lithe movement and dragged a
hand through his hair. For the first time Sophie saw that he
was grey with exhaustion beneath his tan.

'He's been unconscious for about seventeen minutes. He's
breathing again. Pulse is weak but present.'

A female paramedic carrying a defibrillator kit glanced
at him, then did a classic double take. 'Well done,' she said

in a tone that bordered on awestruck. 'That makes our job so much easier.'

'Come on, sweetheart. We can take over now.'

Sophie jumped. One of the other paramedics was kneeling beside her, gently edging her out of the way as he fitted an oxygen mask over Ralph's face.

'Oh, I'm so sorry,' she muttered, attempting to get to her feet. 'I was miles away…I mean, I wasn't thinking…'

Her dress was too tight and her legs were numb from kneeling, making it difficult to stand. Somehow Kit was beside her, his hand gripping her elbow as she swayed on her high heels.

'OK?'

She nodded, suddenly unable to speak for the lump of emotion that had lodged in her throat. Relief, perhaps. Delayed shock. Powerful things that made her want to collapse into his arms and sob like a little girl.

She had no idea why. Even when she was a little girl she couldn't ever remember sobbing so now was hardly the time to start. And Kit Fitzroy, who not half an hour ago had coldly ordered her to leave his family home, was definitely not the person to start on.

Raising her chin and swallowing hard, she stepped away from him, just as Jasper appeared.

'Soph—what's h—?'

He stopped, his reddened eyes widening in horror as the paramedics strapped his father's body onto the stretcher. Quickly Sophie went to his side, putting her arms around his trembling body.

'It's OK,' she soothed, suddenly poleaxed with exhaustion. 'He's alive, he's breathing and he's in the very best hands now.'

Briefly he leaned against her and she smelled the booze on his breath and felt his shoulders shake as he sobbed. 'Sophie, thank God you were here.' He pulled away, hastily wiping his eyes. 'I should go. To the hospital, to be with Mum.'

Sophie nodded.

'I'm afraid there's only room for one person in the helicopter,' the pretty blonde paramedic apologised as they lifted the stretcher. 'The rest of the family will have to follow by car.'

Momentary panic flashed across Jasper's face as he made a mental calculation of alcohol units.

'I can't—'

'I can.' Kit stepped forwards. 'Tatiana can go in the helicopter and I'll take Jasper.' His eyes met Sophie's. 'Are you coming?'

For a long moment they looked at each other. Blood beat in Sophie's ears and her heart seemed to swell up, squeezing the air from her lungs. She shook her head.

'No. No, I'll stay and make sure everything's OK here.'

For a few minutes—seventeen apparently, who knew?—they had shared something. A connection. But it was gone again now. She might just have helped to save his father's life, but that didn't alter the fact that Kit Fitzroy had made it very clear he wanted her out of Jasper's. And his. The sooner the better.

Hours later, standing in the softly lit corridor of the private hospital, Kit rubbed a hand over his stinging eyes.

He could defuse a landmine and dismantle the most complex and dangerous IED in extreme heat and under enemy fire, but he couldn't for the life of him work out how to get a cup of instant coffee from the machine in front of him.

Stabilised by drugs and hooked up to bags of fluid, Ralph was sleeping peacefully now. The hospital staff, hearing that Lord Hawksworth was on his way, had telephoned Ralph's private physician at home. He had arranged for Ralph to be admitted to the excellently equipped private hospital in

Newcastle, which looked like a hotel and had facilities for relatives to stay too. Once she was reassured that her husband wasn't in any immediate danger Tatiana, claiming exhaustion, had accepted the sleeping pill the nurse offered and retired to the room adjoining Ralph's. Jasper, who had obviously knocked back enough champagne to float half the British Navy, didn't need medication to help him sleep and was now snoring softly in the chair beside Ralph's bed.

Which just left Kit.

He was used to being awake when everyone else was asleep. The silence and stillness of the small hours of the morning were tediously familiar to him, but he had found that the only way of coping with insomnia was to accept it. To relax, even if sleep itself was elusive.

He groaned inwardly. Tonight even that was out of the question.

Back in Ralph's room a small light was on over the bed, by which Kit could see his father's skin had lost its bluish tinge. An image floated in front of his eyes of Sophie, lowering her head, her mouth opening to fill Ralph's lungs with oxygen, again and again.

He closed his eyes momentarily. Details he'd been too focused to take in at the time rising to the surface of his mind. The bumps of her spine standing out beneath the pale skin at the base of her neck. Her green gaze fixing on his in a way that shut out the rest of the world. In a way that showed that she trusted him.

He winced. In view of everything that had taken place between them that evening, that was something of a surprise.

But then there was quite a lot about Sophie Greenham that surprised him, such as her ability to make a cheap dress look like something from a Bond Street boutique. The way she'd stood up to him. Fought back. The fact that she could give the kiss of life well enough to make a dead man breathe again.

And another one feel again.

Rotating his aching shoulders, he paced restlessly over to the window, willing away the throb of arousal that had instantly started up inside him again.

The incident in the wine cellar seemed like days rather than hours ago, and thinking about it now he felt a wave of self-disgust. He had told himself he was acting in Jasper's best interests, that somehow he was deliberately seducing his brother's girlfriend *for his benefit*.

Locking his fingers behind his neck, Kit exhaled deeply and made himself confront the unwelcome truth Sophie had flung at him earlier. He had done it to prove himself right, to get some small, petty revenge on his father and score a private victory over the girl who had so unsettled him from the moment he'd first laid eyes on her. He had barely thought of Jasper at all.

But he forced himself to look at him now. Slumped in the chair, Jasper slept on, his cheek resting on one hand, his closed eyelids red and puffy from crying. He looked very young and absurdly fragile.

A pickaxe of guilt smashed through Kit's head.

Always look out for your weakest man—his army training overruled the natural inclination forged by his family circumstances. *Never exploit that weakness, or take risks with it.* Even when it had irritated the hell out of you for as long as you could remember.

Jasper might lack the steel Kit was used to in the men he served with, but that didn't give Kit the right to kiss his girlfriend, just to show that he could. And to enjoy kissing her, so much that he had spent the evening thinking of nothing else but kissing her again. Right up until the moment he'd ordered her to leave.

Horrified realisation jolted through him. He swore sharply.
'Are you OK there?'

Kit spun round.

A plump, homely-looking nurse had appeared on silent
feet and was checking the bag of fluid that was dripping into
Ralph's arm. She glanced at Kit.

'Can I get you anything—coffee perhaps?'

'No, thanks.' Picking up his car keys, he headed for the
door, his need for caffeine paling into insignificance in the
light of this new imperative. To get back to Alnburgh and
make sure that Sophie Greenham was still there. And that
she would stay. For as long as Jasper needed her.

The red tail lights of the last catering van had disappeared
under the archway and the sound of the engines faded into a
thick silence that was broken only by the distant hiss of the
sea. Shivering with cold and fear, Sophie turned and went
back inside, shutting the massive oak door with a creaking
sound that came straight from *The Crypt* and sliding the bolts
across with clumsy, frozen fingers.

She still felt weak with shock and there was a part of her
that wished she were in one of those vans, sweeping down
the drive to civilisation and a warm bed in a centrally heated
home. Going through the hallway beneath the rows of glassy
eyes, she hummed the opening lines of 'My Favourite Things',
but if anything the eerie echo of her voice through the empty
rooms made her feel more freaked out than ever. She shut up
again.

Her mind would insist on replaying events from the moment she'd seen Ralph fall, like one of those annoying TV
adverts that seemed to be on twice in every break. She found
herself hanging on to the memory of Kit's strength and as-
surance, his control of the situation. And the way, when her

resolve was faltering, he'd wrapped her in his gaze and said 'good girl'.

Good girl.

He'd also said an awful lot of other things to her tonight, she reminded herself with a sniff, so it was completely illogical that those two should have made such an impression. But he was the kind of stern, upright person from whom you couldn't help but crave approval, that was why it was such a big deal. And that was the biggest irony of all. Because he was also the kind of person who would never in a million years approve of someone like her.

Miserably she switched the lights out and went into the portrait hall.

Not just the person he thought she was—Jasper's two-timing girlfriend—but the real Sophie Greenham, the girl who had been haphazardly brought up on a bus, surrounded by an assortment of hippies and dropouts. The girl who had no qualifications, and who'd blown her chance to get any by being expelled from school. The girl whose family tree didn't even stretch back as far as her own father, and whose surname came—not from William the Conqueror—but from the peace camp where her mother had discovered feminism, cannabis and self-empowerment.

In her gilded frame opposite the staircase the superior expression on Tatiana's painted face said it all.

Sophie flicked off the light above the portrait and trailed disconsolately into the King's Hall. The chandeliers still blazed extravagantly, but it was like looking at an empty stage after the play had finished and the actors had gone home. She had to steel herself to look at the place where Ralph had collapsed, but the caterers had cleaned up so that no evidence remained of the drama that had taken place there only a few hours earlier. She was just switching the lights off when she noticed something lying on the steps. Her pulse quickened a little as she went over to pick it up.

Kit's jacket.

She stood for a second, biting her lip as she held it. It *was* very cold, and there was absolutely no way she was going to go upstairs along all those dark passageways where the countess's ghost walked to get a jumper. Quickly she closed her eyes and slid it across her shoulders. Pulling it close around her, she breathed in the scent of him and revelled in the memory of his kiss...

A kiss that should never have happened, she told herself crossly, opening her eyes. A kiss that in the entire history of disastrous, mistaken, ill-advised kisses would undoubtedly make the top ten. She had to stop this sudden, stupid crush in its tracks; it was doomed from the outset, which of course was why it felt so powerful. Didn't she always want what she knew would never be hers?

In the drawing room the fire had burned down to ashes. There was no way she was going to brave the ice-breathed darkness upstairs, so she piled logs on, hoping there was enough heat left for them to catch.

In the meantime she would keep the jacket on, though...

It was going to be a long, cold night.

Perched on its platform of rock above the sea, Alnburgh Castle was visible for ten miles away on the coast road, so by the time Kit pulled into the courtyard he already knew that it was entirely in darkness.

Lowering his head against the sabre-toothed wind, he let himself in through the kitchen door, remembering how he'd often done the same thing when he came home from boarding school for the holidays and found the place deserted because Ralph and Tatiana were at a party, or had gone away.

He'd never been particularly bothered to find the castle empty back then, but now…

Lord, she'd better still be here.

His footsteps sounded as loud as gunshots as he walked through the silent rooms. Passing the foot of the stairs, he glanced at the grandfather clock and felt a sudden beat of hope. It was half past three in the morning—of course—she'd be in bed, wouldn't she?

He took the stairs two at a time, aware that his heart was beating hard and unevenly. Outside the door to her room he tipped his head back and inhaled deeply, clenching his hand into a fist and holding it there for a second before knocking very softly. There was no answer, so, hardly breathing, he opened the door.

It was immediately obvious the room was empty. The curtains were undrawn, the moonlight falling on a neatly made bed, an uncluttered chest of drawers.

She might be in bed, he thought savagely. The question was, whose?

Adrenaline was circulating like neat alcohol through his bloodstream as he went back down the stairs. How the hell was he going to break the news to Jasper that she'd gone?

And that it was all his fault?

He headed for the drawing room, suddenly in desperate need of a drink. Pushing open the door, he was surprised to see that the fire was hissing softly in the grate, spilling out a halo of rosy light into the empty room. He strode over to the table where the drinks tray was and was just about to turn on the light beside it when he stopped dead.

Sophie was lying on the rug in front of the fire, hidden from view by the sofa when he'd first come into the room. Her head was resting on one outstretched arm, and she'd pulled the pins from her hair so that it fell, gleaming, over the white skin of her wrist like a pool of warm, spilled syrup. She was lying on her side, wearing a man's dinner jacket, but even though it was miles too big for her it couldn't quite disguise the swooping contours of her hip and waist.

He let out a long, slow breath, unaware until that moment that he'd been holding it in. Tearing his gaze away from her with physical effort, he reached for a glass and splashed a couple of inches of brandy into it, then walked slowly around the sofa to stand over her.

If the impact of seeing her from behind had made him forget to breathe, the front view was even more disturbing. Her face was flushed from the warmth, and the firelight made exaggerated shadows beneath the dark lashes fanning over her cheeks and the hollow above the cupid's bow of her top lip. Tilting his head, he let his eyes move over her, inch by inch, adjusting his jaded perception of her to fit the firelit vision before him.

She looked...

He took a swallow of brandy, hoping it might wash away some of the less noble adjectives that arrived in his head, courtesy of six months spent in the company of a regiment of sex-starved men. *Vulnerable*, that was it, he thought with a pang. He remembered watching her sleep on the train and being struck by her self-containment. He frowned. Looking at her now, it appeared to him more like self-protection, as if she had retreated into some private space where she was safe and untouchable.

He felt a sudden jolt pass through him, like a tiny electric shock, and realised that her eyes had opened and she was looking up at him. Like a cat she raised herself into a sitting position, flexing the arm she'd been sleeping on, arching her spine.

'You're back,' she said in a voice that was breathy with sleep.

He took another mouthful of brandy, registering for the

first time the sheer relief he'd felt when he saw her, which had got rather subsumed by other, more urgent sensations.

'I thought you'd gone.'

It was as if he'd dropped an ice cube down her back. Getting to her feet, she turned away from him, smoothing the wrinkled dress down over her hips. He could see now that jacket she was wearing was his, and a fresh pulse of desire went through him.

'Sorry. Obviously I would have, but I didn't think there would be any trains in the middle of the night.' There was a slight hint of sarcasm in her voice, but it was a pale echo of her earlier bravado. 'And I didn't want to leave until I knew how Ralph was. Is he—?'

'He's the same. Stable.'

'Oh.' She turned to him then, her face full of tentative hope in the firelight. 'That's good, isn't it?'

Kit exhaled heavily, remembering the quiet determination with which she'd kept fighting to keep Ralph alive, reluctant to take the hope away. 'I don't know. It might be.'

'Oh.' She nodded once, quickly, and he knew she understood. 'How's Tatiana? And Jasper?'

'Both asleep when I left. They gave Tatiana a sleeping pill.' He couldn't keep the cynicism from his tone. 'Unsurprisingly Jasper didn't need one.'

Sophie's laugh had a break in it. 'Oh, God. He'll be unconscious until mid-morning. I hope the nurses have a megaphone and a bucket of iced water.'

Kit didn't smile. He came towards the sofa and leaned against the arm, swilling the last mouthful of brandy around his glass so that it glinted like molten sunlight. Warily, Sophie watched him, hardly able to breathe. The fire held both of them in an intimate circle, sealed together against the darkness of the room, the castle, the frozen world beyond.

'He was very emotional. I know he's had a lot to drink, but even so…'

Sophie sat down on the edge of a velvet armchair. 'That's Jasper. He can't help it. He wears his heart on his sleeve. It's one of the things I love most about him.'

'It's one of the things that irritate me most about him,' Kit said tersely. 'He was in bits all the way to the hospital—sobbing like a baby and saying over and over again that there was so much he still needed to say.'

Bloody hell, Jasper, Sophie thought desperately. Coming out to his family was one thing. Getting drunk and dropping heavy hints so they guessed enough to ask her was quite another. 'He was upset, that's all,' she said quickly, unable to keep the defensiveness from her tone. 'There's nothing wrong with showing emotion—some people might regard it as being normal, in fact. He'd just seen his father collapse in front of him and stop breathing—'

'Even so. This is just the beginning. If he can't cope now—'

'What do you mean, this is just the beginning?'

Kit got up and went to stand in front of the fire, looking into the flames. 'Who knows how long this will go on for? The doctors are saying he's stable, which Tatiana and Jasper seem to think is just a stage on the way back to complete recovery.'

'And you think differently,' Sophie croaked. Oh, dear. Something about the sight of his wide shoulders silhouetted against the firelight had made it hard to speak. She tucked her legs up beneath her, her whole body tightening around the fizz of arousal at its core.

'He was without oxygen for a long time,' Kit said flatly.

'Oh.' Sophie felt the air rush from her lungs and felt powerless to take in any more to replace it. She had tried. She had tried so hard, but it hadn't been enough.

'So what are you saying?'

'I'm saying it's highly likely he won't come out of this. That at some point in the next few days Jasper's going to have to deal with Ralph's death.'

'Oh. I see,' she said faintly. 'That soon?' Something about the way he was talking set alarm bells off in some distant part of her brain. He's going to tell me he wants me to leave now, she thought in panic. Tonight, before Jasper gets back...

'I think so.' His voice was low and emotionless. 'And if I'm right, I think it would be better if he didn't also have to deal with the girl he's crazy about running out on him.'

Steeling herself as if against a blow, Sophie blinked in confusion. 'But...I don't understand. You asked me to go...'

Kit turned around to look at her. The firelight gilded his cheekbones and brought an artificial warmth to his cold silver eyes. 'Things have changed,' he drawled softly, giving her an ironic smile. 'And now I'm asking you to stay. You've played the part of Jasper's doting girlfriend for two days. I'm afraid you'll just have to play it a bit longer.'

CHAPTER NINE

KIT was used to action. He was used to giving an order and having it obeyed, working out what needed to be done and doing it, and in the days that followed trying to penetrate the dense forest of bureaucracy that choked the Alnburgh estate tested his patience to the limit.

He spent most of his time in the library, which was one of the few staterooms at Alnburgh to have escaped the attention of Tatiana's interior designer. A huge oriel window overlooked the beach, and on a day like today, when sea, sky and sand were a Rothko study of greys, the bleakness of the view made the inside seem warm by comparison.

Putting the phone down after yet another frustrating conversation with the Inland Revenue, Kit glanced along the beach, subconsciously looking for the slender figure, bright hair whipped by the wind, who had made it so bloody difficult to concentrate yesterday. But apart from a couple of dog walkers the long crescent of sand was deserted.

He turned away, irritation mixing with relief.

It had been three days since Ralph's heart attack, three days since he'd asked Sophie to stay on at Alnburgh, and things had settled into a routine of sorts. Every morning he drove a pale, shaken Jasper and a tight-lipped Tatiana to the hospital in Newcastle to sit at Ralph's bedside, though Ralph remained unconscious and unaware of their vigil. He stayed long enough to have a brief consultation with one of the team of medical staff and then returned to Alnburgh to avoid Sophie and begin to work his way through the landslide of overdue bills, complaints from estate tenants and un-followed-up quotes from builders and surveyors about the urgent work the castle required.

It was a futile task, of that he was certain. Often, as he came across yet another invoice from Ralph's wine merchant or Tatiana's interior designer, he remembered Ralph saying, *I have every intention of lasting a lot more than seven years.*

Now it looked as if he wouldn't make it to seven days, and his inexplicable refusal to acknowledge the existence of British inheritance tax probably meant that the Alnburgh estate was doomed. It would be sold off in lots and the castle would be turned into a hotel, or one of those awful conference centres where businessmen came for team-building weekends and bonding exercises.

Ironically, because in thirty-four years there Kit hadn't formed any kind of bond with the rest of his family.

He walked back to the desk, leaning on it for a moment with his arms braced and his head lowered, refusing to yield to the avalanche of anger and bitterness and sheer bloody frustration that threatened to bury him.

There's nothing wrong with showing emotion—some people might regard it as being normal.

Sophie's voice drifted through his head, and he straightened up, letting out a long, ragged breath. It was something that had happened with ridiculous regularity these last few days, when time and time again he'd found himself replaying conversations he'd had with her, thinking about things she'd said, and wondering what she'd say about other stuff.

It made him uncomfortable to suspect that a lot of the time she'd talked a lot of sense. He'd wanted to write her off as a lightweight. An airhead actress who was easy on the eye, and in other respects too, but who wasn't big on insight.

But if that was the case, why did he find himself wanting to talk to her so badly now?

Because Jasper was either drunk or hungover and Tatiana was—well, Tatiana, he thought wearily. Sophie was the only other person who hadn't lost the plot.

An outsider, just like him.

Sophie dreamed that she was being pulled apart by rough hands. She curled up tightly into a ball, hugging her knees to her chest, trying to stop shivering, trying to stop the hurting deep inside and calling out to Kit because he was the only one who could help her. She needed his strong, big hands to press down and stop the blood from coming.

She awoke to see a thin light breaking through the gap in the curtains. Her body was stiff with cold, and from the cramped position that she'd slept in, but as she unfurled her legs she felt a familiar spasm of pain in her stomach and let out a groan of dismay.

Her mind spooled backwards. Had it really been a month since that December night in Paris? Jean-Claude had called at the apartment in the early hours, reeking of wine and sweat and cigarettes, almost combusting with lust after an evening working on 'Nude with Lilies'. Bent double with period pain, Sophie had only gone down to let him in because she'd known he'd wake the whole street if she didn't. That might have been preferable to the unpleasant little scene that had followed. Jean-Claude had been unwilling to take no for an answer, and it was only thanks to the amount of booze he'd sunk that Sophie had been able to fend him off. He'd fallen asleep, snoring at ear-splitting volume, sprawled across the bed, and Sophie had spent the rest of the night sitting on a hard kitchen chair, curled around a hot-water bottle, deliberately not thinking of anything but the pain blossoming inside her.

Tentatively she sat up now, wincing as the fist in her belly tightened and twisted. Since she was thirteen she'd suffered seven kinds of hell every month with her period. The cramps always came first, but it wouldn't be long before the bleeding started. Which meant she'd better get herself to a chemist pretty quickly, since she hadn't come prepared and neither Tatiana nor Mrs Daniels were the kind of cosy, down-to-earth women she could ask for help. Just the thought of saying the words 'sanitary protection' to either of them brought her out in a cold sweat.

She got out of bed, stooping slightly with the pain, and reached for her clothes.

It was the coldest winter in forty years. The temperature in the castle hardly seemed to struggle above freezing, and Sophie was forced to abandon all ambitions of style in favour of the more immediate need to ward off death by hypothermia. This had meant plundering Jasper's wardrobe to supplement her own, and she'd taken to sleeping in his old school rugby shirt, which was made to keep out the chill of a games field in the depths of winter and was therefore just about suitable for the bedrooms at Alnburgh. She couldn't bear the thought of exposing any flesh to the icy air so pulled her jeans on with it, zipping them up with difficulty over her tender, swollen stomach, and grabbed her purse.

Going down the stairs, clutching the banister for support, she glanced at the grandfather clock in the hall below. Knickers, she'd slept late—Jasper would have gone to the hospital ages ago.

She felt a twist of anguish as she wondered if he'd been hungover again this morning. Sergio had been putting pressure on Jasper to let him come up and be with him through all this, and Jasper was finding it increasingly hard to deal with his divided loyalties. Sophie didn't blame him for trying, though. Kit had given her a hard enough time—what would he do to flamboyant, eccentric drama-queen Sergio?

Not kiss him, presumably...

'Morning. Just about.'

Talk of the devil. His sardonic, mocking voice startled her. That was why her mouth was suddenly dry and her heart had sped up ridiculously.

'Morning.'

She attempted to sound aloof and distracted, but as she hadn't spoken a word since she'd woken up she just sounded bad-tempered. He was wearing a dark blue cashmere sweater and in the defeated grey light of the bitter morning he looked tanned and incongruously handsome, like some modern-day heart-throb superimposed on a black and white background. Maybe that accounted for the bad-tempered tone slightly as well.

His deadpan gaze swept over her, one arched brow rising. 'Off to rugby training?'

She was confused for a second, until she remembered she was wearing Jasper's rugby shirt.

She faked an airy smile. 'I thought I'd give it a miss today and have a cigarette behind the bike sheds instead. To be honest, I'm not sure it's really my game.'

'Oh, I don't know,' he drawled quietly with the faintest smile. 'I think you'd make a pretty good hooker.'

'Very funny.' She kept going, forcing herself to hold herself more upright in spite of the feeling of having been kicked in the stomach by a horse. 'I'm going to the village shop. I need to pick up a few things.'

'Things?'

Bloody hell, why did she always feel the need to explain herself to him? If she hadn't said anything she wouldn't have put herself in the position of having to lie. Again.

'I'm coming down with a cold. Tissues, aspirin—that sort of thing.'

'I'm sure Mrs Daniels would be able to help you out with all that,' he said blandly. 'Would you like me to ask her?'

'No, thank you,' she snapped. The kicked-by-a-horse feeling was getting harder to ignore. She paused on the bottom step, clinging to the newel post as nausea rose inside her. The pain used to make her sick when she was younger and, though it hadn't happened for a few years, her body seemed to have developed a keen sense of comedy timing whenever Kit Fitzroy was around. 'I'll go myself, if that's OK? I wasn't aware I was under house arrest?'

From where she was standing his hooded eyes were on a level with hers. 'You're not.'

Sophie gave a brittle little laugh. 'Then why are you treating me like a criminal?'

He waited a moment before replying, looking at her steadily with those cold, opaque eyes. A muscle was flickering slightly in his taut, tanned cheek. 'I suppose,' he said with sinister softness, 'because I find it hard to believe that you've suddenly been struck with an urgent desire to go shopping when it's minus five outside and you're only half dressed.'

'I don't have time for this,' she muttered, going to move past him, desperate to escape the scrutiny of his gaze. Desperate for fresh air, even if it was of the Siberian variety. 'I'm dressed perfectly adequately.'

'I suppose it depends what for,' he said gravely as she passed him. 'Since you're clearly not wearing a bra.'

With a little gasp of outrage, Sophie looked down and saw that the neck of the rugby shirt was open wide enough to reveal a deep ravine of cleavage. Jasper's fourteen-year-old chest was obviously considerably smaller than hers. She snatched the collar and wrenched it together.

'Because I've just got out of bed.'

'And you're just about to rush into someone else's while Jasper's not here?' Kit suggested acidly.

That did it. The contempt in his voice, combined with another wringing cramp, made her lose her temper. 'No,' she cried, hands clenched into fists at her sides, cheeks flaming. 'I really *am* rushing to the village shop. In minus five temperatures and with stomach cramps that possibly register on the Richter scale, not because I *want* to, but because I'm about to start the period from hell and I am completely unprepared for it. So now perhaps you'll just let me go before it all gets messy.'

For a moment there was silence. Complete. Total. Kit took a step backwards, out of the orbit of her anger, and Sophie saw the spark of surprise in his eyes. And then the shutters went down and he was back in control.

'In that case you're not going anywhere,' he said with a faint, ironic smile. 'Or only as far as the library anyway—at least you won't freeze to death in there. Leave it to me. I'll be back as soon as I can.'

Sitting in the car and waiting for the fan to thaw the ice on the windscreen, Kit dropped his head into his hands.

He had always thought of himself as level-headed. Rational. Fair. A man who was ruled by sense rather than feeling. So in that encounter how come he'd emerged as some kind of bullying jailer?

Because there was something about this girl that made him lose reason. Something about her smile and her eyes and the way she tried to look haughty but could never quite pull it off that made him *feel* far too much. And still want to feel more.

Her body, for a start. All of it. Without clothes.

He started the engine with an unnecessary roar and shot forwards in a screech of tyres. Lord, no matter how incredible he found it, she was his younger brother's girlfriend and the only reason she was still here was because he'd ordered her to stay. That made two good reasons why he should be civil to her, so he'd better start by behaving less like a fascist dictator and more like a decent human being.

After that he could have a look through his address book and find someone who would be happy to supply him with the sexual release he so obviously needed before going back to his unit and channelling his energy into the blessedly absorbing task of staying alive.

Sophie managed to wait until Kit had left the library and shut the door before putting her hands over her burning cheeks and letting out a low moan of mortification.

Saints in heaven, why had she blurted all that out? She was supposed to be an *actress*. Why couldn't she ever manage to act mysterious, or poised, or *elegant*?

Especially around Kit Fitzroy, who must be used to silken officer's-wife types, with perfect hair and manners to match. Women who would never do anything as vulgar as swear or menstruate. Or lose their temper. Or kiss someone without realising they were being set up, or put themselves in a position where someone would want to set them up in the first place...

Women with class, in other words.

She let her hands drop again and looked up, noticing the room properly for the first time. Even seen through a fog of humiliation she could see straight away that it was different from the other rooms she'd been in at Alnburgh. There was none of the blowsy ostentation of the drawing room with its raw-silk swagged curtains and designer wallpaper, nor the comfortless, neglected air of upstairs. In here everything was faded, used and cherished, from the desk piled with papers in the window to the enormous velvet Knole sofa in front of the fire.

But it was the books that jolted her out of her self-pity. Thousands of them, in shelves stretching up to the high ceiling, with a narrow galleried walkway halfway up. Where she had grown up the only books were the few tattered self-help manuals that the women at the peace camp had circulated between themselves, with titles like *Freeing the Warrior Woman Within* and *The Harmonious Vegan*, and even when Sophie had managed to get hold of a book of her own from a second hand shop or jumble sale there had never been anywhere quiet to read it. She had always dreamed of a room like this.

Almost reverentially she walked along the bookcases, trailing her finger along the spines of the books. They were mostly old, faded to a uniform brown, the gold titles almost unreadable, but in the last section, by the window, there were some more modern paperbacks—Dick Francis, Agatha Christie and—joy—a handful of Georgette Heyer. Moving the faded curtain aside, Sophie gave a little squeak of delight as she spotted *Devil's Cub*, and felt a new respect for Tatiana. Maybe they did have something in common after all.

In her embarrassment she'd temporarily forgotten about the pain in her tummy, but the dragging feeling was back again now so she took Georgette over to the sofa and sank down gratefully. At the age of fourteen she'd fallen spectacularly in love with Vidal, and known with fervent adolescent certainty that she would never find a man who could match him in real life.

Her mouth twisted into an ironic smile. At fourteen everything seemed so black and white. At twenty-five, it was all infinitely more complicated. Her teenage self had never considered the possibility that she might meet her Vidal, only for him to dismiss her as…

Her thoughts stalled as a piece of paper slid out of the book onto her knee.

Unfolding it, she saw straight away that it was a letter and felt a frisson of excitement. The date at the top was thirty years ago, the writing untidy, masculine and difficult to read, but she had no trouble making out the first line.

My Darling—

Technically Sophie was well aware that it was wrong to read other people's letters, but surely there was some kind of time limit on that rule? And anyway, any letter that began so romantically and was found in a Georgette Heyer novel was begging to be read. With a sense of delicious guilt she tucked her knees up tighter and scanned the lines.

It's late and the heat is just about bearable now the sun has gone down. I'm sitting on the roof terrace with the remains of the bottle of gin I brought back from England—I'd rather like to finish it all right now, but I couldn't bear the thought of Marie throwing the bottle away in the morning. It was the one we bought in London, that you held underneath your coat when we ran back to the hotel in the rain. How can I throw anything away that's been so close to your body?

Oh, how gorgeous! Sophie thought delightedly, trying to imagine Ralph writing something so intimate. Or doing anything as romantic as dashing through the rain to ravish the woman he loved in a hotel room.

Thank you, my love, for sending the photograph of K in your last letter. He's growing up so quickly—what happened to the plump baby I held in my arms on my last visit to Alnburgh? He is a boy now—a person in his own right, with a real character emerging—such fearless determination! Saying goodbye to him was so much harder this time. I never thought that anything would come close to the pain of leaving you, but at least your letters keep me going, and the memories of our time together. Leaving my son felt like cutting out a piece of myself.

Sophie's heart lurched and the written lines jumped before her eyes. Was K referring to Kit? Thirty years ago he must have been a small boy of three or four. Breathlessly she read on.

I suppose I've learned to accept sharing you with Ralph because I know you don't belong to him in any real sense, but the fact that K will grow up thinking of R as his father makes me rage against the injustice of everything.
Why couldn't I have found you first?

Her mouth had fallen open. Incredulously she read the lines again. After thirty years the sense of despair in them was still raw enough to make her throat close, but her brain couldn't quite accept the enormity of what she was reading.

Ralph Fitzroy wasn't Kit's father?

The sound of the door opening behind her made her jump about a mile in the air. Hastily, with trembling, nerveless fingers, she slid the letter back between the pages of Georgette Heyer and opened it randomly, pretending to read.

'Th-that was quick,' she stammered, turning round to see Kit come into the room carrying a bulging carrier bag. He was wearing the dark blue reefer jacket she remembered from the train and above the upturned collar his olive tan glowed

with the cold. As he moved around the sofa he brought with
him a sharp breath of outside—of frost and pine and ozone.

'I sensed that there was a certain amount of urgency involved.'

He put the bag down on the other end of the sofa and
pulled out a huge box of tampons, which he tossed gently to
her. Catching it, she couldn't meet his eye. The embarrassment of having him buy her sanitary products had paled into
near-insignificance by the enormity of the discovery she'd
just made.

'Thanks,' she muttered, looking round for her purse.

Taking off his jacket, he looked at her, slightly guarded.
'You're welcome. It's the least I could do for being so—' a
frown appeared between his dark brows '—controlling. I'm
sorry.'

'Oh, please—don't be,' Sophie said quickly. She meant it.
The last thing she needed now was him standing here looking like the beautiful hero from an art-house film and being
nice, wrenching open the huge crack that had appeared in her
Kit-Fitzroy-proof armour after reading the letter.

He glanced at her in obvious surprise. 'I anticipated you'd
be harder to make up to,' he said, delving back into the bag,
pulling out the most enormous bar of chocolate. 'I thought
this might be needed, at least. And possibly even this.' He
held up a bottle.

'Gin?' Sophie laughed, though her heart gave another flip
as she thought of the letter, and Kit's mother and her unknown
lover drinking gin in bed while it poured down outside.

Oh, dear. Best not to think of bed.

Kit took the bottle over to a curved-fronted cupboard in
the corner of the room behind the desk. 'Mrs Watts in the
village shop, who under different circumstances would have
had a brilliant career in the CID, looked at the other things I

was buying and suggested that gin was very good for period pains.'

'Oh, God—I'm so sorry—how embarrassing for you.'

'Not at all, though I can't comment on the reliability of Mrs Watts's information.'

'Well, gin is a new one on me, but to be honest if someone suggested drinking bat's blood or performing naked yoga on the fourth plinth, I'd try it.'

'Is it that bad?' he said tonelessly, opening the cupboard and taking down a can of tonic water. Sophie watched the movements of his long fingers as he pulled the ring and unscrewed the gin bottle.

'N-not too bad this time. But sometimes it's horrendous. I mean, not compared to lots of things,' she added hastily, suddenly remembering that he was used to working in war zones, dealing with the aftermath of bombings. 'On a bad month it just makes it, you know...difficult.'

'There's some ibuprofen in the bag.' He sloshed gin into a glass. 'What does the doctor say?'

'I haven't seen one.' She wasn't even registered with one. She'd never really been in the same place for long enough, and Rainbow had always been a firm believer in remedies involving nettles and class B drugs. 'I looked it up on the Internet and I think it might be something called endometriosis. Either that, or one of twenty-five different kinds of terminal cancer—unlikely since I've had it for the last twelve years—appendicitis—ditto—or arsenic poisoning. I decided to stop looking after that.'

Kit came towards her, holding out a large glass, frosted with cold and clinking with ice cubes. 'You should see a doctor. But in the meantime try a bit of self-medicating.'

There was something about the sternness of his voice when combined with the faintest of smiles that made her feel as if she'd had a couple of strong gins already. Reaching up to take it from him, she felt herself blushing all over again.

'I don't have many unbreakable rules, but drinking hard spirits, on my own, in the middle of the morning is actually one I try to stick to. Aren't you having one too?' she said, then, realising that now he'd fulfilled his obligation he might be wanting to escape, added quickly, 'Unless you have something else you need to do, of course.'

'Not really. Nothing that won't keep anyway.' He turned away, picking up another log from the huge basket by the fireplace and dropping it into the glowing grate before going to pour another gin and tonic. 'I'm trying to go through some of the paperwork for the estate. It's in a hell of a mess. My father isn't exactly one for organisation. The whole place has been run on the ostrich principle for decades.'

'So Jasper gets his tendency to bury his head in the sand from Ralph?'

'I'm afraid so.' He sat down at the other end of the massive sofa, angling his body so he was facing her. 'And his tendency to drink too much and rely on charm to get him out of the more unpleasant aspects of life.' He broke off to take a large swig of his drink and shook his head. 'Sorry, I shouldn't be talking about him like that to you. To be fair, the womanising gene seems to have passed him by.'

'Yes.' Sophie's laugh went on a little too long. If only Kit knew the truth behind that statement. 'You're right, though. He and Ralph are astonishingly alike in lots of ways.'

She took a quick sip of her drink, aware that she was straying into dangerous territory. Part of her wanted desperately to ask him about the letter, or more specifically the shattering information it contained, but the rest of her knew she would never dare make such a personal assault on Kit Fitzroy's defences.

Silver eyes narrowed, he looked at her over the rim of his glass.

'Whereas I'm not like him at all.'

It was as if he had read her thoughts. For a moment she didn't know what to say, so she took another mouthful of gin and, nearly choking on it, managed to croak, 'Sorry. It's none of my business. I didn't—'

'It's fine.' Leaning back on the huge sofa, he tipped his head back wearily for a moment. 'It's no secret that my father and I don't get on. That's why I don't feel the need to spend every minute at his bedside.'

The room was very quiet. The only sounds were the hissing of the logs in the grate and the clink of ice in Sophie's glass as the hand that held it shook. Largely with the effort of stopping it reaching out and touching him

'Why?' she asked in a slightly strangled voice. 'Why don't you get on with him?'

He shrugged. 'It's always been like that. I don't remember having much to do with him before my mother left, and after she went you'd have thought we would have been closer.'

'Weren't you?'

'Exactly the opposite. Maybe he blamed me.' Kit held up his glass, looking through it dispassionately. The fire turned the gin the colour of brandy. 'Maybe he didn't, and just took it out on me, but what had previously been indifference became outright hostility. He sent me to boarding school at the soonest possible opportunity.'

'Oh, God, you poor thing.' Just thinking of her own brief boarding school experience made Sophie's scalp prickle with horror.

'God, no. I loved it. I was the only kid in the dorm who used to dread holidays.' He took a mouthful of gin, his face deadpan as he went on, 'He used to call me into the drawing room on my first evening home and go through my report, seizing on anything he could—a mark dropped here, a team captaincy missed there—and commenting on it in this strange, sarcastic way. Unsurprisingly it made me more determined to try harder and do better.' He smiled wryly. 'So then he'd mock me for being too clever and on too many teams.'

Sophie's heart turned over. She could feel it beating against her ribs with a rapid, jerky rhythm. The book, with its outrageous secret folded between the pages, stuck up slightly from the sofa cushions just inches from her right hip.

'Why would he do that?'

'I have no idea,' Kit drawled softly. 'It would be nice to think that he just wasn't someone who liked children, or could relate to them, but his unbridled joy when Jasper came along kind of disproves that. Anyway, it hasn't scarred me for life or anything, and I gave up trying to work it out a long time ago.'

'But you keep coming back here,' Sophie murmured. 'I'm not sure I would.' She looked down at the crescent of lemon stranded on the ice cubes in the bottom of her glass, letting her hair fall over her face in case it gave away how much of a howling understatement that was.

'I come back because of Alnburgh,' he said simply. 'It might sound mad but the place itself is part of my family as much as the people who live in it. And Ralph's approach to looking after the castle has been similar to the way he looked after his sons.'

She lifted her head. 'What do you mean?'

'All or nothing—five thousand pounds for new curtains in the drawing room, while the roof goes unmaintained.'

Their eyes met. He gave her that familiar brief, cool smile, but his eyes, she noticed, were bleak. Compassion beat through her, mixing uneasily with the longing churning in her tender stomach. *I know why it is*, she wanted to blurt out. *I know why he was always vile to you, and it isn't your fault.*

The moment stretched. Their gazes stayed locked together. Sophie felt helpless with yearning. The heat from the fire seemed to be concentrated in her cheeks, her lips...

She jumped out of her skin as the phone rang.

Kit moved quickly. He got to his feet to answer it so he didn't have to lean across her.

'Alnburgh.' His voice was like ground glass.

Sophie's hands flew to her face, pressing against her burning cheeks with fingers splayed. Her heart was galloping. From miles away, his voice reduced to a tinny echo, she could just make out that it was Jasper on the phone.

'That's good,' said Kit tonelessly. Then, after a pause, 'Ask her yourself.'

He held out the phone. Sophie couldn't look at him as she took it.

'Soph, it's good news.' Jasper's voice was jubilant. 'Dad's regained consciousness. He's groggy and a bit breathless but he's talking, and even managed a smile at the pretty blonde nurse.'

'Jasper, that's wonderful!' Sophie spoke with as much warmth as possible, given what she'd just found out about Ralph Fitzroy. 'Darling, I'm so pleased.'

'Yes. Look, the thing is, neither Ma nor I want to leave him while he's like this, so I was wondering if you'd mind very much if we didn't come back for dinner? Will you be OK on your own?'

'Of course.' Unconsciously she found her gaze moving back to Kit. He was standing in front of the fire, head bent, shoulders tensed. 'Don't worry. I'll be fine.'

'The other thing is,' Jasper said apologetically, 'Ma gave Mrs Daniels the day off...'

Sophie laughed. 'Believe it or not, some of us have evolved to the stage where we can survive without staff. Now, go and give Ralph...my regards.'

Her smile faded quickly as she put the phone down. The room was quiet again, as if it were waiting.

'They're not coming back,' she said, trying to sound casual. 'He just wanted to check we'd be OK, since it's Mrs Daniels' day off and I'm not known for my culinary skills.' She gave a nervous laugh. 'Where's the nearest Indian takeaway?'

'Hawksworth.' Kit turned round. His face was blank. 'But forget takeaway. I don't know about you but I need to get away from here. Let's go out.'

CHAPTER TEN

It's not a date, it's not a date, it's not a date.

Sophie looked at herself sternly in the mirror as she yanked a comb roughly through her wet hair. After a walk on the beach this afternoon it had needed washing anyway. She wasn't making any special effort because she was going out for dinner with Kit.

Her stomach dipped. *Period pain*, she told herself.

It would be rude not to make a little bit of effort, and, after being shut up at Alnburgh for days without seeing a soul apart from the odd dog walker on the beach, it was actually pretty good to have an excuse to liven up her corpselike pallor with blusher and put on something that wasn't chosen solely for its insulating properties.

But what?

She stopped combing, and stood still, her mind running over the possibilities. She was sick and tired of jeans, but discounting them only left the black shroud, the vampire corset thing or the Chinese silk dress Jasper had ruled out for Ralph's party on the grounds that it was too sexy. Tapping a finger against her lip, she considered.

It's not a date...

Absolutely not. But she wasn't wearing the shroud. And the corset would look as if a she were meeting a client and charging for it. The Chinese silk it would have to be.

A wave of undeniable nervousness rolled through her and she had to sit down on the edge of the bed. She was being ridiculous, getting dressed up and wound up about a dinner arrangement that was based purely on practical and logical reasons. Jasper wasn't coming back, Mrs Daniels was away, neither of them could cook and they were both going stir-crazy from being cooped up in the castle for too long. Unlike every other dinner invitation she'd ever had, this one very definitely wasn't the opening move in a game that would finish up in bed.

No matter how fantastic she sensed going to bed with Kit Fitzroy would be.

Stop it, she told herself crossly, getting up and slapping foundation onto her flushed cheeks. This was nothing to do with sex. That look that had passed between them in the library earlier had *not* been the precursor to a kiss...a kiss that would have led to who-knew-what if the phone hadn't rung. *No*. It was about finally, miraculously putting their differences behind them. Talking. About her being there at a rare moment when he had needed to offload.

She sighed. The trouble was, in a lot of ways that felt a whole lot more special and intimate than sex.

Her hands were shaking so much it took three goes to get her trademark eyeliner flick right. Then there was nothing else to do but put on the Chinese silk dress. She shivered as the thick crimson silk slid over her body, pulling tight as she did up the zip.

'*It's not a date*,' she muttered one more time, pulling a severe face at her reflection in the little mirror above the sink. But her eyes still glittered with excitement.

In the library Kit put down the folder of Inland Revenue correspondence he'd been going through and looked at his watch.

Seven o'clock—his lip curled slightly—about three minutes later than the last time he'd checked.

He got up, stretching his aching back and feeling fleetingly glad that he didn't have a desk job. He felt stiff and tired and restless; frustrated from being inside all day and surrounded by papers. That was all it was. Nothing to do with the persistent throb of desire that had made concentrating on tax impossible, or the fact that his mind kept going back to that moment on the sofa just before the phone rang.

The moment when he had been about to kiss her. Again. Only this time it wouldn't have been because he was trying to prove anything or score points or catch her out, but because he wanted to. *Needed* to.

Letting out a ragged sigh, he ran his hands through his hair and down over his face.

What the hell was he doing asking her out to dinner?

He was looking after her for Jasper, that was all. Trying to make up a little for the unrelenting misery of her visit, and for boring her with his life story earlier.

Especially for that.

It wasn't a *date* or anything.

Grimly he turned the lights out in the library and strode through into the hall, rubbing a hand across his chin and feeling the rasp of stubble. As he went into the portrait hall he heard footsteps echoing on the stone stairs and looked up.

His throat closed and his heart sank. He had to clench his teeth together to stop himself from swearing.

Because she was beautiful. Undeniably, obviously, hit-you-between-the-eyes beautiful, and it was going to be impossible to sit across a table from her all evening and not be aware of that for every minute. She was wearing a dress of Chinese silk that hugged her body like a second skin, but was high-necked and low-hemmed enough to look oddly demure.

Her footsteps slowed. She was looking at him, her expression uncertain, and it struck him that she was waiting for his reaction.

Swiftly he cleared his throat, rubbing his jaw again to unclench it. 'You look…great,' he said gruffly. He'd been about to say beautiful, but stopped himself at the last minute. It seemed too intimate.

'I'm way overdressed.' She'd come to a standstill halfway down the stairs and turned around, preparing to bolt back up again. 'I didn't really have anything else, but I can put on jeans—'

'No.'

The word came out more forcefully than he'd meant and echoed off the stone walls. Her eyes widened with shock, but she didn't move.

'You're fine as you are, and I'm starving. Let's just go, shall we?'

He took her to a restaurant in Hawksworth. Tucked away in a small courtyard off the market square, it had a low-beamed ceiling, a stone-flagged floor and fires burning in each of its two rooms. Candles stuck into old wine bottles flickered on every table, throwing uneven shadows on the rough stone walls. Thanks to these it was mercifully dark and Sophie felt able to relax a little bit in her too-smart dress.

'You were right,' she said brightly, studying the menu without taking in a single thing on it. 'It is good to be away from the castle. And it's good to be warm, too.'

The maître d', recognising Kit, had shown them to the best table in a quiet corner of the far room, next to the fire. Its warmth stole into Sophie's body, but somehow she couldn't stop herself from shivering.

'Alnburgh hasn't quite lived up to your expectations, then?' Kit asked dryly as he studied the wine list, and Sophie remembered that journey from the station in the back of the Bentley when she'd seen the castle for the first time.

'Let's just say I'm a big fan of central heating. When I was little I used to think that I wouldn't mind where I lived as long as it was warm.'

Oh, dear, that was a stupid thing to say. She looked down, picking bits of fossilised wax off the wine bottle candle-holder with a fingernail and hoping he wouldn't pick up the subject of when she was little. The last thing she wanted to talk about was her childhood.

Actually, come to think of it, there were quite a lot of things she didn't want to talk about. Or couldn't. She'd better not drink too much or she'd be letting skeletons, and Jasper, out of the closet by dessert time.

'So where *do* you live?' he asked, putting the menu down and looking at her directly.

'Crouch End.' Beneath his gaze she felt ridiculously shy. 'I share a flat with a girl called Jess. Or I did, but then I went to Paris for two months for the Resistance film and when I got back her boyfriend had moved in. I guess it might be time to look for somewhere else.'

'Would you move in with Jasper?'

She shook her head, suppressing a rueful smile as she imagined Sergio's reaction if she did. 'I love Jasper, but it's not—'

She stopped as the waitress appeared; a slim, dark-skinned girl who slid a pencil out of her casually piled up hair to take their order. Sophie, who couldn't remember a single thing from the menu, spotted linguine on the specials board behind Kit and ordered that, cursing herself almost instantly for choosing something so inelegant to eat.

No sooner had the waitress sauntered off with catwalk grace than the maître d' brought a dish of olives and the wine, pouring it into glasses the size of goldfish bowls with a great deal of theatre. Sophie's pulse went into overdrive as the incident in the wine cellar came rushing back to her. Looking away, she felt her cheeks flame and wondered if Kit was remembering the same thing.

When they were alone again he raised his glass and said, 'Go on.'

She made a dismissive gesture, deliberately choosing to misremember where she'd got up to. Jasper was probably one of the subjects best placed on the 'Avoid' list.

'So anyway, I'll probably be flat-hunting when I get back to London, unless I stick it out at Love Central until I find out if I've got the vampire film role, because that'll involve about four weeks' filming in Romania...' She picked up her glass and took a huge mouthful, just to shut herself up. The glass was even bigger than she thought and some of the wine dripped down her chin, reminding her even more painfully of the port.

'Is it a big part?'

Kit's voice was low. In contrast to her he was utterly relaxed, his face impassive in the firelight. But why wouldn't he be relaxed? she thought despairingly. He didn't have a thumping great crush to hide, as well as most of the truth about himself.

'No. Lots of scenes but not many lines, which is perfect—' She looked up at him from under her lashes with a grimace of embarrassment. 'The only downside is the costume. My agent is always sending me scripts for bigger parts, but I don't want to go down that route. I'm quite neurotic enough as it is.'

Aware that she was babbling again, she picked up an olive, putting it in her mouth and sucking the salty oil off her fingers while she steadied herself to continue. 'I love what I do now,' she said more slowly. 'It's fun and there's no pressure. I'm not trained or anything and I just fell into it by chance, but it means I get to travel and do interesting things, and pick up the odd useful skill too.'

The waitress arrived and set plates down between them before sauntering off again.

'Such as?'

Kit's eyes were heavy-lidded, dark-lashed, gleaming.

Sophie looked down, knowing for certain there was no way she was going to be able to eat linguine when her stomach was already in knots. She picked up her fork anyway.

'Let me see… Archery. You never know when you might have to face an invading army with only a bow and arrow—especially at Alnburgh. Milking a cow. Pole dancing. Artificial respiration.'

Kit looked up at her in surprise. 'You learned that through acting?'

'I did a season in a TV hospital drama series.' She wound ribbons of pasta around her fork, assuming a lofty tone. 'I'm surprised you don't remember it actually—it was the highlight of my career, until the scriptwriters decided to kill me off in a clifftop rescue scene in the Christmas episode instead of letting me go on to marry the consultant and do another series.'

His smile was sudden and devastating. The firelight had softened his face, smoothing away the lines of tension and disapproval, making him look less intimidating and simply very, very sexy.

'Were you disappointed?'

She shook her head. 'Not really. It was good money but too much like commitment.'

'What, marrying the consultant or doing another series?'

The low, husky pitch of his voice seemed to resonate somewhere inside her, down in the region of her pelvis.

'Both.'

* * *

The place had emptied and the waitress was looking bored and sulky by the time Kit eventually stood up, stooping slightly to avoid the low beams as he went to sort out the bill.

Sophie watched him, her mouth dry, her trembling hands tucked beneath her thighs on the wooden bench. The gaps in the conversation had got longer and more loaded, the undercurrents of meaning stronger. Or so it had felt to her. Maybe he had just run out of things to say to her?

They drove back in silence. The sky was moonless, and veils of mist swathed the castle like chiffon scarves, making it look oddly romantic. Sophie's hands were folded in her lap and she held herself very stiffly, as if she were physically braced against the waves of longing that were battering at her. In the light of the dashboard Kit's face was tense and unsmiling. She gave an inward moan of despair as she wondered if he'd been totally bored by the whole evening.

He pulled into the courtyard and got out of the car immediately, as if he was at pains to avoid drawing the evening out a moment longer than he had to. Sophie followed, misery and disappointment hitting her more forcefully than the cold. For all her self-lecturing earlier, she had secretly longed to break through the barriers of Kit's reserve and rekindle the spark of intimacy that had glowed so briefly between them.

She caught up with him at the top of the steps as he keyed in the number.

'Thank you for a lovely evening,' she said in an oddly subdued voice. 'It seems awful to have had such a good time when Jasper and Tatiana are at the hospital. I hope Ralph is OK.'

'Given the mess Alnburgh's finances are going to be in if he dies, I do too,' Kit said sardonically as he opened the door. Standing back to let her through, he rubbed a hand across his forehead. 'Sorry. I didn't mean it to sound like that.'

'I know.'

She stopped in front of him, instinctively reaching up to touch the side of his face.

He stiffened, and for a moment she felt a jolt of horror at the thought that she'd got it badly wrong *again*. But then he dropped his hand and looked at her, and in the split second before their mouths met she saw desire and despair there that matched her own. She let out a moan of relief as his lips touched hers, angling her head back and parting her lips as he took her face between his hands and kissed her.

It was as though he was doing something that hurt him. The kiss was hard but gentle at the same time, and the expression on his face as he pulled away was resigned—almost defeated. Arrows of anguish pierced Sophie's heart and she slid her hand round his neck, tangling her fingers in his hair as she pulled his head down again.

The door swung shut behind them, giving a bang that echoed through the empty halls. They fell back against it, Sophie pressing her shoulders against the ancient wood as her hips rose up to meet his. Her hands slid over the sinews of his back, feeling them move as their bodies pressed together and their mouths devoured each other in short, staccato bursts of longing.

'Soph? Soph, darling, is that you?'

'Jasper,' she whimpered.

Kit pulled away, jerking his head back as if he'd been struck. They could hear footsteps approaching across the stone flags of the hall. Beneath the light of the vast lantern high above, Kit's face looked as if it had been carved from ice.

Helplessly Sophie watched him turn away, then, smoothing her skirt down, she went forwards, willing her voice not to give her away.

'Yes, it's me. We didn't expect you back so...'

Her words trailed off as Jasper appeared in the doorway.

His face was swollen and blotched from crying, and tears still slid from his reddened eyes.

'Oh, my darling—' she gasped.

Jasper raised his hands in a gesture of hopelessness. 'He died.'

And in an instant Sophie was beside him, taking him into her arms, stroking his hair as he laid his head on her shoulder and sobbed, murmuring to him in a voice that ached with love.

Over his shoulder she watched Kit walk away. She willed him to turn round, to look back and catch her eye and understand.

He didn't.

CHAPTER ELEVEN

AND SO, not quite a week after Ralph's lavish birthday party, preparations were made at Alnburgh for his funeral.

Kit returned to London the morning following Ralph's death. Sophie didn't see him before he left and though Thomas murmured something about appointments with the bank, Sophie, rigid with misery she couldn't express, wondered if he'd gone deliberately early to avoid her.

She was on edge the whole time. It felt as if her heart had been replaced with an alarm clock, like the crocodile in *Peter Pan*, making her painfully aware of every passing second. The smallest thing seemed to set her alarm bells jangling.

The bitter weather continued. The snow kept falling; brief, frequent flurries of tiny flakes that were almost invisible against the dead sky. Pipes in an unused bathroom burst, making water cascade through the ceiling in a corner of the armoury hall and giving the pewter breastplates their first clean in half a century. Thomas, who since Ralph's death seemed to have aged ten years, shuffled around helplessly, replacing buckets.

After that time in the hall Sophie didn't see Jasper cry again, but his grief seemed to turn in on itself and, without the daily focus of sitting at Ralph's bedside and the hope of his recovery to cling to, he quietly went to pieces. He was haunted by regret that he hadn't had the courage to come out about his sexuality to his father, driven to despair by the knowledge that now it was too late.

Sophie's nerves were not improved by a lonely, insecure Sergio ringing the castle at odd hours of the day and night and demanding to speak to Jasper. She fielded as many of the calls as possible. Now was not the time for the truth, but the charade had come to seem pointless and the main difficulty in Jasper and Sergio's relationship was not that it was homosexual but that Sergio was such an almighty, selfish prima donna.

On the occasions when Jasper did speak to Sergio he came off the phone with hollow eyes and a clenched jaw, and proceeded to get drunk. That was something else Sophie was worried about. It was becoming harder to ignore the fact that as the days wore on he was waking up later and making his first visit to the drinks tray in the library earlier.

But there was no one she could talk to about it. Tatiana barely emerged from her room, and Sophie sensed that speaking to Mrs Daniels or Thomas, as staff, would break some important social taboo. Of course, it was Kit that she really longed to talk to, but even if he had been there what could she say? Unless she was prepared to break Jasper's confidence, any concerns she expressed about his welfare would only serve to make Kit think more badly of her. Who could blame Jasper for drinking too much when his girlfriend had been about to leap into bed with his brother, while he was with his dying father?

As the week dragged on she missed him more and more. She even found herself counting the days to the funeral, where she knew she would see him again.

Looking forwards to a funeral, she told herself bleakly, was a mark of a truly bad person.

The day before the funeral Sophie was perched on top of a stepladder in the armoury hall. Taking down the antique pistols that had got soaked in the burst-pipe deluge, she dried them, one by one, as Thomas was anxious that, left alone, the mechanisms would rust. Sophie was very glad to have something to occupy her while Jasper huddled on the drawing room sofa, mindlessly watching horseracing.

Her roots were beginning to come through, and what she would really have liked to do was disappear into the bathroom with a packet of hair dye, but there was a line of shallowness that even she couldn't bring herself to cross. Anyway, the pistol-cleaning was curiously therapeutic. Close up, many of them were very beautiful, with delicate filigree patterns engraved into their silver barrels. She held one up to the light of the wrought-iron lantern, feeling the weight of it in her hand and wondering under what circumstances it had last been fired. A duel, perhaps, between two Fitzroy brothers, fighting over some ravishing aristocratic virgin.

The despair that was never far away descended on her again, faster than the winter twilight. If she was ravishing, or aristocratic—or a virgin for that matter—would Kit feel enough for her to want to fight for her?

Theatrically she pressed the barrel of the gun to her ribs, just below her breasts. Closing her eyes, she imagined him standing in front of her, in tight breeches and a ruffled white muslin shirt, his face tormented with silent anguish as he begged…

'Don't do it.'

Her eyes flew open. Kit was standing in the doorway, his face not tormented so much as exhausted. Longing hit her first—the forked lightning before the rumble of scarlet embarrassment that followed.

'Tell me,' he drawled coolly, picking up the stack of letters that had come in the last few days, 'had you considered suicide before, or is it being here that's driven you to make two attempts in the last week?'

Sophie made an attempt at a laugh, but it dried up in her throat and came out as a sort of bitter rasp. 'It must be. I was perfectly well adjusted before. How was your trip?'

'Frustrating.'

He didn't look up from the envelopes he was sifting through. Sophie averted her eyes in an attempt not to notice how sexy he looked, especially from her vantage point where she could see the breadth of his shoulders and the way his hair curled into the back of his neck, however, her nipples tingled in treacherous recognition. She stared at the pistol in her hand, polishing the barrel with brisk strokes of the cloth.

'I expect you'll be going back to London yourself when the funeral's over,' he said absently, as if it were of no consequence to him.

'Oh.' The idea had come out of the blue and she felt suddenly disorientated, and a little dizzy up there on the ladder. She took a quick breath, polishing harder. 'Yes. I expect so. I hadn't really thought. Are you going to be staying here for a while?'

He took one letter from the pile and threw the rest down again. 'No. I'm going back.'

'To London?'

To give her an excuse not to look at him she put the gun back on its hooks on the wall, but her hands were shaking and it slipped from her fingers. She gave a cry of horror, but with lightning reactions Kit had stepped forwards and caught it.

'Careful. There's a possibility that some of these guns might still be loaded,' he said blandly, handing it back to her. 'No. Not London. Back to my unit.'

For a moment the pain in Sophie's chest felt as if the gun *had* gone off.

'Oh. So soon?'

'There's not much I can do here.' For the first time their

eyes met and he gave a brief, bitter smile. 'And at least it's a hell of a lot warmer out there.'

Sophie's heart was thumping hard enough to shake the stepladder. She could tell from his offhand tone and his abstracted expression that he was about to walk away, and she didn't know when she would see him alone again, or get the chance to say any of the millions of things that flooded her restless head at night when sleep wouldn't come and she lay awake burning for him.

'I only came back to pick this up.' He held up the letter. 'I have an appointment with Ralph's solicitor in Hawksworth, so—'

'Kit—wait.' She jumped down from the stepladder, which was a bit higher than she thought, and landed unsteadily in front of him so he had to reach out a hand to grab her arm. He withdrew it again immediately.

Sophie's cheeks flamed. 'The other night—' she began miserably, unable to raise her head. 'I just wanted you to know that it wasn't a mistake. I knew what I was doing, and I—'

His eyes held a sinister glitter, like the frost outside. Beautiful but treacherous. 'Is that supposed to make it better?'

She shook her head, aware that it was coming out wrong. 'I'm trying to explain,' she said desperately. 'I don't want you to think that Jasper and I— It's not—we're not—'

Kit's mouth twisted into a smile of weary contempt. 'I'm not blaming *you* for what happened—it was just as much my fault. But I don't think either of us can really pretend it wasn't wrong.' Moving past her, he went to the huge arched door and put his hand on the iron latch. 'Like you, I don't have that many unbreakable rules but I wasn't aware until recently that one of them is that you don't touch your brother's woman. Under any circumstances.'

'But—'

'Particularly not just because you're both bored and avail-able.'

The cruelty of his words made her incapable of reply. The door gave its graveyard creak as he opened it and went out, leaving nothing but an icy blast of winter in his wake.

The windscreen wipers beat in time to the throbbing in Kit's head, swiping the snow from in front of his eyes. But only for a minute. No sooner was the glass clear than more snow fell, obscuring everything again.

It seemed hideously symbolic of everything else in his life right now.

In London, trying to make some sense of Alnburgh's nightmarishly complicated legal and financial position, he had come up against nothing but locked doors and dead ends. But at least there he had had some perspective on the situation with Sophie.

Being back within touching distance of her had blown it all out of the water again.

Was it her acting ability or the way she looked up at him from under her eyelashes, or the fact that watching her rub the barrel of that gun had almost made him pull her down off the ladder and take her right there, against the door, that made him want to believe her? Wanted to make him accept it without question when she said that a little thing *like being Jasper's girlfriend* was no obstacle to them sleeping together?

He pulled up in the market square and switched the car engine off. For a moment he just sat there, staring straight ahead without seeing the lit-up shops, the few pedestrians, bundled up against the weather as they picked their way carefully over the snowy pavements.

Since his mother had left when he was six years old, Kit had lived without love. He didn't trust it. He had come to re-alise that he certainly didn't need it. Instead he had built his life on principles. Values. Moral codes. They were what informed his choices, not *feelings*.

And they were what he had to hold on to.

He got out of the car and slammed the door with unnecessary force and headed for the offices of Baines and Stanton.

The Bull was beginning to fill up with after-work drinkers when Kit came out of his meeting with the solicitor. He knocked back his first whisky in a single mouthful standing at the bar, and ordered another, which he took to a table in the corner.

He intended to be there for a while; he might as well make himself comfortable. And inconspicuous. On the wall opposite he noticed the Victorian etching of Alnburgh Castle. It looked exactly the same now as it had done a hundred years ago, he thought dully. Nothing had changed at all.

Apart from the fact it was no longer anything to do with him because *Ralph Fitzroy wasn't his father.*

It was funny, he thought, frowning down into the amber depths of his glass, several whiskies later. He was a bomb-disposal expert, for God's sake. He was trained to locate explosives and disarm them before they did any damage, and all the time he'd been completely oblivious to the great big unexploded bombshell in the centre of his own life.

It explained everything, he mused as the whisky gave a sort of warm clarity to his thoughts. It explained why Ralph had been such a spiteful *bastard* when he was growing up. And why he had always refused to discuss the future of the estate. It explained…

He scowled, struggling to fit in the fact that his mother had left him with a man who wasn't his father, and failing.

Oh, well, it explained some things. But it changed everything.

Everything.

He stood up, his chest suddenly tight, his breath clogging in his throat. Then, draining his whisky in one mouthful, left the bar.

Wrapped in a towel, still damp from the bath, Sophie put her bag on the bed and surveyed the contents in growing dismay.

Out of long habit she hadn't ever bothered to unpack, so she couldn't, even for a moment, enjoy a glimmer of hope that there might be something she'd temporarily forgotten about hanging in the wardrobe. Something smart. And black. And suitable for a funeral.

Black she could do, she thought, rifling through the contents of her case, which was like a Goth's dressing up box. It was smart and suitable where she fell down.

Knickers.

How could she have been so stupid as to spend most of the day looking for displacement activities and polishing pistols when she could have nipped out to The Fashion Capital of the North, which must surely do an extensive range of funeral attire? But it was way too late now. And she was pretty much left with one option.

She'd balled her last unlucky purchase from Braithwaite's in the bottom of the bag, from whence she'd planned to take it straight to the nearest charity shop when she got back to London, but she pulled it out again now and regarded it balefully. It was too long obviously, but if she cut it off at the knee and wore it with her black blazer, it might just do…

Rubbing herself dry, she hastily slipped on an oversized grey jumper of Jasper's and some thick hiking socks and set off downstairs. It was late. Tatiana had retired to her room ages ago and had supper on a tray, Thomas had long since gone back to his flat in the gatehouse and Sophie had helped a staggering, slightly incoherent Jasper to bed a good hour ago, after he had fallen asleep on the sofa watching *The Wizard of*

Oz. However, the fact that all the lights were still on down-stairs suggested Kit hadn't come back yet.

Her heart gave an uneven thud of alarm. Passing through the portrait hall, she looked at the grandfather clock. It was almost midnight. Kit had said something about him going to see the solicitor—surely he should have been back hours ago?

Visions of icy roads, twisted metal, blue lights zigzagged through her head, filling her with anguish. How ridiculous, she told herself grimly, switching the light on to go down the kitchen steps. It was far more likely that he'd met some old flame and had gone back to her place.

The anguish of that more realistic possibility was almost worse.

She switched the kitchen light on. On the long table in the centre of the room a roast ham and roast joint of beef stood under net domes, waiting to be sliced up for the buffet at the funeral tomorrow. After that she'd be going back to London, and Kit would be leaving for some dusty camp somewhere in the Middle East.

Sophie felt her throat constrict painfully.

She'd probably never see him again. After all, she'd been friends with Jasper all these years without meeting him. She remembered the photo in the paper and wondered if she'd catch glimpses of him on the news from time to time. A horrible thought struck her: please, God, not in one of those reports about casualties—

She jumped as she heard a noise from the corridor be-hind her. It was a sort of rusty grating; metal against metal: the noise made by an old-fashioned key being turned in a lock—yet another piece from Alnburgh's archive of horror-film sound effects. Sophie turned around, pressing herself back against the worktop, the scissors held aloft in her hand—as if that would help.

In the dark corridor the basement door burst open.

Kit stood there, silhouetted against the blue ice-light outside. He was swaying slightly.

'Kit.' Dropping the scissors, Sophie went towards him, concern quickening inside her. 'Kit, what happened? Are you OK?'

'I'm fine.'

His voice was harsh; as bleak and cold and empty as the frozen sky behind him.

'Where's the car?' Her heart was pumping adrenaline through her, making her movements abrupt and shaky as she stepped past him and slammed the door. In the light from the kitchen his face was ashen, his lips white, but his eyes were glittering pools of darkness.

'In town. Parked in the square outside the solicitor's office. I walked back.'

'Why?'

'Because I was well over the limit to drive.'

He didn't feel it. No gentle, welcome oblivion for him. The six-mile walk home had just served to sharpen his senses and give a steel-edged sharpness to every thought in his head.

And every step of the way he'd been aware of the castle, black and hulking against the skyline, and he'd known how every potential intruder, every would-be enemy invader, every outsider, for God's sake, for the last thousand years had felt when confronted with that fortified mass of rock.

One thought had kept him going forwards. The knowledge that the six-foot-thick walls and turrets and battlements contained Sophie. Her bright hair. Her quick smile. Her irreverence and her humour. Her sweet, willing body...

'What happened?'

She was standing in front of him now, trembling slightly. Or maybe shivering with the cold. She was always cold. He frowned down at her. She appeared to be wearing a large sweater and nothing else. Except thick woollen socks, which only seemed to make her long, slender legs look even more delicious. They were bare from mid-thigh downwards, which made it hard to think clearly about the question she'd just asked, or want to take the trouble to reply.

'Kit? Was it something the solicitor said?'

She touched his hand. Her skin was actually warm for once. He longed to feel it against his.

'Ralph wasn't my father.'

He heard his own voice say the words. It was hard and maybe, just maybe a tiny bit bitter. Damn. He didn't want to be bitter.

'Oh, Kit—'

'None of this is mine,' he said, more matter-of-factly now, walking away from her into the kitchen. He turned slowly, looking around him as if seeing it all for the first time.

'It all belongs to Jasper, I suppose. The castle, the estate, the title…'

She had come to stand in the doorway, her arms folded tightly across her chest. She was looking up at him, and her eyes were liquid with compassion and understanding and…

'I don't.'

Her voice low and breathless and vibrating with emotion as she came towards him. 'I want you to know that I don't belong to Jasper. I don't belong to *anyone*.'

'And I don't have a brother any more.'

For a moment they stared at each other wordlessly. And then he caught her warm hand in his and pulled her forwards, giving way to the onslaught of want that had battered at his defences since she'd sat down opposite him on the train.

Together they ran up the stairs, pausing halfway up at the turn of the staircase to find each other's mouths. Kit's face was frozen beneath Sophie's palms and she kissed him as if the heat of her longing could bring the warmth back into his body. His jaw was rough with stubble, his mouth tasted of whisky and as he slid his hands up beneath the sweater she gasped at the chill of his hands on her bare breasts while almost boiling over with need.

'God, Sophie…'

'Come on.'

Seizing his hand, she ran onwards, up the rest of the stairs. Desire made her disorientated, and at the top she turned right instead of left, just as she had that first night. Realising her mistake, she stopped, but before she could say anything he had taken her face in his hands and was pushing her up against the panelled wall, kissing her until she didn't care where they were, just so long as she could have him soon.

Her hips ground helplessly against him, so she could feel the hardness of his erection beneath his clothes.

'My room,' she moaned. 'It's the other way—'

'Plenty more.' He growled against her mouth and, without taking his lips from hers, felt along the panelling for the handle of the door a few feet away. As it opened he levered himself away from the wall and stooped to hoist her up against him. She wrapped her legs tightly around his waist as he carried her forwards.

Sophie wasn't sure if this was the same room she'd stumbled into on her first night, or another one where the air was damp and the furniture draped in dust sheets. The window was tall, arched, uncurtained, and the blue light coming through it gleamed dully on the carved oak posts of an enormous bed.

As he headed towards it her insides turned liquid with lust. The room was freezing, but his breath was warm against her breasts, making her nipples harden and fizz. He was still dressed, the wool of his jacket rough and damp against her thighs. As she slid out of his arms and onto the hard, high bed she pulled it off his shoulders.

She was on her knees on the slippery damask bedspread

and he stood in front of her. His face was bleached of colour, its hard contours thrown into sharp relief, his heavy-lidded eyes black and fathomless.

He was so beautiful.

Her breath caught. Her hands were shaking as she reached out to undo the buttons of his shirt. He closed his eyes, tipping his head back, and Sophie could see the muscles quilt in his jaw as he fought to keep control.

It was one battle he wasn't going to win.

Gently now, she slid her hands beneath his open shirt, feeling him flinch with his own raw need. His skin still felt chilled. Tenderness bloomed and ached inside her, giving her desire a poignancy that scared her. She felt as if she were dancing, barefoot, free, but right on the edge of a precipice.

His shirt fell away and quickly she peeled off her jumper. Slowly, tightly, she wrapped her arms around him, pressing her warm, naked body against his cold one, cradling his head, kissing his mouth, his cheekbones, his eyes, his jaw as he lowered her onto the bed.

His heartbeat was strong against her breasts. Their ribs ground together as he undid his jeans with one hand and kicked them off. Sophie reached up and yanked at the damask cover so she could pull it over them, to warm him again. She was distantly aware of its musty smell, but she couldn't have cared less because he was cupping her cheek, trailing the backs of his fingers with exquisite, maddening lightness over her breast until her nerves screamed with desperation.

Reality blurred into a dreamlike haze where she was aware of nothing but his skin against hers, his breath in her ear, his lips on her neck. She kept her eyes fixed on his, swimming in their gleaming depths as beneath the sheets his hands discovered her body.

And with each stroke of his palm, each well-placed brush of his fingers she was discovering herself. Sex was something she was relaxed about, comfortable with. She knew what she was doing, and she enjoyed it. It was *fun*.

And this was as far removed from anything she'd ever felt before as silk was from sackcloth. This wasn't fun, it was essential. As he entered her, gently, deeply, she wasn't sure if it was more like dying or being born again.

Her cry of need hung in the frigid air.

She had never known anything more perfect. For a moment they were both still, adjusting to the new bliss of being joined together, and, looking into his eyes, she wanted to make it last for ever.

But it was impossible. Her body was already crying out for more, her hips beginning to move of their own accord, picking up their rhythm from him. His thumb brushed over her lips, and she caught it between her teeth as with the other hand he found her clitoris, moving his fingertip over it with every slow, powerful thrust.

The thick, ages-old silence of the room pooled around them again. The massive bed was too strong to creak as their bodies moved. Sophie wanted to look at him for ever. She wanted to hold for a lifetime the image of his perfect face, close to hers, as she spiralled helplessly into the most profound chasm of sensation. Their legs were entwined, his muscles hard against hers, and she didn't know where he ended and she began.

She didn't know anything any more. As a second cry—her high, broken sob of release—shattered the stillness she could only feel that everything she'd ever thought she believed was ashes and dust.

Kit slept.

Whether it was the whisky or the six-mile walk or the shattering, deathlike orgasm he didn't know, but for the first time in years he slept like the angels.

He woke as the sun was coming up, streaking the sky with

rose-pink ribbons and filling the room with the melting light of dawn. In his arms Sophie slept on, her back pressed against his chest, her bottom warm and deliciously soft against his thighs.

Or, more specifically, against his erection.

Gritting his teeth, he willed it away as remorse began to ebb through him, dissolving the haze of repletion and leaving him staring reality in the face. He closed his eyes again, not wanting to look at reality, or at Sophie, whose vibrant beauty had an ethereal quality in the pink half-light. As a way of blotting out the anger and the hurt and the shock of his discovery, last night had been perfect—more than he could have hoped for, and certainly more than he deserved. But it was a one-off. It couldn't happen again.

Sophie stirred in his arms, moving her hips a fraction, pressing herself harder against the ache of his erection. He bit back a moan, dragging his mind back from the memories of her unbuttoning his shirt, wrapping her arms around him and holding him when he most needed to be held, folding herself around him as he entered her...

The whisky might have blunted the pain and temporarily short-circuited his sense of honour, but it hadn't dulled his memory. Every detail was there, stored and ready for instant replay in the back of his head. A fact that he suspected was going to prove extremely inconvenient in the nights ahead when he was alone in a narrow bunk, separated from the rest of his men by the thinnest of makeshift walls.

Rolling out of bed, he picked his jeans up from the floor and pulled them on. The pink light carried an illusion of warmth, but the room was like a fridge and he had to clench his teeth together to stop them chattering as he reached into the sleep-warm depths of the bed and slid his arms under her.

She sighed as he gathered her up as gently as possible, but she didn't wake. Kit found himself fighting the urge to smile as he recalled the swiftness with which she'd fallen asleep on the train the first time he'd seen her, and the way it had both intrigued and irritated him. But, looking down into her face as he carried her down the shadowy corridor to her own room, the smile faded again. She was like no woman he'd ever known before. She'd appeared from nowhere, defiant, elusive, contradictory, and somehow managed to slip beneath his defences when he'd wanted only to push her away.

How had she done that?

With one shoulder he nudged open the door to her room. The window faced north, so no dawn sunlight penetrated here, and it was even colder, if that were possible, than the room they'd just left. It was also incredibly neat, he noticed with a flash of surprise, as if she was ready to leave at any moment. Her hair was fragrant and silken against his bare chest as he laid her gently down on the bed, rolling her sideways a little so he could pull back the covers and ease them over her.

Her eyes half opened as he tucked her in and she gazed up at him for a moment, her lips curving into a sleepy smile as she reached out and stroked the back of her hand down his midriff.

'It's cold without you,' she murmured. 'Come back.'

'I can't.' His voice was like sandpaper and he grasped her hand before it went any lower, his fingers tightening around hers for a moment as he laid it back on the bed. 'It's morning.'

She rolled onto her back and gave a little sighing laugh. 'It's over, you mean.'

'It has to be.' He pushed the heels of his hands into his eyes, physically stopping himself from looking at her as he spoke so his resolve wouldn't weaken. 'We can't change what we did last night, but we can't repeat it either. We just need to get through today without giving Jasper any reason to suspect.'

Against the pillow her face was still and composed, her hair spilling around it and emphasising its pallor. She closed her eyes.

'OK.'

The small, resigned word wasn't what he had expected and it pushed knives of guilt into his gut. Why was she making him feel as if this were his fault? Last night they had both been reckless but the result was just the logical conclusion to everything that had happened between them since the moment they'd met. It had felt inevitable somehow, but nonetheless forbidden.

Kit turned away and walked to the door, bracing his arm against the frame before he opened it and saying with great weariness, 'Sophie, what did you expect?'

Her eyes opened slowly, and the smile she gave him was infinitely sad.

'Nothing,' she said softly. 'Nothing.'

After he'd gone Sophie rolled over and let the tears spill down her cheeks.

He had slept with her because he'd finally found a get-out clause in his moral rule book. He no longer had a duty to Jasper, and that made it OK for him. But what about her?

Last night she thought he understood, without making her spell it out, that she wasn't betraying Jasper by sleeping with him.

It seemed he didn't.

She hadn't expected for ever. She hadn't expected declarations of undying love. Only for him to trust her.

CHAPTER TWELVE

'THE cars are here, madam.'

Thomas appeared in the hallway, his face rigidly blank as he made his announcement. But Sophie heard the slight break in his voice and felt the lump of emotion in her throat swell a little.

She mustn't cry. Not when Tatiana was holding herself together with such dignity. Getting into the gleaming black Bentley, she was the picture of sober elegance in a narrow-fitting black skirt and jacket, her eyes hidden by a hat with a tiny black net veil. Jasper got in beside her. He was grey-faced, hollow-cheeked, a ghost of the languid, laughing boy she knew in London. She noticed his throat working as he glanced at the hearse in front, where Ralph's polished coffin lay decked in white flowers, and as he settled himself in the back of the car he had to twist his hands together to stop them shaking.

Poor Jasper. She had to stay strong for him. Today was going to be such an ordeal, and his grief was so much more profound than anything she'd ever experienced. She dug her nails into her palm. And anyway, what did she have to cry about? She'd hardly known Ralph. And it was stupid, *stupid* to be upset over a one-night stand with a man she wasn't going to see again after today.

'After you.'

She looked up and felt her knees buckle a little. Kit was standing behind her on the steps to the castle, his perfectly tailored black suit and tie cruelly highlighting his austere beauty. His face was completely expressionless, and his silver eyes barely flickered over her as he spoke.

His indifference was like knives in her flesh. It was as if last night had never happened.

'Oh. I'm not sure I should go in the official car,' she stammered, looking down at her shoes. 'I'm not family or anything.'

'That makes two of us,' he murmured acidly. 'You're Jasper's girlfriend, that's close enough. Just get in—unless you're planning to walk in those heels.'

She did as she was told, but without any of the grace with which Tatiana had performed the manoeuvre, and was aware that Kit would have got a very unflattering view of her bottom in the tight black dress. She wondered if he'd seen that the hem was stuck up with Sellotape where she'd hurriedly cut it off at the knee this morning and hadn't had time to sew it.

Further evidence of her lack of class. Another reason for him to put her in the category of 'Women to Sleep With' (subsection: Once) rather than 'Women to Date'.

He got in beside her and an undertaker with a permanent expression of compassionate respect shut the door. Sophie found herself huddling close to Jasper so she could leave an inch of cream leather seat between her leg and Kit's. As the car moved silently beneath the arched gateway she bit her lip and kept her head turned away from him, her gaze fixed out of the window. But she could still catch the faint dry, delicious scent of his skin and that was enough to make the memories of last night come flooding back. She wished she could switch them off, as Thomas had switched off the water supply when the pipe had burst. But even if she could, she thought sadly, her body would still remember and still throb with longing for him.

The rose-pink sunrise had delivered a beautiful winter's day for Ralph's send-off—crisp, cold and glittering, just like the day of his party. The leaden clouds of the last grim week had lifted to reveal a sky of clean, clear blue.

Outside the church of St John the Baptist people stood in groups, stamping their feet to keep warm as they talked. Some were smartly dressed in black, but most of them wore everyday outdoor gear, and Sophie realised they must be local people, drawn by the social spectacle rather than grief. They fell silent and turned sombre, curious faces towards them as the cars turned into the churchyard.

'I forgot to bring the monkey nuts,' muttered Jasper with uncharacteristic bitchiness.

'People are curious,' said Tatiana in a flat, cold voice. 'They want to see if we feel things differently from them. We don't, of course. The difference is we don't show our feelings.'

Sophie bit her lip. She was one of those people, with her cheap dress and her Sellotaped hem. She wasn't part of the 'we' that Tatiana talked about. She wasn't even Jasper's girl-friend, for pity's sake. As they got out of the car and Jasper took his mother's arm to escort her into the church, Sophie tried to slip to the back, looking for Thomas and Mrs Daniels to sit with. A firm hand gripped her arm.

'Oh, no, you don't,' said Kit grimly.

He kept hold of her arm as they progressed slowly down the aisle of the packed church, behind Tatiana and Jasper and the coffin. Torn between heaven and hell at his close-ness, Sophie was aware of people's heads turning, curious eyes sweeping over her beneath the brims of countless black hats, no doubt wondering who she was and what right she had to be there. She felt a barb of anguish as she realised people must think she was with Kit.

If only.

'I am the resurrection and the life...'

Beside her Kit's hands were perfectly steady as he held his service sheet without looking at it. Sophie didn't allow herself to glance at him, but even so she knew that his gaze was fixed straight ahead and that his silver eyes would be hard and dry, because it was as if she had developed some supernatural power that made her absolutely instinctively aware of everything about him.

Was that what loving someone did to you?

She lifted her head and looked up at the stained-glass window above the altar. The winter sunlight was shining through it, illuminating the jewel-bright colours and making the saints' faces positively glow with righteousness. She smiled weakly to herself. It's divine retribution, isn't it? she thought. My punishment for playing fast and loose with the affections of Jean-Claude and countless others. For thinking I was above it all and being scornful about love...

There was a shuffling of feet as the organ started and the congregation stood up. Sophie hastily followed suit, turning over her service sheet and trying to work out where the words to the hymn were. She was aware of Kit, towering above her like some dark angel, as he handed her an open hymn book, tapping the right page with a finger.

'I vow to thee my country...'

It was a hymn about sacrifice. Numbly Kit registered the familiar lines about laying down your life for your nation and wondered what the hell Ralph knew about any of that. As far as Kit knew, Ralph had never put his own needs, his own desires anything but first. He had lived for pleasure. He had died, the centre of attention at his own lavish party, not alone and thousands of miles from home on some hot, dusty roadside.

He would never have sacrificed his happiness for the sake of his brother.

Was that yet another item on his list of character flaws, or evidence that he was a hell of a lot cleverer than Kit after all?

Kit let the hymn book in his hands drop and closed his eyes as the hymn reached its stirring climax. Everyone sat down again, and as Sophie moved beside him he caught a breath of her perfume and the warmth of her body on the arctic air.

Want whiplashed through him, so that he had to grip the back of the pew in front to steady himself. Kit had attended too many funerals, carried too many flag-draped coffins onto bleak airfields to be unaware that life was short. Rules and principles didn't help when you were dead.

Joy should be seized. Nights like the one he'd just spent with Sophie should be celebrated.

Shouldn't they?

In the elaborately carved pulpit supplied by another long-gone Fitzroy, the vicar cleared his throat and prepared to start his address. Kit forced himself to drag his attention away from Sophie's hands, resting in her lap. The skin was translucent pale against her black dress. They looked cold. He wanted to warm them, as she'd warmed him last night.

'We come together today to celebrate the life of Ralph Fitzroy, who to those gathered here was not just the Earl of Hawksworth, but a husband, father and friend.'

It was just sex. That was what she'd said on the phone the first time he'd seen her, wasn't it? Just sex. He had to forget it. Especially now, in the middle of a funeral...

'Let's just take a few moments of silent reflection,' the vicar encouraged, 'to enjoy some personal memories of Lord

Fitzroy, and reflect on the many ways in which he touched our lives...'

Ye Gods, thought Kit despairingly, rubbing at the tense muscles across his forehead. In his case, remembering the ways in which Ralph had touched his life really wasn't such a good idea. All around him he was aware of people reaching for tissues, sliding arms around each other in mutual support while he sat locked in the private dungeon of his own bitterness. Alone.

And then, very gently Sophie put her hand over his, lacing her cold fingers through his, caressing the back of his hand with her thumb with a touch that had nothing to do with sex, but was about comfort and understanding.

And he wasn't alone any more.

'Lovely service,' people murmured, dabbing their eyes as they filed out into the sharp sunlight to the strains of The Beatles singing 'In My Life'. That had been Jasper's idea.

'You OK?' Sophie asked him, slipping her arm through his as Tatiana was swept up in a subdued round of air-kissing and clashing hat brims.

'Bearing up.' He gave her a bleak smile. 'I need a drink.'

'What happens now?'

'We go back for the interment.' He shuddered. 'There's a Fitzroy family vault at Alnburgh, below the old chapel in the North Gate. It's tiny, and just like the location for a low-budget horror film, so I'll spare you that grisly little scene. Mum and I, and the vicar—and Kit too, I suppose—will do the honours, by which time everyone should have made their way back up to the castle for the drinks. Would you mind staying here and sort of shepherding them in the right direction?'

In spite of the sunshine the wind sweeping the exposed clifftop was like sharpened razor blades. Jasper was rigid with cold and spoke through clenched teeth to stop them chattering. Weight had dropped off him in the last week, Sophie noticed, but whether it was from pining for his father or for Sergio she wasn't sure. Reaching up, she pressed a kiss on his frozen cheek.

'Of course I will. Go and say your goodbyes.'

He got into the car beside Tatiana. 'Save a drink for me,' he said dismally. 'Don't let the hordes drink us dry.'

Sophie bent to look at him through the open door. 'Of course I will.'

She turned round. Kit was standing behind her, obviously waiting to get into the car, his eyes fixed on some point in the far distance rather than at her rear.

'Sorry.' Hastily Sophie stepped out of the way. 'Are you going to the interment too?' she added in a low voice.

A muscle twitched in his cheek. 'Yes. For appearance's sake. At some point Jasper and I need to have a proper talk, but today isn't the right time.' He looked at her, almost reluctantly, with eyes that were as bleak as the snow-covered Cheviots stretching away behind him. 'At some point you and I should probably talk too.'

An icy gust of wind whipped a strand of hair across Sophie's face. Moving her head to flick it out of the way again, a movement in the distance caught her eye. Someone was vaulting over the low wall that separated the graveyard from the road, loping towards them between the frosty headstones.

Oh, no... Oh, please, no... Not now...

Sophie felt the blood drain from her head. It was a familiar enough figure, although incongruous in this setting. A bottle of vodka swung from one hand.

'Today might not be the best time for that either,' she said, folding her arms across her chest to steady herself. 'You should go—I think they're waiting.'

It was an answer of sorts, Kit thought blackly as he lowered himself into the Bentley and slammed the door. Just not the one he'd hoped for.

As the car began to move slowly away in the wake of the hearse Kit watched her take a few steps backwards, and then turn and slip into the cluster of people left behind outside the church. He lost sight of her for a few seconds, but then caught a glimpse of her hair, fiery against the monochrome landscape. She was hurrying in the direction of someone walking through the churchyard.

'Such a lot of people,' said Tatiana vaguely, pulling her black gloves off. 'Your father had so many friends.'

Jasper put an arm around her. 'It was a great service. Even Dad, who hated church, would have enjoyed it.'

Kit turned his face to the window.

The man's clothes marked him out as being separate from the funeral-goers. He was dressed neither as a mourner nor in the waterproofs and walking boots of the locals, but in skintight jeans, some kind of on-trend, tailored jacket with his shirt tails hanging down beneath it. Urban clothes. There was a kind of defiant swagger to the man's posture and movements, as if he was doing something reckless but didn't care, and as the car waited to pull out onto the main road Kit watched in the wing mirror as Sophie approached him, shaking her head. It looked as if she was pleading with him.

The car moved again, and for a few seconds the view in the wing mirror was a blur of hedge and empty sky. Kit stared straight ahead. His hands were clenched into fists, his heart beating heavily in his chest.

He waited, counting the beats. And then, just before the bend in the road when the church would be out of sight, he turned and looked back in time to see her put her arms around him.

When she'd taken his hand in church like that, it had

changed something. Or maybe that was wrong—maybe it hadn't changed, so much as shown him what was there before that he hadn't wanted to admit.

That possibly what he wanted from her—with her—wasn't just sex. And the hope that, at some point, when she had settled things with Jasper, she might want that too.

It looked as if he'd been wrong.

'Please, Sergio. It won't be for long. A couple of hours—maybe three, just until the funeral is over.'

Sergio twitched impatiently out of her embrace. 'Three hours,' he sneered. 'You make it sound like nothing, but every hour is like a month. I've waited over a week already and I've just spent all day on a stupid train. I *need* him, Sophie. And he needs me.'

'I know, I know,' Sophie soothed, glancing back at the church with its dwindling crowd of mourners, and sending up a silent prayer for patience. Or, failing that, forgiveness for putting her hands round Sergio's elegant, self-absorbed neck and killing him.

What had Kit meant, they needed to talk? And why did bloody Sergio have to choose the very moment when she could have asked him to stage his ridiculous, melodramatic appearance?

'You don't,' Sergio moaned theatrically. 'Nobody knows.'

'I know that Jasper's in despair without you,' Sophie said with exaggerated patience. 'I know he misses you every second, but I also know that his mother needs him right now. And he needs to get closure on this before he can be with you properly.'

It was the right thing to say. 'Closure' was the kind of psychological pseudoscience that Sergio lapped up.

'Do you think so?'

'Uh-huh.' Sensing victory, Sophie took the bottle out of

his hand and began to lead him through the gravestones back in the direction from which he'd just come. 'And I also think that you're tired. You've had a horrible week and an exhausting journey. The pub in the village has rooms—why don't we see if they have anything available and I'll tell Jasper to join you there as soon as he can? It would be better than staying at the castle, just for now.'

Sergio cast a wistful glance up at Alnburgh Castle, its turrets and battlements gilded by the low winter sun. Sophie sensed rebellion brewing and increased her pace, which wasn't easy with her heels snagging into the frosty grass. 'Here—I'll come with you and make sure you're settled,' she said firmly. 'And then I'll go to Jasper and tell him where you are.'

Sergio took her arm and gave it a brief, hard squeeze, in the manner of a doomed character in a war film. His blue eyes were soulful. 'Thank you, Sophie, I do as you say. I *trust* you.'

The hallway was filled with the sound of voices and a throng of black-clad people, many of whom had been here only a week earlier for Ralph's party. After the surreal awfulness of the little scene in the Alnburgh vault Kit felt in desperate need of a stiff drink, but he couldn't go more than a couple of paces without someone else waylaying him to offer condolences, usually followed by congratulations on the medal.

His replies were bland and automatic, and all the time he was aware of his heart beating slightly too fast and his body vibrating with tension as he surreptitiously looked around for Sophie.

'Your father must have been immensely proud of you,' said an elderly cousin of Ralph's in an even more elderly fur coat. The statement was wrong in so many ways that for a moment Kit couldn't think what could have prompted her to make it. 'For the George Medal,' she prompted, taking a sip of sherry and looking at him expectantly.

It was far too much trouble to explain that such was his father's indifference that he hadn't told him. Oh, and that he wasn't actually his father either. Instead he gave a neutral smile and made a polite reply before excusing himself and moving away.

Conversation was impossible when there was so much that he couldn't say. To anyone except Sophie.

He had to find her.

'Kit.'

The voice was familiar, but unexpected. Feeling a hand on his arm, Kit looked around to see a large black hat and, beneath it, looking tanned, beautiful but distinctly uneasy, was Alexia.

'Darling, I'm so sorry,' she murmured, holding on to her hat with one hand as she reached to kiss each of his cheeks. 'Such a shock. You must all be devastated.'

'Something like that. I wasn't expecting to see you here.'

Kit knew that his voice suggested that the surprise wasn't entirely a pleasant one, and mentally berated himself. It wasn't Alexia's fault he'd seen Sophie falling into the arms of some tosser in a girl's jacket amongst the headstones, or that she'd subsequently disappeared.

'Olympia and I were in St Moritz last weekend, but when her mother told us what happened I just wanted to be here. For you, really. I know I wasn't lucky enough to know your father well, but...' Beneath her skiing tan her cheeks were pink. 'I wanted to make sure you're OK. I still care about you, you know...'

'Thanks.'

She bent her head slightly, so the brim of her hat hid her face, and said quietly, 'Kit—it must be a horrible time. Don't be alone.'

Kit felt a great wave of despair wash over him. What was this, International Irony Day? For just about the first time in his life he didn't *want* to be alone, but the only person he wanted to be with didn't seem to share the feeling.

'I'll bear that in mind,' he said wearily, preparing to make his escape. And no doubt he would, but not in the way she meant.

'Hello, Kit—so sorry about your father.'

If they were standing in the armoury hall, Kit reflected, at this point he would have had difficulty stopping himself grabbing one of the pistols so thoroughly polished by Sophie and putting it against his head. As it was he was left with no choice but to submit to Olympia Rothwell-Hyde's over-scented embrace and muster a death-row smile.

'Olympia.'

'Ma said you were an absolute *god* at the party, when it happened,' she said, blue eyes wide with what possibly passed for sincerity in the circles she moved in. 'Real heroic stuff.'

'Obviously not,' Kit said coolly, glancing round, 'since we find ourselves here...'

Olympia, obviously unaware that it was International Irony Day, wasn't thrown off her stride for a second. Leaning forwards, sheltering beneath the brim of Alexia's hat like a spy in an Inspector Clouseau film, she lowered her voice to an excited whisper.

'Darling, I have to ask... That redhead you sat next to in church. She looks terribly like a girl we used to know at school called Summer Greenham, but it *can't* be—'

Electricity snapped through him, jolting him out of his apathy.

'Sophie. She's called *Sophie* Greenham.'

'Then it *is* her!' Olympia's upper-crust voice held a mixture of incredulity and triumph as she looked at Alexia. 'Who can blame her for ditching that embarrassing drippy hippy name? She should have changed her surname too—apparently it came from the lesbian peace camp place. Anyway, darling, none of that explains what she's *doing* here. Does she work here, because if so I would *so* keep an eye on the family silver—'

'She's Jasper's girlfriend.' Maybe if he said it often enough he'd accept it.

'No way. No. *Way!* Seriously? Ohmigod!'

Kit stood completely still while this pantomime of disbelief was going on, but beneath his implacable exterior icy bursts of adrenaline were pumping through his veins.

'Meaning?'

Beside Olympia, Alexia shifted uneasily on her designer heels. Olympia ploughed on, too caught up in the thrill of gossip to notice the tension that suddenly seemed to crackle in the air.

'She came to our school from some filthy traveller camp—an aunt took pity on her and wanted to civilise her before it was too late, or something. Whatevs.' She waved a dismissive hand. 'Total waste of money as she was expelled in the end, for stealing.' She took a sip of champagne before continuing in her confident, bitchy drawl. 'It was just before the school prom and a friend of ours had been sent some money by her mother to buy a dress. Well, the cash disappeared from the dorm and suddenly—by astonishing coincidence—Miss Greenham-Extremely-Common, who had previously rocked the jumble-sale-reject look, appears with a *very* nice new dress.'

A pulse was throbbing in Kit's temple. 'And you put two and two together,' he said icily.

Olympia looked surprised and slightly indignant. 'And reached a very obvious four. Her aunt admitted she hadn't given her any money—I think the fees were quite enough of a stretch for her—and the only explanation Summer could give was that her mother had bought it for her. Her mother who lived on a *bus*, and hadn't been seen for, like, a *year* or something and so was conveniently unavailable for comment, having nothing as modern as a *telephone...*'

Looking down at the floor, Kit shook his head and gave a soft, humourless laugh. 'And therefore unavailable to back her up either.'

'Oh, come on, Kit,' said Olympia, in the kind of jolly, dismissive tone that suggested they were having a huge joke and he was spoiling it. 'Sometimes you don't need *evidence* because the truth is so obvious that everyone can see it. And anyway—' she gave him a sly smirk from beneath her blonde flicky fringe '—if she's Jasper's girlfriend, why would she have just been checking into a room in the pub in the village with some bloke? Alexia and I went for a quick drinkie to warm ourselves up after the service and saw her.' The smirk hardened into a look of grim triumph. 'Room three, if you don't believe me.'

If Sophie had known she was going to walk back from the village to the castle in the snow, she would have left the shag-me shoes at home and worn something more sensible.

It was just as well her toes were frozen, since she suspected they'd be even more painful if they weren't. Unfortunately even the cold couldn't anaesthetise the raw blisters on her heels and it was only the thought of finding Kit, hearing what it was he had to say that kept her going.

She also had to find Jasper and break the news to him that Sergio had turned up. Having ordered an enormous break-fast for him to mop up some of the vodka and waited to make sure he ate it, she had finally left him crashed out on the bed. He shouldn't be any trouble for the next hour or so, but now the formal part of the funeral was over she knew that Jasper wouldn't want to wait to go and see him. And also she was guiltily keen to pass over the responsibility for him to Jasper as soon as possible. Sitting and listening to him endlessly talking about his emotions, analysing every thought that had flickered across his butterfly brain in the last week had made her want to start on the vodka herself. She had found herself thinking wistfully of Kit's reserve. His understatement. His emotional integrity.

Gritting her teeth against the pain, she quickened her steps.

The drive up to the castle was choked with cars. People had obviously decided they were staying for a while, and parked in solid rows, making it impossible for anyone to leave. Weaving through them, Sophie could hear the sound of voices spilling out through the open door and carrying on the frosty air.

Her heart was beating rapidly as she went up the steps, and it was nothing to do with the brisk walk. She paused in the armoury hall, tugging down her jacket and smoothing her skirt with trembling hands, noticing abstractedly that the Sellotaped hem was coming down.

'Is everything all right, Miss Greenham?'

Thomas was standing in the archway, holding a tray of champagne, looking at her with some concern. Sophie re-alised what a sight she must look in her sawn-off dress with her face scarlet from cold and exertion, clashing madly with her hair.

'Oh, yes, thank you. I just walked up from the village, that's all. Do you know where Jasper is?'

'Master Jasper went up to his room when he got back from the interment,' said Thomas, lowering his voice respectfully. 'I don't think he's come down yet.'

'OK. Thanks. I'll go up and see if he's all right.' She hesitated, feeling a warm blush gather in her already fiery cheeks. 'Oh, and I don't suppose you know where I could find Kit, do you?'

'I believe he's here somewhere,' Thomas said, turning

round creakily, putting the champagne glasses in peril as he surveyed the packed room behind him. 'I saw him come in a little while ago. Ah, yes—there he is, talking to the young lady in the large hat.'

Of course, he was so much taller than everyone else so it wasn't too hard to spot him. He was standing with his back half to her, so she couldn't see his face properly, only the scimitar curve of one hard cheekbone. A cloud of butterflies rose in her stomach.

And then she saw who he was talking to. And they turned into a writhing mass of snakes.

CHAPTER THIRTEEN

A CHILDHOOD spent moving around, living in cramped spaces with barely any room for personal possessions, being ready to move on at a moment's notice, had left its mark on Sophie in many ways. One of them was that she travelled light and rarely unpacked.

Once she'd seen Jasper it didn't take her long to get her few things together. It took a little longer to get herself together, but after a while she felt strong enough to say goodbye to her little room and slip along the corridor to the back staircase.

It came out in the armoury hall. As she went down the sound of voices rose up to meet her—less subdued and funereal now as champagne was consumed, interspersed with laughter. She found herself listening out for Kit's voice amongst the others, and realised with a tearing sensation in her side that she'd never heard him laugh. Not really laugh, without irony or bitterness or cynicism.

But maybe he would be laughing now, with Olympia.

She came down the last step. The door was ahead of her, half-open and letting in arctic air and winter sunshine. Determined not to look round in case she lost her nerve, Sophie kept her head down and walked quickly towards it.

The cold air hit her as she stepped outside, making her gasp and bringing a rush of tears to her eyes. She sniffed hard, and brushed them impatiently away with the sleeve of her faithful old coat.

'So you're leaving.'

She whirled round. Kit was standing at the top of the steps, in the open doorway. His hands were in his pockets, his top button undone and his tie pulled loose, but despite all that there was still something sinister in his stillness, the rigid blankness of his face.

The last glowing embers of hope in Sophie's heart went out.

'Yes.' She nodded, and even managed a brief smile although meeting his eye was too much to attempt. 'I saw you talking to Olympia. It's a small world. I suppose she told you everything.'

'Yes. Not that it makes any difference. So now you're going—just like that. Were you going to say goodbye?'

Sophie kept her eyes fixed on the ivy growing up the wall by the steps, twining itself around an old cast-iron downpipe. Of course it didn't make any difference, she told herself numbly. He already knew she was nothing. Her voice seemed to come from very far away. 'I'll write to Tatiana. She's surrounded by friends at the moment—I don't want to barge in.'

'It was Jasper I was thinking of. What about him?'

Sophie moved her bag from one hand to the other. She was conscious of holding herself very upright, placing her feet carefully together, almost as if if she didn't take care to do this she might just collapse. She still couldn't bring herself to look at him.

'He'll be OK now. He doesn't need me.'

At the top of the steps Kit made some sudden movement. For a moment she thought he had turned and was going to go inside, but instead he dragged a hand through his hair and swung back to face her again. This time there was no disguising the blistering anger on his face.

'So, who is he? I mean, he's obviously pretty special that he's come all this way to claim you and you can't even wait until the funeral is over before you go and fall into bed with him. Is it the same one I heard you talking to on the train, or someone else?'

After a moment of confusion it dawned on Sophie that he must have seen her with Sergio. And jumped, instantly, to the wrong conclusion.

Except there wasn't really such a thing as a wrong conclusion. In her experience 'wrong conclusion' tended to mean the same thing as 'confirmation of existing prejudice', and she had learned long ago that no amount of logical explanations could alter people's prejudices. That had to come from within themselves.

'Someone else.'

'Do you love him?' Suddenly the anger that had gripped him seemed to vanish and he just sounded very tired. Defeated almost.

Sophie shook her head. Her knees were shaking, her chest burning with the effort of holding back the sobs that threatened to tear her apart.

'No.'

'Then why? Why are you going to him?'

'Because he'd fight for me.' She took a deep breath and lifted her head. In a voice that was completely calm, completely steady she said, 'Because he trusts me.'

And then she turned and began to walk away.

Blindly Kit shouldered his way through the people standing in the hall. Seeing his ashen face and the stricken expression on it, some of them exchanged loaded glances and murmured about grief striking even the strongest.

Reaching the library, he shut the door and leaned against it, breathing hard and fast.

Trust. That was the last thing he'd expected her to say.

He brought his hands up to his head, sliding his fingers into his hair as his mind raced. He had learned very early on in life that few people could be trusted, and since then he had almost prided himself on his cynicism. It meant he was one step ahead of the game and gave him immunity from the emotional disasters that felled others.

It also meant he had just had to watch the only woman he wanted to be with walk away from him, right into the arms of someone else. Someone who wore designer clothes and left his shirt tails trailing and *trusted* her. Someone who would fight for her.

Well, trust might not be his strong suit, but fighting was something he could do.

He threw open the door, and almost ran straight into the person who was standing right on the other side of it.

'Alexia, what the—?'

'I wanted to talk.' She recovered from her obvious fright pretty quickly, following him as he kept on walking towards the noise of the party. 'There's something I need to tell you.'

'Now isn't a good time,' he said, moving through the groups of people still standing in the portrait hall, gritting his teeth against the need to be far more brutally honest.

'I know. I'm sorry, but it's bothered me all these years.' She caught up with him as he went through the archway into the armoury hall and moved in front of him as he reached the door. 'That thing that happened at school. It wasn't Summer, it was Olympia. She set it all up. I mean, Summer—Sophie— did have the dress and I don't know how she got the money to pay for it, but it certainly wasn't by stealing it from the dorm. Olympia just said it was.'

'I know,' Kit said wearily. 'I never doubted that bit.'

'Oh.' Alexia had taken her hat off now, and without it she looked oddly exposed and slightly crestfallen. 'I know it's ages ago and it was just some silly schoolgirl prank, but hearing Olympia say it again like that, I didn't like it. We're adults now. I just wanted to make sure you knew the truth.'

'The truth is slightly irrelevant really. It's what we're prepared to believe that matters.' He hesitated, his throat suddenly feeling as if he'd swallowed arsenic. 'The other thing—about her checking into the hotel with a man. Was that one of Olympia's fabrications too?'

'No, that was true.' Alexia was looking at him almost imploringly. 'Kit—are you really OK? Can I help?'

From a great distance he recognised her pain as being similar to his own. It made him speak gently to her.

'No, I'm not. But you have already.'

He wove his way through the parked cars jamming the courtyard and broke into a run as he reached the tower gate. At the sides of the driveway the snow was still crisp and unmarked, but as he ran down he noticed the prints Sophie's high-heeled shoes had made and they made her feel closer—as if she hadn't really gone. When he reached the road through the village they were lost amongst everyone else's.

The King's Arms was in the mid-afternoon lull between lunchtime and evening drinkers. The landlord sat behind the bar reading the *Racing Times*, but he got to his feet as Kit appeared.

'Major Fitzroy. I mean Lord Fitzr—'

Kit cut straight through the etiquette confusion. 'I'm looking for someone,' he said harshly. 'Someone staying here. Room three I believe? I'll see myself up.'

Without giving the flustered landlord time to respond he headed for the stairs, taking them two at a time. Room three was at the end of the short corridor. An empty vodka bottle stood outside it. Kit hammered on the door.

'Sophie!'

Kit listened hard, but the only sounds were muted voices

from a television somewhere and the ragged rasp of his own breathing. His tortured mind conjured an image of the man he'd seen earlier pausing as he unzipped Sophie's dress and her whispering, *Don't worry—he'll go away...*

But he wouldn't. Not until he'd seen her.

'Sophie!'

Clenching his hand into a fist, he was just about to beat on the door again when it opened an inch. A face—puffy-eyed, swarthy, unshaven—peered out at him.

'She's not here.'

With a curse of pure rage, Kit put his shoulder to the door. Whoever it was on the other side didn't put up much resistance and the door opened easily. Glancing at him only long enough to register that he was naked except for a small white towel slung around his hips, Kit pushed past and strode into the room.

In a heartbeat he took in the clothes scattered over the floor—black clothes, like puddles of tar on the cream carpet—the wide bed with its passion-tumbled covers and the room darkened, and he thought he might black out.

'Kit—' Jasper leapt out of the bed, dragging the rumpled sheet and pulling it around himself. Blinking, Kit shook his head, trying to reconcile what he was actually seeing with what he had expected.

'Jasper?'

'Look, I didn't want you to find out like this.' Jasper paused and ducked his head for a moment, but then gathered himself and raised his head again, looking Kit squarely in the eye while the man in the white towel went to his side. 'But it's probably time you knew anyway. I can't go on hiding who I really am just because it doesn't fit the Fitzroy mould. I love Sergio. And I know what you're going to say but—'

Kit gave a short, incredulous laugh as relief burst through him. 'It's the best news I've had for a long time. Really. I can't

tell you how pleased I am.' He turned and shook hands with
the bewildered man in the white towel, and then went over
to Jasper and embraced him briefly, hard. 'Now please—if
Sophie's not here, where the hell is she?'

The smile faded from Jasper's face. 'She's gone. She's
getting the train back to London. Kit, did something happen
between you, because—?'

Kit turned away, putting his hands to his head as despair
sucked him down. He swore savagely. Twice. And then strode
to the door.

'Yes, something happened between us,' he said, turning
back to Jasper with a suicidal smile. 'I was just too stupid to
understand exactly what it was.'

The good news was that Sophie didn't have to wait long for
a train to come. The bad news was that there was only one
straight-through express service to London every day, and
that was long gone. The one she boarded was a small, clank-
ing local train that stopped at every miniature village station
all along the line and terminated at Newcastle.

The train was warm and virtually empty. Sophie slunk to
a seat in the corner and sat with her eyes closed so she didn't
have to look at Alnburgh, transformed by the sinking sun into
a golden fairy tale castle from an old-fashioned storybook,
get swallowed up by the blue haze.

She was used to this, she told herself over and over. Moving
on was what she did best. Hadn't she always felt panicked
by the thought of permanence? She was good at new starts.
Reinventing herself.

But until now she hadn't really known who 'herself' was.
Sophie Greenham was a construction; a sort of patchwork of
bits borrowed from films and books and other people, fragments of fact layered up with wistful half-truths and shame-

less lies, all carried off with enough chutzpah to make them seem credible.

Beneath Kit's cool, incisive gaze all the joins had dissolved and the pieces had fallen away. She was left just being herself. A person she didn't really know, who felt things she didn't usually feel and needed things she didn't understand.

As she got further away from Alnburgh her phone came back into signal range and texts began to come in with teeth-grating regularity. Biting her cheeks against each sledgehammer blow of disappointment, Sophie couldn't stop herself checking every time to see if any were from Kit.

They weren't.

There were several from her agent. The vampire film people wanted to see her again. The outfit had impressed *them*, at least.

'Tickets from Alnburgh.'

She opened her eyes. The guard was making his way along the swaying carriage towards her. She sat up, fumbling in her broken bag for her purse as she blinked away the stinging in her eyes.

'A single to London, please.'

The guard punched numbers into his ticket machine with pudgy fingers. 'Change at Newcastle,' he said without looking at her. 'The London train goes from platform two. It's a bit of a distance so you'll need to hurry.'

'Thank you,' Sophie muttered, trying to fix those details in her head. Until then she'd only thought as far as getting on this train. Arriving at Newcastle, getting off and taking herself forwards from there felt like stepping into a void.

She dug her nails into her palms and looked unseeingly out of the window as a wave of panic washed over her. Out of nowhere a thought occurred to her.

'Actually—can you make that two tickets?'

'Are you with someone?'

For the first time the guard looked at her properly; a glare delivered over the top of his glasses that suggested she was doing something underhand. The reality was she was just trying to put something right.

'No.' Sophie heard the break in her voice. 'No, I'm alone. But let's just say I had a debt to pay.'

The station at Alnburgh was, unsurprisingly, empty. Kit stood for a moment on the bleak platform, breathing hard from running and looking desperately around, as if in some part of his mind he still thought there was a chance she would be there.

She wasn't. Of course she wasn't. She had left, with infinite dignity, and for good.

He tipped his head back and breathed in, feeling the throb of blood in his temples, waiting until the urge to punch something had passed.

'Missed your train?'

Kit looked round. A man wearing overalls and a yellow high-vis jacket had appeared, carrying a spade.

'Something like that. When's the next one to London?'

The man went over to the grit bin at the end of the platform and thrust the spade into it.

'London? The only straight-through London train from here is the 11.07 in the morning. If you need to get one before that you'll have to get to Newcastle.' He threw the spadeful of grit across the compacted snow.

Hopelessness engulfed Kit. Numbly he started walking away. If he caught a train from Newcastle, by the time he'd got to London she'd be long gone and he'd have no way of finding her. Unless…

Unless…

He spun round. 'Wait a minute. Did you say the only straight-through train was this morning? So the one that just left…'

'Was the local service to Newcastle. That's right.'

'Thanks.'

Kit broke into a run. He didn't stop until he reached the tower gate, and remembered the cars. The party was evidently still going on, and the courtyard was still rammed with vehicles. Kit stopped. Bracing his arms against the shiny black bonnet of the one nearest to him, letting his head drop as ragged breaths were torn from his heaving chest, almost like sobs.

She had gone. And he couldn't even go after her.

'Sir?'

Dimly he was aware of the car door opening and a figure getting out. Until that point he hadn't registered which car he was leaning against, or that there was anyone in it, but now he saw that it was the funeral car and the grey-haired man who had just got out was the undertaker.

'I was going to ask if you were all right, but clearly that would be a daft question,' he said, abandoning the stiff formality of his role. 'A better question would be, is there anything I can do to help?'

'Yes,' Kit rasped. 'Yes, there is.'

Sophie stood on the platform and looked around in confusion.

Newcastle Central Station was a magnificent example of Victorian design and engineering. With its iron-boned canopy arching above her, Sophie felt as if she were standing in the belly of a vast whale.

Apart from the noise, and the crowds, maybe. Being inside a whale would probably be a blissfully quiet experience compared to this. People pushed past her, shouting into mobile phones to make themselves heard above the echoing announcement system and the noise of diesel engines.

Amongst them, Sophie felt tiny. Invisible.

It had been just a week and a half since she'd dashed onto

the 16.22 from King's Cross but now the girl with the stiletto boots and a corset dress and the who-cares attitude could barely bring herself to walk away from the little train that had brought her from Alnburgh. After the space and silence of the last ten days it felt as if the crowds were pressing in on her and that she might simply be swept away, or trampled underfoot. And that no one would notice.

But the guard had said she needed to hurry if she was going to catch the London connection. Adjusting her grip on her broken bag, holding it awkwardly to make sure it didn't spill its contents, she forced herself to move forwards.

Platform two. Where was platform two? Her eyes scanned the bewildering array of signs, but somehow none of the words made sense to her. Except one, high up on the lit-up board of train departures.

Alnburgh.

Sophie had never been homesick in her life, probably because she'd never really had a home to be sick for, but she thought the feeling might be something like the anguish that hollowed out her insides and filled her lungs with cement as she stared at the word.

She looked away. She didn't belong there—hadn't she told herself that countless times during the last ten days? The girl from nowhere with the made-up name and the made-up past didn't belong in a castle, or in a family with a thousand years of history.

So where did she belong?

Panic was rising inside her. Standing in the middle of the swarming station concourse, she suddenly felt as if she were falling, or disappearing, and there was nothing there to anchor her. She turned round, desperately searching for something familiar...

And then she saw him.

Pushing his way through the crowds of commuters, head

and shoulders above everyone else, his face tense and ashen but so beautiful that for a moment Sophie couldn't breathe. She stood, not wanting to take her eyes off him in case he disappeared again, unable to speak.

'Kit.'

It was a whisper. A whimper. So quiet she barely heard it herself. But at that moment he turned his head and looked straight at her.

His footsteps slowed, and for a second the expression on his face was one she hadn't seen before. Uncertainty. Fear. The same things she was feeling—or had been until she saw him. And then it was gone—replaced by a sort of scowling ferocity as he crossed the distance between them with long, rapid strides. Gathering her into his arms, he kissed her, hungrily and hard.

There were tears running down Sophie's face when she finally pulled away. She felt tender and torn with emotions she couldn't begin to unravel—gratitude and joy and relief, undercut with the terrible anguish she was beginning to realise went with loving someone.

'My train...' she croaked, steeling herself for the possibility that he'd just come to say goodbye.

Slowly he shook his head. His eyes didn't leave hers. 'Don't get on it.'

'Why not?'

He took her face between his hands, drawing her close to him so that in the middle of the crowd they were in their own private universe. Under his silver gaze Sophie felt as if she were bathed in moonlight.

'Because then I would have to get on it too,' he murmured gravely, 'and I'd have to sit opposite you for the next two and a half hours, looking at you, breathing in your scent and wanting to take your clothes off and make love to you on the table.' He gave her a rueful smile that made her heart turn over. 'I've done that once before, so I know how hard it is. And because I hijacked a hearse and committed several civil and traffic offences to find you, and now I have I don't want to let you go again. Not until I've said what I have to say. Starting with sorry.'

Tears were still spilling down her cheeks. 'Kit, you don't have to—'

'I've been rehearsing this all the way from Alnburgh,' he said, brushing the tears away with his thumbs, 'so if you could listen without interrupting that would be good. I saw Jasper.'

'Oh! And—'

He frowned. 'I'm horrified...'

Sophie's mouth opened in protest, but before she could say anything he kissed her into silence and continued softly, '...that he ever thought I wouldn't *approve*. Lord, am I such a judgmental bastard?'

Sophie gave a hiccuping laugh that was half sob. 'I think you're asking the wrong person.'

He let her go then, dropping his hands to his sides and looking down at her with an expression of abject desolation. 'God, Sophie, I'm so sorry. I've spent my whole miserable life not trusting anyone so it had become something of a habit. Until Olympia told me what she did to you at school and I wanted to wring her neck, and it made me realise that I trusted you absolutely.'

'But what about with Sergio—you thought—'

Out of his arms, without his touch Sophie felt as if she were breaking up again. The crowed swelled and jostled around them. A commuter banged her leg with his briefcase.

'No.' It was a groan of surrender. An admission of defeat. He pulled her back into his arms and held her against him so that she could feel the beat of his heart. 'I was too bloody deranged with jealousy to think at all. I just wanted to tear him limb from limb. I know it's not big or clever, but I can't help it. I just want you for myself.'

Tentatively she lifted her head to look up at him, her vision blurred by wonder and tears.

'Really?'

In reply he kissed her again, this time so tenderly that she felt as if he were caressing her soul.

'It'll never work,' she murmured against his mouth. 'I'm not good enough for you.'

'I think…' he kissed the corner of her mouth, her jaw '…we've already established that you're far too good for me.'

She closed her eyes as rapture spiralled through her. 'Socially I mean. I'm nobody.'

His lips brushed her ear lobe. 'So am I, remember?'

It was getting harder to concentrate. Harder to think of reasons why she shouldn't just give in to the rising tide of longing inside her. Harder to keep her knees from buckling. 'I'd be disastrous for your career,' she breathed. 'Amongst all those officers' wives—'

He lifted his head and gazed at her with eyes that were lit by some inner light. 'You'll outshine them all,' he said softly, simply. 'They'll want to hate you for being so beautiful but they won't be able to. Now, have you any more objections?'

'No.'

He seized her hand. 'Then for God's sake let's go and find the nearest hotel.'

Still Sophie held back. 'But I thought you had to report back for duty…'

'I called in some favours.' Gently he took her face between his hands and kissed her again. 'I have three weeks' compassionate leave following my father's death. But since Ralph wasn't actually my father I think we can just call it passionate leave. I intend to make the most of every second.'

EPILOGUE

It was just a tiny piece in the property section of one of the Sunday papers. Eating brioche spread thickly with raspberry jam in the crumpled ruins of the bed that had become their world for the last three weeks, Sophie gave a little squeal.

'Listen to this!

'Unexpected Twist to Fitzroy Inheritance.

'Following the recent death of Ralph Fitzroy, eighth Earl of Hawksworth and owner of the Alnburgh estate, it has come to light that the expected heir is not, in fact, set to inherit. Sources close to the family have confirmed that the estate, which includes Alnburgh Castle and five hundred acres of land in Northumberland as well as a sizeable slice of premium real estate in Chelsea, will pass to Jasper Fitzroy, the Earl's younger son from his second marriage, rather than his older brother, Major Kit Fitzroy.'

Putting the last bit of brioche in her mouth, she continued,

'Major Fitzroy, a serving member of the armed forces, was recently awarded the George Medal for bravery. However, it's possible that his courage failed him when it came to taking on Alnburgh. According to locals, maintenance of the estate has been severely neglected in recent years, leaving the next owner with a heavy financial burden to bear. While Kit Fitzroy is rumoured to have considerable personal wealth, perhaps this is one rescue mission he just doesn't want to take on...'

She tossed the newspaper aside and, licking jam off her fingers, cast Kit a sideways glance from under her lashes.

'"Considerable personal wealth"?' She wriggled down beneath the covers, smiling as she kissed his shoulder. 'I like the sound of that.'

Kit, still surfacing from the depths of the sleep he'd been blessed with since he'd had Sophie in his bed, arched an eyebrow.

'I thought as much,' he sighed, turning over and looking straight into her sparkling, beautiful eyes. 'You're nothing but a shallow, cynical gold-digger.'

'You're right.' Sophie nodded seriously, pressing her lips together to stop herself from smiling. 'To be honest, I'm really only interested in your money, and your exceptionally gorgeous Chelsea house.' The sweeping gesture she made with her arm took in the bedroom with its view of the garden square outside. 'It's why I've decided to put up with your boring personality and frankly quite average looks. Not to mention your disappointing performance in bed—'

She broke off with a squeal as, beneath the sheets, he slid a languid hand between her thighs.

'Sorry, what was that?' he murmured gravely.

'I said...' she gasped '...that I was only interested in your... money.' He watched her eyes darken as he moved his hand higher. 'I've always wanted to be a rich man's plaything.'

He propped himself up on one elbow, so he could see her better. Her hair was spilling over the pillow—a gentler red than when he'd first seen her that day on the train—the colour of horse chestnuts rather than holly berries—and her face was bare of make-up. She had never looked more beautiful.

'Not a rich man's wife?' he asked idly, leaning down to kiss the hollow above her collarbone.

'Oh, no. If we're talking marriage I'd be looking for a title as well as a fortune.' Her voice turned husky as his lips moved to the base of her throat. 'And a sizeable estate to go with it...'

He smiled, taking his time, breathing in the scent of her skin. 'OK, that's good to know. Since I'm fresh out of titles and estates there's probably no point in asking.'

He felt her stiffen, heard her little gasp of shock and excitement. 'Well, there might be some room for negotiation,' she said breathlessly. 'And I'd say that right now you're in a pretty good bargaining position...'

'Sophie Greenham,' he said gravely, 'I love you because you are beautiful and clever and honest and loyal...'

'Flattery will get you a very long way,' she sighed, closing her eyes as his fingertips trailed rapture over the quivering skin on the inside of her thighs. 'And *that* will probably do the rest...'

His chest tightened as he looked down at her. 'I love you because you think underwear is a better investment than clothes, and because you're brave and funny and sexy, and I was wondering if you'd possibly consider marrying me?'

Her eyes opened and met his. The smile that spread slowly across her face was one of pure, incredulous happiness. It felt like watching the sun rise.

'Yes,' she whispered, gazing up at him with dazed, brilliant eyes. 'Yes, please.'

'I feel it's only fair to warn you that I've been disowned by my family...'

Serene, she took his face in her hands. 'We can make our own family.'

He frowned, smoothing a strand of hair from her cheek, suddenly finding it difficult to speak for the lump of emotion in his throat. 'And I have no title, no castle and no lands to offer you.'

She laughed, pulling him down into her arms. 'Believe me, I absolutely wouldn't have it any other way...'

* * * * *

GIRLS' GUIDE TO FLIRTING WITH DANGER

BY
KIMBERLY LANG

Kimberly Lang hid romance novels behind her text-books in secondary school, and even a Master's programme in English couldn't break her obsession with dashing heroes and happily ever after. A ballet dancer turned English teacher, Kimberly married an electrical engineer and turned her life into an ongoing episode of *When Dilbert Met Frasier*. She and her Darling Geek live in beautiful North Alabama, with their one Amazing Child—who, unfortunately, shows an aptitude for sports.

Visit Kimberly at www.booksbykimberly.com for the latest news—and don't forget to say hi while you're there!

To Dee, who taught me how to plant flowers, flute a pie crust, and form proper jazz hands. Despite her best efforts, I do none of these things well.
Thankfully, she loves me anyway.

CHAPTER ONE

FIFTY MINUTES COUNSELING Mr. and Mrs. Martin left Megan Lowe's head pounding. She needed to talk with Dr. Weiss about getting their meds adjusted, or else one of them would end up killing the other soon enough.

Megan made a few notes in their file while the session was still fresh in her mind, and added it to the stack in her in-box. She then went in search of aspirin.

Julie, another of the three interns who handled most of the actual counseling here at the Weiss Clinic, held the aspirin bottle in her direction as Megan pushed through the swinging door of the lounge.

"I heard that all the way in here. You should be getting combat pay."

Megan laughed as she opened a bottle of water and popped two pills gratefully. "Their volume is just set on eleven this week. I don't think there's any actual danger to anyone or anything—except my eardrums."

"A thousand years in grad school and you end up the equivalent of a referee for pro wrestling." Julie shook her head sadly.

"Only it doesn't pay as well."

Julie tapped the sheet of newspaper under her hand, calling attention to the full-page, full-color ad for Devin

Kenney's book. "Well, if you can't sort them out, at least you can recommend a good divorce attorney."

Megan felt her eye begin to twitch. "That is not funny, Julie. Not funny at all." Why couldn't Devin toil away in obscurity like everyone else? She'd fielded a bit of press interest last year when Devin's radio show, *Cover Your Assets,* had gone into syndication, but since his book of the same name had hit the top of every bestseller list, she'd felt like the most famous ex-wife in America. Or at least Chicago.

"Actually, it is kind of funny." Julie's smile wasn't in the least bit sympathetic. "And the irony is just delicious."

"Don't make me hate you. It's annoying, not ironic. Plus, it's ancient history." History that should have been lost in the mists of time, only Dev had to make it part of his career.

"A marriage counselor whose starter marriage left Devin Kenney so bitter he made it his life's work to get other people out of their marriages? Sorry, Megan, that's delicious. And newsworthy."

"You have a very liberal definition of news." Megan flipped the paper over so the ad no longer stared at her. "New topic. Did you get your grant paperwork in?"

She didn't miss the eye roll that accompanied Julie's dramatic sigh as Megan went to get her lunch from the fridge, but Julie did pick up the new topic, thank goodness. The amount of time she spent thinking about Devin these days simply wasn't good for her mental health, and talking about it wasn't going to help either. Strangling Devin for putting her in this position *might,* but that wasn't really an option. No matter how tempting the thought.

They were joined a minute later by Alice, the clinic's receptionist, who brought a stack of messages for them both. Megan flipped through the papers absently, until one caught her interest. "The Smiths canceled?" Allen and Melissa Smith were her most fanatical clients. They had a standing Monday appointment promptly at one o'clock. They never missed it. "Did they say why?"

Alice winced as she put her lunch in the microwave. "Yeah, they did."

There was that eye twitch again. She wasn't going to like this. "And?"

"They're very uncomfortable with the level of notoriety you've reached lately, especially since that blogger who's been lurking around here called them at home yesterday to ask about you."

"That guy identified and called one of my clients?" She caught Julie's shocked face out of the corner of her eye. "*Please* tell me you're kidding."

"I wish."

"Oh, my God. That's...that's..."

"An invasion of the Smiths' privacy and a black mark on the reputation of this clinic." Dr. Weiss— the Weiss of the Weiss Clinic—spoke from behind Megan, making her jump.

"Dr. Weiss, I'm *so* sorry. This is just insane."

"I agree." Dr. Weiss looked unperturbed and calm, but Megan knew that might just be her "counselor face." Dr. Weiss had been a therapist for more than thirty years; she wouldn't show surprise if Megan jumped up on the table and danced a naked cha-cha. At the moment Megan sincerely wished Dr. Weiss wasn't quite such a master of the poker face. It was simply impossible to tell how much trouble—if any—she was in at the moment. Strangling Devin was sounding better and better.

"I'm sure this will blow over soon. I'm just not that interesting, you know. And we all know how fickle people's interest can be," she finished with a lame attempt at humor.

"I'm glad to hear you feel that way, Megan." Dr. Weiss's voice was understanding and kind, but that didn't stop the sinking feeling in Megan's stomach. "I think you should take some time off until it does."

The sinking feeling became a twenty-story drop. "What?"

Dr. Weiss joined them at the table and sipped her coffee. "You have plenty of vacation time, and now might be a good time for you to take it."

"But my clients..."

"We can handle them for a couple of weeks."

"*Weeks?* Dr. Weiss, I know this isn't a great situation, but..."

"Megan, I will not have my clinic turned into a three-ring circus. And I will not have our clients embarrassed or inconvenienced."

She felt like a chastised child—which was probably exactly what Dr. Weiss was going for—and anger at Devin boiled in her stomach. Julie and Alice were feigning attention to their lunches, but she could feel their pity and it tossed fuel on that fire. She fiddled with a pencil, focusing on it as she forced herself to remain outwardly calm.

"I understand. I'll work with Alice to get everything rearranged after I finish with my anger-management group this afternoon...." She trailed off as Dr. Weiss shook her head.

"I'll handle your group."

The pencil snapped.

Dr. Weiss's eyebrows went up. "Perhaps you might wish to join the group this afternoon."

"No." She forced her jaw to unclench and tried to smile. "It's okay. I'll start getting everything together. Alice, when you're finished with your lunch, will you have a few minutes to look at my schedule?"

Alice nodded, and Dr. Weiss looked pleased—or maybe not. It was very hard to tell.

"This isn't a punishment, Megan. As you say, this will die down soon, and you can work on those journal submissions while we wait for it to pass."

"That's a wonderful idea, Dr. Weiss." *And I'll get right on that, right* after *I kill Devin Kenney.*

Megan managed to walk out of the break room with some small measure of dignity, but she couldn't get her fists to unclench. Her nails were digging painfully into her palms by the time she made it back to her office and shut the door.

Trying to focus on something other than Devin, she checked her calendar and started pulling files and making notes for Julie and Nate, the other therapist, who'd been with a client and missed the fun. But she was sure he'd be brought up to speed about thirty seconds after his client left.

I'm not fired. I'm not being punished. This will blow over.

Damn Dev. How many more times would she have to reorganize her life because of him?

This will blow over soon enough.

She kept repeating that phrase until she heard the soft knock and looked up to see Julie and Alice tiptoeing in.

"We're so sorry," Julie said.

"There's nothing to be sorry about. This will pass."

Julie sat in the chair across from her desk as Alice took the files from Megan's hands. "We all know hate is a very negative emotion," Julie began, "but I think we'd all agree that it's not an inappropriate one in this situation."

"Thanks, Jules." She sighed. "You know, I've never hated anyone before in my entire life."

"Not even Devin?"

"Oddly enough, no." At Julie's obvious disbelief, she tried to explain. "It wasn't like that. I was bitter and angry and hurt, but I didn't hate him. I was disappointed, disillusioned, heartbroken…but it never crossed over into actual hate." She shrugged. "And then I moved on. Dev's obviously the one with lingering issues."

"Sounds like he could use a good therapist." Julie smirked. "Know any?"

"Sadly, I'm off the clock for the foreseeable future." She rested her head on her hands. "All that time patting myself on the back because I'd moved on. Now *I'm* angry. The man is dead meat if I ever get my hands on him. Like I could," she scoffed. "I'm sure he's unlisted these days, and I doubt his firm would let me in the front door."

"You could just go to his book signing, you know," Alice offered.

That caught her attention. "His book signing?"

Alice nodded. "There was an ad in the paper today. He's signing books downtown today from three to five."

"Really. Hmm." Devin was in town—not off doing the talk-show rounds in New York or L.A. "Interesting…"

"Megan…" Julie's voice held a warning tone. "Do *not* make this worse."

Megan was already running a search on Google for the bookstore. "How could it possibly be any worse? He's already destroying my career, my reputation, my *life*."

"Nothing's in complete ruins just yet. Let's not build a bonfire in the rubble prematurely."

"I'm a professional, Julie. I think I can confront my ex-husband in a positive, appropriate manner."

Julie snorted. "You really think that?"

Megan lifted her chin. "I do."

"You know that means you can't kill him, right? Or even throw a punch?"

She leaned back in her chair and closed her eyes. "Unfortunately, yes. But I've got to put a stop to this somehow. Before it gets any more out of hand."

"You, Devin Kenney, are a force of nature, my friend. Incredible. You need anything? Water? A soda? By the way, love the shirt. It looks great on you."

Devin wasn't even slightly bolstered by Manny Field's exuberance or insulted that Manny bolted off before those words were fully out of his mouth. It was just part of the job. Manny saw everything in terms of his 15 percent, and Devin knew he was the biggest cash cow in Manny's herd at the moment; therefore, he was worth milking. *And sucking up to, as well,* he thought darkly. But Manny was his agent, not his friend—the kowtowing notwithstanding—and as his agent, Manny had made Devin a hell of a lot of money.

And vice versa—hence the pandering.

The last person in line approached. He scrawled his name one more time and handed the book over with a nod, trying to ignore the overbright smile and overenhanced cleavage of the woman gushing at him. She looked as if she was in the market for a husband—not looking to leave one. Just as the feeling registered, her next words confirmed that hypothesis.

"You know, Mr. Kenney—or can I call you Devin?— even after my last divorce, which your book would have helped me considerably with, I still think I'm a bit of a romantic at heart." She smiled coyly and leaned forward, offering him another view right down the front of her blouse.

"What about you? Are you still looking for true, lasting love?"

His on-air persona of Bitter Divorced Guy helped—a little—to avoid situations like this, but some women saw that as a challenge instead.

"If I—or anyone else—really believed in true, lasting love, I'd be out of a job."

That should have shut her down midflirt, but instead she leaned closer and murmured huskily, "Maybe you haven't met the right woman yet."

Maybe Manny needs to get his ass back over here and run some interference. He heard the quiet whir of a camera and knew this woman and her breasts were about to make the front page of someone's blog. *Great.* He didn't want to insult a fan with his rebuff, but he didn't want to hear the next offer either. *Where the hell is Manny?*

He scanned the store until he found Manny engaged in a conversation with a small blonde. Her back was to him, so he couldn't see her face, but Manny certainly looked aggravated. The woman spoke animatedly, the motion causing a long ponytail to sway against her shoulders. She was casually dressed, the white T-shirt skimming over a lovely back and narrow waist before it disappeared into the waistband of faded jeans. Those jeans hugged her butt in a way that got his body's attention—much more so than the cleavage nearly under his nose.

The woman hitched a battered brown bag over her shoulder, and something about the movement seemed oddly familiar. A moment later she turned to look in his direction and pinned him with a stare.

Megan.

Aware she now had his attention, she turned to face him, crossed her arms over her chest and tilted her head to one side. As her weight shifted onto her back leg, two realizations hit him at once.

First, the years had been very, *very* good to her.

Second, she was madder than hell.

Manny tapped Megan on the shoulder. Old instinct kicked in, and he was on his feet before he knew it. Manny could be caustic and slice people apart with mere words, and from the look on his face, Megan was seconds from getting the full Manny treatment. He barely glanced at the woman in front of him as he stood. "Enjoy the book. Hope it helps next time."

The woman's sputter barely registered as he crossed the bookstore, dodging a table full of his books, and got closer to Megan. As he closed the distance, her blue eyes narrowed, but not before he saw the cold fire burning there.

So the anger was directed at him, personally. Interesting. He should let Manny handle it, but his conscience wouldn't let Megan's feelings be hurt like that. It would be letting a bully kick a puppy, and regardless of anything else, he couldn't let that happen.

Plus, he was too curious now to see what had brought Megan intentionally back into his universe after seven years.

The freshman fifteen she'd battled in college was long gone, bringing out her cheekbones and giving her a delicate look that was at odds with the angry jut of her chin. That T-shirt scooped low on her chest, snuggling tightly against the curves of her breasts—breasts that the position of her arms were pressing together and up as if they were begging for his attention.

As if she realized the direction of his thoughts, Megan shifted, bracing her hands on her hips and pressing her lips into a thin line. With her light blond hair, big blue eyes, tiny stature and ticked-off look, Megan resembled an angry Tinker Bell at the moment.

Manny stood behind her, still talking, but Megan didn't spare him a glance. Her eyes bored into his as he approached.

"Sorry, Devin, but this woman says—" Manny started.

He waved Manny silent. "Not a problem." Manny sputtered, and Megan seemed to be grinding her teeth. Aware of their audience, he turned on his best media-honed charm and smile. "Megan, this is a surprise. I'm flattered you'd come."

She shook her head. "Don't be. You're a dead man, Dev." Her voice was quiet, but the heat behind it was fierce.

Manny took a step back. "I'll get security."

"No need. This is Megan Lowe. My ex-wife."

Manny scowled at Megan. "You didn't mention that."

She rolled her eyes in response. "Could you excuse us for a minute? I need to talk to Devin. Privately," she forced out between gritted teeth.

Manny looked at him for confirmation, obviously still ready to get security to remove a half-crazy woman. It wouldn't be the first time. Devin nodded. "It's fine, Manny. Give us a minute. I'm sure Megan doesn't actually plan to attack me."

"Wanna bet?" she snapped.

"I'm sure you wouldn't want to make a scene in front of fifty people, would you?" he warned. Megan was fired up about something, but he didn't want this to make the papers.

She looked around, then blew out her breath in a long sigh. The most fake smile he'd ever seen crept over her face as she turned to Manny again. "Of course not. I just need a few minutes of Devin's time." The sugary sarcasm dripping off her words didn't bode well for whatever she needed those few minutes for.

Manny backed off a few steps, and Devin reached for Megan's elbow. She jerked away before he could touch her. Lord, she really was mad, but why had she decided to confront him *here?* Whatever bee was in her bonnet, the middle of a busy bookstore during one of his signings wasn't the place to discuss it. With a sigh he indicated the stockroom he'd been stashed in earlier before the signing began. "How about in there?"

Megan hitched her bag up again and squared her shoulders. She walked stiffly, that fake smile fixed on her face until the stockroom door swung shut behind them. Then she turned on him. "How *could* you, Dev?"

"How could I what? You'll need to be more specific."

Megan pulled a copy of his book out of her bag and tossed it at him. *"This."*

He caught it reflexively and looked at her. When she didn't elaborate, he prodded her. "Should I make it out to you, or is it a gift for a friend?"

"Neither." She snorted. "I've got your autograph already. On my divorce papers."

"Then what?" She didn't answer, but he could see the muscle in her jaw working. "Need some legal advice?"

She tilted her head, and the end of her ponytail fell to rest on the heaving swell of her breasts above the neckline of her shirt. A faint flush colored the skin there, barely noticeable in the dimness of the stockroom. "Actually, I could use some legal advice. What's the difference between slander and libel?"

He pulled his attention from her cleavage. "What?"

"How about defamation of character? Can I sue you for that?"

Meggie rarely made sense when she got good and mad,

but this seemed to be extreme, even for her. "Why don't you calm down and tell me—"

"Don't you dare patronize me, Devin Kenney. Your radio show was bad enough, but this book…"

Old habits warred with each other. Placate or fight back? "I don't think—"

"And therein lies the problem. Did you never once think that people *might* be interested in the ex-wife of America's most popular divorce attorney?" Megan began to pace, her hands moving agitatedly as she spoke. "That people *might* think that some of the things you mention on the radio or the stories in this book are based on your *personal* experience? Or that they might come looking for *me,* wanting dirt or backstory or something?"

Ah, unwanted notoriety. "You're all spun up because some tabloid wants you to dish the dirt on me?"

She crossed her arms on her chest again as she stared at him, eyes snapping. "Not just *some* tabloid. *All* the tabloids. All the cable news channels. Half a dozen talk shows and every damn blogger in the universe. Do you not keep up with your own press? Haven't you seen *my* name next to yours recently?"

He didn't keep up with his own press; he didn't have time. That's why he had Manny. And they'd be having a conversation about *that* later on. After he finished with Megan.

Her anger made a bit more sense now. Megan was so shy, the media hounds would be too much for her to deal with without major stress. Feeling a twinge of guilt that Megan had been pulled into this media circus at all, he reached for her arm out of habit, simply to calm her. When she stepped back, he remembered he didn't have the right to touch her anymore. He leaned back against a stack of boxes instead. "The fact we were married once is public record. I can't change that." She took a deep breath, and he held up a hand, trying to be diplomatic. "But I *am* sorry you're being bothered by the press. It'll blow over soon." Something about that phrase made her nostrils flare and the color in her cheeks deepen. "Feel free to milk this any way you want, though."

"I don't want to milk this. I want it to go *away*. My career may never recover as it is, but if this continues..."

He tried to follow the change in topic. "Your career?"

"I realize it was never high on your radar, but surely you remember I wanted one of those, too."

Oh, he remembered, all right. She'd moved to Albany and filed for divorce in pursuit of her precious career. The bitter taste of *that* memory settled on his tongue and made his next words sharper than intended. "I don't see how a little fame could have any detrimental effect on your career."

"I'm a therapist." He shrugged in question and Megan's jaw clenched again. "Primarily a *marriage* therapist," she managed to grit out.

He felt his eyebrows go up, and a small chuckle escaped before he could stop it.

Megan rolled her eyes and sighed. "Yes, yes, I'm aware of the irony. As are all the people contacting me about you. But I'm damn good at what I do. And I was building a nice client list and decent reputation. Until now."

"And?"

"Let's see. The press won't leave me alone. They call my office and my house at all hours. My email overflows, and one even tried to pose as a new client. I could handle that, but now my *clients* are being harassed by the press, which is a horrible invasion of their privacy, not to mention embarrassing for them and the clinic I work for. The speculation in the tabloids about our marriage makes me look like some kind of psychotic harpy, which tends to make people think twice about listening to my advice." She was pacing again, working that head of steam back up. "Oh, and there's the little issue of being placed on extended leave because all of this interferes with the entire clinic's ability to do business. So, thank you, Devin, for screwing up my life. Again."

That accusation rankled, but he wasn't going to argue who had screwed up whose life in the first place. He'd win that battle. But that was ancient history. He did feel slightly bad Megan was catching flak—and that he'd been unaware of any of it. Regardless of his reputation, he wasn't completely heartless. Even when it came to her. "I didn't know. I'll try to do some damage control, if you want. Make it clear that we were so long ago that nothing of us is part of the book."

Her shoulders dropped. "It's a start. But I doubt it will help."

Old frustration edged its way back in. "Then exactly what *do* you want me to do?"

The question hung between them in the dim stockroom, and Megan didn't have an answer.

Anger and indignation had brought her this far and now she regretted giving in to either emotion. So much for "positive confrontation." All those "I" statements—*I think, I feel*—she was *supposed* to use in this situation had evaporated under the heat of her emotions. Good God, if Dr. Weiss had heard that outburst… She cringed inwardly. She'd be sent back to Psych 101 to start over again. The outrage drained away, leaving her feeling hollow and foolish.

It was a familiar feeling. One she didn't like.

She just hadn't been properly mentally prepared to see

Devin again. Face-to-face, at least. She'd debated taking this internship simply because Devin was so famous, and she wasn't sure she wanted to be in the same town. But an internship at the Weiss Clinic was too prestigious to turn down over an ex-husband. Not in a town this size, where she was practically guaranteed to never run into him.

Then she'd moved here and his picture was all over town: on the sides of buses, on billboards, in magazines. Devin's I'm-up-to-something smile was *everywhere*. It was wreaking havoc on her psyche, but she'd learned how to ignore it—for the most part.

But all that practice hadn't prepared her to be in the same room with him. *Alone.* His long, lean body took up way too much space, and her nerve endings seemed to jump to high alert. Devin appeared to suck up all the available oxygen in the room, leaving her with nothing to breathe except the unique scent of him that she—and something inside her—recognized immediately. Those liquid brown eyes, the way his dark hair curled just slightly behind his ears... Those hands—oddly elegant for a man who oozed testosterone from every pore—brought visuals she didn't need right now.

It was terribly unfair to discover that after all these years Devin still had an effect on her—especially when she obviously had no effect on him at all. Her inner eighteen-year-old was stuttering and stammering just being this close to him, and it irritated her to no end.

And now she'd stormed in here and acted exactly like some kind of crazy ex. And considering how reasonable *he* was being... She wanted to go hide under a rock for the next five years or so. She might recover her pride and get over the embarrassment by then.

Devin repeated the question, and the exasperation in his tone drove home how ridiculous she was being.

I should have listened to Julie.

"Well, Meggie?"

You could start by not calling me Meggie. It caused another one of those heartbeat stutters and brought back memories she was doing her damnedest to suppress. But the question did deflate the last bit of the outrage that had sent her storming downtown to confront him. She sighed and dropped her shoulders in defeat. "I don't know. I guess that's all you *can* do. Eventually my fifteen minutes will be up, right?"

Biting her lip, she reached deep inside for a bit of the professional behavior she'd lost in her tirade. Without the anger and indignation fueling her, she felt foolish. And Dev's proximity was just too much. "I apologize. I shouldn't have come here in the first place, so I'll go now." A small laugh at the absurdity of the situation escaped her. "I won't say it was nice seeing you again, but at least I can offer you my congratulations on your success in person." There. She could end on a less embarrassing and slightly more mature note.

Dev nodded, but he had the oddest look on his face— rather as if he was concerned she wasn't all there mentally. She couldn't really blame him for that. "Bye, Dev. And good luck." She held out her hand.

Seeming surprised and not bothering to hide it, Devin took her offered hand. *Damn it.* His touch caused her fingers to tingle, and it took all she had not to jerk her hand away.

"You, too, Meggie."

Pulling herself together by force of will, she released his hand and refused to look back as she walked away. She pushed the door with a little too much force, causing it to swing wide. That annoying agent jumped back to avoid being hit.

"Eavesdropping? Really? Lovely."

Manny had the sense to look a little abashed at being caught, but then he shrugged and grinned. It was a fake, practiced grin, and she wasn't the least bit fooled by it. Or by the false friendliness that followed. "You know, you really shouldn't take any of this personally. It's just showbiz."

She pretended to think about that statement. "Showbiz. Yeah. Well, for those of us who didn't sign up for it, it sucks."

Much like her life at the moment.

CHAPTER TWO

TWENTY-FOUR HOURS under the covers and more ice cream than any adult should ever eat hadn't solved anything. Megan didn't feel better about any of it. And now her stomach hurt, as well.

She was tired of hiding in her apartment, mainly because seeing Devin had awakened every old repressed memory, causing her to relive their entire history. She was a complete mess now, thanks to him.

When the phone rang, *again,* she flipped back the quilt to check the number. No name. *Damn.* Not answering wasn't an option, since it could be a client calling. They all had her cell-phone number in case of an emergency. She mentally crossed her fingers, then immediately felt bad for hoping one of her clients was having an emergency.

"Dr. Lowe?"

"Speaking."

"My name is Kate Wilson. I'm a producer—"

She sighed. "No comment. Goodbye." The press was driving her crazy.

"Wait! Don't hang up, please." Something in the woman's voice caused her to pause. "I'm Devin Kenney's producer for *Cover Your Assets.*"

That's why the voice sounded vaguely familiar. She'd heard it on the radio the once or twice she'd tuned in to

Devin's show—strictly for research purposes, of course. "And I still have no comment."

It wasn't for lack of trying, though. She'd spent hours trying to come up with the perfect comment. One that would be pithy and quotable yet shut down any further questions. Sadly, such a comment did not exist.

"I understand your reluctance, but please hear me out. I'm not looking for a quote or a story." The woman laughed. "That's not my job."

Megan focused on the water stain on the ceiling and prayed for patience. "Ms. Wilson, I'm extremely busy today, so—"

"So I'll get to the point. I understand you're getting a lot of unwelcome attention from the media right now."

That was an understatement.

"I don't know how much you've dealt with the media in the past, but I do know one way to get this circus under control."

That would be too much to ask, especially since this woman worked for the media—and Devin. Therefore her offer to help sounded suspicious at best. "And that would be…?"

"You beat them to it. Put yourself out there in a way you can control."

"Ms. Wilson—"

"Call me Kate."

"Kate, I'm really not interested in doing interviews or anything of that nature."

"Exactly. That's why I think you should come on Devin's show."

What part of "no interviews" does this Kate not understand? "I'm sorry, what?"

Excitement oozed out of the woman's words. "You could tell your side with Devin right there to corroborate the truth of the stories. You could take questions, even, and end the speculation. If you show that you and Devin aren't on opposite sides—and that you two think it's a nonissue—that issue will no longer be interesting. Problem solved."

That sounded way too good to be true. Too easy. "What makes you think anyone would—"

"Dr. Lowe, you have to know the fact you're a marriage counselor and Devin is a divorce attorney is the stuff blogs eat up. It just feeds on itself, and the more that's not said about it just gives rise to more speculation."

"I am aware of that." *Blindingly aware,* she thought as her eye began to twitch again.

Kate seemed to miss the sarcasm. "Then come on the show tomorrow night. You and Devin can address this issue head-on. Get the truth out there and end everyone's curiosity."

It couldn't be that easy. Plus... "I've never done anything on the radio before."

"Don't worry about that. You have a great voice, and Devin and I can walk you through the specifics."

"I don't know. Maybe I should talk to Devin first." Oh, the thought made her stomach hurt again.

"It'll be great for Devin's ratings, too. I think a lot of folks will tune in to hear you two sort things out. And think, you could become the most popular marriage counselor in Chicago. It would probably increase your patient list."

Something didn't quite feel right. "Why didn't Devin call me himself with this grand idea?"

"He's in Atlanta today for a book signing and won't be back until tomorrow afternoon."

It was tempting. Very tempting. Except for the talking-to-Devin part. And the being-near-Devin part. That hadn't gone so well yesterday. She cringed again.

Kate did have a point about taking control instead of being pushed along. And wasn't she always telling her clients to act instead of react?

But the radio? Devin had a coast-to-coast audience. She wasn't the same wallflower she used to be, but still... Who *wouldn't* be nervous at the idea of being heard by that many people? The possibilities for humiliation were *huge*.

But if it went the way Kate seemed to think it would... Maybe she could shut this down before it got any bigger and get back to work. Put Devin out of her life once and for all.

"Dr. Lowe? If this is going to work, we need to jump on it now. Before it gets any bigger."

Megan took a deep breath. "Then I guess I'll come on the show."

"Wonderful! You'll need to be here by six so I can brief you. Do I need to send a car for you...?"

Kate rattled off questions and instructions, but Megan was questioning her sanity and barely heard them over the sound of her head gently banging against the headboard.

Devin made the mistake of heeding Megan's advice about reading his own press just as his flight began its descent into O'Hare. He put his seat and tray table in the upright position, stowed his electronics and changed to printed media to occupy the last few minutes of the flight.

There, on the front of the entertainment section, in type large enough to be read from Coach, was a promo for tonight's show.

And Megan's name was right next to his.

What the hell?

According to this, tonight's very special guest would be his ex-wife, Dr. Megan Lowe. His surprise at Megan's doctor title was quickly swamped by the news that she was coming on his show.

Whose bright idea was *that?*

He reached for his phone, only to remember he couldn't use it. Waving over the flight attendant, he asked, "How long until we land?"

"Hard to say, Mr. Kenney. There's a bit of a line and we're going to have to circle for a while. I'll let you know when we get an updated ETA, though."

He didn't know who to call first when they landed— Kate, Manny or Megan. Scratch Megan, since he didn't have her number. This stunt reeked of Manny's machinations, but Kate could've had a hand in it, as well. They were probably in collusion to drive him insane. Ratings and money: the two things Kate and Manny could be guaranteed to jump on any possibility of.

He shifted in his seat as the pilot announced the delay to the rest of the passengers.

How had they talked Megan into this idea? She had a fear of public speaking. She hated being the center of attention. Their small, family-only wedding hadn't been all about finances—Megan just couldn't face the idea of being the focus of that many people. She was an introvert, uncomfortable outside her zone.

That protective instinct that had appeared out of nowhere yesterday swooped back in again. The feeling was both familiar and odd at the same time. He'd been trapped by that feeling the very first time she'd turned those huge baby-blue eyes on him, awakening some caveman instinct to protect and shelter her from the big, bad world.

But it should be long gone by now, beaten down by the way she'd walked out on him, buried by her selfishness and immaturity.…

There was the feeling he was used to getting on those

rare occasions Megan crossed his mind. That older instinct had just been shaken loose by the surprise at seeing her the other day. That twinge of guilt he'd felt at the bookstore had been easily tamped down, even as several tenacious reporters had questioned him about their marriage in interviews yesterday. He'd evaded the questions as much as possible.

Megan wasn't a part of his life. She needed to go back to whoever she was and whatever she did when not crashing his book signing. She certainly wasn't relevant to his career.

And he sure as *hell* didn't want her on his show.

No man should have to deal with his ex-wife on a national platform. What drugs were Manny and Kate on to even consider it?

He should fire both of them.

And he just might, if this plane ever hit the tarmac and he could use his phone.

The high-rise building that housed Broad Horizons Broadcasting looked like any other office building on the Chicago skyline. Megan wasn't sure what she'd expected when the shiny black town car had pulled up at her door earlier to ferry her downtown, but she didn't feel as if she'd been brought to a radio station. It looked rather more like an insurance company or something. She thanked her driver as he held her door, feeling a bit like a celebrity herself from his deferential treatment.

As she walked into the building and read the company listings on the wall, she stifled a laugh when she saw the building was, indeed, an insurance company. And an investment firm, a law firm and several other things on different floors. She signed in at the front desk, and the elderly security guard's eyebrows went up when he read her name and destination.

"You're not what I was expecting, Dr. Lowe."

She wasn't sure if that was a compliment or not. "You were expecting me?"

"Ms. Wilson told me to send you straight up to fifteen when you arrived."

Ms. Wilson. Kate. *Not Devin.* She still hadn't heard from him, although Kate had promised to pass along a message for him to call her. They went live on the air in less than an hour, and she'd like to talk to Devin before then. They needed ground rules, a plan of action.... And she needed to be sure she had worked past all those stammers Devin seemed to cause in her *before* she made a fool of herself on air.

The guard walked her to the elevator bank. "I have to release the floor for you. Otherwise you'll have to go to fourteen first." At her look, he elaborated. "It's a security measure for the hosts and their guests." He inserted a key, pressed the button and gave her a friendly smile as he stepped out and the doors closed. "Good luck."

"Thanks," she answered, but the doors were shut and the elevator lurched upward. Megan tried to tell herself that the sinking feeling in her stomach was caused by the swift ascent, but she wasn't a very good liar. Especially to herself.

When the elevator dinged and the doors opened, she stepped out carefully. Once again she hadn't been sure what to expect, but so far, Broad Horizons looked a lot like every other corporate-type office she'd ever seen—gray cubicles, fluorescent lighting, sturdy carpet and the faint lingering odor of coffee and microwave popcorn. Most of the cubicles were empty, and the quiet of the post-five-o'clock workday had already begun to settle.

She stood there, feeling rather foolish and unsure what to do.

"Dr. Lowe!"

She recognized the voice as Kate's and turned. Like everything else, Kate was completely *not* what Megan had expected. Tall and willowy with long black hair that curled in perfect unruliness around her shoulders, Kate looked like a supermodel. Someone that beautiful should be on TV, not hiding on the faceless radio.

At the very least, she should be sharing a couple of Dev's billboards.

Megan felt plain and frumpy—and rather underdressed in a simple skirt, tee and cardigan. Kate looked as if she belonged on a catwalk.

A perfect smile nearly blinded her as Kate extended her hand and introduced herself. "I'm so glad you're here, Dr. Lowe. Tonight's show is going to be fantastic."

I'd settle for not horrific. "Why don't you call me Megan?"

Kate nodded before she indicated Megan should follow her through the labyrinthine offices. She had to trot to keep up with Kate's longer strides.

"I have to admit, Kate, you're not how I pictured you." Realizing how that might sound, Megan tried to clarify. "Your voice, I mean. It seems like you'd be—" *Yikes. That sounds even worse.* "I mean…"

Kate laughed. "I understand. No one looks like you think they should once you've heard them on the radio." She shot Megan a sly smile. "Except for Devin, of course. People expect a panty-ripper when they hear his voice, and he doesn't disappoint."

"Excuse me, a what?"

"Panty-ripper. You know, the kind of man you'd rip your panties off for."

Megan stumbled slightly over her own feet. She couldn't quite argue with that statement, but she certainly wasn't going to agree out loud. Hell, she'd been guilty of some panty-ripping on more than one occasion…. She stopped that train of thought. *Ancient history.*

Kate continued talking, thankfully unaware of the heat stealing over Megan's face. "But that's the key to Devin's cross-demographic appeal. The men like his content, and the women like his package." She winked. "What's the saying? Men want to be him and the women just want him."

Did Kate want him? Was there something going on between Dev and his beautiful producer? Megan told herself it was strictly professional curiosity, but that didn't explain the little pang in her stomach. "So where is he? Did you give him my message?"

"Devin's plane was delayed and he's been frightfully busy all afternoon. He must not have had a chance to call. But you'll see him shortly." Kate held open a door for her. "We don't have a Green Room or anything, but you can hang out here for a few minutes and make yourself comfortable. I'll be back in a couple of minutes to start prepping you."

Prepping? That sounded as if something painful was coming. Megan wished she had a clue what went on at a radio station.

As the door closed, she realized Kate had left her in a break room. Table, fridge, couch, coffeepot—it could have been in any office anywhere, except for the pictures on the walls. She assumed many of them were on-air personalities, but she didn't recognize their faces. Except Devin's, of course. She did, however, recognize the people they posed with—sports stars, celebrities, politicians. Dear Lord, was that the vice president shaking Dev's hand?

The realization hit her a little too late. Some of America's most popular and controversial talk-radio shows broadcast out of this very building. Possibly using the same microphones and everything she was about to use. It was a little intimidating.

She settled on the couch and ran a hand over her hair. A snort escaped. She was going to be on the *radio;* it didn't matter what she looked like since only a few people would see her.

And one of those people would be Devin. It wasn't vanity or wanting to look good for *him* that sent her digging for lipstick. She was about to go talk to thousands—possibly hundreds of thousands—of people. She needed to feel confident. Even if they couldn't see her, the confidence of knowing she looked decent would come through in her voice.

It had nothing to do with Devin.

Hard on that thought, the door opened. Expecting it to be Kate, she finished with her lipstick and dropped it into her bag before turning.

Devin stood there, a slightly mocking look on his face. "It's radio, you know. No one can see you."

Do not take the bait. "It's a pleasure to see you again, as well." *Pleasure* might not be exactly the right word, since her stomach felt a little unsteady as he closed the door behind him, but at least her voice sounded normal enough to her ears.

Devin acknowledged the small slam against his manners with a mocking nod. He didn't seem happy she was here. Was he regretting inviting her on the show? Holding a grudge for her behavior the other day? He crossed to the fridge and took out two bottles of water. Handing one to her, he confirmed her earlier feeling. "I can't believe Kate convinced you to do this."

"Kate made some very valid points about controlling the press and putting the proper spin on things."

"Kate would sacrifice kittens on the air if she thought it would improve our ratings."

"So your plan is to sacrifice me?" A dread settled in her chest. Had she just walked into an even bigger disaster? Was this going to make things worse?

He shook his head. "This isn't *my* plan. Not by a long shot. I only learned of this bright idea as I was landing at O'Hare today. I've had to rearrange several things to accommodate you."

"Accommodate me? Kate said—" *Damn.* She should've... "Why didn't you return my call? We could have avoided this."

He shrugged. "The publicity was done. And I've been a bit busy today."

That remark reminded her how busy she *wasn't* at the moment, thanks to him and his stupid book. "I can imagine. A radio show, a book tour—it must be exhausting. How do you find the time to practice law?"

"I don't. Much."

"What?" That seemed impossible. Dev *loved* the law. Loved the tactics, the arguments, the logic required. Way back when, he'd spend hours explaining the nuances of a case or a statute to her, and his passion for law and justice had been one of the things she'd loved about him. She'd been floored to hear he'd ended up a high-priced and notorious divorce attorney, but to give it up altogether?

"My name may be on the door of the firm, but it doesn't mean I'm on every case. That's what partners and paralegals are for."

"Do you miss it?" The question was out before she could stop it.

"I don't have time for that either." She wanted to respond

to that, but Devin rushed ahead. "Sounds like you've done pretty well for yourself, *Dr.* Lowe. You became a psychiatrist after all."

"Clinical psychologist—" *no thanks to you* "—but you're close enough." As was she—just a few more months and she'd be official.

"And is it everything you hoped it would be?"

She could hear a small undercurrent in his voice that made her wonder if he was trying to pick a fight. No one else would notice it, but she knew that tone all too well for it not to send her hackles up. She lifted her chin. "And more."

"Good for you." He finished the bottle of water in one long drink and tossed it into the recycling bin.

Megan battled with herself. She'd sworn she wouldn't let her temper or her emotions control her and drive her to say or do anything that remotely resembled that debacle at the bookstore. She knew he was needling her. Intentionally. "Dr. Lowe" recognized that and knew how to handle it both properly and professionally. "Meggie," though, wanted to smack back.

Meggie won. "So how do you like being the country's divorce guru? Is it everything you hoped for while you were in law school?" She feigned confusion. "Oh, wait, that's not why you went to law school in the first place. Let me guess, there's more money in divorce than in protecting the Constitution."

"Lots more money." Dev had the audacity to grin at her and she felt childish for giving in to the urge to snark back. "Bit more excitement, too."

"And to think you used to be an idealist." The disappointment in her voice wasn't all fake.

"Blind idealism is dangerous."

"Ergo *Cover Your Assets?*"

"Exactly."

"And it doesn't bother you?"

"What?"

"The pessimism you dish out. Anyone listening to you would begin to believe that all marriages end in divorce."

He arched an eyebrow. "Wonder where I got that idea?"

She shouldn't have started this. They were already falling back into bad habits, and they hadn't even been around each other a full fifteen minutes yet. At this rate, they'd be at each other's throats by the time they went on the air. Time to be a professional—and the bigger person—and make a graceful retreat. "I tell you what—let's not make this personal." Dev's other eyebrow joined the first, and she quickly amended her statement. "Or more personal than it has to be, at least."

He nodded his agreement. "That's my plan."

"Good. I'm glad you have one. Why don't you fill me in on the details of this plan?"

"It's not too complicated, but if we're lucky it just might work out for you."

"And for you?"

That seemed to amuse him. "Megan, this actually has very little to do with me. I'm fine no matter what you say or do."

"In other words, you're doing me some kind of a favor?" She did *not* want to be indebted to him on top of everything else.

He just shrugged again.

"But you'll get a boost to your ratings, too."

"I'm number one in my time slot. My ratings don't really need a boost."

"But Kate said—"

"Kate's obsessed with our ratings. You know, maybe you could help her with that."

"If this works, and I get to go back to work, then I'll give her all the free counseling she needs." Biting her tongue to keep anything else from coming out, she faced him again. "So. The plan?"

"Simple, actually. First you'll need to bottle some of that hostility." Megan felt her jaw tighten. "Be friendly, but not too friendly. Polite. Noncommittal. Kate culled some of the more inflated speculations from the tabs and the blogs—we'll have a good laugh over that." That was an instruction, not a prediction, so she nodded. "The trick is to describe to the listeners how boring and mind-numbingly average our marriage really was and then make our divorce sound even more so. We'll take calls for a while, and then it will be over."

Over. She'd thought she and Dev were over long ago, but here they were. And to hear Dev describe their marriage as "boring" and "mind-numbing" felt like a slap across the face. Granted, they'd had problems—obviously—and that last year had gotten pretty ugly at times, but the early days had been far from boring or average. At least for her.

They'd been living on little more than love, but they'd been happy.

Dev obviously felt differently.

All her education and training had given her insight into why their marriage had failed, and she'd come to terms with that. She even knew what to say to couples going through the same things that split up her and Devin. She had perspective. She had distance. She had closure.

But hearing Dev dismiss their good times opened up all kinds of old wounds she didn't realize could hurt anymore.

Until right now.

Thankfully, Kate choose that minute to return, giving Megan a much-needed moment to get hold of herself while Kate and Devin discussed show-related things she didn't understand.

If she was smart, she'd back out of this crazy idea and go back to Plan A: lie low and ride it out. Plan B—changing her name and moving to Canada—was starting to gain traction, as well.

But then something beeped, and Kate and Devin were gathering up the few papers and bottles of water.

Kate turned her supermodel smile on Megan. "You ready? It's showtime."

Devin held the door open, waiting for her, and when she didn't move, that eyebrow arched up again. Irritation crawled over her, forcing her feet into motion.

She was walking to the gallows out of pure spite.

Dr. Lowe's official diagnosis? She was certifiably insane.

CHAPTER THREE

SHE'D MISSED THE FOURTH-grade field trip to the radio station, so Megan had spent last night trying to find out what she could about radio stations and how they worked. A couple of movies, so hopelessly out of date the disc jockeys were spinning vinyl records, some video clips posted on the internet…she still didn't have a clue. And she hated not having a clue. Research was her friend; it made her feel comfortable and confident. But the how-to's of radio were still a mystery, and she felt at a distinct disadvantage going into this.

That bothered her a lot. She didn't want to be at a disadvantage—of any kind—when it came to Devin. She needed to feel like an equal. She was, she reminded herself. She wasn't the same person she'd been all those years ago. She could hold her own—intellectually, professionally, sarcastically—against Devin Kenney.

She squared her shoulders as Devin opened a door marked Studio A. *I can do this.*

Two chairs facing each other across a small desk, two microphones, some computer screens—the booth looked a lot like what she'd expected from her research. Kate was on the other side of a large glass window that ran perpendicular to their table, settling into her chair and sliding large headphones over her ears. Somehow Megan knew Kate wasn't the kind of woman who would have "headphone hair" two hours from now. She, on the other hand...

Dev's "ahem" brought her back to the present. He was indicating a chair. "You'll sit here. That's your mic—be sure you get close to it, or folks won't be able to hear you. Here—" he handed her a set of headphones "—put these on. And don't touch anything."

Megan bristled. "I'm not five. I think I can handle that." Trying to look as if she did things like this all the time, she settled into the chair and smiled through the window at Kate.

"This is your last chance to back out, Megan. We're going to be live, and while there's a five-second delay, I won't be able to walk you through one of your panic attacks."

She almost let a sarcastic comment fly before she realized Dev had every right to be concerned about his show. It was the sign of a professional. She needed to respect that—at least while they were on the air. She'd keep her tongue behind her teeth if it killed her in the process.

She tried for a noncommittal tone. "I haven't had a panic attack in years, but thanks for your concern."

Dev looked surprised. "You haven't? That's a surprise."

"Do you think I could help other people if I couldn't learn to help myself first? I wouldn't have lasted long in this business if I couldn't talk to people."

"That's impressive, Meggie. Good for you."

She couldn't quite tell if that was grudging admiration in his tone or more sarcasm. She chose to accept the compliment, regardless of its sincerity. "Thank you. It means I should be able to get through this just fine." *At least I hope so.* She could feel all kinds of old insecurities bubbling up to the surface, and they felt much like a panic attack.

As Devin pulled his chair up to the desk, she realized how small the booth was. Not claustrophobic small, but not large enough to be in with your ex-husband sucking up all the oxygen, either. By the time she got her chair in place, only about a foot of space separated them. She tucked her feet under the chair, not wanting her legs and feet to accidentally tangle with his. *No footsie under the table tonight.*

Kate signaled them, and Devin put his headphones on. She did the same, and a panicky flutter started in her stomach. She took deep, calming breaths, trying to focus.

Through her headphones she heard Devin's theme music and intro. Then Devin leaned into the mic and started to speak.

It was as if his lips were only inches from her ear. She jumped, and her hands flew to her headphones, nearly pulling them off her ears in response to that baritone seeming to speak only to her.

She caught herself and pretended to adjust the headphones instead. Just another thing she hadn't prepared herself for. Her need to stammer seemed right on the end of her tongue, but Kate and Devin were bantering a bit, and the mention of her name returned her attention to the proper place.

"...welcome Dr. Megan Lowe, my ex-wife, to the show."

Both Devin and Kate looked at her, obviously expecting a response, and for a moment she faltered. Her heart thudded in her chest. How many people were listening? Every old insecurity she thought she'd buried was clawing its way to the surface.

Then Devin smirked at her.

A little spark of ire flared in her stomach, and that helped her gain control of herself. Trying to match his mock, she plastered a smile on her face, leaned into the microphone and prepared to meet the nation. "Thanks, Dev. I can't say I'm *pleased* to be here, but I appreciate the invitation, nonetheless."

He'd expected Megan to fold long before now. *Saying* she'd outgrown her shyness was a far cry from actually doing so, and he'd been ready to kill her mic and go to tape if she had a total meltdown. But twenty minutes into the show she sounded cool and poised, and her voice carried just a touch of mocking cynicism.

He'd seen the tiny flare of panic rise, but only someone who knew her very well would know that the wrinkle in her forehead was a warning sign of her discomfort. But the panic was gone as quickly as it had risen, and she managed to sound both amused and bored with the circus the media had made of her life and the outlandish speculation Kate had found on the blogs.

Megan's voice slid a notch down on the register as she leaned into the mic, giving her a seductive, husky tone that had to have half his male listeners at attention. He certainly was. When Kate commented on the main talking point— the fact Megan counseled couples to stay together when she herself was divorced—Megan chuckled.

She might as well have run a hand over him. The sound seemed to hum through his headphones directly through his body as if they were alone. Intimate.

He tried to shake off the feeling, but when Megan tilted her chin half an inch in his direction, he wondered if she'd done it on purpose.

No, Megan couldn't think she'd still have an effect on him after all these years. Hell, he wouldn't have dreamed it was possible if he hadn't felt the electric shiver over his skin.

Through the window Kate beamed an I-told-you-so grin,

but she would have been equally glad to have Megan crash and burn. Kate pointed at her computer, meaning the callers were lining up. A glance at his screen confirmed it.

Seemed as if Megan was on her way to fifteen minutes of fame instead of shame. He was oddly, *inexplicably* proud of her.

He brought the first caller on. "Caller, you're on the air."

"This is Andrea from Las Vegas. I'm a big fan of your show, Devin, but my question is actually for Dr. Megan."

Megan covered an amused snort with a small cough before she turned to him and mouthed, "Dr. Megan? Really?"

He shrugged.

Megan shook her head and leaned into the mic. "Hi, Andrea. What's your question?"

"So why'd you two get divorced? Who left who?"

Oh, he couldn't wait to hear her answer to this. When Megan looked to him, question written all over her pixie features, he folded his arms over his chest and shrugged.

Megan stuck out her tongue at him before she answered. "Devin and I were young when we got married—college sweethearts, in fact—and we had some maturity issues and some disagreements about what we wanted from our lives and each other. Those differences proved to be irreconcilable."

"So Devin left you?" It was more of a statement than a question. Maybe he should have warned her his listeners wouldn't accept vagueness.

He saw Megan's shoulders straighten. "Actually, I left Devin and filed for divorce."

At the caller's gasp of disbelief, he cut in, challenging Megan with a grin. "Hard to believe, huh?"

She rolled her eyes, but picked up the gauntlet. "Trust

me, Andrea, he totally deserved it." Her grin turned slightly evil, but her voice sounded conspiratorial. "He wasn't always this charming, you know."

"But surely he was still this hot, even back then. You had to be crazy to walk away from *that*," the caller continued, and through the booth's window he could see Kate practically crowing in glee as the queue of callers grew longer.

Megan cleared her throat. "There's a lot more to a good marriage than the hotness of one partner. Lust can only hold a couple together for so long—at some point there has to be something more. Some commonality. Some kind of meeting of the minds. I'm not implying that Dev's just a pretty face...." She trailed off, doing exactly that.

Kate was about to fall off her chair in excitement, and Megan shot him a look of triumph. The computer in front of him flashed as listener emails started flooding his in-box. It was time for him to take his show back in hand, damn it.

"Emotional stability helps a relationship, too. Both partners need to be mental adults." Megan's jaw dropped at the insult, and her eyes narrowed at him. He ignored her. "Thanks for your question, caller. Kate, who's next on the line?"

The next few callers were predictable—folks commenting on the hype and irony, asking them to confirm or deny more rumors—but as the show went on, there were a few callers who were, amazingly enough, more interested in getting out of their own marriages than how or why he ended his.

He was trying to explain—for the thousandth time—that covering one's assets did not mean hiding assets, since hiding assets was illegal in all states. The caller kept interrupting with bitter condemnations of his wife, as if that would allow him freedom with financial disclosure laws.

Pete-from-Tennessee harrumphed when Devin stopped to take a breath.

"Excuse me, can I butt in for a second?"

It was the first time Megan had commented on any question not directed at her or their past. He'd seen her shake her head a few times, and she'd probably bitten holes in her tongue, but she'd stayed off his "turf."

When he turned in her direction, he could see the frown between her eyebrows. She was drumming her fingers lightly on the desktop. "You have something to add, Dr. Megan?"

She frowned at his use of her new nickname, but she nodded to him before turning to the mic. "Pete, I'm hearing a lot of anger and a lot of bitterness. I'm not saying it's not justified, and without talking to you more or hearing your wife's side of the story, I can't offer any advice. *But,*" she stressed as both Devin and the caller tried to interrupt, "I'm also hearing hurt and jealousy, and that tells me there's something else going on. Have you talked about some of these issues with your wife? Or a counselor?"

"Megan..." Devin started, but she held up a hand to stay him.

"Well, Pete?"

Pete-from-Tennessee muttered something unintelligible. Then he cleared his throat. "Not everyone needs—or wants—therapy, Dr. Megan."

"I understand that. But something tells me you and your wife have some communication problems. You might benefit from a few sessions with a counselor."

"You're a shrink. That's how you make your money. Of course you don't think people should get divorced," Pete-from-Tennessee grumbled.

"On the contrary, I'd never advocate anyone stay in a marriage where they were mentally, emotionally, or physically in danger of any kind. There are some marriages that can't be saved." She met Devin's eyes evenly. "And there are some that shouldn't."

Then Megan's voice took on an earnest and almost hypnotic quality. The combination of compassion and concern tempered with a no-nonsense tone had even him listening carefully. "But from what you're saying, Pete, I'm not sure your marriage is firmly in either of those camps. Marriage isn't easy. Sometimes you have to fight for it. But it can be worth the battle."

They must have taught Megan that idea in graduate school, because that certainly wasn't her thinking when she walked out on *him*. The caller's sputters had lapsed into silence, so Devin asked the question hanging in the air. "You agree, though, that divorce is sometimes the best thing?"

Megan met his eyes again, and the mood in the booth shifted. "I do. Sometimes divorce is the best and the healthiest option for both partners. Some people just shouldn't be together. It's a cold, hard fact that can be difficult to admit, but once those couples split, they usually find themselves to be happier."

"What? No romantic notions about happily-ever-after or psychobabble—"

"Happily-ever-after isn't a romantic notion—but it's not guaranteed, either. Love and passion will only get you so far—like to the altar. It isn't always enough for a successful marriage."

Oh, he knew all about love and passion, and from the look on Megan's face, she was remembering a few choice moments from their history, too. But they also both knew the reality of it not being enough. He didn't break the stare, but he did try to inject a lighter tone to his next words for the sake of his audience. "Isn't *that* the truth."

Megan's brows drew together in a frown, and the intense stare changed to a dirty look. "Pete, do me a favor, okay? Talk to your wife before you get any more advice from a divorce lawyer. You may be partly right—I do tend to look for ways to heal a marriage. It's my nature and my job. But a divorce lawyer makes his money off your unhappiness and therefore has an unhealthy interest in your attempts to reconcile with your spouse."

Devin heard the caller take a deep breath. "I'll think about what you said, Dr. Megan."

Megan was good—he'd give her that—but the smug smile tugging at the corners of her mouth and the mocking lift of her eyebrows told him *she* knew it, too. He'd had a lot thrown at him in the past forty-eight hours, but this new side of Megan was the hardest of all to grasp.

"That's all I ask. Good luck, Pete, to both you *and* your wife. I hope you can figure out what's best for you both in the long term."

Kate took the opportunity to break in. "And on that note, we need to take a short break for your local news update and a message from our sponsors." A second later she indicated they were clear, and Kate began to gush. "You two are fabulous together! The chemistry is just amazing and the audience is eating it up. Have you seen the call queue? The mail piling up in the show's in-box? You guys are a hit! I knew you would be!" Kate wiggled in her chair, something he recognized as her "ratings dance." "Oh, and you have three minutes."

He took off his headphones and Megan did the same, a confused look on her face. "Three minutes of what?"

"A break." He moved the mics out of the way. "What the hell was that about?"

She'd started reaching for her water when he mentioned

a break, but his angry question had her responding in an equally snide tone. "What was what about?"

"Counseling my callers?"

"Sorry, but that's my job." Megan didn't sound the least bit sorry, and that tweaked his ire a little more.

"Not on my show, it's not. My callers want advice about breaking up, not psychobabble about making up."

"There was absolutely no psychobabble at all in anything I said to that caller. Just the truth. Maybe divorce is the best thing for that guy and his wife, but I'm not going to sit here and let you dish out all that bitterness on someone who might be able to be happy if you didn't egg him on and make him believe a divorce is the best idea ever."

"Sometimes it is. You said so yourself. And you would know, of course."

Megan's eye began to twitch. "You're not wrong about that. Trust me when I say that divorcing *you* was certainly the best idea *I* ever had."

I really do need some anger-management classes. Megan winced inwardly at the nasty remark that hung in the air between them.

Being around Devin—and the tension that proximity caused—was doing bad things to her brain and releasing the brake on her tongue. What had she expected? Things to be different?

Doing the same thing and expecting different results was the classic definition of insanity. *Doctor, heal thyself.*

But the words were out there now, and she couldn't see a graceful retreat from them. Too much of their past had been stirred up for that.

Dev's eyes narrowed, telling her she'd scored a direct hit with that outburst. "And yet you claim to be a marriage advocate. The hypocrisy doesn't bother you?"

Oh, now he'd crossed a line. "Hypocrisy? You're getting on your soapbox about hypocrisy? That's a laugh. You're the biggest hypocrite on the planet. And, again, I'm in a position to know *that* for a fact. Too bad it's not grounds for divorce in Illinois. I'd have gotten more alimony."

Kate's voice came over a small speaker. "Um, guys? I hate to interrupt—this looks, um, fascinating—but you've got one minute."

A muscle in Dev's jaw twitched. Oh, he was really itching for a fight now. But then, so was she. Going back on the air with him now might be a big mistake, considering how loose her tongue was today. But walking out now? In the middle of the show? That would only undo every bit of damage control she'd managed to accomplish tonight. There was no good to be found anywhere in this situation now. She was damned if she did, damned if she didn't.

Dev glared at her as he scooted his chair to the table and grabbed his headphones. "We'll finish this conversation later." He motioned her to silence as the red light came back on and Kate brought them back from commercial.

Megan had to give him credit—no one in Listener Land would know he was shooting daggers at her as she moved her chair and positioned her microphone. His voice carried none of the heat he'd just blasted her with as he started back into his show.

That lack sent warning shivers up her spine.

Kate motioned to her to put her headphones on. With a sigh, she did.

"Hi, caller, you're on the air."

"Hi, Devin. This is Terri from Albuquerque. I'm a long-time listener, but a first-time caller. And I just have to ask you and Dr. Megan something."

"Go ahead, Terri. Megan and I are open books tonight."

Dev raised an eyebrow at her in challenge. "No holds barred."

Megan shifted uncomfortably in her seat.

"What's the story with you two? You haven't really told us what the problem was."

Devin gave her a look that made her regret she'd let Kate talk her into this in the first place.

She was definitely moving to Canada.

CHAPTER FOUR

MEGAN KEPT UP A GOOD GAME for the listeners for the remainder of the show, but Devin could tell something was going on. She avoided eye contact unless absolutely necessary and when she did meet his eyes, she couldn't hold it for long. The technology in the booth seemed to fascinate her, but he could tell that interest was feigned. During the breaks she asked questions about how everything worked and even chatted with Kate some, but after that first heated exchange, all the fire seemed to drain out of her.

"Great show, guys." Kate cut the feed from the studio, ending their broadcast and turning it over to *Lola's Late Night Love Show* from a station in New York. "The mucky-mucks at corporate are going to be beyond thrilled. I got several calls from morning shows there toward the end."

Megan had been busily rooting in her bag, but her head jerked up sharply at Kate's words. "What do you mean, morning shows?"

"I mean you two were a hit and everyone is dying to know more. I'm going to be up all night cutting and redubbing to get the clips ready." Kate sighed dramatically, but the glee in her words couldn't be easily masked.

Megan, however, paled visibly at Kate's words. "This was supposed to be the end of it. 'Give them what they want so they'll go away,' remember?"

He laughed, causing Megan to finally meet his eyes directly. The anger and accusation there… "What gave you the idea the media would go away?"

"*She* did." Megan pointed at Kate, who shrugged and made a show of killing the mics and speakers, effectively bailing from the conversation by virtue of soundproof rooms.

He had no doubt Kate had led Megan to believe exactly that. "She lied."

Megan shot a killing look through the window at Kate, who was busy reviewing the tape and didn't see it. Then Megan rounded on him. "And *you* did, too."

"I never said anything like that."

"Yes, you did. 'We'll take calls for a while, and then it will be over.' Your words, in the lounge, not two and a half hours ago."

He thought back for a moment. "I was referring to the *show*."

"Oh, my God." Megan began to pace, her hands tugging at her hair, a sign of frustration he recognized from days past. "The morning shows…this is just going to make things *worse*."

Okay, this was an overreaction, even from Megan. "Media attention doesn't go away overnight, you know. This will take the nasty edge off, though, until it does."

Megan dropped into her chair with a groan and buried her face in her hands.

"That could happen sooner than you think, especially if something more interesting breaks."

"And what's more interesting than Devin Kenney?" she muttered into her hands. It wasn't a real question, so he didn't bother to respond. It wasn't his fault the book and the show were so popular, but Megan was acting as if he'd done all this to spite her somehow. Hard on that thought,

Megan lifted her head, spun the chair and faced him. "I hate you, Devin. I really, really do."

Actually hearing the words cut deeper than expected. "I'm supposed to be surprised? I figured that out a long time ago, Meggie. It's hardly news."

Megan's attitude changed. Her shoulders dropped, and while she was still obviously angry, somehow not all of it was directed at him anymore. "It's news to me. I didn't realize I was capable of that emotion until now."

"Really? If you walk out on people you *don't* hate, I'm curious to see what you do to the people you do."

Megan's jaw tightened. "I didn't just walk out on you. I *had* to leave because you were so caught up in yourself you forgot there was anyone else deserving of a thought from you."

"You're implying I somehow forgot we were married? That I mistook you for a roommate?"

"Pretty much." The sarcasm from Megan was new. Unexpected. It seemed graduate school had taught her a lot more than how to come out of her shell. It had given her teeth, as well.

"That's insane, Meggie."

"First of all, please do not call me Meggie," she snapped.

The heat behind what seemed like a simple statement caught him off guard.

She pushed to her feet to face him. "Secondly, I think I'm a bit more qualified to decide what's insane and what's not. And since I was there, since *I* was the one being treated like nothing more than a roommate, I know what I'm talking about."

Memories crashed in—vivid visuals of Megan's thighs straddling his hips, that long blond hair falling around them both like a curtain, her eyes closed and mouth open slightly in pleasure as she moved against him. A familiar, if almost forgotten, heat built under his skin. He fought to tamp it down. "I'm suddenly rather intrigued by your definition of *roommate*. Do you sleep with all your roommates, Megan?"

She gasped and her cheeks turned pink as she obviously got a similar visual. Then she swallowed hard and bit her bottom lip. Her arms crossed over her chest, pulling her thin cardigan closed, but not quickly enough to hide the sight of rigid nipples pressing against the cotton tank. The small success he'd had getting himself under control faltered.

"There's no need to be crude, Devin."

"It's a fair question. Personally, I'm not in the habit of having sex with my roommates, so I'm curious to see where you got *wife* and *roommate* confused."

Her chin went up. "A wife is normally afforded greater respect than a roommate," she lectured, ice dripping off her words. "Especially when it comes to big, important issues like where you're going to live, or what you're going to do with your future—your *joint* future. Your roommate can't expect you to take their plans into consideration when making yours. Your wife, however, should get a say. Since that seemed to be shocking news to you, I can only assume *you* were the one with vocabulary problems."

"And *I* think a wife would be happy her husband had been offered such a plum job after so many years of eating Ramen noodles and scrimping to pay the rent. I wasn't asking you to move to Cambodia, for God's sake. It's not like you couldn't have gone to school here in Chicago. And, hey, look where you ended up anyway."

"And you're still missing the point, Dev. I moved for you so you could go to law school—losing credits and pushing my graduation back—because you promised you'd do the same for me. But when the time came, I was supposed to walk away from *my* plans and dreams in favor of yours."

"And the obvious solution to a disagreement about jobs is, of course, divorce. I'm surprised you're allowed to counsel couples at all considering how quickly you found a divorce lawyer." The bitterness was back, surprising him with its intensity, but he had no reason to hide it now.

"Oh, grow up, Devin." Megan was good and mad now, and it was a completely different attitude and posture than he remembered. The pissy-pixie was gone, as was the big teary-eyed guilt-tripping he remembered. Somewhere along the line she'd found a steel backbone that had her in his face. "It was never just about your job or my school or anything else. It was the fact you were too freaking self-ish to realize my plans should have any relevance in the discussion. I couldn't stay married to someone who could so blithely disregard me and my dreams...."

"I'm the selfish one? Listen to yourself—everything coming out of your mouth is 'me, me, me.' That much hasn't changed about you. It's still all about you. Hell, this whole situation is practically a rerun. You don't like something, so you come to me and expect me to fix it."

"Son of a—" Megan bit the words off and took a deep breath. "Yes, I freely admit I was young and immature when we got married, and I probably did rely on you way too much. But I had to grow up pretty damn fast after I moved out."

"You moved out because you wanted to go to Albany and I wanted to go to Chicago. And instead of looking for a solution, you filed for divorce."

"Had you come to me and *asked* me to move to Chicago, I'd have done it in a heartbeat because I lov—" She caught herself and cleared her throat. "I would've moved to Chicago for you. Rearranged my life *again*. But you didn't ask. You just expected, and you went all sexist caveman when I didn't just roll over and do it."

"I thought your major was psychology, not revisionist history. How convenient for you."

Megan's eyes widened, and the flush coloring her cheeks and neck darkened. "Excuse me?"

"You've convinced yourself it was all my fault. I was the big fat jerk and you were the poor innocent victim."

Her jaw dropped and she quickly snapped it shut. "Stop. Just stop." The words barely escaped the hardened line of her lips. "I swear, Dev…"

Megan seemed to catch herself at that moment. Closing her eyes, she took a deep breath and let it out slowly. Then she did it again. When she opened her eyes and spoke, she seemed calmer. "Good Lord, I can't believe we're rehashing this. It's not beneficial to either of us. And it's certainly not healthy. We're way off topic." The angry crease in her forehead smoothed out and she sat.

The absurdity of the situation finally filtered through the adrenaline Megan caused to rush through his brain and body. "Agreed." They'd moved from spinning the media to spinning their wheels about the past. "If the APA or the Bar Association had witnessed that, they'd pull both our licenses."

Megan shook her head. "And the sad thing is that I know better." She leaned back in the chair and blew out her breath noisily. "There's now about four chapters of my dissertation I may want to revise before I publish."

"Megan," he began.

"Look, Dev—" she said at the same time. She interrupted herself and yielded the floor. "Sorry, go ahead."

"Ladies first."

She took another of those deep breaths. "You know, I do appreciate what you tried to do tonight. It's my fault I didn't quite understand what would happen. In retrospect, if I'd thought it all the way through, I'd have realized this wasn't quite the magic bullet I hoped it would be. But that's not your fault. Hopefully, it will help a little, maybe make it die down a little faster." She reached for her bag and settled the strap on her shoulder. "But now I'm going to go home and pack for Canada."

"That's a good idea. A vacation would do you some good. Maybe this will all be over when you get back." He doubted it, but Megan would be better off believing that. She could enjoy her vacation and be better prepared to face whatever was still being churned around in the press when she did get back.

Megan snorted and rubbed her hands over her face. She stood, then turned back to him, a question on her face. "I'm sorry. It's your turn now. What were you going to say?"

He thought for a moment. Megan seemed to be calming down, and spinning her up again wouldn't help anything. Neither would continuing their delightful trip down memory lane. The past was past, and as an adult, he should let it go and move on.

He'd show her who'd grown up and who hadn't. He would be the mature one if it killed him in the process.

"Do you need a ride home?"

Megan finally understood what drove some of her clients to drink. She'd always told them it was an excuse or a crutch, but at this moment she knew why so many people sought solace and calm in a bottle. She desperately needed a drink to calm her nerves, soothe her brain and numb a little of the unbelievably powerful and conflicting emotions tumbling through her.

But Devin… After everything that had happened to-night—including the amazingly painful opening of old scars—he seemed able to brush it all aside. Was Devin really that unfeeling now? Or did that coldness extend only to her? The idea bothered her a little at the same time she envied that ability. He'd gone from looking at her as if he'd gladly strangle her to calmly offering her a ride home without missing a beat.

"No, thank you. Kate sent a car...." She trailed off when Devin shook his head.

"Kate may have sent a car for you, but I promise she didn't arrange for one to take you home."

Every friendly feeling she'd had toward Kate had died off quite a while ago, and Megan was rapidly moving toward wanting to rip out Kate's beautiful shampoo-ad-quality hair now. She shot a dirty look through the window into the producer's booth, but Kate was busy with her computer. "I'll get the guard at the front desk to call me a cab, then."

"Don't be ridiculous. I drove myself in tonight, and I can run you home."

She wasn't about to admit to Devin that she didn't want a ride from him. She didn't want to put herself in another, even smaller enclosed space with him tonight. Although the tension built from their arguing and their past was making her desperately crave a glass of wine, she could handle that. She would be fine once she had a little time and distance to process the violent whirlpool of emotions in her stomach.

No, she didn't want to get into a car with Devin, because the one thing she couldn't process or even address right now—especially while he was in the same room with her—was the disturbing reaction of her body. Getting into the close confines of a car? Where it was dark and intimate? She had enough memories crashing in on her at the moment to deal with, and his flat-out remark about sex had made it impossible to ignore them. It was difficult enough to keep her mind away from their history, but to know that Dev was fully capable of—and probably *was* at that very second—picturing her naked and…and… She nearly lost it completely at that point.

And now she couldn't shake off the images of an equally naked Devin that were foremost in her mind and shaking up her libido.

"I appreciate the offer, but I'm sure it's out of your way.…"

"I don't mind. It's probably the least I can do."

Decision time. Continuing to argue with him over this would be juvenile, but there simply wasn't a graceful way to decline without sounding petty and petulant. Then there was the voice of her inner accountant who had calculated the fare for the trip home and was screaming to accept the ride if she wanted to make rent this month. Financial recklessness in order to make a stand? That was more than juvenile. It was stupid. And after the mess he'd put her in, he did at least owe her cab fare.

"Then I accept." She forced herself to smile as Devin opened the studio door and held it for her. Kate waved as they left, and it was all Megan could do not to make a rude gesture in return.

She really was losing her grip on her sanity.

Thankfully, Devin was quiet on the long elevator ride down to the garage under the building. He pulled out his phone and began checking messages, so she did the same. None worth responding to, but it kept her hands and eyes occupied and made being trapped in a small box with Devin a little easier.

The parking garage was all but deserted, and the hum of fluorescent lights bouncing off the gray concrete walls seemed like the setup for something in one of those bad horror movies Dev used to love to watch. It gave her the willies.

Devin must have noticed, because he called her on it.

She shrugged. "I just can't help but feel like that blonde girl in every horror movie right before the serial killer jumps out with a chain saw."

That caused Dev to laugh, and the sound had a disturbing effect on her stomach. "The blonde girl who dies is always alone. And usually wearing substantially less than you are."

The way Devin's eyes roamed over her as he spoke sent her mind back to earlier uncomfortable thoughts about states of nakedness. She tried to think of something witty to say, but her thoughts were a bit too scrambled. She settled for the nonwitty "Good point."

When she heard the beep of Devin unlocking his car, she finally took notice of the car he was headed toward. Low-slung, sleek and red, the car was every teenage boy's fantasy. As he opened the door for her, she let out a low, appreciative whistle. "Nice car. Divorce does pay well, it seems."

"That it does," he answered, then closed the door on any further comment she might have made. She didn't know much about cars, but even she could appreciate the butter-soft leather seats and dashboard that resembled a cockpit. When Devin slid into his seat and brought the engine to life, she could feel the horsepower rumbling under her feet.

Devin braced his hand on the back of her seat as he backed out of the space, and she got an unwelcome reminder of why this was such a bad idea. He was only inches away, and even the tiniest movement of his hand would cause his fingers to brush against the nape of her neck. Goose bumps rose on her skin and she fought back a shiver.

Of course Devin couldn't drive one of those huge SUVs, where a couple of feet would have separated them. Oh, no, the tiny sports car meant his arm brushed hers as he shifted gears, and every time she inhaled, the familiar scent of his aftershave tickled her nose. Once upon a time the scent had been comforting and calming. Not now. Tonight it jangled her nerves and made her palms sweat.

She had to get control of herself. "A red sports car is a cliché, don't you think?"

Devin shrugged. "I always wanted one. Don't you remember?"

She did, now that he mentioned it. A fancy car much like this one had always been Dev's wish when they played "One Day When We Are Rich." They'd drink off-brand beer and pretend it was champagne while they planned the fabulous vacations they'd take and the house in the country they'd buy.

It all seemed a little silly in retrospect, but it brought a small smile to her face before a feeling of sadness and loss for the kids they were and the dreams they'd had settled on her shoulders.

The feeling passed, though, when she realized Devin had achieved part of their dreams without her. "But now I know that sports cars are overcompensation devices for men who are, ahem, *lacking*."

Dev's smile was wicked in the half-light of the car, and she knew instantly she shouldn't have gone there. "I don't remember you complaining about my lack of anything. In fact, you seemed more than satisfied with my compensation."

Heat rushed to her face, and she could feel her ears burning. She refused to take the bait, though, and chose instead to move to the neutral topic of directions. Dev's eyebrow went up when she told him her address, but thankfully, he didn't press further.

They rode in silence for a few minutes, and Megan stared out the window at the familiar scenery to keep from trying to watch Devin's face out of the corner of her eye. It was ridiculous to be so uncomfortable. This was just Dev, for goodness' sake. At the same time, this was *Dev,* and that did funny things to her heart rate.

When he spoke, she jumped. "Everything else aside, you did well tonight. On the air, I mean."

She turned in time to see the side of his mouth curve upward at the last sentence. *Small talk. Excellent idea.* "Thanks. It was both easier and more nerve-racking than I thought. If that's possible."

"I understand. Not everyone does so well their first time."

"You're very good at what you do—on the air, at least," she qualified, and that got another smirk from Devin. "I can't say I agree with even half of what you said to your callers, but I'm impressed nonetheless."

Devin nodded at the compliment, and the question that had been on her tongue all night couldn't be held back any longer. "What happened to you, Dev?"

He looked surprised. "Happened how?"

"You used to have all this passion for justice and now you're a divorce attorney."

"Are you saying that there's no need for justice to be served in divorce proceedings?"

"Not at all. But I know you came to Chicago to do something bigger than argue alimony."

"Things work out differently than we plan sometimes." There was an undertone of bitterness to his words. She was familiar with the taste herself, so she couldn't blame him. "I was asked by my boss to help with a divorce for a client. It wasn't our usual thing, but we were doing it as a personal favor for that client. It was supposed to be simple and low-key. Instead it exploded, spinning completely out of control and hitting all the papers."

"That football player, right? I remember seeing your name tied up in that."

He nodded. "The longer it dragged on, the more salacious it got—mistresses and illegitimate children and accusations of abuse and extortion. And that's only what made the papers. The stuff that didn't would curl your hair. The division of property was a nightmare. I spent the better part of two years sorting out that one divorce." He snorted. "So much for simple and low-key. When the papers were finally signed and the dust settled, I had a line of folks with equally high-profile or messy divorces begging me to represent them."

She turned sideways in the seat to face him. "You're trying to tell me this was an *accident?*"

"Specializing in divorce, yes."

"And the show? The book?"

"Amazing opportunities I'd have been a fool to pass up."

Her perspective shifted uncomfortably with this new information. "So it's purely business, then. Not personal," she said partly to herself.

"What is?"

There was no good way to say this, but she was in too far now to back down. "There's that one blogger who insists your entire career was launched by *our* marriage and divorce."

That caused a laugh. "I had no idea you were so egotistical, Meggie."

Trust Dev to jump to the worst conclusion. "It would hardly be something I'd be proud of. I'd hate to think…"

"That you'd broken my heart and left me bitter and cynical?" Devin's sarcasm was back, but she couldn't deny it was appropriate.

"You can't deny you're bitter and cynical about *something*. I'm just glad to hear it's not me."

"If you'd witnessed what I'd witnessed in the last seven years, you'd be a cynic about marriage, as well."

Was he kidding? "You do remember what I do for a living, right? I've seen some of the worst marriages in the universe—and some of the worst people, I might add. I'm not all pessimistic and angry at the world."

"You always were an optimist."

"And you were an idealist."

"People change."

So neither one of them was quite who they used to be. "You're right about that."

"And you're certainly living proof of that." Dev shifted gears and his arm brushed hers. The hairs on the back of her neck stood at attention. Megan tried to unobtrusively move over and put a little more space between them.

"I'm not sure I'm following you."

"You've grown a pretty impressive backbone. And lost a lot of that shyness." There was admiration in his tone, but no trace of sarcasm this time.

"Like I said earlier, I had to in order to do my job. Getting out on my own and moving to Albany was a huge wake-up call. I had to find my spine. And my voice. I couldn't hide behind you anymore." She looked over in time to see Dev's jaw tighten slightly. "I don't mean that as any kind of insult to you. I was a different person then, and that wasn't your doing. It's just who we were. Who I was. But once we were over… In some ways, I owe you for who I am today. I'm sorry if you see that as some kind of insult."

The streetlights kept throwing Dev's face in and out of shadow, making it hard for her to read his face. Maybe that was a good thing.

"Well, Meggie, it's certainly worked out well for us both, then." His voice was as tight as her stomach.

The statement might be true, but the truth didn't lessen that feeling in her stomach. Thankfully, the conversation was about to end, and she grabbed the moment. "Turn left here, and I'll be the first on the right."

Devin expertly slid his flashy car into a space between two cars that added together probably wouldn't equal the value of one of his hubcaps. He shifted into Park and peered through the windows as she gathered her bag and unbuckled her seat belt.

"Thanks for the ride—"

His hand landed on her wrist. "*This* is where you live?"

She'd grown used to the shabby buildings, overgrown lawns and general dilapidation, but Devin's appalled tone brought back her own initial feeling about the neighborhood. "Yeah. Good n—"

The grip tightened. "I'm not sure it's safe for you to get out of the car."

She really wasn't in the mood for this. "Your car's in more danger than I am. So you should probably get it out of here before…"

Dev wasn't listening. "That building looks like it should be condemned. Tell me it's nicer inside."

She should, but the lie stalled on her tongue. "Where I live is none of your business."

"I'm not letting you out of this car, Megan, until I…"

God, she hated that tone. It brought back old, anger-inducing memories. As if to prove his point, Dev hit the button that locked her door. Irritation crawled over her skin. "What? You're going to kidnap me from my own front yard?"

"I'd probably be doing you a favor if I did. Jesus, Megan, why are you living like this? You have a job."

"I have an internship," she corrected, hating this entire conversation.

"And?"

She sighed. "You really didn't pay any attention at all to anything I ever said, did you?"

He didn't take the bait this time. Instead, his eyes bored into hers as he waited for an explanation. *I don't owe him one,* she reminded herself, but she found herself providing it anyway. "I have to do a two-year internship before I get my license. Internships are politically correct, modern forms of slavery—except that the slaver is doing me a favor by letting me work long hours for little or no pay. I'm lucky the Weiss Clinic pays enough for me to live *here.*"

"If you need money…"

"I'm paying my dues, the same as everyone else. In a couple more months I'll have my hours complete and I'll sit my exam. Then I'll be able to get a job that pays a living wage. Until then, I'm treating this as a character-building experience."

"So your newfound backbone actually came from living in poverty?"

"It's hardly squalor." She tried to sound upbeat. "In fact, it's not much worse than our first apartment."

He made an odd choking noise. "Our first apartment was a hellhole."

In retrospect, it had been exactly that. It just hadn't felt like it—unlike her current place. And she didn't need a

PhD in anything to tell her why her perception had been rose-colored back then.

Devin's grip on her arm tightened incrementally, bringing back those old feelings to tangle with the current ones. And that memory rush was simply too much to handle in the small, dark, cozy confines of Devin's car.

He was so close. Too close. She could feel the heat of his body warming the air around them, see the pulse in his neck. If she inhaled when he exhaled, they'd share the same breath. But she wasn't sure she could breathe.

And Dev seemed to realize that, too. His attention had moved from her neighborhood to her face and now seemed focused on her lips. Her heart skittered, skipping a couple of beats. Just another inch and she... *What the hell am I thinking?* She pulled back, putting as much distance between them as the car would allow, and Dev frowned.

She cleared her throat and chose her words carefully. "I appreciate your concern, but my life is not your business or your problem anymore. Good night, good luck and hopefully we'll never have to see each other again."

Feeling rather proud of her little speech, she reached for the door handle. Devin still held her wrist, and she stared at his hand pointedly until he released his grip.

The sounds and, unfortunately, smells of her neighborhood rushed in as she opened the door, destroying the quiet cocoon, and the intimacy evaporated. *Thank goodness.* "Bye, Dev."

"Damn it, Megan—" Dev began, but she closed the door on his words.

She climbed the stairs on unsteady legs, the imprint of his hand still burning into her arm. She didn't hear the engine start, so she assumed he was watching her make her way safely inside. That thought kept her head high. She just needed to get inside, get a drink and crawl under the covers to forget this hellish, hellish day.

The urge to look over her shoulder was almost impossible to resist, but she kept her eyes straight ahead as she opened the door. Leaning against it, eyes closed, she waited for the sound of Dev's engine revving and pulling away. It seemed to take forever.

As the rumble faded, Megan grabbed a bottle of wine from the fridge and headed to her bedroom. Then, for the first time ever, she changed the voice-mail message on her phone to have clients with emergencies call the clinic's answering service.

She couldn't deal with anyone else's problems or pain tonight.

She had enough of her own.

CHAPTER FIVE

MANNY'S AVARICIOUS GLEE was not what Devin wanted to face at ten o'clock in the morning. Not after the night he'd had.

Dealing with Megan and all the history they'd stirred up had left him with much to think about, and it had been nearly impossible to concentrate on anything else. After years of *not* thinking about her, having her that much on his mind was slightly disconcerting. When he'd finally given up and gone to bed, different memories awaited him. Making love to Megan in every position known to mankind for hours on end had left him grouchy this morning from lack of rest and the residual frustration of erotic dreams.

And now Manny had decided to show up first thing this morning, throwing off what little ability to concentrate he'd managed to find. To make matters worse, it seemed Manny had only one topic of conversation available to him today: Megan.

"My phone started ringing off the hook five minutes after you two hit the airwaves. The show was incredible. You guys were a hit."

"Kate would agree with you." Devin reached for the nearest file, not knowing or caring what it contained, and flipped it open purposefully. "Now, I've got a few..."

Manny was oblivious to the hint and got comfortable in

the chair next to Devin's desk. "Kate is a genius, a complete freakin' *genius,* for putting you two together. You know, with the offers I've heard this morning, you should seriously consider partnering with Megan for more projects."

That got his attention. "Have you lost your mind?"

"I'm serious as a heart attack. You should take your show on the road—do some rounds with the talk shows, some special appearances...."

"No thanks. I'm not interested, and I think it's safe to assume Megan isn't either." *But considering Megan's living situation, she could benefit from some paying stints....*

Manny didn't seem to hear him. "And The Powers That Be are giddy this morning. They want Megan to be a regular guest on the show."

He closed the file with a snap. "Absolutely not. Last night's freak show doesn't need to be repeated."

"Freak show or not, you and Megan together are magic."

Devin choked. Magic. *Yeah, right.* They'd had some magic years ago, but that was definitely gone. "Kate lied to Megan, and that's the only reason she was on the show to begin with. Megan would like this whole situation to die a quick death, and I can't say I object to that. For slightly different reasons, mind you."

"But—"

"No buts. This ends now. You work for me—not Kate, not The Powers That Be—and I want you to find something else to make money from. Something that doesn't involve Megan Lowe."

"I can't control the media. I'm good, but I'm not that good. Until something better comes along, you and Dr. Megan are what the world wants to see."

"Then *make* something better come along. Surely one of your other clients could be convinced to go into rehab.

Maybe one could pick a bar fight and get arrested? I'd be willing to make it worth their while." *Anything to end this.* "And yours, too."

Manny seemed to ponder his words, then shook his head. "Dream on, Devin. You're the media's darling right now."

He felt more like the media's bitch at the moment. And fortune's fool. A strong mental slap brought him back to earth. He couldn't get Megan off his mind because he'd never expected to cross paths with her again, much less twine his life with hers—however temporarily—and create a circus. The edge of frustration cutting him…well, that was just a side effect of the long, crazy hours he'd kept recently and the resultant celibacy caused by those long hours and ridiculous schedule. In a couple of weeks the hype around the book would die down, and life would return to normal.

Megan had just landed in his life at exactly the wrong moment, and that was the reason for his headache.

As Manny babbled on, he amended that statement. Megan wasn't solely to blame for his headache.

"Look, I have things to do today—other people's marriages to dissolve, people who are depending on me to end their misery. In order to do that, I need to file papers before close of business. You, the book and the show will have to wait your turn." He grabbed Manny by the biceps and hauled him to his feet. "In fact, I'm forbidding you to contact me—at all, in any way—until Monday. No email, no calls, no texts, no telegrams, not even a smoke signal from you until noon Monday. It will give you plenty of time to think of something else."

"But, Devin…"

"No buts. If I hear a peep out of you before twelve noon

Monday—not eleven fifty-nine, twelve—you're fired. Understand?"

Manny sputtered, but Devin was feeling pretty good as he guided Manny to his office door and out into the hallway.

"Devin—"

"This is the only warning you're going to get. Not a word from you."

They passed Kara, one of his paralegals, in the hall, and she dissolved into giggles as Devin frog-marched Manny to the reception area. "Kara, do me a favor and look up the termination clause in Mr. Field's contract." He tossed the words over his shoulder. "We might need it."

"Of course, Mr. Kenney. I'll get right on that."

In the tasteful, designed-to-impress reception area, he released Manny's biceps. "I'll talk to you Monday. Enjoy the long weekend."

Manny merely nodded, and Devin choked back a laugh. Manny's silence, however coerced, was both amusing and welcome. In fact, the prospect of an entire Manny-less weekend improved his mood considerably and he felt almost chipper as the door closed behind his overzealous agent.

His receptionist was openmouthed in shock when he turned around. She closed her mouth with a snap, but the smirk of satisfaction had him wondering how much his staff had resented Manny's constant intrusions on his office—and therefore everyone's time. A couple of his junior attorneys, several paralegals and a few secretaries—also wearing looks of amusement and satisfaction—lined the hallway as he made his way back to his office. "Now that we're less distracted, let's see if we can't get something accomplished today."

On that note, everyone disappeared into their offices and cubicles.

Blissful silence awaited him as he closed his office door behind him. He should've threatened to fire Manny months ago.

But as he started working his way through his in-box, an earlier thought kept pushing its way to the forefront of his concentration. Megan obviously needed money. Whatever her internship was paying, it was barely enough to keep a cat alive. Maybe she *could* benefit from this mess. Devin was sure Manny would know a way to make "Dr. Megan" some quick cash from appearances or something.

Without him, though. Megan and Devin were not a package deal. Not anymore.

If Megan was interested, he could drop Manny a quick email; it would smooth Manny's ruffled feathers to have something to wrangle into profitability over the weekend.

Oddly pleased, he whistled as he picked up the phone. This was a win-win situation. Any lingering guilt he felt over Megan would be appeased, and he'd make his agent happy, as well. Then he'd be able to catch up on things here and enjoy his weekend.

He loved having a plan.

"Are you *trying* to get fired? Is that your plan?"

Had she not heard Julie's ring tone, Megan would have continued to ignore her phone. The damn thing had been ringing nonstop all morning, disturbing her much-needed pity party. Dev had done a number on her head last night, and all the self-therapy in the world wasn't making it easier to cope. The last thing she needed was Julie's dramatics on top of everything else.

"What makes you think I have a plan for anything?" she

grumbled, debating whether she wanted to bother making coffee. Nah, the caffeine would only wake her up, and she had every intention of going back to sleep as soon as she could get Julie off the phone. If she could just sleep until this was over, that would be *grand*. "Anyway Dr. Weiss said I wasn't in danger of being fired."

"That was before. I think it's a distinct possibility now unless Dr. Weiss calms down."

"What?" That sent a jolt through her, chasing away every last bit of sluggishness in a way no amount of caffeine ever could. "Why?"

"You left here Monday with instructions to lie low. To let this blow over."

That feeling of dread she was beginning to think had taken up permanent residence in her stomach started to flow into her entire body. "Um, well…"

"What part of 'lie low' did you translate as 'go on the radio and stir up the whole country'? Dr. Weiss is having a duck this morning."

Dr. Weiss was emotionally incapable of having a duck. Or anything else. But if Julie seemed to think Dr. Weiss was remotely close… "Ah, damn it. Since when did she start listening to Dev's show? Did she hear it?"

"She has now. She missed the segment on *Chicago A.M.* this morning, thank goodness."

"Chicago A.M.?" Her voice came out as a squeak.

"Oh, yeah. It was a great piece." Julie's sarcasm cut to the quick. "Complete with a picture of you and a mention of the clinic."

Oh, no.

"The phone has done nothing but ring since eight this morning," Julie continued as Megan felt a chill settle into her blood. "The waiting room is buzzing because the clients are talking about it. It didn't take Dr. Weiss long to get the drift and then go online to get all the details."

The adrenaline of panic shot through her, making her hands shake slightly. "This is not good, Julie."

"That's an understatement. *Why* did you go on his show?"

She'd asked herself the same question a thousand times with no good answer. "Temporary insanity?" she offered weakly.

"Try that with people who don't know what that term actually means."

"I was trying to help...."

"Megan, honey, get real. There's no help for this but time."

"I know that *now*. I just thought—I mean, I *hoped*..." She scrubbed a hand over her face and tried to regroup. "Should I call Dr. Weiss? Try to explain?"

"I wouldn't if I were you. She's a little unhappy with you at the moment." Julie fell silent and Megan prayed she was thinking of a brilliant idea. "Let me plead your case. Temporary insanity won't fly, but maybe I could argue for diminished capacity or something."

"Thanks."

"Don't thank me yet. I'm not sure Dr. Weiss is open to much discussion about you right now. We've heard your name a lot this morning, if you get my meaning."

Megan did. All too well. "Apologize to Alice for me, too. Let her know I'm sorry about all the phone calls she's having to take."

"Oddly, I think Alice is getting a weird thrill out of hanging up on them. It's not something she gets to do often." Megan could almost hear the smile in Julie's voice. At least there was something about this situation that didn't suck.

"Look," Julie added, "don't do anything else to rile Dr. Weiss. Stay home. Stay away from the media. And stay off Devin Kenney's show, for God's sake."

"Not a problem. I won't even call in to tomorrow morning's show. I promise." *Not that that would help.*

"Good. By the way, he's looking for you this morning."

She was still trying to force out of her head the image of her career going down the toilet. "Who is?"

"Devin. He called here and asked us to pass along a message to you."

Huh? "Why would he call there?"

"According to Alice, he knows you're not answering your phone this morning, so he called us figuring we'd talk to you at some point."

Lovely. "And the message?"

"He wants you to call him."

"Did he say why?"

"Does it matter? Didn't we *just* agree you were going to stay away from him?"

"I'm only curious," she argued, but she sounded weak.

She heard Julie sigh. "He didn't say why. Is that curiosity going to cause you to do something stupid now? Like call him?"

"Nope." Although she'd love to know what Dev was up to, she could resist. "Obviously it's not important or life threatening."

"Good girl. Keep that attitude and just stay home for the next few days. I'll try to calm Dr. Weiss down today—downplay what I can and put a positive spin on the rest. Maybe she'll calm down over the weekend and have a different attitude on Monday."

"I will. And *thanks*. I owe you."

"Oh, you definitely do. If I get fired for this, I'll never forgive you."

Megan flipped the phone closed, fully intending to get back to her wallowing, but instead she opened it again and scrolled through the call log. She had several voice-mail messages, but thankfully not everyone who'd called this morning had left a message. She scanned the numbers, wondering if one of them was Dev's. Would he have left her a message explaining why he was looking for her this morning?

It doesn't matter, remember? She had no need to talk to Devin about anything. Nothing good could come of it.

On that thought, she forced herself to get out of bed. Wallowing and moping weren't going to change anything, nor would they help, either. She knew that. She might have screwed up by going on Dev's show, but she could make the most of these unplanned days off and the forced seclusion. She'd revise and submit those journal articles, do some research she'd been putting off, maybe even paint her kitchen if she got really bored,

When this was over, she'd be able to go back to work with something positive to show—or maybe even impress—Dr. Weiss. All those projects she'd been putting off until she had time? Well, now she had it.

She went to her tiny kitchen to make coffee, and while it brewed, she made a mental to-do list. The pity party was over. By the time she had a full cup of caffeine ready, she'd shaken herself out of her funk.

Learn from this and grow from the experience. Think of possibilities. What doesn't kill me only makes me stronger. This was a learning experience, and though she'd stumbled coming out of the blocks, she could still finish well and salvage some of her pride.

And, hopefully, save her career, too.

* * *

Devin couldn't put into words why it bothered him that Megan hadn't returned his call. But it bothered him. A lot more than he liked to admit.

Surely she'd checked her voice mail or called in to her office. She had to know he wanted to talk to her. Of course, he could tell from speaking with the receptionist at her clinic that Megan was a hot topic today and that no one was happy about it, either. The woman had all but hung up on him.

Granted, they hadn't exactly parted as friends last night, but Megan wasn't the type to hold a grudge. Or she didn't used to be. Maybe she'd learned how to do that, too.

Regardless, he wanted to talk to her, and she wasn't returning his calls. This was business, and beneficial to her, so it was juvenile for her to ignore him when he was only trying to help.

And that was the *only* reason he was currently climbing the stairs to her apartment.

This place looked even worse in the daylight. While the neighborhood might have started off as working-class thirty or forty years ago, suburban flight and the ensuing income slide had taken its toll. *Seedy* was the nicest adjective he could muster.

And Megan lived here. She had a PhD, had graduated top of her class—if the press could be believed—and *this* was the best she could do. She'd left him to pursue her career and her dream, and she was living in a dump now. *This* was what she'd traded him in for. It was insulting. It boggled the mind.

The door rattled in its frame as he knocked. A moment later he could have sworn he heard a sigh before the rattle of multiple locks disengaging. Not that the locks would keep anyone out—a strong kick to the flimsy door would render them useless.

Finally the door opened and Megan leaned against it, annoyance written across her face. "What do you want, Dev?"

His comeback died on his tongue. Megan's hair was swept up and back into a messy coil, a pencil holding it in place. Her face was scrubbed clean, the sprinkling of freckles across her nose and cheeks dark against her fair skin. A pair of horn-rimmed glasses perched on the bridge of her nose.

He'd never harbored the sexy-librarian fantasy, but as the blood in his head rushed south, he could picture Megan taking off those glasses, pulling that pencil out and shaking her hair loose....

"Dev?"

The irritation in her voice snapped him out of his adolescent daydream and back to the present. The librarian fantasy stopped at her neck, as she was wearing cutoffs and a SUNY T-shirt, but the expanse of toned thigh revealed by those shorts awakened a new fantasy. After starring in last night's erotic dreamfest, Megan looked way too good for his loose grip on his sanity to handle.

He cleared his throat and tried to shake off the images haunting him. "I've been trying to get in touch with you."

"I realize that."

Her matter-of-fact admission she'd been intentionally ignoring him rankled. *"And?"*

She folded her arms across her chest. "And nothing. Can't you take a hint? I don't want to talk to you."

"But I want to talk to you."

Her eyebrows went up, reigniting that naughty-librarian vibe. "And that takes precedence over my desires because…? Oh, yeah, because you're Devin Kenney."

Desires. She should have chosen a different word. That

one was too dangerous to hear for someone still waiting for his blood to circulate freely again. Her desires, his desires...his body would like nothing more than to explore their *mutual* desires.

"I'm here to proposition you." Megan's jaw dropped, and he quickly caught himself. "I mean, I have a proposition for you. A business proposition."

"I'm not interested."

Was she *trying* to annoy him? "Don't be like that. You haven't even heard it yet. Aren't you at least curious?"

She sighed. Removing her glasses—but, sadly, *not* shaking out her hair—Megan pinched the bridge of her nose. "Fine," she conceded. "Come on in."

He was treated to an excellent view of her backside as Megan crossed the tiny living room and bent to lift a stack of books out of a chair. She added those books to a teetering pile on the floor and indicated he should sit. "Would you like something to drink? Water? Diet soda?"

He declined as he sat, and Megan took her seat on the sofa angling him. She curled her feet under her and leaned against the overstuffed arm.

The room, while bright with the afternoon sun, was depressing. The upholstery had once been floral, but it had faded long ago into an unrecognizable and threadbare gray. The apartment was clean, but decades of neglect showed in the cracked plaster and dingy linoleum. He recognized some of the artwork on the walls as being from their old apartment, but despite Megan's clear attempts to make the place homey or cheerful, nothing could overcome the sense of hopelessness that seemed to seep out of the walls.

Hell, the laptop on the opposite end of the couch probably cost more than the furniture in this room. He couldn't deny the small sense of schadenfreude that crept in. If she'd stayed married to him, she'd be living a much different lifestyle.

Megan picked up on his appraisal of her apartment. "Yes, I know it's a dump. But it's cheap, and it's clean and, most important, it's temporary."

"I didn't realize you were still an intern. When will you get your license?"

"I'll sit the exam in three or four months, depending on how long it takes me to get my hours finished, of course." She sighed and shook her head. "It will take a few weeks to get the official results, but I can start looking for a job immediately."

"That sure you'll pass, huh? That's kind of cocky of you."

She shrugged. "It's not cockiness. I'm damn good at what I do. You were pretty sure about the bar exam, remember?"

"Pure bravado."

"Liar." But she grinned as she said it, and it softened the pinched look around her eyes. "So what brings you by, Dev?"

Right. On to business. "You were quite the hit last night." At her smirk, he amended, "With the listeners and the corporate types, at least. Are you aware of your new popularity?"

"Oh, yeah." She didn't sound pleased about it.

"You obviously need some additional income." He gestured to the furniture. "And I could hook you up with the people who could turn that new popularity into a revenue stream for you."

"By...?" she prompted.

"By just being 'Dr. Megan.'"

She nodded her understanding. "I see. No, thank you."

God, she was frustrating. "You're jumping ahead again. You haven't even heard me out."

"I don't need to. I'm not going to be the equivalent of a newspaper agony aunt."

"It's lucrative."

"But it's not real. It's called psychotainment for a reason. You can't solve people's problems with a ten-minute sound bite." He started to counter that, but she held up a hand. "The people who call in to radio shows or go on TV don't really want help. They want a quick fix, and they usually get a pithy piece of psychobabble. Then they go back to their lives. Does it make a difference? There's no way to know. There's no follow-up. No aftercare. No actual solutions for these people. That's not me. It's not what I want to do with my life."

Megan could be so single-minded that the bigger picture often escaped her. "So you do a few appearances, make a name for yourself. That fame will build your real practice. I know that from experience."

She shook her head. "Most people who seek counseling—who *need* counseling—don't want anyone to know they are in counseling. Real clients would be afraid my notoriety would expose their weaknesses. They'd be afraid their problems would be fodder for my next appearance. I can't build a real career on a foundation that's all juicy show-and-tell."

"So you'd rather live like this?"

Her jaw tensed. "At least it's honest. And it will be worthwhile in the end. And at least I haven't sold out my principles." The defiant lift of her chin made that last sentence an accusation.

Anger pricked at him. "And you think I have?"

Megan clasped her hands together and leaned forward. Her voice dropped its edge and took on a smooth, impartial tone. "More important, Devin, do *you?* How do *you* feel about the choices you've made?"

Frustrated, he waved away her analysis attempt and leaned back in his chair. "Oh, don't try that with me. I'm not going to lie on your couch and tell you about my relationship with my mother."

"You don't have to. I know all about your mother already." She sat back with an exasperated sigh. "Unfortunately. Talk about someone who needed serious therapy." She shook her head. "I know she probably celebrated after our divorce became final, the grumpy old bat. How's she doing these days?"

The question caught him off guard, but there was no good way to soften the truth. "She died three years ago."

Megan's face fell, and she paled. "Oh, my God. I'm *so* sorry," she whispered. "I had no idea. What happened?"

"Heart attack. Seems she did have one after all."

"Dev," Megan chided.

This was yet another reason not to hang out with his ex. She knew way too much. "Don't worry, Dr. Megan, I'm good."

"You aren't talking to Dr. Megan. You're talking to me, and while I probably know more than you're comfortable with, I'm still willing to listen."

He regretted snapping at her. Megan's sympathy seemed genuine. "Mom and I made our peace before it happened." A flash of surprise crossed her face before she nodded. "So there's no need for me to go into therapy."

"I'm glad to hear that. Really I am." Considering how his mother had treated Megan, he was surprised at her sincerity. "What about your dad?" she continued. "And your sister?"

"Both fine. Dad moved to Arizona to be closer to Janice and her kids."

Megan's eyes widened. "Janice has kids?"

"Three boys." This conversation now bordered on

surreal—the how's-the-family catch-up—but it felt rather nice at the same time.

"Wow. Tell her I said hi the next time you talk to her."

"Will do. I think she missed you after the divorce."

"I missed her, too."

Anyone else? Did you miss me? Did you miss us? The questions popped into his head, but he pushed them aside. It was his turn for the small-talk questions. "And your folks?"

"Both fine. Hale and hearty. Mom's trying to talk Dad into moving to Florida when they retire."

Roger Lowe was too set in his ways. "Your dad's not going to move south."

"I know that and you know that." She smirked. "I think Mom knows that, too, but she's not willing to give up the fight just yet."

"Good for her."

Megan laughed—a real laugh this time—and adjusted her position, relaxing against the cushions, stretching her legs out and propping her feet on the coffee table. The table wobbled ominously, on the verge of collapsing on itself.

That brought him back to the purpose of his visit. He wasn't here to wander down memory lane or catch up on each other's families. "About that offer…"

Megan tensed a little, and the conversation lost its easy tone. "Again, thanks, but no thanks. I know a lot of people would welcome the chance in the spotlight, but surely you realize I'm not one of them. I'm not comfortable being 'out there.'"

"You fooled me. You seemed like a natural. No one would ever be able to tell you used to hate any kind of public speaking."

"I appreciate the vote of confidence, but just because I'm not that painfully shy mouse anymore, that doesn't mean

I'm ready—or willing—to let it all hang out. But it means a lot to me that you think I even could."

Megan's hand landed on his and squeezed. She probably meant it to be a friendly, meaningless gesture, but the contact rocketed through him. The first deliberate touch in over seven years, and it set his skin on fire in a flash.

Megan jumped, and when her eyes flew up to meet his, he knew she felt it, too. Belatedly, she tried to move her hand away, but he caught it easily.

A slow flush rose out of the neckline of her shirt, creeping its way up her neck until her cheeks turned red. Her thumb moved slightly against his skin, a faint caress he doubted she even realized, but it fanned the flames licking his skin. He returned the movement, his thumb teasing lightly over the skin of her palm, and her breath caught.

The silence stretched out, neither of them moving except for the gentle stroke of their fingers. It was ridiculous, this connection and the sensations it caused, but he couldn't bring himself to break the contact. Megan seemed to have a similar problem as her pupils dilated and her teeth worried her bottom lip.

It would be easy, so easy to… One tug, and she'd be in his lap.…

"D-Dev…I…um…I…" she whispered, and he felt her tremble ever so slightly. Megan closed her eyes as her tongue moistened her lips. She shifted her body forward as he reached for her.

The coffee table collapsed from the increased weight, sending books and papers crashing to the ground. With the table supporting her feet gone, Megan overbalanced and landed on the floor with a thud and a colorful curse.

Her hand was still in his, and he pulled, helping her right herself. "Are you okay?"

Big blue eyes met his and he watched as several emotions

battled for dominance. The desire was still there, but banked, while amusement and embarrassment and annoyance seemed to be gaining ground.

She pulled her hand away and used it to push back the hair that had escaped its containment when she fell. "I swear, Dev, being around you is a disaster looking for a place to happen."

CHAPTER SIX

MEGAN HAD MEANT THE WORDS to be light considering the embarrassing position she was in—and the even *more* embarrassing position she'd just escaped—but somehow they seemed to come out all wrong.

She'd known the moment she'd seen him on her step that nothing good could—or would—come from letting him in. She'd spent the day convincing herself of that and focusing on the future instead of the past. But she could no more close the door in his face than sprout wings and fly.

Dev just had some kind of unholy control over her. She thought she'd broken it when they split up, but if anything, the past couple of days had proven *that* notion false. Hell, the past five minutes had proven it to be a bald-faced lie.

And now Dev was in her tiny living room, filling the space and leaving her light-headed and shaky. Even worse, the heat in his stare didn't abate as she untangled herself from the mess on the floor and the remains of her coffee table.

She picked up a table leg and examined it, eager for something to distract Devin while she got her own hormones under control. "The apartment came furnished. I wonder how much they're going to charge me to replace this."

"I'll pay for it." The growl in his voice sent shivers over her skin and kicked her pulse into high gear. "Megan—"

"That's okay." She cut him off before that growl could go somewhere else, and hated herself for taking the cowardly way out. What happened to standing up to him? "I'm sure any local garage sale will have a replacement for a couple of dollars." She laughed weakly, but Devin didn't join her. He was still staring at her, his eyes raking over her body and leaving heated skin in their wake. Dev might have shown up at her door with a business proposition, but she knew that look well enough to know he had something entirely different on his mind now.

So did her body. It was completely on board with the idea, conveniently forgetting that they weren't a couple anymore. She could feel the early trembles of arousal in her thighs, the sensation traveling up to make her core muscles clench in anticipation.

Even worse, she knew Devin knew it, too. Electricity snapped through the air between them, the tension growing thick and heavy. She had to do something to break the spell or else...

"Meggie..."

That husky tone nearly did her in, pouring gasoline on the fire he'd started with just a look. *No,* she told her libido. *This is not going to happen.* She had enough problems without compounding them by getting naked with Devin.

She levered herself to her feet, only to find her knees weren't steady enough to support her. As she wobbled, seeking her balance, Devin's hand closed around her wrist, pulling her gently yet purposefully toward him.

Be strong. What had happened to the anger, the outrage, the indignation that had kept a nice safe wall between them? It had crumbled under one passionate look. *So much for being over him.*

It took every bit of strength she had to override her hormones, pull her wrist out of Devin's grasp and dig her heels into the floor. "Dev," she started, but her voice sounded thick. She cleared her throat and tried again. "Devin, I, um…I appreciate your offer."

His eyebrows went up and she hurried to clarify. "The offer to help. Business, I mean. You've done all you can and you were right last night when you said it would just take time. I think I'll go back to that plan and wait this out."

With the moment of connection broken, the heat started to fade from Devin's eyes. Then, with a quick shake of his head, it was gone entirely. Envious, Megan wished she could do the same, but at the same time she felt a little hurt he could turn it off so quickly. She, on the other hand, still wasn't steady on her feet and parts of her were throbbing along with her rapid heartbeat.

He cleared his throat. "That's probably a wise choice."

Damn it. "Yeah." She squatted and began sliding the papers and books into slightly more orderly piles. It gave her something to do with her hands, something to look at other than him, while she shored up her already faltering resolve. "So…I'm going to get back to work. I've got a ton of research to go through…."

"So I'll let you get back to it." He stood, looming over her position on her knees on the floor.

She quickly scrambled to her feet. "Thanks."

"If you change your mind…"

I'm about to, if you don't leave. "I won't," she answered quickly, clutching a psychiatric manual to her chest like a shield.

His lips twitched slightly. "I meant about exploring some of those other media options."

Kill me now. Her ears burned with embarrassment. "I'll keep it in mind and let you know. Okay?"

"Okay. Bye, Megan."

"Bye, Dev." She closed the door behind him and threw all the locks. Only then did she release the breath she was holding.

She made her way to the bedroom on unsteady legs and fell face-first across the bed. Disgust at herself churned the acid in her stomach. Embarrassment and humiliation had her skin crawling. But under that, she *burned.*

For Devin.

She was not some teenager without control over her hormones. She was an adult, damn it.

An adult who knew exactly what Dev could do to her.

Exactly, she told herself as she pulled a pillow over her head. Physically, yes, Dev could do amazing things. Things that made her shiver at the thought. Her body was screaming at her to call him back and take him up on the unspoken yet blatantly obvious offer. She could practically feel his hands sliding over her skin, and gooseflesh rose in anticipation. Devin was generous, thorough, often insatiable.… Ah, yes, *physically,* there was no downside.

But she also knew what Dev could do to her emotionally. And her reaction to him proved beyond a doubt that her emotional state wasn't as stable as she'd thought. The tug on her heart couldn't be ignored and it scared the hell out of her. The magnetic pull she'd felt had been more than physical, more than just a chemical reaction or memories of how good it could—would—be. *That* was something else entirely.

Her whole life was in too much upheaval to add *that* to the mix.

Deep breaths and rational pep talks weren't helping. She focused on the only thing that might—the anger and hurt that had driven them apart last time. When she had no luck with that, she flipped to her back and concentrated on the present—her problems that wouldn't be helped by giving in to the chemistry between them.

That was no use either. With a sigh of disgust, she pushed herself off the bed and headed for the bathroom.

She'd try that old standby, the cold shower.

Learn from your mistakes. Devin couldn't count the number of times he'd lectured his listeners on that very topic. For that reason alone, he had no excuse for what had almost happened. If Megan hadn't chickened out and all but thrown him out of her apartment, it wouldn't have been *almost.*

And while he could beat himself up over the fact he should know better, he also knew he wouldn't have regretted it for a second. Whatever lie he'd told himself on his way to Megan's, the real reason he'd gone to her had become crystal clear the moment she touched him.

Getting involved with Megan—in any way, for any reason—was just plain stupid, but that knowledge wasn't damping his raging erection or blurring the erotic images in his mind. Between the two, he was getting nothing done tonight.

Something had to give, or he was going to lose his mind.

Sure, he felt sorry for her, for the situation she was in. Her notoriety was partly his fault; even if he hadn't directly caused it, he'd compounded it, and any decent human being would want to help.

But this other need… That had nothing to do with being a decent human being. In fact, a decent human being wouldn't compound a bad situation by acting on what he was feeling at the moment.

It wasn't going to stop him, though. He'd just have to accept he wasn't a decent human being. He'd been called worse. By Megan, in fact.

But Megan's reaction proved this wasn't one-sided. She wanted him—that much had been very clear—but she was fighting it. Probably for all the same reasons he'd examined and rejected already.

Devin scrolled through the messages in his in-box again. There were many things he should be working on, but none really captured his interest.

He could be at Megan's exploring his new naughty-librarian fantasy. Or multiple other fantasies. Other people's soon-to-be ex-wives weren't nearly as interesting as his, so he clicked the email window closed and gave up the pretense.

This was sick. This was twisted. It was nuts to even consider.

But it was going to happen. That much he was sure of. And he was pretty damn sure Megan felt the same way.

Maybe if they could both get it out of their systems, then they could go back to their separate lives.

Now to get Megan to see it that way.

"I'm fine, Mom. Really." The lie got easier each time Megan told it. Another three hundred times and maybe she'd begin to believe it, as well.

"Well, if it makes you feel any better, I think you did great on Devin's show. I'd sign on as a client of yours any day." Her mom was in cheerleader mode—had been since the first whiff of trouble.

"Thanks, Mom. But please tell me you and Daddy aren't having problems."

"Nothing a move to Florida won't solve."

"Together, I hope."

"Of course, honey. Don't worry about us. We've been married so long divorce isn't an option. I might kill him, but I won't divorce him."

"Good. But try not to kill him, either. Call me first and I'll talk you down."

"Speaking of killing people…" Her mom's voice took on a too-casual tone and Megan braced herself. "How are you getting along with Devin?"

Argh. "What do you mean?"

Mom sighed. "You've obviously had to spend some time with him—during the show, if nothing else. How'd that go?"

"Fine," she managed to get out in a normal tone. Thank goodness her mother couldn't see her face. She'd be busted for that lie for sure. "We've both grown and changed and we're different people now, and this was a professional setting and situation, so it—" Megan broke off midramble as her mother laughed. "Okay," she admitted, "so I've had better moments. You just said it all sounded fine on the radio, and that's what matters."

"If you say so."

"I do." *I need to change the subject.* "So, Mom—"

"Did you listen to his show this morning?"

She had, but she wasn't going to admit it. "Are you telling me you did?"

"Of course. I wanted to see which way the wind was blowing. Make sure he didn't undo any of the progress you'd made. He didn't, by the way."

"I didn't think he would." But she'd listened to be sure. "Devin's being great about this. He understands my predicament."

"So did you two talk about anything…?"

Not subtle, Mom. Not subtle at all. "Oh, Mom, there's someone at the door. Can I call you later?"

"Of course, honey. Take care."

Megan hung up and spent a brief moment feeling bad about lying to her mother. After all the Devin-related drama of the past, though, of course Mom was twitchy about her being anywhere near him again.

And boy, did Mom have good reason to be. Megan was very twitchy about it, too, but after a long, sleepless night spent thinking, she had it under control now. The current emotional upheaval made her vulnerable. That vulnerability had her looking for a safe anchor. Years ago that anchor had been Devin, and with him here now, she was misplacing all that angst and emotion and need. That was the explanation for yesterday's close-call chemical reaction.

Now that she'd identified it, she could avoid it. She felt much better today with her newfound understanding of the situation. Sadly, that understanding hadn't completely squelched the ache inside her, but it had damped it down a bit. Once she managed to rein in her subconscious's need to explore every old fantasy she'd ever harbored, she'd be in good shape. It would just take a little time. And effort.

Maybe in a couple of days—or months—she'd be able to articulate that to her mother. Until then, avoiding discussing the issue seemed wise.

She left the phone on the couch, stepped over her laptop and headed for the kitchen for a refill. As she opened the fridge, she heard a knock at the door.

Spooky. Either she'd gained ESP recently or something was telling her not to lie to her mother about things unless she wanted them to come true.

At the door, she looked through the peephole and nearly fell back in shock.

Devin. Here. Again.

Why?

She weighed her options. Honestly, she had only two—open

the door or pretend not to be home. After yesterday… She took a careful step backward.

"Megan, I know you're home." Dev's voice carried easily through the flimsy door. "I can hear you moving around."

Damn it.

"C'mon. Open up."

She took a deep breath to steady herself. Blowing it out slowly, she opened the door.

Dev grinned at her. "Hi."

"Hi, Dev, what's…" She trailed off as she saw what he was holding. "What's that?"

"What does it look like? It's a coffee table."

Like that's normal? "Well, yes, I see that. But…but… *why* do you have a coffee table?"

"To replace the one you broke yesterday."

Her head was spinning. "That's not neces—"

"This is where you say, 'Thanks, Dev,' and invite me in. It's heavier than it looks."

She stood there gaping as Devin turned sideways to pass her and stepped inside. He carried the table to the center of the room and set it down carefully. "There. It doesn't match the sofa, but then nothing in here does."

I've snapped. The stress has gotten to me and this is a hallucination. She closed her eyes, and when she opened them, Devin was still standing in her living room. With a coffee table. *Okay. Reality is just weird.* Closing the door, she tried again to make sense of the situation. "It's lovely, Devin, and that's very kind of you, but…"

"You're welcome." Devin looked at the mess covering her floor. "You certainly need it. How are the articles going?"

Confusion reigned supreme. "Devin…um…I mean,

what…" She scrubbed a hand across her face. "What is going on?"

Devin frowned at her, obviously assessing her sanity and getting a big question mark. "This—" he indicated the table "—is a gift. For you. Why are you looking at me like that?"

"Because you showed up on my front step with a coffee table for some unknown reason. I think I'm allowed to be a little thrown by this."

That got her a shrug in response. "I don't see why."

She held on to her last shred of sanity. "Devin…"

"Okay, so I'm feeling a little bad about the stress you're under, so I thought I'd try to do something nice for you."

"So you bought me a *table?*"

Devin's smile bordered on sheepish, but she wasn't buying it for a second. "It seemed like a better idea than flowers or something. I knew you needed a table."

A laugh bubbled up without warning. It felt good after all the tension of the past few days. "You're certainly full of surprises, Dev."

He looked pleased with himself. "I try. Now, are you going to invite me to sit and stay awhile?"

She shouldn't. She knew that much for sure. But he'd brought her furniture; she couldn't just send him off like a delivery guy with a smile and a wave. With all her new-found answers gleaned from her self-therapy last night, surely she could handle a polite conversation with the man. After all, he was trying to be nice. "Would you like to sit? Can I get you something to drink?" When he shook his head, she went to the couch and sat, trying to shake off the déjà vu with simple, harmless small talk. It proved harder than expected, though, as she fumbled for a topic. "I listened to your show today. It's a bit different than the nighttime version."

He seemed shocked at her revelation, but then he shrugged. "Different target demographic. There's some overlap, of course." With a level stare, he added, "And you still don't approve."

"I don't have to approve. Or agree with what you're saying. I may think you're wrong, but it's your show. Your listeners." She shrugged.

"And you'd tell them something different?"

"Not necessarily. I mean, if people are definitely getting a divorce, then they really do need good advice on the legal aspects. It's the folks calling you who seem on the fence that I worry about."

"And yet you look down on psychotainment. For some folks, that sound bite is the best they're going to get."

He had a point. "True," she conceded, "but I don't have to like it. On the other hand, it's not my show, and it's a free country. You're obviously popular, so I'm in the minority. I'm okay with that, and I'll keep my objections to myself." To prove it she folded her hands in her lap and smiled.

Dev's eyes widened in surprise, and she was treated to one of those dangerous grins. "Boy, if I get this just from bringing a coffee table, what will I get if I show up with a couch?"

"Do *not* show up at my front door with a couch, Devin Kenney. Or any other furniture, for that matter."

"So it's the furniture you object to, not the delivery guy?" Dev winked at her.

Busted. "Well, um…I wasn't really expecting you at all. Much less with a table." *Nice recovery.*

Dev simply laughed.

Time to get this back in hand. "Okay, I know why I'm home on a Friday afternoon, but don't you have a job you need to be at?"

To her utter amazement, Dev leaned back in the chair

and got comfortable, propping his feet on the new table, which on second glance looked very expensive. "Yes, but I also have plenty of people to take care of the grunt work. They'll call if they need me. I thought you might need the company, though. You seem determined to be a recluse."

The sight of him settling in unnerved her. "Staying in is often good for people. Gives you time to think. Accomplish things. Do stuff." *Stop babbling.* "Things you normally wouldn't do."

"So I can talk you into having dinner with me, then."

"No!" She caught herself and tried again. "I mean, thanks, but no."

"Why not? That's not something you'd normally do."

Because I'm not that crazy. Lord, she had to get control of this situation. Fast. "Is there a particular reason you're here, Dev? Other than furniture delivery?"

She regretted the question immediately. A dangerous spark lit in Devin's eyes as they met hers, and that was all the answer she needed. She should feel insulted, irritated, maybe even outraged, but her traitorous body was too primed not to react to the electric current flowing between them.

That electricity sent a jolt through her that had her jumping to her feet. "Damn it, Dev."

The slow, sensual smile she got in return caused her knees to wobble. *Oh, no. No, no, no.* So much for all those answers and explanations and reasons she'd worked out so carefully. They toppled like dominoes after one look from him. It was ridiculous, frustrating...

"Come here, Meggie." He softened the command by wrapping his hand around her fist, causing her fingers to release so they could twine through his. Palm to palm, the connection was complete. Electric. It hummed through her, bringing dormant cells back to life and making them pulse with need.

He lowered his feet to the floor and tugged her arm, bringing her a step closer. To him. Into the energy that radiated off him like a sexual aura.

Yesterday she'd been strong. Dug in her heels and stood her ground. Until this moment she wouldn't admit—not even to herself—that she regretted that stance.

She could make a different choice today.

The part of her brain that could quote the textbook on why it was a really, *really* bad idea to even consider what she was considering launched a protest, but her body wasn't listening.

One more tiny step and she was standing between his thighs. Dev's head was at eye level with her cleavage, and her nipples hardened in anticipation. He released his grip on her wrist, only to slide both hands up the backs of her thighs, causing her to lean ever more slightly toward him and the promise in his eyes. His thumbs brushed under the hem of her shorts, teasing the sensitive skin at the curve of her bottom.

"Dev—" Her voice was a broken whisper, so she cleared her throat to try again. "Dev, I'm not sure this is a good idea."

"It's a *great* idea." His voice was husky with need, hypnotizing her. "We've been heading here since you crashed my book signing on Monday. I know you, Meggie. And I know you want me as badly as I want you right now."

CHAPTER SEVEN

DEVIN'S BALD WORDS affected her as strongly as the fingers caressing her inner thighs. *Walk away, Meggie, walk away.* But the message wasn't reaching her legs. They wobbled again, and she had to place a hand on Devin's shoulder for support. The heat of his skin burned her, even through his shirt, but she couldn't let go. "This isn't about want." She wasn't sure which of them she was trying to convince.

Devin called her bluff simply by placing his lips at the hollow of her throat, letting his tongue sneak out to feel the frantic beat of her pulse. Her breath seemed trapped in her lungs.

His hands slid up to her waist as he lifted his head. "You're right," he said, and disappointment caused her stomach to clench painfully. "It's about need."

That was all the warning she got before he pulled her head down and captured her protest in his mouth.

With one touch of his tongue, everything she'd told herself since the day she left was proven a lie.

She recognized his taste and the weight of his lips. Like magic, she slipped back into the rhythm she thought she'd forgotten long ago, matching the movement of his kiss. The hand on his shoulder slid up along the tight cords of his neck, finding the soft, fine hairs at his nape.

His hands cupped her jaw, holding her head steady, but

there was tenderness under the pressure that caused her heart to skip a beat. When Devin released her face, letting one hand tangle in her hair while the other slid slowly to the hem of her shirt, the poignancy of the loss was quickly replaced by the flash of heat from his bare hand against the small of her back.

Her body seemed to remember and respond without reservation, eager to receive his touch and the pleasure it knew would follow. As Devin tugged her shirt up, her arms floated up without hesitation, offering him access. Once the fabric cleared her head, Dev's eyes were on hers as he swept his hands down her ribs and up to cup her breasts through the thin cotton of the simple bra she wore. Every stock phrase she'd perfected with her clients came screaming into her head.

This is all misplaced—emotions dragged out of the depths of her psyche due to the happenings of the past couple of days. Digging through the past had awakened all kinds of memories, and this was simply a side effect.

She felt the clasp of her bra give way. *This isn't real.*

Devin's tongue traced her collarbone as he slid the straps down her arms and off. *This is a really bad idea.*

She arched as Devin's thumb scraped across her nipple, and his mouth found the sensitive place just below her earlobe. *You'll regret this later.*

Her hands pulled at Devin's shirt, working it up and off, and exposing the hard planes of his chest for her to trace with her fingers. *It won't solve anything. In fact, it will only complicate the issue and make things worse.*

Then Devin's hot mouth was on her breast, closing around an aching nipple and tracing it with his tongue.

And she no longer cared about the possible repercussions.

She gripped Devin's shoulders for support and gave herself over to the moment.

Devin knew the moment Megan quit arguing with herself and gave in, and the knowledge electrified his skin. *This.* Seeing Megan again, having her haunt his dreams—even rehashing their past—it had all been leading to this. To having Megan's skin under his hands and pressed against him again. Having her scent on him, her taste in his mouth. The intoxicating combination made him light-headed as he moved to tease her other breast, then burned him as the old flame kindled a raging inferno.

He pushed to his feet, wrapping Megan's legs around his waist and holding her hips as he headed for her bedroom. She groaned softly as she tightened her legs and moved restlessly, nearly causing his knees to buckle as pleasure shot through him.

Megan's bed was a tangle of covers, the pillows tossed haphazardly against the headboard, her quilt sliding half-way off the edge to the floor. Some things didn't change, it seemed, but Megan's unwillingness to ever make the bed saved him a step today. He lowered her onto the sheets, and the grip around his waist pulled him down with her. Here in the bed, her scent was even stronger, enveloping him even as he sat back on his heels and went to work on the snap of her shorts.

The quiver of stomach muscles against the backs of his hands nearly caused his fingers to fumble as desire shot through him. Megan arched, lifting her hips to assist as he slid the last of her clothing off, and his eyes widened.

A small blue butterfly nestled in the hollow beneath her right hip bone.

Megan had a tattoo.

It was beautifully done, this tiny work of art, the detail and shading carefully designed to capture the moment right before flight. The colors contrasted with Megan's fair skin, drawing his fingers like a magnet to smooth over the butterfly's wings.

Seeing it on her body was shocking. And unbelievably arousing.

She hissed softly as he traced the wings, and gooseflesh rose under his seeking fingers, then trembled under his tongue. Capturing his head, she pulled, bringing him level with her body again and meeting his eyes as she worked the snap and zipper of his jeans.

The release brought both pleasure and pain: relief from the confinement mixed with an overwhelming need to bury himself in her. *Now.*

He echoed her earlier hiss of pleasure as she palmed him, and his eyes closed as she stroked him with the practiced ease she'd learned years ago, remembering exactly how to drive him insane.

The pleasure bordered on torment as Meggie fitted into the curve of his body, her leg draping over his and her hips moving restlessly in contrast to the steady stroke of her hand.

He was too close to bear much of her touch, and with a push he flipped her to her back to reacquaint himself with her body.

So many subtle differences, yet it was all so familiar, as well. The faint sprinkle of freckles between her breasts, the indentation of her waist, the long, lean muscle of her thigh... The rediscovery of the curves and planes felt like coming home, only to find something new.

But that wasn't a new feeling either. He hadn't been Megan's first lover, but she'd come to him with only the fumblings of high-school boys forming her experience. Her inherent shyness had masked deep passion waiting to be plumbed, and they hadn't left the bed for nearly two days. Even then, his hands on her skin had felt as if they belonged there, and he'd known...

That memory stirred his blood, but not as much as the gloriously naked woman before him now. This wasn't the same Meggie he'd married, and he was eager to find out who she'd become.

As if she read his mind, Megan's lush lips curled into a seductive smile. Without opening her eyes, she reached for his wrist, stopping his lazy exploration. "You're driving me crazy."

He grinned, knowing she couldn't see it. "That was the plan."

"Touch me, Dev."

The words slammed into him, causing his breath to catch this time. "But I am."

She growled low in her throat, and the frustration fueling the sound rocketed through him like an electric current. "Dev..."

His free hand slid over the butterfly tattoo to her thatch of pale curls, and her thighs opened in welcome. He let his fingers tease gently, enjoying the sight of her hands fisting in the sheets and the sheen of sweat that caused her skin to glisten in the dim half-light of the room. A very un-Meggie-like curse burst from her lips and she finally met his eyes. "Devin!" she demanded, desire choking her words.

"Like this?" he asked as he cupped her sex and felt the heat of her arousal.

Her teeth caught her lip as she tried to press against his hand. He couldn't keep up the game; he needed to feel her. His thumb slipped into the wet heat, and a strangled cry escaped as he found the stiff nub and circled it.

Meggie's response left his hands shaking as he slid one finger inside her body. A moment later her inner muscles gripped him powerfully as she began to tremble from the approaching climax.

Megan was drowning in the sensations, the pleasure Devin's touch brought. The hedonistic side she'd forgotten she had came out in full force, and she wanted more.

She was close, so close to the edge. But she didn't want to go there alone. Not this time. Not after so long. "Dev," she whispered, causing his hooded eyes to meet hers.

He seemed to understand, sliding his big body up to cover hers as he kneed her thighs apart. His weight was welcome, blissful, and she held her breath in anticipation as he sought entrance.

Oh, yes, her body seemed to sigh as he filled her, and she felt her trembles of pleasure echo through Dev's shoulders and arms.

She couldn't hold his stare. It caused her heart to stutter, and she only wanted to enjoy this moment. Closing her eyes, she met his first thrust, and stars burst behind her eyelids.

Then she couldn't think at all. She could only hold on to Dev as the wave took her higher. Vaguely she could hear Dev's breath labor, hear him mumble her name into her hair as he pulled her tightly to him. Dev's arms held her together as she began to shatter, prolonging the pleasure until she felt Dev join her on that precipice.

Devin claimed her mouth in a kiss that scorched her, and Megan exploded in white-hot pleasure as he sent them tumbling over the edge together.

Reality was slow to return, and Megan wasn't encouraging it. She didn't want to have to face the unpleasant thoughts starting to niggle at the edges of her conscience. The dreamy, fuzzy weightlessness of afterglow, the feel of Devin's breath against her neck as it evened out to normal, the lazy sweep of his hand over her hip and thigh… Reality could wait. It would only spoil the moment, and she wanted this moment to last as long as possible.

Forever, something whispered, and she pushed the thought away. She and Devin weren't meant to be forever; she'd learned that the first time. But she was more than willing to enjoy this small interlude from reality without expectation of something more.

She could salve her conscience with the knowledge she was being realistic about *that,* at least.

"Nice tattoo," Dev mumbled against her ear as his fingers traced the butterfly. She'd noticed the way the tattoo had drawn his attention—and his hands and his mouth—repeatedly.

"Thanks." Her voice seemed rusty and thick, but then, so did Devin's. "It hurt like hell getting it, but I love it."

"I never dreamed you'd get a tattoo. You just…"

"Don't seem like the type?" she finished for him. "You and everyone else." Dev stiffened a little for some reason, and his hand stalled briefly on her hip. The moment passed quickly, though, and Megan didn't comment. "The artist in Albany was dating my roommate at the time, so we knew each other a little bit. He did everything to try to talk me out of it, and I think he was surprised when he couldn't."

There was that tension again. Was Dev somehow disapproving of her tattoo? Was that why he was so fascinated by it? "Very talented guy."

"I think so. If you're thinking about getting one yourself, I'll give you his name and number. He'd be worth the trip."

"I'll pass." Dev used his hand to pull her even more snugly against him, and she curled happily into his warmth. "I've heard that's a painful place to get ink."

"Well, I put it on my hip so I can see it but my clients can't. Most people don't think 'Accomplished Professional I Can Tell My Problems To' when they see a tattoo. Regardless of the quality," she added.

"And when did you become a great fan of butter-flies?"

Dev knew her, that was for sure. She'd never been a girlie-girl type liking unicorns and butterflies and rainbows. She tried to shrug it off with a casual "It just seemed appropriate at the time."

"Why?"

She hesitated. Her usual response to the few people who knew about her tattoo wouldn't really work now. Not without sounding like a slam against him. "Well," she hedged, "it was about a year after…after…"

"Us?" he supplied.

"Yeah, about a year after us. I had just moved to Albany, and I really felt like I was starting a whole new life. I'd grown and changed so much in that year, I didn't feel I was the same person I used to be."

She felt Devin's nod of understanding, and she worried he'd taken offense. "Transformation," he said.

"It's a trite image, I know. A cliché. But it felt right on the money. And Keith—the artist—understood. He'd watched me come out of my cocoon, but knew I hadn't started to fly yet. That's why he made it look like it's about to take off." She sighed. "It's more about the possibilities that come from change."

A low chuckle rumbled in his chest, and the vibrations moved through her, as well. "Spoken like a shrink."

She elbowed him in response, but it did bring a smile to her face she knew he couldn't see.

Then Devin sobered, his hand pausing on her waist like

a weight. "Regardless of what you may think, I assure you it wasn't my intention to hold you back somehow."

She rolled over and met his eyes. "I know," she said honestly, but Dev frowned at her in disbelief. "At least, I do *now*. Time has given me some perspective. And regardless of what I've said recently, I don't hold you fully responsible for us. I made some mistakes, too."

"The folly and hubris of youth."

"*Hubris?* Did you really just use the word *hubris?*"

Dev propped his head on his fist. "I'm a lawyer. I'm allowed to use arcane words in idle conversation for no good reason."

She shook her head and sighed in censure, but Dev was unmoved and his cheeky grin didn't fade. "Some people hide their insecurities behind big vocabularies, using those big words to make themselves sound superior to others." Dev arched an eyebrow at her and she wanted to smack him. "You're the most arrogant person I've ever met."

"Thank you, Megan."

This was the most comfortable she'd felt around Devin in ages. The barriers between them seemed to have disappeared with their clothes....

Good Lord, she'd never let a client get away with this line of reasoning and kind of rationalizing to excuse their behavior. "You are terrible, Devin Kenney." *And I'm even worse.* "What am I going to do with you?"

A wolfish grin spread across his face, and her heartbeat kicked up in response. Every nerve ending jumped to life at the promise in that grin. "I guess that depends. When do you leave?"

Huh? "I'm sorry? What?"

"On vacation?"

She racked her brain and came up empty-handed. "What

makes you think I'm going somewhere?" *Like I could afford a vacation.*

"The other night you said you needed to pack. For Canada."

"Oh, that." She giggled. "Changing my name and moving to Canada was my backup plan for solving this whole mess."

Dev smirked at her.

"Hey, I was catastrophizing, so it—"

"That's not even a word."

"Yes, it is."

There was that smirk again. "Now who's overcompensating with a big vocabulary?"

She gave in to the urge to smack him. Grabbing the pillow from under her, she swung it at his head. Dev blocked the blow easily, pulling the pillow out of her hand and tossing it to the floor as he wrestled her onto her back and pinned her hands over her head.

Her body reacted instantly, heat pooling in her belly and nipples hardening as Dev settled comfortably between her thighs.

"And now we're back to the earlier topic. What to do…?" Dev's lips found her earlobe and the tiny nibbles sent chills shivering down her body. "Hmm…" The sound vibrated against her throat. "Since you're not going anywhere, I'm thinking I shouldn't either."

Was he planning on staying the night?

"My weekend is free.…"

Weekend? Oh, she knew *that* wasn't a good idea. Giving in to a little ex-sex for old times' sake wasn't uncommon, but a weekend would be—

Her inner hedonist quickly stopped that line of thought, stomping it into oblivion and answering before her brain could regroup. "I don't have any plans."

Dev's smile warmed her heart. But his next words warmed her blood.

"Now you do."

Devin heard his phone beep again, but he wasn't interested in anything other than the woman curled around him.

He ran his hands through the blond strands that snaked across his chest and listened to Megan's even breaths of very deep sleep. The dark circles around her eyes testified to her exhaustion, but considering what had caused that exhaustion…

He smiled as Megan mumbled something in her sleep and shifted.

Sleep, though, escaped him. He should be equally exhausted, but while he was enjoying the bone-deep satisfaction and the languid feeling it brought to his body, he wasn't all that tired. Only the knowledge that Megan *was* kept his hands in her hair and off the rest of her.

Hunger had driven them from bed to order a pizza shortly before ten, and even during their impromptu naked picnic Megan had refrained from discussing any of the reservations he could see written on her face during unguarded moments. He hadn't brought them up either.

It was selfish.

He didn't care.

If there were going to be repercussions or regrets or anything else in the morning, he'd deal with them then. *No,* he amended, *I'll deal with them Monday.* They had the weekend, and he fully intended to keep the world at bay until then. He wasn't going to question whichever of the fates had thrown Megan back into his arms.

He rubbed his fingers over Megan's butterfly again. How such a small tattoo affected him…unreal. From the strange erotic kick it landed on his libido, to the jealousy that flared at the thought of how many men might have been in a position to see it, to the unsettling knowledge that their divorce had, in the end, been such a positive change in Megan's life that she had decided to commemorate it with a permanent mark, that tattoo was seared on his mind.

The tattoo was a very colorful reminder of exactly what this was all about. Any nostalgia awakened in him, any strange ideas that this would—or could—be more were quickly dismissed. This was what it was—nothing more.

Megan stirred, and her arm bumped his. She jumped and sat straight up, pushing her hair out of her face as she turned. The shocked gasp became an embarrassed chuckle. "Sorry. I'm not used to sleeping with someone and when we bumped…" She rubbed a hand across her face to chase the sleep away. "Sorry if I woke you."

Megan sleeps alone. That message was the only one that registered. And for some reason he didn't want to explore—with or without a therapist—he was oddly pleased to hear it. "I wasn't asleep."

"No?" Megan's jaw dropped. "You're not tired? Not after…?"

It was hard to tell in this light, but Megan might have been blushing. "It's barely past midnight, and I'm not that tired."

A wicked grin tugged at Megan's mouth. "That sounds like a challenge." Her hand began to trace over his ribs and stomach, causing him to catch his breath.

"Might be."

"I love a challenge," she said as she lowered her head and swirled her tongue around his navel.

The past few years definitely had wrought changes in Megan.

And he was rapidly coming to appreciate that.

CHAPTER EIGHT

LAST CHRISTMAS, Megan's parents had given her a ladies' tool kit—hammer, screwdriver, pliers, all sized a bit smaller and clad in hot-pink-and-purple polka dots. It had come in handy in this apartment, allowing her to do minor repairs without involving her landlord.

Devin had protested using such girlie tools, and she had to admit that watching him try to put the bathroom door back into its frame with a pink-and-purple screwdriver was quite funny to watch. She perched on the edge of the bathtub, providing unsolicited and unhelpful advice.

"You need real tools," Dev grumbled as he forced a screw back into the frame. The flex and pull of his biceps and shoulders had her full attention, and she was glad he'd not seen the need to put on a shirt while he worked. The small screwdriver slipped, and he cursed. "And a real door in a real apartment. Hand me the hammer."

She stood and her quads lodged a protest at the movement. Her thighs simply weren't used to the level of activity they'd seen last night. And this morning. And this afternoon. "There's nothing wrong with this apartment." Handing him the hammer, she added, "You have no one to blame but yourself for the damage."

That got her a smile that melted her knees. "Really? Who jumped who in the shower?"

She shrugged, trying to seem unaffected by the memory that heated her skin. "But it was your, um, *exuberance* that destroyed my door." The ancient hinges hadn't been able to withstand the force of Dev's thrusts as she was pinned against it.... She cleared her throat. "You break it, you buy it."

"Deal." Dev handed her the tools.

The door still hung at a drunken angle. "Um, hello? Door still not fixed."

"I choose to buy. I'll send a carpenter out here first thing Monday morning." He slipped out behind her, leaving her staring at her broken door.

"Devin…"

He wrapped his arms around her waist from behind, pulling her against his chest. Hard evidence of what Dev would rather be doing pressed against her lower back. "Anyway, there's a good chance we'll break something else before we're done here. Might as well start a running list of repairs—coffee table, bathroom door…" His fingers toyed with the hem of the baggy T-shirt she'd put on shortly after they'd crashed through the bathroom door, snaking under to smooth across her hips and stomach. Her head fell back against his chest as one hand moved up to cup her breast, teasing the nipple to a hard point. Dev's other hand slid lower, those long fingers wringing a moan from her with just a touch.

It was easy, and getting easier, to forget everything that wasn't Devin. The real world seemed like an abstract notion existing only in her mind. Only right now—and only this man—seemed real. Concrete. She was in dangerous territory and going deeper as she angled her neck to give Devin better access to the sweet spot under her ear.

She knew all that. But it was very hard to remember at a moment like this.

Dev was dangerous to her sanity and mental health. His words—*before we're done here*—should have been a reminder that this little interlude from reality wouldn't last. In a way they were a wake-up call, causing a pang in her chest she didn't want to explore.

Because if she did, she'd have to give this up: the magic of Dev's hands on her body, the odd comfort and security she felt just having him here. She didn't want to probe those feelings either.

She just wanted to feel.

As her legs began to tremble and lose the strength to hold her upright, Dev's arm tightened around her, supporting her.

It felt good on so many levels and in so many ways it scared her. Not badly enough to ask Dev to leave, but enough to worry her.

More than her apartment was in danger of getting damaged.

All interludes from reality must come to an end, and something in Dev's sigh and the way he dropped a kiss on the top of her head as he passed told Megan it was time.

They'd been sipping coffee over the remnants of a late Sunday brunch, and between the lengthening periods of silence she couldn't call completely comfortable and the choppy conversation, she'd known it was coming. Hell, she'd known it was coming as she cooked his favorite breakfast frittata for old times' sake this morning. Like so many times before, the frittata had burned due to Devin's ability to distract her. And like so many times before, they'd scraped off the burned bits and eaten it anyway.

It might have seemed like old times, but it wasn't. She knew that. And she was prepared for the words.

"I have to leave soon."

Ouch. Not as prepared as I thought. "I figured."

"I'm doing a morning show in Cincinnati tomorrow and my flight leaves…"

"It's fine, Dev. You have a life. So do I," she lied. "And we should probably get back to them." Proud of how nonchalant she sounded about the situation, she stood and grabbed some dishes off the table. "I'm so far behind on those articles.…"

Devin followed her into the kitchen. "This week's schedule is a nightmare for me. I'm triple booked practically every day."

Let the excuses begin. Was there a phrase book guys got in high school just for the gotta-go-I'll-call-you-sometime moment? "I understand. Just don't forget to send the carpenter, okay?"

A furrow appeared on Devin's forehead. "What's wrong, Megan?"

"You're busy. I get that. You don't need to give me the particulars. I'm just trying to tell you I don't expect anything from you beyond a carpenter to fix my door."

"So that's it?"

"This weekend has been great, but we both know it doesn't mean anything."

Devin actually looked offended at her comment. "I must've missed that memo. I was trying to explain that if you wanted to do dinner—or anything else this week—it would have to be late. After the show."

"Oh." She felt about a foot tall.

Devin's hands closed around her upper arms, and he massaged them lightly. "You know, I'm always advising people to stay away from their exes."

Oh, the irony. "Yeah. Me, too."

The corner of his mouth twitched in amusement. "So neither of us is good at taking our own advice." Then his voice dropped a notch and turned serious. "But I'm not sorry this weekend happened. Are you?"

"Nope. No regrets." *Yet.*

"Then dinner tomorrow night?"

"Okay." A little happy campfire warmed her heart.

Then Dev's kiss fanned the flames, leaving her breathless when he finally broke the kiss with a heartfelt groan. "I wish I didn't have to go."

"Me, too," she admitted as she grabbed the countertop for support.

"I'll call you later." He winked. "Seriously."

Then he was gone, and her apartment felt empty. The tiny rooms seemed bigger now that Dev wasn't filling them, and Megan almost expected them to echo.

As she walked to her bedroom she took stock of the damage they'd done to the apartment: one broken table, one broken door, one lamp that had been kicked off her bedside table. The lamp had survived, but the shade needed to be bent back into shape.

Later, she thought as she crawled back under the covers. Dev's scent still clung to the pillows, and she breathed it deep into her lungs. It was hard to focus on current damage or potential future disasters when caught in residual afterglow.

It had been one crazy week. Not even a full week, she realized after a quick mental count. After years of avoiding everything Devin-related, she'd gone from reading him the riot act on Monday to cuddling his pillow on Sunday. Somehow it seemed like much longer than six days.

Devin just had a knack for turning her life upside down. He always had. Since the day he'd tripped over her step stool in the library stacks and caused her to literally fall into his arms... She smiled at the memory.

And while life with Devin hadn't always been easy, it

had never been dull. It was disconcerting to think how col-
orless her life had been over the past years. She'd been so
focused on one thing that she'd gotten unbelievably boring.
Only, she hadn't realized that until Dev had livened up this
week considerably.

She should really get up and do something. Work
on those articles. Tidy the kitchen. Fix the lampshade.
Something other than lie there and obsess over her ex-
husband.

But she was warm and comfy and enjoying the obsess-
ing. Which only proved she really was certifiable.

Fate was strange sometimes. Just when she'd thought
she had everything all worked out, it had thrown Devin
back into the mix. It wasn't an ideal situation—and if she'd
ever harbored any wild fantasy about Devin walking back
into her life it wouldn't have been like this—but she felt
hopeful about the possibilities.

The possibilities that come from change.

The problem, though, was that there was so much change
and so many possibilities, it made her head hurt to think
about it. That was a lie; it actually made her *heart* hurt
to think about it. Because there were so many things that
could go horribly wrong.

But there were so many things that could go amazingly
right, as well.

She wondered if her apartment would survive the
ride....

He'd left Megan's for this? To spend the night alone in a
Cincinnati hotel just to get up before dawn to answer the
same seven questions he'd answered a hundred times across
the country? He had to be insane.

He'd been chafing against the publicity machine for a
while now, but tonight drove the point home. This crossed

a line into ridiculous. He and Manny and the publicist were going to have a chat about his schedule. It was time to get his life back.

He debated calling Megan just to talk, but he knew she was trying to work on some research she wanted to publish in one of those academic journals. It wouldn't be fair to interrupt her work because he was bored and lonely in Cincinnati.

Especially since he'd kept her from working at all over the weekend. He should feel bad about that, but he didn't. Not in the least.

He could use this time to get some work done, as well. Instead, he pulled the file Simon had passed to him Friday morning.

He'd hired Simon to work part-time last year as a favor to a friend to give the young man some real-world experience before he started law school. Privately, Devin found Simon's zeal a refreshing break from the day-to-day realism of his job, so he always made time when Simon came to him with an interesting case or sticky law to discuss. It kept his brain from atrophying.

But this was different. Simon was moving past theory and discussion of the past and into more current and complicated issues: a local college student's case involving right to privacy, which seemed to be struggling in the system. Simon had copious notes scrawled in the margin of the printout: questions, statute references and a very insightful invoking of the Ninth Amendment to back up his argument.

The kid was sharp. Granted, his reading of the 1969 Supreme Court decision wouldn't hold up long under pressure, but the 1990 decision *would*.…

An hour later Devin realized the student in question had one hell of a case but a lawyer who wasn't quite on the ball enough to get it done. And where was the media? Where was the outrage at the blatant disregard of this student's constitutional rights? Why was this flying under the radar?

He booted up his laptop and started sending emails. One to an old classmate who worked for the American Civil Liberties Union now, one to his assistant and one to another radio personality who'd love to break a story like this. That would get everyone started, and by the time he got home tomorrow...

Then he remembered what his schedule for the week was like and grumbled under his breath. He probably didn't have the time to get his hands into something this complicated.

And he knew now that he *wanted* to be in this fight.

Well, he had been planning to make some changes, and this was just more reason to do so. There was no real need for him to continue this junket anyway.

The need to call Megan was really strong now. She'd always been the one to catch the brunt of his enthusiasm. How appropriate he and Megan were back together at the same time he'd found this case. He grinned. Definitely fate trying to tell him something.

But it was late; Megan was probably asleep and he had to be up in a few hours anyway. He'd tell her all about it tomorrow at dinner.

The call had come earlier than expected, but when Megan had seen the clinic's number on her phone she'd known it was over. It hadn't stopped her from hoping, though, that it might work out differently.

At least Julie had called her last night to give her the heads-up so she hadn't been blindsided by it. In the time it had taken to do one search on Google, the rosy afterglow of her weekend and her hopeful outlook had been scrubbed away by internet notoriety and its viral nature.

Dr. Weiss had been calm and measured, never raising her voice as she lectured Megan on professional behavior, privacy issues, the clinic's reputation and bad decision-making. She'd even allowed Megan a chance to explain, raising Megan's hopes before shooting them down in flames.

Then, in that same calm voice, Dr. Weiss had fired her. Megan could come clean out her desk and return her keys after the clinic closed this evening.

Shell-shocked, she'd sat cross-legged on her bed and stared at the phone for a long while, unable to completely process that her career was, for all intents and purposes, over.

But now Megan's pity party was in full swing. Everything she'd worked for was in the toilet, and it wasn't her fault. So she'd acted a little recklessly and made a bad decision, but *this*... This was beyond belief.

Her first response was to blame Devin, but on second thought, this wasn't his style. Plus, after the weekend they'd just shared, she couldn't bring herself to believe Devin would callously sow the seeds to destroy her and then crawl into her bed.

No, this had Kate's manicured fingers all over it. She had to have some kind of personality disorder to do something like this. She wished there was an official diagnosis of Narcissistic Self-Serving Evil Witch Disorder. Antisocial Personality Disorder just didn't seem quite strong enough.

But knowing who to blame didn't change the situation. She was screwed. No matter how she tried to look at it, there was no way to salvage her career. She'd worked so hard in school, fought tooth and nail to get a good internship and now she was at a dead end. Tears burned her eyes and rolled down her cheeks, but they didn't offer any catharsis.

Masochist that she was, she went back to the computer and checked the file on the *Now Hear This* website. She wouldn't torture herself by listening to the clip again, but the counter showed another two hundred clicks in the past hour. Dozens more pingbacks from other sites. The speed of the internet was a dangerous force, but at least she could track the downward spiral of her reputation in real time.

She clicked over to her email to find a message from Devin.

Tried to call, but you're still not answering the phone.

That wasn't entirely true. She'd seen his number on the caller ID, but she didn't trust herself to talk to him at the moment. She might not blame him for this mess, but he was still hip-deep in it.

Still under siege?

That was one word for it.

I'll pick you up after I finish the show. Be thinking about where you want to eat. Oh, and pack a bag. Your place isn't sturdy enough.

Either Dev didn't realize the extent of what that audio clip had done or else he was completely insane. Either way, she didn't plan on leaving the house tonight. She'd go pack up her office as directed, but then she was going back under the covers for a good long wallow in her misery.

Megan debated what to tell Devin. She decided the easiest way out was avoidance. If she confronted him, she'd break down; everything was just too raw right now. Maybe tomorrow she'd feel up to it.

Dev—
Not tonight. Maybe we can talk tomorrow.
M

Megan's short, uninformative email left Devin confused, but since it hadn't arrived until he was about to go on the air, he couldn't follow up. Was she sick?

His intro was playing and he had about four seconds—not enough time to send her an email. He was still planning to go to her place straight from here tonight, and he'd get some answers then, but he'd be left wondering for the next two hours.

He plugged the book, discussed a couple of the celebrity divorce cases making the news, chatted with Kate about upcoming appearances and special guests, but he couldn't shake the uneasy feeling something wasn't right with Megan.

But the listener queue was growing, and Kate was connecting his first caller. He needed to get his mind back on what he was doing.

Thankfully, none of the first few callers had complicated or sticky problems. Devin could fall back on stock answers, recited from memory. Oddly, the question he'd been expecting didn't come until just before the first break.

"So where's Dr. Megan tonight?"

"Living her life, saving marriages, that kind of thing." He tried to sound friendly and casual about it. "She might come back and visit at a later date, but this isn't exactly her area of expertise." He laughed. "Or interest, for that matter. What can I help you with?"

"My ex-wife is about as psycho as yours, but my ex has no problem pulling out the crazy in public."

Psycho?

"So what I want to know is how you manage to keep that crazy under control in front of other people. I don't care what she says to me, but I'm tired of having an audience. You two were fine on the show last week, so how'd you get her to act normal?"

This wasn't the question he'd been expecting. He looked at Kate for confirmation this caller was off his rocker. Her shrug and grin set alarm bells ringing.

He chose his words carefully. "If your ex is truly mentally ill—"

"No, just bitchy like yours."

"Excuse me?"

The caller laughed. "Dude, we all heard the clip. I give you major props for keeping your cool the way you did, 'cause *damn*—"

Devin was missing a piece of the puzzle, but thanks to the caller, he now had a clue where to find it. He disconnected the call. "Caller? You there? Kate? We seem to be having some technical difficulties. I've lost the caller."

Kate looked at her board. "I'm not sure what happened...." She looked up, saw his signal and nodded in understanding. "Sorry, folks, something's weird here. We're going to go to break while I sort it out."

While Kate scrambled, Devin was already typing in the URL to the website where Kate uploaded what she called his "greatest hits"—the craziest or funniest or most ridiculous calls. It didn't take him long to see which clip was getting the most traffic: "Behind the Scenes with Devin and Dr. Megan." The counter showed thousands of listens, and the comment tail...

"Okay, we went to tape." Kate's voice came through the studio's speakers. "What's going on?"

His anger was simmering already, so he ignored her as he clicked play. Ten seconds later he understood the caller's words. Ten seconds after that, he knew why Megan wasn't in the mood for dinner.

And the clip was five and a half minutes long. His blood was boiling by the one-minute mark.

Kate was lucky she was on the other side of the glass and not where he could get his hands on her immediately. She might have killed the live feed on their mics the other night, but the ratings-chasing bitch had kept the recording going. With a little splicing and dicing, Kate had turned his and Megan's private, off-air discussions into a juicy sound clip, totally distorting what actually happened. Thanks to Kate's editing, Megan did sound a bit like a psycho.

"Take it down." Kate opened her mouth to argue, but he wasn't interested. "Take it down *now*."

She pressed her lips into a thin line, but turned to her computer. A few seconds later she nodded, and when he refreshed the page, the clip was gone.

"It's still out there, you know. The internet never forgets."

"Then you'd better get busy on some kind of retraction or apology."

"Devin," she argued through the glass separating them, "it's been the number-one clip on *Now Hear This* since Saturday morning. It's viral and people can't get enough of it—or you. The hits to your site have gone through the roof. Your book is number one on Amazon today."

Kate's blindness to anything that couldn't be ranked, rated or re-tweeted had never been so clear. Or so dangerous. She might not care about people, but she definitely cared about her job. He targeted his comment to that care. "Are you *trying* to get us sued?"

Kate shrugged. "Megan has no grounds to sue us for anything. She agreed to be on the show. She agreed to be taped and possibly used for promotional purposes."

"She didn't agree to have you edit her words into something damaging to her reputation, though. Somewhere there's an attorney trying to get her to sue even as we speak."

"Good! Let her sue. The added publicity—"

He leaned close to the microphone and spoke carefully. "You're fired."

"What?"

"You heard me."

"We're in the middle of a show, Devin."

"I'll handle it."

Kate turned mutinous, crossing her arms over her chest. "I work for this station, not you. You can't fire me."

"Exactly who do you think this station values more? Me or the person who answers my phone?"

That statement hit home and Kate turned an unflattering shade of angry red. "You son of a..." Her eyes narrowed. "I made this show a hit, you know."

"Then you won't have any problem finding someone else to work for. But you no longer work on *my* show."

Kate tossed her headphones on the desk as Devin opened the door between the booths. "Go to hell, Devin Kenney."

She flounced out the door past him, leaving a trail of expensive perfume in her wake. He had no doubt he'd hear from the studio's Powers That Be in the morning, pleading her case.

He'd produce his own damn show before he had her back in the booth again.

Speaking of, his show was currently running on tape and the listeners had to be confused.

Sliding into Kate's chair, he paused the tape and pulled the mic close. "Sorry, folks, but we're having major technical difficulties this evening. Must be the full moon or something. Apologies to everyone on hold and out there listening, but we're going to have to rely on some old favorites for the rest of tonight's show."

Oh, he'd be hearing about this tomorrow, too, but right now he had bigger tigers to tame.

Down the hall he found one of the sound techs messing with some ad spots. "Do you know how to run a board?"

The young man nodded.

"Good. Babysit my show, will you?"

Devin waited only long enough for the shocked tech to nod again before he continued on. With *Cover Your Assets* covered, he dialed Manny's number as he waited for the elevator.

"Devin! Great show tonight. You were fab, as always...."

Manny's butt-kissing grated his last nerve. "The show is still on, you jackass. Why didn't you tell me Kate had posted some hatchet-job clip on the web?"

"Because you told me not to call you until noon today, and by then it was old news." Manny's sniff said he wasn't over that insult. "But the good news is that your book has jumped to number one on Amazon."

Damn. What kind of idiots had he surrounded himself with? "You'd better come up with a stellar form of damage control for this."

"Devin, you have nothing to worry—"

"For *Megan,* you fool. Could you think beyond your fifteen percent for just a minute?" The elevator started its descent to the parking garage. "You and Kate have the ethical standards of mob bosses."

"Kate and I only want to do what's best for you and your career. And look! You're the hottest thing right now."

"And Kate is looking for a new job." He waited for Manny to connect the dots to the precarious position he was in at the moment.

"Look, I know you and Megan are revisiting your younger years, and you're feeling all nostalgic and lovey-dovey after your weekend..."

How does Manny know where I'd spent the weekend? Damn tabloids.

"But, Devin, you have a public image to uphold. A persona you've created that you have to honor for your fan base."

"I'm an attorney. My public image can't be 'screw everyone over.' Do you even know what the term *ethical* means?"

"Your fans don't see you as an attorney."

"Then you definitely have some major work ahead of you fixing *that* situation." Manny started to sputter something again, and Devin cut him off. The elevator doors opened, and Devin was nearly at his car. "We will talk tomorrow about future plans for my career and public image. In the meantime, you need to get busy with your spin machine and generate some pushback."

Not waiting for Manny's agreement, Devin hung up and cranked the engine. He looked at his phone, then tossed it in the passenger seat. No sense calling Megan now; she wouldn't answer and he'd be there in a few minutes anyway.

He'd lost control over a large part of his life without realizing it, and this was his wake-up call.

CHAPTER NINE

As DEVIN PARKED IN front of Megan's apartment, a feeling of dread settled in his stomach. At least a dozen photographers had set up camp in front of Megan's—drawing an interested crowd of neighbors to gawk at the circus. They converged on him before the car came to a complete stop, turning the short trip up to her building into a gauntlet of shouted questions and flashbulbs.

He didn't doubt the crowd had a lot to do with Megan's earlier message. His fault or not, there was a very good chance Megan blamed him for this latest fiasco. If she'd been *trying* to become the most infamous ex in Chicago, his people couldn't have done a better job achieving it for her. No wonder she didn't want to see him tonight. Had she been dealing with this all day?

He knocked on the door, calling her name so she'd know it was him and not another tabloid looking for a story. Then he held his breath. Moment-of-truth time. Would she even open the door? If she didn't, they'd both be fodder for the tabloids tomorrow.

Megan opened the door, but she didn't look overly happy to see him. She was pale, with dark half-moons under her eyes as if she hadn't slept last night, and he knew Kate—and by extension, he, too—was to blame. "Dev, I—"

"Kate's evil. I had no idea what she'd done until half an hour ago."

"I believe you." She sounded sincere, but she didn't open the door wider and invite him in.

"I fired her." Megan's eyebrows rose in shock. "And I have Manny at work on damage control even as we speak. I'm sorry about this."

Megan nodded, accepting his apology, and her lips pressed into a line as she seemed to weigh it against the damage already done.

"You have to let me in. Otherwise we'll be on every gossip blog in minutes."

"You think we won't be anyway?" She sounded disgusted, but she stepped back and held the door open for him.

First major hurdle cleared. But Megan kept plenty of distance between them as she closed the door and crossed to the couch on the other side of the room. Changing her mind, she took the chair instead, presumably to keep him from joining her on the couch. *So, the cold barrier circling Megan like a razor-wire fence will be my next challenge.* Before he could decide how to approach her, though, he noticed the four boxes next to the door. Boxes that hadn't been there yesterday when he left. That didn't bode well. "What's all this? Still planning that trip to Canada?" he joked.

Megan's humorless laugh chilled him. "I wish. Those would be the contents of my office. Kate isn't the only one who lost her job today over this."

What? "You got fired?"

She braced her elbow on the arm of the chair and propped her chin on it. "You sound surprised."

"Well, *yeah*. Some stupid audio clip makes the internet rounds and you lose your job?" He claimed the corner of the couch closest to her chair. "That's insane." But it did explain much more about her attitude and the pinched look around her eyes.

"No, that's what happens when you work in a profession where discretion is paramount and reputation is everything. My lack of the first has destroyed the second." The even cadence and tinge of sarcasm made him think that might have been a direct quote from her boss.

"The clip has been removed."

She nodded. "I appreciate that, but the damage is done."

"So you get another job, start rebuilding your reputation...." He trailed off as Megan shook her head. "Why not?"

"I guess I didn't explain this clearly the other night. Internships are really hard to come by. Good ones are even more competitive." She leaned back with a sigh as she continued. "Internships paying a decent wage are few and far between, and unless I want to starve and default on my student loans, I'm not in a position where I could work at one of the nonpaying ones, even if there was one available. There's no place for me to go to rebuild my reputation." She snorted. "Not that it matters now."

Megan had to be overreacting—nothing was unfixable—but considering the day she'd had, he wouldn't call her on it now. "Why?"

"Dr. Weiss isn't the only one concerned with the reputation of her clinic. No reputable therapist is going to hire an intern who's been outed on the internet with borderline personality disorder."

"But you don't. That was all Kate, and she's going to admit it in public."

"Yeah, well, a retraction won't spread nearly as wide or as quickly, and it will still sound fishy to anyone hiring."

She sighed. "And even if I could find someone to hire me and let me finish my hours, the state licensing board isn't going to be impressed. They do background checks, you know. This mess has brought everything—my abilities, my education, my ethics, even my mental stability—into question. Even if they could look past the fact I was fired from an internship, do you think the state is going to grant a license to the infamous and possibly crazy Dr. Megan?"

She was obviously hurting, but... "There are plenty of doctors far more infamous than you. Who's the one with the TV show?"

Calmly—almost too calmly—Megan shook her head. "They got their licenses before they became famous. Most of them don't have licenses now because they weren't able to get them renewed. But there's no requirement that they need one to do those kinds of shows, so..."

He could strangle Kate, but he also had to admit he wasn't fully innocent either. He hadn't known what the repercussions could be, and he hadn't torpedoed her career intentionally, but he definitely shared the blame. "So what do we do?"

"*We* don't do anything. Tomorrow *I* will go find a job—"

"Good. Where?"

She shrugged. "I can tend bar, wait tables..."

With her skills? "You have a PhD."

"So do a lot of other people. You'd be surprised at the educational levels of the folks serving your dinner. Just one of many reasons to tip your servers well—they probably have enormous student loan debt." Her attempt at humor fell flat, and her wan smile told him she knew it, too.

"This is ridiculous. Kate is going to confess that she doctored the clip. If anyone is going to look bad, it's her.

Manny is working his spin right now. And if you need money—".

"You'll loan it to me?" she scoffed.

"Forget loan." She stiffened, and he looked for a non-insulting way to give her the money. "Manny has been quick to tell me how much I'm making off this fiasco, so it's fair to say you've earned it."

She shook her head again. For someone who seemed to be on the edge of disaster, she was oddly calm and rational. "Dev, I'm not looking for a sugar daddy. I'll figure something out."

Stubborn woman. "Why won't you let me help you?"

"Because my problems are not your problems."

It sure felt like it, though. He tried to inject some humor. "Just last week you said I was the source of your problems."

A small smile tugged at her cheek. "True."

"Then let me help you get through this."

She fell silent and the beginnings of the smile faded. He recognized the look on Megan's face. She was having an interesting internal debate, coming to a decision about something. He just wasn't sure which decision about what. A long moment later, Megan took a deep breath. He braced himself.

"I kind of got the impression when you left yesterday— and correct me if I'm wrong—that this past weekend was some sort of new start for us. Was I wrong about that?"

The brutal honesty in her words caught him off guard. Whatever he'd prepared himself for, that wasn't it.

Asking Devin that question had taken all the bravado she could muster. The look of shock he wore now made her want to take the question back. *No, it's a fair question. I jumped into bed with him again, so I have a right to know what he's thinking this is about.* Megan ignored the obvious addendum that she should have asked that *before* they had sex.

Don't back down. She straightened her spine. "Well, Dev?"

Devin cleared his throat. "Is that what you want?"

"Don't play games. I'm not expecting you to drop to your knees and propose or anything. I just need to know if this is fun and games for old times' sake or if there's a possibility this might go somewhere. Eventually."

A long moment passed and her heart began to stutter in her chest. Had she read this situation all wrong? "I told you I have no expectations of you, but I think it might be helpful to be sure we're on the same page."

Dev nodded. "There's always a possibility, right?"

That wasn't exactly a ringing endorsement of any future, but considering their past... No, she couldn't hide behind Devin again now. She'd worked too hard to make something of herself, to be someone other than just Devin's wife. She couldn't do it. Not now. "Then there's no way I can take money from you."

That brought Dev's irritation back to the forefront. He pushed to his feet and began to pace. "That makes no sense at all, Megan."

"As you noted before, I'm a different person from the one you used to know. I've worked hard, and there's no way I can go into any, ahem, 'possibilities' as anything less than an equal. If I let you play knight-with-a-big-fat-wallet then we're not equals."

"So you'll accept nonfinancial help? Like if I put Manny to work?"

"Only if Manny wants to sign me as a client, too."

Dev rubbed a hand over his face in exasperation. "You're being ridiculous."

"And you're being overbearing." She caught herself and

tamped down her temper. "Try to see this from my point of view. If I'm ever going to salvage my career, then I need to salvage my pride first."

Dev shook his head and snorted. "You're wrong."

It was getting much more difficult to keep her ire under control. "Excuse me?"

"If you want to salvage your career, you're going to have to swallow your pride. Your ego is bruised and your feelings are hurt, but—"

What the...? "Hang on, which one of us is the shrink?"

"This has nothing to do with psychology. This is PR, and I understand the circus you're caught in better than you do. Forget about your pride for the moment. Do whatever you have to do to get through this and your pride will recover with your career."

"You talk a good game, Dev, but—"

"No buts. How do you think my clients get through ugly public divorces where all of their dirty little secrets make the papers and still have careers on the other side?"

He had a point. And he knew she knew it. She could tell by the smirk on his face. "Fine. I'll bite. What do you suggest?"

He stood in front of her and crossed his arms over his chest. "Now that you don't have to worry about your boss, take control of your press. For real this time."

She waved the advice away. "This from the person who doesn't even read his own press." When Dev continued to stare at her expectantly, she elaborated. "I tried that already, remember? It's why this is worse, not better."

"Meggie, Meggie, Meggie." Dev shook his head sadly. "You went into it with the wrong attitude. Now, go put on a dress."

"Are you bipolar now? Why would I do that?"

"Because we're going to dinner. That's the first step in discrediting Kate's little hatchet job. Plus, I'm hungry."

"I'm not in the mood to go out." Even to her own ears she sounded like a petulant five-year-old.

"Tough." Devin leaned forward and placed his hands on the arms of the chair, effectively caging her. He let his eyes roam down her body in a way that left her wiggling slightly in her seat. "As much as I'd rather stay in, you need to be out in public. You need to give that crowd out front a picture of you with your head held high and going on with your life. Right now you're acting like you've done something to be ashamed of, and they'll feed on that. Anyway, you're going to need the energy a good, well-balanced meal provides," he promised with a wicked grin.

Her career was in tatters and she'd spent the day wallowing in it without ever coming up with a solution. She didn't necessarily believe Devin's plan would work, but it was still nice to have a plan. To have someone in her corner staying optimistic—not with "tomorrow is another day" platitudes, but with actual plans—when she couldn't. "Okay. I'll get dressed."

Devin grinned and leaned in for a kiss that lingered long enough to shake the last of the sluggishness off and bring her body to life. And when Dev offered her a hand to help her to her feet, she realized how much lighter she felt. How odd. Today was the worst day of her life, but it didn't seem insurmountable anymore.

Something was terribly wrong with her. This feeling, though...

Megan didn't let go of the hand pulling her out of the chair. She twined her fingers through his instead and tugged him closer. Based on their history, she and Dev probably weren't a good idea, and getting more involved with him now was an even worse one, but with her road map and game plan totally shot to hell, she had nothing but possibilities ahead of her.

Devin was one she was willing to explore.

Dev's eyes lit as she slid her other hand over his chest to his neck, pulling his head closer to hers. "Before I get dressed, I need to get undressed, and if I'm getting undressed..."

She didn't get to finish the statement. Or the thought. Or any thoughts for a long *wonderful* while.

Years ago, Megan had worshipped Dev. His strength, his passion, his charisma—in her eyes, he'd been just a rung down from deity. Over the next week, though, she began to wonder if Dev had moved up the celestial ladder while she hadn't been looking.

Devin spoke; people listened. He wanted something done; it got done. He had minions and assistants and interns at his beck and call. He had hangers-on and yes-men genuflecting and seeking his approval or support.

He could walk into any restaurant and immediately get a table. Random strangers in a bar would send drinks to him or pick up the tab. He played poker with the mayor and golf with the governor's son. She half expected to find he had the president on speed dial.

She'd known he was famous. She'd known he was popular. She just hadn't realized how popular and famous and rich and influential he was.

And it bothered her a little bit. More than a little bit.

The reasoning behind her unease didn't hold up under close scrutiny because Devin didn't seem overly affected by it. Aside from his disparaging comments about her apartment, of course. When she called attention to it, he'd just shrug and brush it off as being the nature of the business. This attitude worked—at least for him—but Megan still felt uncomfortable in the spotlight. Granted, it was Devin's spotlight and she just happened to be sharing it, but that light illuminated all the problems and inequalities and potential issues in getting involved....

And it gave her an excuse, however flimsy and annoying Dev found it to be, to continue to return to her own apartment on a regular basis. As she was now.

Only one photographer waited for her this morning—down from four at the start of the week—so she smiled and waved as she climbed the steps.

The blogs had a field day with their public reconciliation, just as Dev had predicted, especially coming so quickly on the heels of Kate's disastrous—and now discredited—audio clip. Another appearance on Dev's show, several very public dinners and a few pictures of her leaving Dev's building in the early-morning hours had the media buzzing in a whole new direction. She'd gone from "psycho ex" to "the woman who might tame Devin Kenney" in a matter of days. Dev had been right about that much.

But she still didn't have a job or a plan for what she'd do next. The focus of the media attention had turned positive, which was nice on a personal level, but the attention was still there. No job meant no money, and she couldn't float for long on her meager savings. She couldn't—wouldn't—allow Dev to give her money, so something had to give one way or the other.

That was a more solid reason behind her return to her apartment every day. She and Dev might be "exploring possibilities," but there was no sense in getting used to Dev's fancy condo on Lakeshore Drive or the limos or the box seats. Coming back to her place kept her from getting too complacent, reminding her nothing right now was permanent.

It also reaffirmed her commitment to not get into anything

serious while they were on such different playing fields. She'd done that before, and look how that had ended up....

No, she and Dev were having a good time, healing some old wounds and burying some ghosts from the past. That was healthy. That was positive. The fact it was repairing some damage to her ego and professional image was also a plus.

But she refused to read anything else into it.

She also *had* to find a job. Megan dropped her bag onto the couch and logged on to her email to see if she had any responses to the feelers she had out.

At the core of all this was the uncertainty, and that uncertainty was getting to her. Too much was up in the air for her to feel comfortable about anything. Her "possibilities that come from change" line wasn't at all comforting, and she was beginning to think it was the stupidest mantra she'd ever adopted. Much less tattooed on her body.

Her email in-box had plenty of messages, but none of any help. However, against her better judgment and over Manny's protests, Devin had put Manny to work on her behalf, and Manny's name in the return address of one message caught her attention.

Sorry, Megan. No one is biting. Honestly, you're just not as interesting now that you and Devin are a couple.

Being pronounced uninteresting stung a bit, but all things considered, that wasn't unexpected. Manny's casual use of "couple" to describe her and Devin, however, *was*. Some blogs had speculated about their possible couple-ship, mainly because Divorce Attorney and Marriage Counselor Reconcile made interesting headlines, but Manny?

No. Manny is just quoting public feeling about my uninteresting self, that's all.

But this was ridiculous. As she expected, she was too notorious to land another internship with any reputable clinic, and the amount of time she had to get her internship hours completed if she still planned to sit the licensing exam anytime soon was ticking away. Her first instinct on that was proving correct. The irony was kicking her, because now she wasn't notorious enough to get a job providing even weak psychotainment for the masses.

It was frustrating. Annoying. Scary. Normally, any one of those things would have her scuttling to get out and restore order to her universe. The only thing unnerving her now was her tepid response and inability to get overly worked up over it. She could blame—or was it credit?—the Dev-caused endorphins for the lack of overachiever response this should be causing.

Speak of the devil… Dev's ring tone sounded from the depths of her bag.

"Where are you, Meggie?"

"Home."

"I just tried that number. Why didn't you pick up?" He sounded distracted.

She sighed. "*My* home, Dev. Not yours."

"Why do you insist on going back there every day? My place is plenty big enough—"

"We've had this conversation, Dev," she interrupted, and heard his exasperated sigh. "So what's up?" Clicking her email client closed, she set the computer on the coffee table and leaned against the cushions.

"Crazy day and I left a file in the kitchen…."

"Yeah, I saw one when I went to make coffee."

"I was hoping I could convince you to bring it to me."

She could hear the wheedle in his voice. "I'll take you to lunch after."

Drive back to Dev's, get the file, drive to his office... It would be way past lunchtime by the time she got there. She looked around. It wasn't as if she had much of anything else to do today. "I guess I could do that."

"I appreciate it. See you in a little while."

She hadn't even had a chance to take off her shoes. She grabbed her keys and bag, locked the door and waved at the photographer again on her way out.

Halfway to Devin's she remembered his army of assistants and minions. Why didn't he send one of them to his apartment to get the file if it was so important? It would have been quicker and easier for everyone.

The next thought sent a chill through her veins. He was treating her like his wife again. And not in a good way. Belatedly she realized she'd set herself up for this exact thing—doing some cooking, running a different errand for him yesterday on her way home. They'd fallen back into some older habits, so why was she surprised about this one? After all, why send an assistant to do a job your wife could do—and had done—hundreds of times? What was next? Picking up his dry cleaning?

Talk about unequal playing fields...

Oh, no. This did not bode well at all.

The receptionist buzzed Devin to let him know Megan was on her way to his office. He looked at his watch. *That was quick.* Good. He could give the file back to Simon and send him over to meet with Mark from the ACLU. As soon as the publicity junkets surrounding his book ended—and he had Manny working on that—he'd be able to devote some time to this young man's case. Until then, Simon would get some real-life experience being Devin's assistant in the preliminaries.

He called out when he heard Megan's knock. She'd been curled up under the covers when he left this morning, mumbling about catching up on her sleep. The stress was getting to her, he knew. The job hunt was going nowhere, she was worried about money and the state licensing exam, and even the adjustment of the media's attitude hadn't been able to lift that from her shoulders. She had a good game face, but he knew her too well.

If she'd just accept his help… No, Megan seemed determined to dig in her heels and go it alone. It was a bit insulting when he thought about it. She'd play his arm candy for the press, and she happily warmed his bed and body in the evenings, but she had a concrete wall around her that he couldn't breach when it came to anything more.

There was a pinched look on her face when she stuck her head around the door, and he knew not only had there not been any developments in the search for another internship, something else had gone wrong, as well.

"You okay?" he asked, knowing he probably wouldn't get a real answer.

"Great. Here's the file you left. And another one I found on the coffee table. I wasn't sure if you needed it."

"Thanks, Meggie. You're a lifesaver." She accepted the light kiss he pressed against her lips, but didn't respond otherwise. "Let me give this to Simon and I'll take you out for a quick bite to eat."

"I'm not hungry. Thanks anyway."

Oh, he knew that tone. He leaned against the desk. "Okay, what's wrong?"

"Nothing."

He waited.

"I'm not your lackey. Next time you need your errands run, ask one of your assistants."

"I didn't realize it would be an inconvenience—"

"Because I don't have a job?" she challenged.

That might have figured into his request a small bit, but only a fool would admit that now. Not with Meggie getting her dander up already. "Would you believe it was an excuse to get you to come down here and have lunch with me?" That was true as well, and wouldn't give Meggie a reason to hand him his head.

"No, but you get points for trying."

"You could've said no if you were busy."

"I think we've established I'm not busy," she grumbled. "I just don't think we should be falling back into any old habits one or both of us might resent."

She'd been practicing that statement. And while he could tell Megan might not actively be looking for a fight, the set of her shoulders told him she wouldn't back down from one either. "Next time I'll send someone, okay?"

"Thank you." Her shoulders relaxed. "Now you can buy me lunch."

That was a turnaround. "So you're hungry after all?"

"Maybe."

"Are we playing some kind of game?"

"No games." She cocked an eyebrow at him. "I think we're both a little old for that, don't you?"

"And we know each other a little too well for it to work."

Megan smiled. "That, too." She pointed at the file. "I assume that's the case you were telling me about?"

He nodded. Poor Megan had had to listen to his lecture on the privacy doctrine and the Fourteenth Amendment for an hour the other night. And she'd done so wearing nothing but a sheet and a smile he hadn't seen since he'd done the same thing in law school. "I'm sending Simon over to the ACLU office today."

"It's nice to see you so excited about this."

He *was* excited. It was an unusual feeling. "It's been a while, that's for sure."

"But there are only so many hours in the day. When will you have time for it all? Your practice, the show, the book and now this."

"Some things are going to be rearranged in the future." He took the file to the hallway and waved down a paralegal with instructions to find Simon. Then he closed the door carefully behind him, making sure it latched. "I've been so caught up in show business—both mine and my clients'—I forgot I was a lawyer."

"Good for you, Dev. This kid is very lucky—your smarts will help the case, but your name recognition will help, too."

"Well, it definitely won't hurt." He leaned against the desk. "The media seems to have ignored this case, but…"

She perched on the edge of his desk, as well. "But we know what happens to anyone who gets in your orbit. Instant headlines." The small laugh Megan finished with couldn't mask the dry tone.

"Do you regret being back in my orbit?"

"No." She looked at him sideways and smiled weakly. "Well, maybe a little," she corrected. "I wish I hadn't lost my job over it, but being with you again…"

He waited as she thought.

"Honestly? Hmm, well, being with you doesn't suck, either." The hand on the desk slid over to close around his.

It wasn't exactly the enthusiastic response his ego had hoped for, but he'd take it. A small tug was all it took to pull Megan into his arms, and she rose on her tiptoes to capture his lips with hers.

Megan's kiss, whether she meant it to be carnal or not, instantly heated his blood. His hands tightened on her waist, pulling her closer, fitting her body to his.

Her shirt wasn't tucked in, and it was easy to slide his hand under the hem to find soft, warm skin. Megan jumped and broke away. "Dev! Someone could—"

"No one will."

She gasped as he released the clasp of her bra, then sighed as his hands cupped her breasts. "I didn't come here for a nooner on your desk," she protested weakly.

"Okay," he said, then nearly laughed at the disappointed look on her face. He levered himself off the desk and led her to the other side of his office. "However, as you'll notice, shrinks aren't the only ones with couches in their offices."

CHAPTER TEN

"HAVE YOU TRIED CALLING Dr. Kincaid's clinic?" Julie brought Megan a glass of wine and tried a little too hard to sound upbeat. "I hear…" She trailed off when Megan shook her head.

"I've tried *everyone*. No one will touch me with a ten-foot pole. Well," she amended, "Dr. Hearst at that clinic in Elgin seemed interested, but he's a bit of a quack. And I got the feeling he wanted to…" She couldn't finish.

"Wanted to what?"

"Touch me."

"Ew." Julie shuddered slightly.

"Tell me about it."

"What can I do?" The concern was genuine. Julie had gone above and beyond Megan's expectations in trying to help. First by advocating with Dr. Weiss, then by sending out requests to her contact list to see if anyone needed an intern. Julie hadn't had any more luck than Megan herself.

"You've done everything you can, and I'm very appreciative. So this—" she indicated the wine and snacks "—is exactly what I need. Girl talk. Drinks without the sympathy. A chance to just hang out."

"Mi casa, su casa." Julie's eyes turned sympathetic anyway. "And that can be literal, if necessary."

"I'm not in danger of being evicted. Yet." But it was still nice to know she had a place to go if it came to that. Julie's apartment was a castle compared to hers, but then, Julie's family was more well-off and she was still on their payroll. Megan didn't want to go to her parents for help just yet, even though they'd offered, because she wasn't willing to admit defeat. "Actually, I called one of my professors and he's got a possible lead for me."

"Really? That's great."

"It's a small clinic with low-income clients, and I'd be doing mostly substance-abuse work."

"I hear a *but*," Julie said.

"But the money is tiny. And it's in Carbondale."

The wrinkle in Julie's nose said a lot. "That's like, what? Four hours from here?"

"Five and a half." She tried to sound enthusiastic. "But the cost of living would be a lot less, so if I picked up a part-time job on the side, I might be able to make it work."

Julie looked over the edge of her wineglass. "What did Devin have to say about this?"

"I haven't told him anything about it yet. He doesn't understand why I don't just move into his place as it is."

"Honestly, neither do I."

"Jules, would you move back in with your ex-husband?"

"I don't have an ex-husband."

"Touché. But moving in with Dev isn't a great idea." At Julie's doubtful look, she added, "Aside from obvious benefits, of course. Just because we lived together before, that doesn't mean we should be rushing right back into it. Anyway—" she took a long drink of her wine "—I'm not sure where Dev and I are heading at the moment, and I don't think he is either. Even if I did have an idea, it's still not an option."

"Why not?"

She couldn't stop the pitiful tone that crept into her voice. "Because I'd feel like I'd failed at my own life and gone crawling back to him."

"So you'd rather move away?"

"No, but at least I'd be succeeding or failing on my own."

"You were succeeding just fine until Devin's career intersected with yours so disastrously. This isn't a failure, and even if it was, it wouldn't be your fault."

"I know. But if I let Dev ride to my rescue, I'll never get my feet back under me. It would be like I hadn't accomplished anything over the last seven years, because I'd just be Meggie again. I can't do it. I *won't* do it."

Julie looked at her oddly. "Is there something you haven't told me about your marriage?" she asked cautiously.

"It's nothing like what you're thinking." She drank deeply from her glass while she tried to find the right words. "Part of what drove us apart was that I was just 'Devin's wife.' He might not have been *the* Devin Kenney back then, but he wasn't much different than he is now. Popular. Important. On a smaller scale, of course, but still… I always felt like the sidekick—and not even a useful sidekick with my own superpowers and cool toys. More like the useless one you feel sorry for and can't understand why the hero puts up with them. I can't live the rest of my life as the sidekick."

"It doesn't have to be like that. I didn't know you then, but I know you now, and you definitely aren't just a sidekick."

"Thanks." She fiddled with her glass some more. "Then, of course, there's also the very real possibility Dev and I could fall apart again. I can't risk my future on…on…on whatever this is we're doing."

"*Is* that a possibility?"

"Anything's a possibility, but think about it, Dr. Moss. What do you think our chances are? Realistically."

Julie frowned.

Megan swirled the wine in her glass. "Exactly. Reuniting with your ex is all about remembering why you got together in the first place."

"And the hot sex."

Megan rolled her eyes. "I never should have told you that. Yes, there's fabulous hot sex, but I know better than to assume anything about any kind of future based on the hotness of the sex. You and I both know the problem with reunions is that all the reasons you broke up are usually there, too, lurking beneath the surface, just waiting to blow the whole thing to hell again."

"But you know all the lurking problems, so…"

"If I was your client, would you be encouraging this?"

"Probably not." Julie leaned over to refill both glasses. "But you're not my client. You're Dr. Megan." She lifted her glass in a mock toast.

"I can't tell you how much I hate that name and what it implies."

"Don't be such a snob. So four or five months in Carbondale, huh?" Julie shuddered delicately.

"You make it sound like I'm being exiled to Siberia. Carbondale isn't the ends of the earth."

"But it's not Chicago, either."

"It may take a crowbar to get you *out* of the city, but I'm a bit more flexible. Six months, tops, and I'll be back. Plus, there's the added perk of giving all of this time to really die down and be forgotten. I'll come back, get my license and we can start our own practice just like we planned. Only with one small detour."

"You sound like your mind is made up."

"Almost. I can't dither around with this. The clinic needs someone ASAP and I need a job ASAP. Something has to happen soon."

"Which brings me right back to my earlier question. What about Devin?"

Megan didn't have a ready answer. Julie, good counselor that she was, sat quietly and patiently while Megan thought. "I've made a lot of decisions in my life where Devin was a weight on the scale. I moved to Urbana for him so he could go to law school, then I moved to Albany in spite of him. I'll admit Devin is one of the factors in this equation, but I really need to make this decision based on what *I* want and what's best for *me* in the long term."

"And that is…?"

Megan took a deep breath and blew it out noisily. "I wish to God I knew."

Megan was being uncharacteristically quiet tonight. She'd been getting less talkative for two days now, but had lapsed into almost complete silence tonight. Something was up, but Devin knew he wasn't any more likely to get an answer now than he had been yesterday or the day before.

But she was here, at least. She wouldn't stay at his place full-time, but she was spending more time here than at her apartment these days, so she might be coming around to the idea. It was progress.

Megan was curled up on one end of the couch watching the news while he stretched out with his laptop on the opposite end. They'd fallen back into what Megan used to call "old married people mode" as if they'd never been apart. It was familiar and oddly pleasant, and for the first time in a long time he'd started looking forward to his evenings off. He even found himself looking for ways to clear his schedule to have more free time and actually have a life again.

So he was content to wait for her to talk. Whatever was going on inside her head, it couldn't be his fault, or he knew she wouldn't be here. *She might,* he amended, *but she wouldn't be silent about it.* He'd be getting an earful if it was his fault, so he knew the best approach to Megan's silence was to wait it out until she was ready to talk.

As if she heard his thoughts, Megan turned off the TV and nudged him with her foot. "I got offered a job. A chance to finish out my internship almost on schedule."

He set the laptop aside. "That's great, Meggie. I told you you'd find one. There's a bottle of champagne still in the fridge...." He trailed off when she shook her head, and he belatedly, *stupidly,* realized she should be far happier about this news than her mood expressed. And since she'd waited so long to tell him about it, he probably wasn't going to be thrilled either. Tiny alarm bells went off inside his head.

"It's not perfect. The pay's not great and hours will be hellish, but I can't be too picky."

"And?" he prompted, waiting for the other shoe to drop.

She lifted her chin. "And it's in Carbondale."

Now he understood her mood. "Please tell me that's a little neighborhood in the suburbs I've just never heard of before."

"No, it's actually the Carbondale."

He chose his words carefully, not liking the sense of déjà vu that settled around this conversation. "Have you accepted it already?"

"No, I told them I needed to think about it, and I'd let

them know by Friday. If I take it, I'd have a week to get settled and start the next Monday."

If she hadn't accepted it, then maybe she was giving him the chance to confirm his last offer. "You don't have to move to Carbondale. I've already told you—"

"That you'd help me out. I know. But I've told *you*—repeatedly—that I'm not looking for a sugar daddy to support me. I want to—I *need* to—accomplish this on my own."

God, she was stubborn. "So you'd rather move to the opposite end of the state instead of accept money from me?"

She shrugged, and his irritation grew. "It's six months, tops."

Here we go again. "What about this?" He indicated the two of them.

That sparked her temper. "*This?* I don't even know what this *is*. It's certainly not enough to give up the opportunity to salvage my career."

Of course. Her precious career was always the most important thing. "It never is, is it?"

"Oh, please. We're going to play *that* song again?" She rolled her eyes at him. "Grow up, Devin. Not everything can be about you. Some things have to be about me, you know? It's six months. Nothing can ever come of *this* if you can't handle six freakin' months." Megan swung her legs off the couch and stood staring down at him. "Just once it would be nice if you could think for a moment beyond your life and your convenience. I put up with a hell of a lot more than six months in Carbondale for you and your career. Moving across the state, switching schools, delaying my graduation because all my credits wouldn't transfer…"

He'd heard this all before, and now she wasn't the only

one getting angry. "Yeah, and nothing was going to stand between you and your career. So you left."

"Damn it, Dev. I'm not asking *you* to move to Carbondale."

Of course not. "Good."

She made a face, but otherwise ignored his comment. "All I'm asking for is your support. Maybe a little cooperation. Just a little inkling that getting involved with you again isn't setting myself up for another crash. I had to choose last time—"

"And you chose your job then, too."

"Because you weren't willing to look for ways to compromise so we could both be happy."

"Compromise?" He snorted. "My choice was Albany or nothing."

Her jaw dropped. "That's not true and you know it."

"Really, Megan? Exactly where did I—or us, for that matter—rank on your list? Couldn't have been very high."

"Don't even *try* to—"

"Oh, I tried. Back then *and* now. I kind of hoped your priority list might have changed a little. Guess I was wrong."

"And I thought *you'd* changed. That you'd try to understand how grown-ups act in a relationship. An *equal* relationship." She tilted her head in that way that annoyed him. "Guess we were both wrong."

He'd been fooling himself that she'd changed. That she'd lost her tunnel vision and was willing to value something more than her job. Like maybe him, for once. But no. They were right back where they'd ended last time. "You got that right."

Megan took a deep breath and her eyes narrowed. "You know, let's just forget it."

"Forget what?"

"All of it. Everything that's happened since I made the mistake of getting anywhere near you again. You go back to your fabulous life and I'll see if I can salvage anything of mine. In Carbondale."

He'd fallen into a time warp. She was walking out on him *again*. At least this time it had happened before he'd gotten all wrapped up in her like a lovesick fool. "If that's what you want, Megan, so be it."

So be it. The same words he'd used when she said she was leaving him last time. His jaw was even set at the same angle and his eyes held the same bitter coldness. Talk about déjà vu. She was twenty-two again, and her heart felt as if it had been slashed with a rusty blade. How could it hurt like this a second time? Had her heart forgotten it had been seven years? Had she just been fooling herself all this time that she was over him? As Devin stared at her, the twitching muscle in his jaw showing his anger, the pain in her chest spread until it was hard to breathe.

She swallowed hard and spoke carefully to keep her voice from shaking. "I'm so glad we had this conversation, Devin. It's nice to know for sure absolutely nothing has changed between us." The pang that shot through her emphasized the underlying truth of that statement. Oh, yeah. She'd been fooling herself. And doing a damn fine job of it until now.

She'd thought about this—Devin, the job in Carbondale, her, her career—from every angle possible the past couple of days. Obviously she'd managed to ignore the great big question right in front of her.

She had her answer now, though.

And she knew what she needed to do.

* * *

"And you just walked out? No more discussion?" Julie's jaw had been hanging open for most of this conversation, but when she did manage to get it working, Megan didn't like the questions. Julie was supposedly there to help her pack, but any packing on her part had come to a screeching halt as soon as Megan started relaying the showdown at Devin's.

"What more was there to discuss? Devin doesn't want me to take this job, even though it's the only way I'll get to finish something that's *very* important to me. It's so selfish of him." She closed the box of glassware and strapped tape across the top. Thankfully, she didn't own a lot of stuff, and anything she didn't absolutely need, Julie had offered to store at her place while she was gone. "Last time around, I supported his goals, and he didn't support mine. I expected better this time."

"May I point out that you didn't really give him a chance?"

Megan sat back on her heels. "I think I did. Devin sees this as a black-and-white issue. Either I stay or I go. No middle ground. I'm not playing that game again."

"Look, I totally agree that Devin is being a bit of a schmuck, and personally I'd love to put him on a spit and slow roast him over hot coals for putting you through all of this. But honey..." Julie's mouth twisted. "I think you're being a bit irrational."

"And I don't think I asked you."

"Someone's testy." Julie shook her head in censure.

"Wouldn't you be? I've had a rough couple of weeks, and I've earned my testiness. My whole life has been turned upside down."

"And Devin's hasn't?"

"Maybe, but not as much as mine. *He* has a successful law practice, a hit radio show and a bestselling book. The poor dear isn't exactly suffering from a little bad press caused by his ex-wife. I, on the other hand…" She sighed and rubbed her temples, trying to release the building tension. "I don't think it's too much to ask, but Devin acts like any ambition I have is some kind of direct slap to him."

Julie tsked. "Sorry, honey, but that sounds like old baggage and self-pity talking."

The barb stung. "You're not a very good counselor, you know," she grumbled.

Unrepentant, Julie smirked at her. "You get hand-holding and 'how does that make you feel?' when you pay for it. Since this is friendly—and free—girl talk, I'm allowed to tell you when you simply have your panties in a twist."

Megan couldn't believe her ears. "You're really telling me to just get over it?"

"Hmm, maybe not get over it, but definitely grow up and act like a big girl."

It was Megan's turn to go slack jawed. "And to think I'm the one looking for a job. You're the worst counselor I've ever met. I'm calling Dr. Weiss."

Julie waved away the criticism. "But I'm a good friend, honey. I know you want this to be a Feel My Pain conversation—and I do, honestly, I do—but surely you know that you're not thinking clearly."

Another sting. "So since this is girl talk and not actual counseling, tell me what you think I should do."

"You know what you should do."

Of course I do. "Yeah."

"Then call Devin. Apologize for acting like a child and clearly tell him what you want. Give him the opportunity to act like an adult, and maybe you two can work this out." Julie raised an eyebrow at her. "You *do* know what you want, right?"

"I know what I don't want," Megan mumbled, feeling a little sick inside.

"No wonder you two are flailing all over the place. Here's my unsolicited take on the situation. You two got divorced when some really good counseling would have been a better option. Then things go crazy, and you two are thrown back together again. Unsolved problems, emotions not laid to rest, some hormones and you're all messed up again. Am I right?"

The muscles in her stomach clenched around the rock settled there, but she nodded.

"But you know better now. You've worked with couples who were far worse off than you two are and straightened them out. There's nothing here that's unfixable if you're *both* willing to work on it." She cleared her throat. "Solely in my opinion as the world's worst counselor."

"But the bestest friend." Megan thought for a minute. "Do you really think Dev and I can—could, maybe—make this work this time?"

"It'll be tough, but I don't think it's unrealistic to try. And at this point, do you have anything to lose?"

Yeah, I do. Megan grasped for one last lifeline. "If I were your client—a paying client," she amended, "what would you say?"

"I'd recommend some honest conversation about expectations, maybe with a counselor present to assist in keeping you both on topic.... You know the drill, Megan. This is pretty basic stuff."

"I know. No wonder Dr. Weiss fired me. I suck."

"Nah." Julie patted her shoulder. "You're just in the middle of it. Where's Devin now?"

Megan looked at her watch. "Seven-fifteen on a Wednesday night... The studio. I guess I could call him after the show."

"Excellent plan." Julie swung her legs off the couch and slid her feet into her shoes. "I will get out of your way. You should shower and put on something pretty." She eyeballed Megan's battered shorts and ratty T-shirt and frowned. "Or at least presentable. Invite him over tonight and work this out. Like adults."

Megan considered the possibilities. The little spark of hope caused by Julie's pep talk began to glow and grow and relax the painfully clenched muscles in her stomach. "Thanks, Jules."

"You're welcome." Julie picked up her purse and headed for the door. "Call me tomorrow and let me know how it goes. I'll get the spit and fire pit ready, just in case. Good luck, honey." She winked. "My bill will be in the mail."

Once the door closed behind Julie, Megan reached over and turned on her stereo. Devin's voice filled the room, causing little tingles to dance across her skin. Now she didn't want to wait until after the show. She couldn't call the listener line for this, and Dev wouldn't answer his cell while he was on the air, but she could send him a text asking him to call during the break or once he finished. Maybe an email would be better?

The more she thought about it, the more excited and impatient she became. She could be at the studio before the show ended. She could wait outside until he was off the air....

The mention of her name cut through her buzzing thoughts and she froze. She'd been caught in the sound of his voice and ignored the words. But hearing the clipped "Megan" narrowed her focus. She turned up the volume.

"...and I'm telling you it's not worth it. You and your ex are exes for a reason. It's easy sometimes to forget that, maybe even get caught up in the good ol' days, but the truth of the situation never goes away."

"But," the female caller interrupted, "you and Dr. Megan seemed to be—"

Dev's bitter laugh pained her. "See, there's the proof that anyone—it doesn't matter that they know better—can get caught in that trap. Temporary insanity can affect even the best of us."

Her knees felt a little weak.

"My ex swears he's changed, and he really does seem to be different now."

"People don't really change." Devin turned sarcastic. "They tell themselves that, and they'll tell you that, but don't believe it. The truth is that people—at their core—can't change."

In any other situation, Megan would challenge that statement, but the sick feeling in her stomach outweighed any professional outrage.

"Learn from my mistake, folks. It was certainly public enough." He laughed. "Seriously, though, that's the danger of exes. Megan and I had a good run for a while when we were kids, but we shouldn't have gotten married in the first place. I felt sorry for her when the publicity from the book caused her problems—"

The sick feeling started to turn and churn as her anger began to rise.

"—and I let that plus the 'everything old is new again' idea mess with my head. Yeah, hooking up with your ex is fun and exciting for a little while, but nothing good will come of it. That's stupid thinking, folks, and we've talked about stupid thinking on this show dozens of times. Stupid thinking causes you to lose the house *and* the car."

Stupid thinking, indeed. Seems I'm guilty of that.

The caller tried to plead her case. "But sometimes, when we're together, it just seems so right and meant to be."

She didn't think Devin's voice could turn any nastier, but it did. "You mean you're sleeping with your ex again."

"Well…"

"That really *is* stupid. I don't care how good your ex is in bed—and honestly, half the time the reality isn't going to be as good as the memory anyway."

A cold anger slithered down Megan's spine.

"Look, caller, I know I broke one of my top ten rules, and that probably confused a lot of you. But let's just look at this as a good lesson for everyone. We're all susceptible to the heat of an old flame—including me. And while I don't recommend anyone get mixed up with their exes again, if you are—or are looking at your ex and wondering if you should—accept that you made a stupid mistake and run for the hills, folks. Cut your losses."

She wanted to throw something at the speakers. She wanted to smack herself for her stupidity. *I am an idiot.* She shouldn't have let Julie talk her out of her original plan, even for a minute. She'd been right all along.

"You're right, Devin. Thanks."

"You're welcome, caller. We're going to take a short break, and when we come back, we're going to talk more about exes and when you should file for a modification to your original divorce agreement. I'm Devin Kenney, and I'm here to help you Cover Your Assets."

I may be an idiot, but Dev's a jerk. "Way to cover your butt with your listeners by throwing me under the bus, Dev," she said to the radio.

Her earlier excitement had been replaced by indignation and strengthened resolve. She was going to use this as a learning experience and a stepping stone. She'd go into exile in Carbondale, but she'd be back in Chicago soon enough. And when she did return...

Oh, she probably wouldn't be able to do much to Dev—at least nothing on a scale of what he'd done to her recently—but she wouldn't have her hands tied the way she did now.

She'd been right. Dev wasn't good for her—not then, and not now.

So be it.

CHAPTER ELEVEN

AFTER WEEKS OF HEARING nothing but Megan this and Megan that—as well as having Megan in his life and bed again—the absence of all things Megan seemed very strange to Devin. With Megan gone there was little to feed the media circus, and when combined with a local politician's breaking sex scandal, Megan was off the city's radar completely. Her fifteen minutes were finally over.

His life went back to what would be considered normal for him: days at his practice, three shows a week and the occasional appearance for either the show or the book. But even the book's hoopla was dying down now as an organic-gardening-as-spiritual-self-help book made its rise up the lists.

But back to normal felt wrong somehow. It was disturbing because everything was exactly as it should be, yet it all felt hollow and empty. He was getting testy and short-tempered with his callers, even taking one to task on air for being superficial and greedy. *That* hadn't gone over well. He could trace his reaction and lecture right back to Megan—in fact, he might have quoted her at least once— so he held her responsible for his discontent.

The one bright spot in his life—the only thing really holding his interest at the moment—was his involvement with the student's case, which had now almost taken on a life of its own. That involvement had been met with skepticism at first—after all, Devin had staked his professional claim as a divorce attorney, not a constitutional one—but he soon had the skeptics eating crow. That was exhilarating, except he had no one to share the thrill with.

Megan might have accused him of screwing up her life, but he wasn't exactly lovin' his right now either. They were even.

But that didn't make him feel better.

The only person more unhappy than Devin at the moment was Manny, a fact he reminded Devin of constantly. Like now. Devin had Manny on speaker phone, listening with only half an ear while he went through his email in-box.

"That organic-gardening girl is knocking you off the lists."

"I'm still at number eight. I'm hardly toiling in obscurity."

"We need to get you back out there meeting the people and making the papers."

"I don't have time for that right now. This case is taking up what free time I have."

"And that's my point. Pro bono do-gooding doesn't pay the bills." He could almost hear Manny's pout.

At least Manny was consistent. Money talked. "Loan sharks on your case, Manny?"

"Plus, it's even less interesting than it is profitable."

"We are in a sorry state in this country when the denial of a citizen's constitutional rights is considered uninteresting. I thought you could spin anything into headlines."

"That is beyond even my abilities, Devin. Folks aren't interested, and I can't make them be. I'm rather hoping you have another ex-wife tucked away somewhere."

"Dear God, no. One is plenty." The horror in his voice was genuine, as was the pang that shot through him.

"Come on, Devin, give me something meaty to work with."

"The Fourteenth Amendment is pretty enigmatic. Lots of meatiness."

Manny groaned. "You're trying to kill me, right? What say we call Dr. Megan up and see if she's interested in—"

"No."

"When you two are at each other's throats, you're golden. I think a regular He Said–She Said night might be a sellable idea. Maybe just once a week. What do you think?"

"No."

"Can I at least see if Megan is interested?"

"No." *So much for not hearing Megan's name every five minutes.* "End of discussion."

"Fine." Manny sighed dramatically. "Would you be interested in participating in a bachelor auction?"

A bachelor auction? "You really shouldn't drink early in the day, Manny. It's affecting your judgment. Call me when you're sober. Bye."

Manny was still sputtering when Devin disconnected the call. That brought a little smile to Devin's face. For some sick reason, he got a kick out of needling Manny.

Mostly because it was so easy to do. Manny was acting as if the world was ending just because Devin didn't want to renew his contract for *Cover Your Assets*. At least not in its current incarnation. It took up a lot of his time, and honestly, the pessimism was getting to him. If Manny wanted to continue as his agent, he needed to start thinking outside the box.

"Mr. Kenney." His receptionist buzzed in, interrupting

his thoughts. "Dr. Julie Moss is here with a delivery for you."

Julie Moss. She was one of Megan's friends. This was the closest thing to contact he'd had since Megan had stormed out of his place three weeks ago. His first worry—that Megan was sick or hurt—was relieved by the mention of a delivery. Maybe the delivery was a peace offering of sorts? No, he wasn't that lucky. But there was only one way to find out for sure. "You can send her in."

"Um, okay."

It was a strange response from his normally very professional employee, and he wondered if this Julie person was crazy or something. He got his answer when a woman opened his door, nodded a greeting, then held the door open for a man carrying a table.

The coffee table he'd given Megan.

The man set the table down with a grunt of relief, then extended his hand. "Nate Adams. I worked with Megan at the Weiss Clinic."

"And I'm Julie Moss."

Nate seemed friendly enough, but Julie's mouth pulled into a disapproving frown. This was going to be interesting. "Megan mentioned you both."

"Good." Julie replied tersely. "So you can assume she mentioned you to us as well, and we can skip over all the niceties."

Blatant hostility. As a friend of Megan's, he didn't blame her. "What can I—"

"We're just returning the table. I'd have brought it sooner, but I needed Nate's help. It's heavier than it looks."

"Indeed."

Julie cleared her throat. "So Megan asked me to return this to you, and now I have. We'll go, and you can get back to your big, important, famous life."

Sarcasm to go with the hostility. Julie was definitely on Megan's team.

He almost asked why Megan hadn't taken the table with her, but decided against it. "I haven't heard from her since she left." Ignoring Julie's derisive snort, he directed his comment at Nate. "How's she doing?"

The younger man looked distinctly uncomfortable. "Um, fine, I guess. I really don't talk to her that much, you know." He cut his eyes at Julie, as if she would jump in with an answer.

Julie was currently eyeballing him as if he was something she'd found stuck to her shoe, so the chances of any good information on Megan coming from that source seemed slim at best.

In the ensuing silence Nate cleared his throat. "Megan's in Carbondale. Working. Doing great stuff at their clinic. Or so I hear…"

"Good for her."

"Yes, good for her," Julie interrupted. "She's doing quite well in Carbondale. No thanks to you at all." Julie turned to the other man with a false smile. "Nate, could you wait for me in the lobby? I need to talk to Mr. Kenney for a minute."

Profound relief crossed the young man's face. "Of course. Nice meeting you." He beat a hasty retreat, closing the door behind him.

Julie's smile faded when she turned back to him. "Let's cut to the chase."

He leaned against his desk and crossed his arms over his chest. "By all means."

"I don't like you."

"Obviously."

"In fact, I think you're a bit of a jerk. But, in your defense, Megan hasn't exactly been firing on all cylinders lately, so part of that might be a simple reaction to her irrational behavior. Since you're mostly to blame for that behavior, though, you're still a jerk."

"Is there a point you'd like to make, Dr. Moss, or do you just expect me to stand here and allow you to continue to insult me in my own office?"

"As delightful as that sounds, I know that's not likely to happen. Granted, Megan hasn't been the poster child of mental health recently, but I was actually on your side."

"You'll pardon me if I find that difficult to believe."

"I was at first. I even argued on your behalf. Told her how irrational she was being, and we had a major breakthrough."

That would have been after *Megan left me. For the second time. Interesting.*

"Of course, then you went and threw her under the bus on your show."

Guilt nagged at him. He'd been hurt and lashed out. It didn't make anything less true, but the execution had lacked finesse.

"After that," Julie continued, ice dripping off her words, "I couldn't get her out of town fast enough. Hence me being stuck with this table in my living room where I've been tripping over it for the last couple of weeks."

A slightly guilty conscience didn't require him to listen to more of this. "And now you've done your job." He walked to the door and opened it. "Thank you, Dr. Moss."

Julie opened her mouth as if she wanted to say more, then closed it with a snap. "You're welcome, Mr. Kenney."

As she passed him, though, she stopped and eyed him from head to toe as if she was sizing him up for a fight. "Know, however, that Megan does plan to come back to Chicago. And if she's still after your blood then, I won't talk her down."

"Why do I get the feeling you'll drive the getaway car?"

Julie shrugged. "Whatever she needs." With a toss of her hair, she disappeared down the hall.

Devin closed his door and went back to his desk. Between Megan and her friend Julie, he had serious doubts about the relative sanity of so-called mental-health professionals. Craziness seemed to be a prerequisite for the job.

At least at one point, someone—other than him—had been trying to convince Megan she was overreacting. He could take a small bit of satisfaction in that.

However small. And cold.

But Julie's words about Megan being out for blood shocked him more than he wanted to admit. That side of Megan was new. Along with that backbone she'd grown in the past few years, she'd learned to carry a grudge, as well. She wasn't the same Megan he used to know, that was for sure.

That thought stopped him. Megan *wasn't* the same. She was a different person. He'd accepted and appreciated her new confidence but not that she wanted to be treated as an equal, instead of being taken care of. How had he managed to miss that?

He hadn't missed it; he'd ignored it. She'd told him directly numerous times and it hadn't sunk in. Seemed he was as hardheaded as Megan accused him of being. When faced with the possibility of reconciliation, he'd expected them to pretty much pick up where they'd left off—at least where they'd been before he asked her to move to Chicago. He'd enjoyed her new backbone and attitude, but hadn't processed the fact that it meant she wasn't the Megan he used to know.

Insanity was doing the same thing over again and expecting a different result. He'd expected something different and then been surprised when he'd gotten the exact result as last time: Megan gone.

Either the crazy was contagious or he deserved every insult Megan hurled his way.

And it was pretty clear he wasn't crazy.

The only real question was whether or not there was anything left to salvage out of this mess.

Thursday was becoming Megan's least favorite day. There was a sound reason she didn't like a client list packed full of substance abusers, and Thursday was the day she had groups back-to-back-to-back. The host of other problems the substance abuse caused—with spouses, children, the law—was both depressing and demoralizing. Depressing because she got so tired of seeing families torn apart over it, and demoralizing because there was often so little she could do to really help. Most of the time the damage was done and she was just trying to help pick up the pieces. Not every counselor was made to counsel every kind of client. She knew that.

But it was tougher than usual right now. Rationally, she knew her feelings were being compounded by the sad state of her personal life. She didn't really have much of one to speak of.

She'd been so busy at the clinic since she arrived she hadn't had time to make any friends or even explore the town. What little free time she had, she was usually so exhausted or brain dead all she wanted to do was watch TV. She talked to her mom, and Julie called to keep her up-to-date on things in Chicago, but otherwise…

She was bored. She was lonely.

And she was pregnant.

It seemed there really was no end to the upheaval and chaos Devin Kenney could bring to her life.

Moving here hadn't gotten Dev off her mind; no matter how much she tried to focus on her job and lose herself in the work, he was always there, poking around the edges of her concentration. And if that wasn't enough, he seemed to haunt her dreams, leaving her feeling empty and frustrated in the mornings.

In fact, she'd almost ignored the fact she'd missed her period, assuming it was just stress and obsession over Dev manifesting in physical ways. How wrong she was.

She couldn't get Dev out of her mind, and now she was carrying his baby in her body, as well. His hold on her was permanent now.

Like it wasn't already.

They'd talked about having kids. Even discussed some baby names, although to no one's surprise, they'd never managed to come to an agreement.

Did the universe hate her? After falling in love with Devin, spending seven years trying to get over him, then falling in love with him again only to lose him again, she got pregnant with his child *now?*

It was enough to make her want to pull her hair out.

At least she was being honest with herself. She was in love with Devin again and realizing she'd probably never really gotten over him in the first place. Having that understanding would help her get through this—even if it didn't make it hurt any less.

And this hurt a lot. No amount of self-therapy could help. Even having Julie admit she'd been wrong and come fully onto her side didn't help. The misery ran deep.

Somehow, amazingly enough, this time seemed to hurt more than last time. Even though she was fueled by the same righteous indignation, it didn't provide much solace this time. Being right in principle had helped before, but now it was cold comfort—and not even much of that, since she wasn't even sure she was right in principle now. Or that she cared who was right or wrong in the first place.

She was completely miserable, and the only thing that kept her from driving back to Chicago to tell Devin that was the knowledge—in his own words—that he considered her a mistake.

That cut to the quick.

She wondered how long it would take for the pain to lessen enough for her to talk to Devin without admitting she'd been stupid and wrong and begging for another chance. She'd have to talk to him eventually. She had to tell him about the baby. This wasn't the kind of thing she could just keep to herself. It wouldn't be fair to Devin or the baby—or her, either. She'd just have to suck it up and deal.

Eventually. Right now she wanted to wallow. It was easier. Going to bed and getting today over with sounded like the best plan ever. She could wallow herself to sleep.

Julie's ring tone blared on the end table behind her. Without opening her eyes she reached for her phone.

"What's up, Ju—"

"Turn on your radio. *Now.*"

The urgency in Julie's voice spurred her into action even as she sputtered questions. "Why? What's going on?"

"It's Devin. You've got to hear this."

"Dev's show isn't on tonight," she argued even as she searched for the channel.

"He's doing an interview with Bruce Malaney and now they're talking about *you.*"

Megan's heart crawled into her throat. Bruce Malaney shared his philosophy of anything-for-ratings with Kate and her ilk. Was there no end to this? The static finally cleared, and she turned the volume up.

Devin's voice came out of the speakers and curled through her as he spoke. At least he didn't sound angry. "...not really speaking to each other right now, as I'm sure you can imagine, but I hear she's doing well."

"That info came from me," Julie said.

"Shh! I can't hear."

"Of course," Bruce said, "your recent relationship with her was major news."

Dev laughed. "I'm not sure I'd use the word *news,* but it was something people took an interest in. I'm feeling more sympathy for celebrities and their relationships now, though, that's for sure."

Bruce and his listeners might not catch the edge to Devin's voice, but Megan heard it loud and clear.

"People are speculating that Megan Lowe might be indirectly or directly responsible for ending your show."

What? "Julie, what's this about Devin's show?" Megan asked.

"They talked about that earlier." Julie spoke quickly. "*Cover Your Assets* is being overhauled somehow. Devin was cagey about what it would be when it returned...."

Megan couldn't listen to Julie and Devin both. "Shh."

"The only thing Megan is responsible for," Devin said, "is opening my eyes to details I've been missing, both personally and professionally. In its current format, *Cover Your Assets* has really outlived its original purpose. I've found out you can't really help people with quick, pithy sound bites during a ten-minute radio conversation."

Megan bit her lip in disbelief.

"So what is next for you, Devin?" Bruce asked. "You evaded the question earlier, so I'm going to pin you down now."

Devin took a deep breath. "I don't want to get stuck in a rut. This situation with Megan showed me I was headed there. People fear change, but change opens doors and adds possibilities. I'm going to explore some possibilities."

Megan was feeling light-headed and realized it was because she was holding her breath. Somehow, though, she couldn't get her lungs working properly.

Bruce laughed. "Sounds like your next book will be a self-help tome."

"I think the last few weeks have proven beyond a shadow of a doubt that I'm the last person who should be handing out advice to people on how to manage their lives. I'll leave that to the experts like Megan."

"Megan, did you hear that?" Julie asked breathlessly, but Megan couldn't find her voice through her shock. "Megan?"

"We're going to take a short break. We'll be back with more from divorce expert and newly minted legal crusader Devin Kenney in a few minutes. I'm Bruce Malaney and this is *Clear the Air*."

Megan couldn't believe her ears. There was no way she'd heard that right. Wishful thinking obviously led to auditory hallucinations. Or maybe early pregnancy had her hearing what she wanted to hear. Because if what Dev had just said was real...

"Megan!" Julie's shout finally broke through, and Megan slapped the volume down as the show went to commercial.

"I'm here. Did you hear what I just heard?"

"Oh, my God, *yes*. That was practically a public apology. Not to mention a hell of a shout-out to the counseling prowess of Dr. Megan."

"So you don't think I'm reading too much into that."

"Read *more* into it, honey. There's no way Devin could

be sure you were listening, so that wasn't for your benefit. You need to call him."

"And say what?"

"Start with 'I'm sorry for being psycho' and go from there."

Now that the paralysis had passed, Megan felt full of restless energy. She hauled herself to her feet and started to pace. "I have his cell. I could call him tonight after the show. Apologize. See if any of that was an olive branch."

"Excellent idea."

"But what if it's not? What if he's just putting a good face on all this for the sake of the masses? Like you said, there's no way he could guarantee I'd be listening tonight."

"You won't know until you talk to him, now, will you?"

She needed to find out. Especially considering... She laid a hand on her stomach. She needed to find out what Dev meant with all of that before she told him about the baby.

And out of nowhere, a little spark of hope flared in the darkness.

Possibilities, indeed. Suddenly there were a whole lot of possibilities to explore, and some of those possibilities now held a golden, promising glow.

"I do need to talk to Devin." *But I need to see his face while I do it.*

"Duh. That's what I've been saying."

"Let me make a few phone calls." Megan was already mentally rearranging her schedule. "Can I crash at your place tonight?"

"You're coming in? Tonight?"

"Yeah. I'll go see Devin in the morning before his show."

"You're a brave girl."

She didn't feel brave. If she was reading the wrong meaning into Dev's words, she would regret it—horribly—tomorrow.

But right now there was the possibility she wouldn't.

Devin had one eye on the clock as he halfheartedly dispensed advice to his listeners. So far, the calls had been pretty evenly split between questions about his announcement that the show would be undergoing some major changes and the news of Hollywood's latest power-couple breakup.

Despite his best attempts to steer the discussion away from the couple's private life, that was exactly what the audience wanted to speculate about. He wasn't going to add fuel to that fire if he could at all help it, so he was trying to shift the focus to prenuptial agreements in general.

Paula-from-Milwaukee seemed awfully distraught for someone who had no real stake in the possible settlement, and he bit back the urge to tell her to seek counseling about her overinvestment in the lives of people she didn't even know. "Paula, I haven't seen their prenup, so I have no idea how it's worded, but California law does not recognize adultery as grounds for divorce."

"But if she's sleeping with her costar..."

Twenty more minutes and this show would be over. He still had a long drive to Carbondale ahead of him and possibly a long night if Megan decided to be stubborn or nurse her grudge. His patience was wearing thin, and he motioned to Mike, Kate's replacement, that this call needed to be wrapped up. "Let's not speculate about the private lives of others, okay? I think the point we need to take away from this is that prenuptial agreements aren't always ironclad."

Mike was quick on the draw. "Let's find a new caller

and see what other topics are out there. I personally would like to talk about that case in Michigan where the couple is fighting over custody of the parrot, but…"

Sixteen minutes left. "Pick a caller, Mike."

"Here's a lady who's been waiting patiently in the queue for a while now. You're on the air, caller."

"Finally," a voice Devin recognized muttered. "This is Megan, and, um, I'm from Carbondale."

Astonished, Devin looked through the window at Mike, who simply shrugged unhelpfully. After all this time, Megan called his show? What the…?

"Hello? Hello? Did I get disconnected? Damn."

"No, you're on the air, Megan." *Treat her like you would any other caller.* "Do you have a question or a comment?"

"Both, actually. I heard your interview last night." She laughed, but it lacked any real humor. "Since I'm not exactly a regular listener, most of that was news to me."

"And?" he prompted.

"So my question is about possibilities. Like the ones you mentioned last night."

Devin tried to remember exactly what he'd said.

"I'm usually a big fan of possibilities, and in my line of work I kinda have to be, but recently I've had some trouble with the idea."

"That's the thing about possibilities. Once you start questioning them, you start cutting off options."

"Yes, Devin, I know that," Megan snapped, but then seemed to remember where she was. "I mean—" she tried again with a different tone "—how do you know when you've totally crossed a possibility off your list?"

Outside the booth's main window, a crowd was gathering. Staff had come out of their cubicles to gather around the booth and its speaker. In his booth, Mike moved at high speed between phone and computer, looking as if he was under siege. A glance at his own computer screen told him why: Mike *was*.

The call lines were lit up like a Christmas tree and the hold queue had reached new lengths. Comments were already getting posted on his website bulletin board under a brand-new thread titled "Dr. Megan is back—now!"

This is not how I planned to have a conversation with Megan today. He was still forming his plan of attack and had rather counted on the ride to southern Illinois to flesh it out. But what he said here could have massive repercussions later tonight. "I'm not sure I'm the right person to come to with that question, Megan. I specialize in divorce, not—"

"No, you're the right person. I'm not using a generic 'you' here in my question. I mean how do you, Devin Kenney, decide a possibility has been totally removed from the list?"

The booth might have been soundproof, but he could still see the crowd outside take a collective breath, even if he couldn't hear it. Everything seemed to freeze.

"Megan, I'm not sure this is the right forum—"

"I'm sorry, Dev. I was wrong and I'm sorry and I miss you and I'd really like to talk about possibilities." She paused, and her voice seemed to shrink. "If you're still willing, that is."

Devin swallowed hard, unsure if he'd heard her right. "Megan—"

Mike's voice came through his headphones. "Damn, they just crashed the server. Your site's down."

Devin ignored him. "We need to talk, but this probably isn't the best venue."

"God, you're right. I'm sorry, Dev. I'll wait down here until you're done."

Down here? "Megan, where are you?"

"The lobby on fourteen. The security guard wouldn't let me up and the receptionist—"

"Stay there." He was on his feet and taking off his head-phones before the words were fully out of his mouth. "Go to commercial," he barked at Mike, who nodded, his eyes wide. Outside the booth he passed his slack-jawed audience without pausing on his way to the stairwell.

When he opened the door to the fourteenth-floor lobby, Megan was easy to spot. She stood in the middle of the room with half a dozen people staring wordlessly at her, keeping a safe distance as if she was a ticking time bomb. When she spied him, a small smile tried to form, then faded.

Every eye in the room turned to him at that moment, and he froze, unsure of what to do next.

Dev looked much like the wrath of God bearing down on her, and Megan worried she'd handled this situation all wrong. Devin stopped about five feet from her and those rich brown eyes nearly stared her into the ground.

"Hi, Dev," she said feeling lame and embarrassed at the same time.

"What are you doing here?"

"I tried calling you all morning, but you never answered and you never called me back...."

"You're not the only one who can ignore a telephone after an interview draws attention."

"And then the receptionist was supposed to tell you I was here and I just couldn't wait any longer. So I called. I didn't mean to raise a ruckus on your show. I'm sorry about that, too. Jeez, can I just do a blanket apology for everything and start over?"

For the first time she could ever remember, Dev seemed shocked speechless. Finally he managed, "What?"

Their audience was now staring openly, avidly hanging on every word. Somewhere a phone rang, unanswered. She could feel heat creeping up her neck. "Umm... Well..."

Dev looked at the crowd, then reached for her hand. "Come on."

She followed him without question as he led her back into the stairwell. The gray walls echoed the sound of the door closing, and she turned to find Dev leaning against it. *Now or never.* "Dev, I'm sorry about everything. You were right about—"

Devin moved like a streak of lightning, pinning her against the wall before she realized it. A second later his mouth landed on hers in a kiss that stole her breath and made her scalp tingle in delight.

She was left gasping when he finally broke away and ran a hand over her hair. "I'll accept your apology if you'll accept mine."

"Yours?"

"You were right about a few things, too. In fact, I was headed to Carbondale after the show to tell you exactly that."

Hope kindled in her chest. "You were?"

"I was being a selfish jerk. Again."

"Well, I wasn't doing much better," she admitted.

"See, we're meant to be together. No one else would put up with us."

"About Carbondale, though..."

"As you said, it's six months, maybe less. We'll work it out. You tell me what you need, and I'll do my part."

That was too easy. "Just like that?"

"Just like that."

Her world clicked into place. Maybe it was that easy. "I love you, Dev. I don't think I ever stopped."

"Good. Because I know I never stopped loving you." Dev's smile made her heart melt into a warm puddle. She wrapped her arms around his neck and pulled him close for another kiss. As the kiss deepened, Dev pressed her back against the cinder block wall. She threaded her fingers through his hair and let him catch her happy sigh in his mouth. Then his lips moved to her neck....

The loud crash of the door above opening forcefully into the wall caused her to jump. Devin's flustered producer started down the stairs two at a time before he saw them and skittered to a stop. The shocked look on his face melted into a grin. "Well, this answers one question." He cleared his throat. "Devin, it's a zoo up there. What do you want me to do?"

Devin pressed a kiss to her forehead, but didn't move from his position or even look behind him. "Megan, you remember Mike?"

Feeling a little embarrassed at the position she was currently in, Megan managed to lift her hand and wave her fingers. "Hi, Mike. Sorry about the commotion."

"Hi, Dr. Megan. Glad you're back. Well, Devin?"

"Tell the listeners Devin and Dr. Megan will be back in a few minutes with a—" Dev paused and smiled at her "—big announcement."

Speaking of big announcements...

"Will do." Mike was gone before the words stopped echoing off the walls.

When Devin leaned in for another kiss, she stopped him with a hand on his chest. He changed direction and went for her earlobe. She fought back her shiver at the touch. "Dev, there's something I need to tell you."

"Now?" he murmured against the sensitive skin of her neck.

She debated, but the need to lay everything out on the table won. "Yeah."

Concern was etched on his face as he pulled back and his eyes met hers. "What?"

Cupping her hands under his jaw, she met his eyes steadily. "Before I tell you, though, know that it has *nothing* to do with anything I've just said. I'd be here regardless. I just want you to know everything before we go any further."

She could tell her words worried him. His eyebrows drew together in a V. "What's wrong?"

"Nothing's wrong. At least not to me. I mean, I'm okay—more than okay, actually. It's just…"

"Then quit dancing around the subject and tell me."

She took a deep breath and prayed this happy moment wasn't going to be short-lived because of her announcement. "I'm pregnant."

This time Dev really did seem speechless. In fact, as his jaw dropped, Megan was afraid she'd really stepped in something.

"You're sure?"

"Positive." When Devin didn't say anything, her heart started to crumple in on itself. "Dev? Are you okay?" Devin's frown reversed itself into a smile that caused her stomach to flutter. "I know we'll need to talk about the whole where-I'm-living issue, but—"

He cut her off with another soul-stirring kiss that removed all her doubts. "Like I said earlier, we'll work it out."

Yesterday she wouldn't have believed it, but today she did. It was that simple.

"Marry me."

It was her turn to be shocked nearly speechless. She swallowed hard. "I didn't tell you about the baby to get a proposal."

"And I'm not proposing because of the baby. He's just a bonus."

"It could be a girl," she reminded him.

Dev grinned. "I guess anything is possible." With a sigh, he looked at the stairs and the door above. "Come on," he said, threading his fingers through hers. "Let's go save Mike and tell the listeners the news."

Last month, even contemplating such a thing would have convinced her she was certifiably insane. But things had changed, and, as always, change brought possibilities.

Anything is possible.

Maybe even a happy ending for them.

EPILOGUE

WHEN MEGAN CAME OUT of the bedroom in search of something to drink, she was surprised to find Devin fully dressed as he flipped through the paper. She'd heard him get up and she'd promptly gone back to sleep, but she didn't think she'd snoozed for *that* long. She was sleeping almost as much now as she had in her first trimester. So much for those "bursts of nesting energy" she was supposed to be getting the closer she got to her due date.

He looked up as she waddled in. The deep gold of his tie brought out the color of his eyes, and the starched white shirt contrasted nicely with his dark hair. "Good morning."

"Look at you, all dressed up to impress the judges. You look sexy in a tie, you know."

He pulled at the knot at his throat as if it was uncomfortable. "Rumor has it you have to wear a tie when you appear in front of the State Supreme Court. I sincerely hope it's *not* because the judges find it sexy. That's just too disturbing to think about."

"Doesn't matter. It's still sexy to me." To prove her point, she tugged on the tie until his lips met hers for a good-morning kiss. "Good luck today."

"Thanks, but I don't need luck. I have the Constitution backing me up." Devin reached for something next to his briefcase. "This came for you yesterday. You fell asleep before I could mention it."

The sight of the long white envelope had her heart pumping before she even confirmed the return address as the Department of Professional Regulation. *This is it. Moment of truth.* Her mouth went dry and she refused to take it. "I can't open it. You read it."

"Eight months ago you were positive you'd ace this thing with your eyes closed and your couch tied behind your back."

"That was bravado talking. Now I'm not so cocky about it."

Dev studied the envelope. "I don't even need to open it. Congrats, Meggie."

Aw. "Thanks for the vote of confidence, but…"

He held it out again, an exasperated look on his face. "Read who it's addressed to."

She took the envelope and looked at it. Her heart started to beat double time. She looked again to be sure and read it aloud. "'Dr. Megan Lowe, LCP.'"

"Nice set of letters you got there."

"I did it." She could feel the goofy grin stretching across her face. "I actually did it. Dr. Megan Lowe, Licensed Clinical Psychologist, at your service. How can I serve your mental-health needs today?"

Dev put his arms around her waist—or what was left of it. "Well, you could give me some reassurance."

"My pleasure. Want some positive affirmations?" She looked into the beautiful brown eyes she hoped the baby would inherit and grinned. "Repeat after me. 'I am a great lawyer. I will knock the Supreme Court dead with my arguments today.'"

Dev shook his head. "I was thinking more along the

lines of 'Yes, Dev, I will marry you *before* I give birth to your child.'"

"Yes, Dev, I will marry you before I give birth to your child," she parroted. "Now that I have this—" she shook the envelope "— checked off my to-do list, you can name the date."

"Next week," he challenged.

If he was trying to bluff her, he was in for a big surprise. "Deal. But I can't change my name until it's time to renew my license."

"Fair enough."

"Really?" That was too easy.

"I don't care which name you use professionally—Dr. Lowe, Dr. Kenney, Dr. Megan... Hell, call yourself Dr. Zhivago, for all I care."

She smacked his arm. "Not Dr. Zhivago. Or Dr. Megan. Although it's going to be weird to be Megan Kenney again."

"Weird how?"

"How many times can one person change her name back and forth? It took me forever to get everything switched back to Lowe last time. I was still getting catalogs addressed to Megan Kenney last year."

"Well, whatever you decide, you'll never have to change your name again." He winked. "Or move to Canada."

For someone who'd made a small fortune from being the world's biggest cynic on marriage, Dev had pitched his tent in the other camp pretty quickly. "You really don't have a preference about me changing my name?"

Devin placed a kiss on her forehead. "You can call yourself anything you want. I just want to call you mine."

Tears burned in the corners of her eyes. "That's probably the sweetest thing you've ever said to me." *Great, now this baby is making me all weepy, too.*

Dev looked shocked. "That's very sad. No wonder you divorced me."

"No, I divorced you because I thought you weren't giving me what I needed."

"And now?" he prompted.

She pretended to think on his question, but the answer really didn't require thought, soul-searching, or discussion with a counselor of any sort.

"I couldn't ask for anything more."

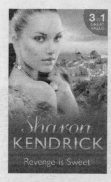

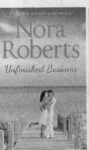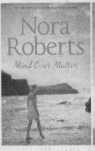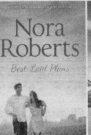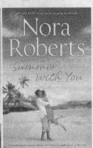
0415_ST_11